CONTEMPORARY
GEORGIAN FICTION

Library of Congress Cataloging-in-Publication Data

Contemporary Georgian fiction / edited and translated by Elizabeth Heighway.
-- 1st ed.
    p. cm.
 ISBN 978-1-56478-716-3 (pbk. : alk. paper) -- ISBN 978-1-56478-751-4 (cloth
: alk. paper)
 1. Short stories, Georgian--Translations into English. 2. Georgian fiction--20th
century--Translations into English. I. Heighway, Elizabeth.
 PK9168.2.E6B47 2012
 899'.969--dc23
                            2012004231

This book is published thanks to the support of the Ministry of Culture and
Monument Protection of Georgia

Partially funded by the National Lottery through Arts Council England, and a
grant from the Illinois Arts Council, a state agency

www.dalkeyarchive.com

Cover: design and composition by Sarah French
Printed on permanent/durable acid-free paper and bound in the United States
of America

CONTEMPORARY GEORGIAN FICTION

TRANSLATED AND EDITED BY ELIZABETH HEIGHWAY

Dalkey Archive Press
Champaign | Dublin | London

CONTENTS

INTRODUCTION

IX

MARIAM BEKAURI
Debi

3

LASHA BUGADZE
The Round Table

9

ZAZA BURCHULADZE
The Dubbing

21

DAVID DEPHY
The Chair

35

TEONA DOLENJASHVILI
Real Beings

38

GURAM DOCHANASHVILI

The Happy Hillock

64

REZO GABRIADZE

The White Bridge

95

KOTE JANDIERI

Cinderella's Night

99

IRAKLI JAVAKHADZE

Kolya

114

DAVIT KARTVELISHVILI

The Squirrel

148

BESIK KHARANAULI

Ladies and Gentlemen!

163

MAMUKA KHERKHEULIDZE

A Caucasian Chronicle

174

ARCHIL KIKODZE

The Drunks

183

ANA KORDZAIA-SAMADASHVILI

Rain

212

ZURAB LEZHAVA

Love in a Prison Cell

216

MAKA MIKELADZE

A Story of Sex

233

AKA MORCHILADZE

Once Upon a Time in Georgia

247

ZAAL SAMADASHVILI

Selling Books

297

NUGZAR SHATAIDZE

November Rain

305

NINO TEPNADZE

The Suicide Train

351

AUTHOR BIOGRAPHIES

357

INTRODUCTION

When I was approached about translating an anthology of contemporary Georgian literature I was both delighted and intrigued. My studies in the Georgian language had introduced me to many of the nation's great authors—Shota Rustaveli (c. 1165–?), Vazha Pshavela (1861–1915), Ilia Chavchavadze (1837–1907), Akaki Tsereteli (1840–1915), Galaktion Tabidze (1891–1959)—but my knowledge of Georgian literature from 1950 onward was rather limited. From a personal standpoint, then, I was very pleased to be offered the chance to devote my time to a project of this breadth and in doing so to acquaint myself with the contemporary literary scene within Georgia. I was also very enthusiastic about playing a part in making Georgian literature accessible to an English-speaking readership. There are only relatively few published works and journal articles in translation, mostly centering on classic texts, with almost nothing that could be considered "contemporary." It is my hope that this anthology will go some way toward addressing this shortfall by bringing to the English-speaking reader a selection of stories from some of the best Georgian authors of the last fifty years.

In collaboration with the Georgian Ministry of Culture, a selection was made with an eye toward including a very comprehensive mix of writers and a broad range of literary styles. Some of these authors are well established, with long publishing careers, while others are young writers who are just emerging onto the literary scene. Some have previously been translated into English or other languages, while for others this will be their first published translation. Some lived large portions of their adult lives under Soviet rule, others just their childhoods, and a few have no memory of Georgia being anything other than an independent country. Indeed, the majority of the works included here were written in the years since the restoration of Georgia's independence in 1991. While the stories deal with universal human themes—love, belonging, betrayal, loss—the range of settings reflects the many transitions Georgian society has undergone in recent years.

Georgia's literary history is long; the first works date back to the fifth century and even before then the region had generated a wealth of oral folklore. The number of references in this anthology's stories to historical Georgian authors, as well as characters from their work, is evidence of the pride with which this literary heritage is viewed by the Georgian people. In this brief introduction I will mention only some of these authors, mainly those mentioned in this anthology or else who have been translated into English, and have included a bibliography at the end of this section for readers wishing to learn more. Sadly, a number of the translated works were published only within Georgia or the Soviet Union, or appeared only in literary journals. To date, the most accessible and wide-ranging selection of translations is to be found in Donald Rayfield's *The Literature of Georgia: A History*, of which a fifth of the text consists of translated extracts of literature from all periods.

Arguably the most well-known work of Georgian literature outside Georgia is the epic poem *The Man in the Panther's Skin* (*Vepkhistqaosani*; also known as *The Knight in the Tiger Skin*), written by Shota Rustaveli, poet in the court of Queen Tamar at the end of the twelfth century, during the golden age of Georgian literature. It was translated at the start of the twentieth century by the English translator Marjory Wardrop, who produced a prose version of the poem, and again by Katharine Vivian in the 1970s. Among Katharine Vivian's other translations was an eighteenth-century work by the writer and lexicographer Sulkhan Saba Orbeliani, *The Book of Wisdom and Lies* (*Tsigni sibrdzne-sitsruisa*), a collection of folk tales, fables, and sayings (also translated by Marjory Wardrop's brother Oliver in 1894). Two other collections of Georgian folklore have also been translated by Kevin Tuite and Marjory Wardrop.

One of the most respected of all Georgian writers emerged in the 1860s; the realist Ilia Chavchavadze, so revered within Georgia that in 1987 he was canonized as "Saint Ilia the Righteous" by the Georgian Orthodox Church, and is widely considered one of the founding fathers of the Georgian nation. His narrative poem *The Hermit* (*Gandegili*) was translated by Marjory Wardrop in 1895. After Chavchavadze came Vazha Pshavela, at the end of the nineteenth century, and whose narrative poems such as *Host and Guest* (*Stumar-maspindzeli*) and *The Snake-Eater* (*Gvelis mchameli*)— translated by Donald Rayfield for publication within Georgia—are firmly rooted in the myth and folklore of the Caucasian highlands.

During the first decades of the twentieth century there was a sudden resurgence of poetry and prose that coincided with Georgia's brief period of independence between 1918 and 1921, after which it was annexed by the Soviet Union. Galaktion Tabidze and the Georgian symbolist poets and prose writers Titsian Tabidze, Paolo Iashvili, and Grigol Robakidze (known collectively as "the Blue Horns") took literature in innovative new directions inspired by Modernism, Russian Symbolism, and French poets such as Verlaine, Baudelaire, and Mallarmé. In the 1930s, Beria's purges resulted in the arrest or death of many of Georgia's writers and it took some time for Georgian letters to recover. Some of the more noteworthy writers of the remainder of the Soviet period are the poets Ana Kalandadze and Mukhran Machavariani, and the prose writers Chabua Amirejibi and Otar Chiladze. In the first years after independence, publishing in Georgia was severely affected by the country's civil war and subsequent economic collapse, but writing and publishing started to re-emerge from the mid-1990s onward as Georgia regained relative political stability. It was that period in which most of the works in this anthology were written.

And so to the process of translating the present anthology. The first issue that needed to be decided was precisely what language I would be translating into; my native language is, after all, British English, but the anthology was being produced by a publisher with offices in Dublin, London, and Champaign, Illinois, in the United States—and my own editors located at the latter! It is a relatively simple matter for a speaker of British English to adopt US spelling and punctuation, and even vocabulary, but it is a lot harder not to betray one's origins through subtler regional differences in idiom, metaphor, and nuance. I was very aware, though, of the danger of producing some kind of overly neutral, bland "mid-Atlantic English" if I was over zealous in my attempts to deregionalise my translations. By avoiding overtly British phraseology and working with the US editors at Dalkey to iron out other regional inconsistencies I hope we have achieved our goal of producing a text that sits comfortably with English-speaking readers from a variety of geographic backgrounds, but not at the expense of depth of expression.

The sheer variety of narrative styles contained in this anthology meant that each story presented its own distinct challenges to the translator. I hope I have succeeded in recreating the various different voices and styles, for example Dochanashvili's biblical tone, Bekauri's almost childlike voice, and Burchuladze's increasingly manic narrator. Some of the challenges I faced were at a purely linguistic level: Kharanauli's dense, non-linear prose, Jandieri's complex structures, and Mikeladze's heavy use of metaphor meant that even the first drafts were very time-consuming and labor-intensive. Some of the other stories were much simpler at a structural level, and here the first draft was a relatively quick process, but then the challenge presented itself as to how to establish distinct authorial voice within the confines of that simplicity of form. One particularly interesting linguistic challenge that arose in one of the stories related to the lack of gender-marking in Georgian grammar. The Georgian pronoun does not vary according to the gender of the subject or object, such that there is no grammatical difference between *he*, *she*, and *it*. This does not normally pose a particular problem to the translator, who uses context to determine whether she needs to use *he*, *she*, or *it* in English. One of the stories in this collection, however, used Georgian's lack of gender marking as a central narrative device, and it was necessary to find ways to avoid all references to gender in the translated text, which required quite considerable and innovative restructuring of sentences.

Several texts presented me with the age-old problem of how to translate words or concepts that have no ready equivalent in the target language. In such instances the translator has to decide when to let the reader deduce the meaning from the context, when to substitute a term familiar to the reader, and when to give explicit explanation of the term. Different situations require a different approach; I do not think it is possible to adopt a single strategy for all instances. For example, when it came to mention of Georgian foods, at times it was enough to use a broadly equivalent translation. At others, it was appropriate to use the Georgian name for the food on its own, on the grounds that context would provide enough information for the reader to deduce roughly what kind of food was meant. However, in instances where the food item was more central to the text for one reason or other, the reader might require a little more information as to its precise nature. For example the *khinkali* in Kikodze's story "The Drunks." The word on its own doesn't give the reader enough information in the context of its frequent recurrence in the story. Still, I didn't want to use a description of the item in place of its name as I felt this would be making the text "less Georgian." To translate *khinkali* as "meat dumpling" in the text changes it from being that specific food, one of Georgian cuisine's most popular signature dishes, to being just a generic dumpling, a vague, culturally nonspecific foodstuff. I could have used a combined approach and provided the name *and* a description (for example "khinkali, a meat dumpling") but I felt that this sounded cumbersome and artificial. The remaining alternative, to use a footnote, again breaks the flow and to a certain extent pulls the reader out of the fictional word she has immersed himself in. This last solution was in fact the one chosen in the end; for all its flaws it allows the text to flow and retain its Georgian feel while at the same time allowing the reader to access the information needed. Elsewhere, the problem of words without exact equivalents could be dealt with differently. Several stories contained vocabulary relating to Soviet infrastructure and concepts, where I felt able to either modify the concept slightly into another term more acceptable and understandable to foreign readers, without betraying the original concept, or else to use an explanatory gloss in place of the original term (as with words for different forms of Soviet prison transportation and types of prisoner in Lezhava's story "Love in a Prison Cell").

In fact, the frequency with which Soviet and Russian terms appeared in the texts raised other questions as well. On a practical level the prevalence of non-Georgian words causes obvious difficulties if the translator doesn't speak the language those words come from. Perhaps somewhat unusually, I did not come to Georgian through studying Russian, and my knowledge of Russian is in fact quite limited. I started learning Georgian in the early 1990s, by which time Georgia was already an independent nation. And yet Russian was still widely, if not universally, spoken within Georgia and even now, while its influence may have diminished, it can nonetheless still be assumed that most Georgian readers would understand the Russian words in these stories. Of course the same can't be said of the English-speaking reader, and so for the most part I simply translated the Russian into English as I had done with the Georgian, and hope that the reader will be alerted to any instances in which the use of Russian was particularly significant, either by context or by an explicit reference to that effect (possibly inserted by me). I say "I *simply* translated the Russian"—in fact, translating those fragments of Russian was not always straightforward; the stories contained not only instances of Russian speech but also Russian loan words, colloquialisms, and slang, along with Russian titles of books and films used interchangeably with the Georgian titles. And almost all of these were written not in Cyrillic but had been transliterated into Georgian script, which meant the original spelling had to be worked out from the phonetic Georgian rendering before they could be looked up. More often than not in these cases I chose to consult someone with knowledge of both Georgian and Russian; this was both less time-consuming and less subject to error. In places, however, it wasn't possible to deal with the use of Russian by translating it directly into English. In the stories by Morchiladze and Lezhava, the relationship between Russian and Georgian is referred to explicitly, and a significant portion of text devoted to a discussion thereof; on those occasions it was necessary to find a way to explicitly address this within the confines of a text that has been translated into a third language.

Tracking transliterated foreign words and names back to their original spelling was actually one of the most time-consuming tasks after the first draft of translations had been completed. Mikeladze's "A Story of Sex," for example, contains a number of Romanian words that had to be put back into the original Latinate script, complete with the appropriate Romanian diacritics. Although for the purposes of the story it was not necessary to translate the words themselves, I had no way of knowing how the words would be spelled in Romanian from their phonetic rendering in Georgian, and so once again I had to work with a native speaker, this time of Romanian, to reconstruct the words in their original form. Other examples of this kind were working out the spellings of the names Rybczynski, Doña Isidora Covarubio de los Llanos, and various Russian gangsters from their Georgian phonetic transliteration, and trying to work out whether an author was referring to the French poet Rimbaud or Stallone's Rambo (spelled identically in the Georgian script).

A final point to make is that the sheer number of foreign names and titles in these stories gives some idea as to how much of the prose in this anthology is outward-looking. In the course of translating this anthology I found myself doing an enormous amount of research into the literature, history, and culture of countries outside Georgia. This was, of course, in addition to research relating to the history and culture of Georgia itself. For me this sums up the anthology as a whole: the expression of a strong Georgian identity situated within a much broader context.

As a non-native speaker of Georgian living in the UK, I was very aware of the gaps in my knowledge of Georgian language, culture, and history. Of course, modern technology has made it much easier to conduct research, access resources, and communicate with colleagues across the world than it was even ten years ago, and I am extremely grateful for the help and assistance I had from so many different sources. I must thank those authors who willingly answered my queries relating to their texts, gave me more context for unfamiliar references when I requested it, and who helped me clarify my understanding of problematic phrases and constructions. It was both interesting and educational to work with them to ensure my translations followed the intentions of their original texts as far as possible. I am grateful, too, to the many native speakers who assisted me in checking the meaning of words I could not locate in my Georgian dictionaries: Russian loan words, contemporary Georgian slang, colloquialisms, regional variations on words, Soviet-era acronyms. I must also thank Professor Donald Rayfield who was kind enough to read through some of the translations that I found most challenging. I received a great deal of support and advice regarding general translation decisions from various faculty members at the University of Birmingham, where I am currently studying for my MA. Last but by no means least my thanks must go to my family, who were incredibly patient for months on end and without whose support I would not have been able to participate in this most worthwhile project.

ELIZABETH HEIGHWAY, 2012

BIBLIOGRAPHY

Chavchavadze, I., *The Hermit*, trans. M. Wardrop, London, 1895.

Orbeliani, S.-S., *A Book of Wisdom and Lies*, trans. K. Vivian, London, 1982.

Orbeliani, S.-S., *The Book of Wisdom and Lies*, trans. O. Wardrop, London, 1894.

Rayfield, D., *The Literature of Georgia: A History*, 2nd rev. edn., London, 2000

Rustaveli, S., *The Knight in the Panther Skin*, trans. K. Vivian, London, 1977

Rustaveli, S., *The Man in the Panther's Skin*, trans. M. Wardrop, London, 1912

Tuite, K., *An Anthology of Georgian Folk Poetry*, London/Madison, NJ, 1994.

Vazha Pshavela., *Three Poems: Aluda Ketelauri, Host and Guest, The Snake Eater*, trans. D. Rayfield, Tbilisi, 1981

Wardrop, M., *Georgian Folk Tales*, London, 1894

CONTEMPORARY GEORGIAN FICTION

MARIAM BEKAURI
Debi

We are playing with pebbles. Debi is so thin I worry sometimes that she might break in half. We don't speak. We throw pebbles into each other's "territory" and count them up to see who has the most. Mom's warned me that Debi is sick and I should always let her win. We mingled our blood and swore to keep it a secret that we don't believe in God. Debi says if God existed she wouldn't be so thin. At night, when Mom perches on Debi's bed and quietly says her prayers, we pull the blanket up over our heads and laugh. Then Mom bends down and kisses us: me twice, Debi four times. She turns out the light and leaves the room. Soon after I feel something touching me. Debi holds my hand tight and whispers a warning in my ear: "Go to sleep or the bogeyman will get you!" We cling to each other in fright. I press my lips against my sister's eyelids and am surprised by how salty her eyes are.

"I'm a statue," Debi insists. She stands motionless in the middle of the room and won't look at me. I make lots of noise. I want her to react. But she won't look at me, just gets paler and paler. I hold two fingers right in front of her eyes and wait. She doesn't move. I get angry. "Look at me!" I yell at her, but she gives no reaction. "Look at me!" She says nothing. I grab hold of her shoulders and shake her. She's so pale I start thinking there's no blood left in her. Mom runs in when she hears the shouting. She goes as white as a sheet.

"Leave her alone!" She comes over to me.

"Make her look at me then!"

"What was it I told you?" Mom slaps me across the face.

I let go of my sister and try with all my might to hold back the tears. I mustn't cry now, I know it. My mother and I stand in silence. Debi slowly raises her hands and starts to clap.

"Did it hurt?" she says in a strange voice.

Now it's me who stays silent.

"Did it hurt?" she shouts and starts to laugh. "It hurt, didn't it?"

"Are you not a statue anymore, then?" I can't hide my anger.

"Now you get it, don't you? You won't hurt me anymore!" Her laughter falls away and she starts to cough.

Mom kisses me quietly on the head. She does it so Debi doesn't see, and I notice that Mom's crying.

Debi sits on my back. I go from room to room on all fours. She's happy. "I've got a horse," she shouts. I don't like this game. I stop and wait for her to get off my back. I've got dirty knees and dirty palms. Debi brings a jug of water. She pours it over my hands and rubs my palms as hard as she can.

"Now I'll be your horse," she offers, laughing, not realizing we can't do it that way around.

I cut her off. "I don't want to."

"But I want to," she sulks.

"We can't, Debi."

"Because I'm thin, is that why?"

"Yes."

Her face brightens. "Then lick my stomach."

"We can't do that either."

"Why?" She's gone pale again.

"We'll get told off."

"They won't find out. Please?"

"No, Debi." I turn around. I can't look at her paleness anymore and I'm tired of following her stupid wishes, too. She runs over, comes up to me with a frightened look in her eyes and asks me, "Don't you love me anymore?"

"Of course I do."

"Then why won't you play with me?"

"I'm tired."

She thinks for a moment, then tilts her head to one side for a second as if she's just worked something out and says, haltingly, "No, you don't love me anymore. I know it."

"Don't be stupid."

"It's true."

She's sitting on the floor. She puts her hands behind her head and stares at me so hard I almost yell at her to stop.

"You must love me more than anyone else, do you understand?" Her voice is frantic.

"I do love you, Debi."

"No! That's not what I'm saying. You must love me, and nobody else."

"So what if I love somebody else?"

"You mustn't. Other people don't know our secrets. Promise me!"

"Debi, don't be stupid!"

"No! Promise me!" She's very pale.

I sit down next to her, try to calm her down.

"Listen . . ."

"I don't want to. You can't love anyone but me! Promise!"

Right then I really wish I believed in God, but I don't anymore. If God existed Debi wouldn't be so thin.

"Promise!"

Debi presses her face against mine.

"This is mine. Both are mine. And mine is yours. Don't you get it?"

Her lips are pressed against my lips and it's almost as if both of us are speaking.

And then I feel that familiar saltiness spill once more from Debi's eyes into mine. We smell of the sea.

Debi stands in front of the mirror, a smile on her face. Her shirt's pulled up under her chin and she's prodding her slight, budding breasts.

"Can you see them?" She turns around toward me.

"Pull your shirt down." Instinctively, I turn my head away. I somehow know it's not right.

"No. They're pretty."

"It's not right, Debi."

She ignores me. Then it's as if she's forgotten I'm there. She sings something very quietly. I've never heard the song before. She's probably made it up. Suddenly she turns white as a sheet. She walks over to me with rapid little steps and pulls my T-shirt right up. I try to stop her, gently. I'm scared I might hurt her. She doesn't give up. She stares at my chest curiously and asks me in amazement, "Why haven't you got any?"

"Only girls get them."

Suddenly she gets it. "Aaaah," she says, drawing the sound out thoughtfully. Then she presses her hands around my neck.

"Does that hurt?"

"No."

"It must hurt."

"In that case it hurts."

"There is no God, do you understand?" She's paler than death.

"I know."

She moves away from me. She rubs her hands together and, smiling, says to me, "I nearly broke my fingers."

Mom lets us go down to the yard. She only does so when I promise not to leave Debi's side. Debi takes long steps. She jumps down two steps at a time. She's not usually this excited. "Lord, have mercy on your child Debi," she repeats senselessly. She heard it last night when Mom was praying. She doesn't know that "Lord" is the same as "God," otherwise she wouldn't say it. I sit her on a bench under the tall poplar tree and warn her not to go anywhere, to behave herself, and wait for me. And I go out onto the square, right by where she's sitting, where the boys play soccer. I'm so happy. It's as if I've broken free. I run fast, chase after the ball, use my sleeve to wipe away the sweat pouring from my temples. Suddenly everyone stops. They're looking at something and laughing. I turn around and I see her: Debi is holding a small puppy, her T-shirt's pulled up around her neck again and she's telling it to suck. The puppy is howling pitifully and trying to get away. But Debi's holding it tight. Then she starts howling just like it, she seems unaware of what's going on around her. I leave the ball and run over to my sister. Behind me I hear voices saying, "Debi, you're mad!" and, "Debi, you dog!" Those voices tear me apart inside and I finally understand what pain is. "Don't you dare!" I scream, and shake my fists. All I know is that they are all my enemies and I must beat them all so that they too feel pain and know that God does not exist . . .

I grab Debi and start dragging her home. "No, I don't want to go! He hasn't fed yet!" she wails and tries to break free. Silent, I pull her along and think that I may never speak again.

Debi lies down on the bed. She pulls her T-shirt up again and, laughing, points at her chest.

"Do you want to touch them?" she asks with interest.

I sit down on her bed. I lay my head beneath her chest and once again force myself not to cry. Debi's naked skin has a particular scent to it. The saltiness has dried up. I start to feel sure that my sister is right. I can love nobody but her. It comes to me as a sort of childlike intuition and I run my rough tongue over her stomach. "Again, again!" she cries at the top of her voice. I wet her bony flesh again. I want her to understand that it hurts me. That she got what she wanted and that now it hurts me more than it hurts her. And so I lick Debi again and again until her paleness fades away . . .

"What are you doing?" I hear my mother's quivering voice. I turn around. I look at my mother and I know that this time I am allowed to cry. But I do not cry.

Silence spreads through the room like fire. Nobody in the room speaks but Debi. It's as if there's a law against it. Mom stares at me strangely, tears in her eyes. I feel guilty because it's Debi who is ill and not me. But I already know the most important thing, the thing I should have known before. We all know that something is going to change, and the change frightens us. Debi isn't pale because she doesn't believe in God. It's because of her illness.

I lurk by the window, watching unobserved as they take Debi to live somewhere else, somewhere where they're all like her. Debi cries and calls out my name, again and again. I can almost taste the saltiness of her eyes. "Oh God, have mercy on your child Debi!" I intone. For the first time I cry, and know that I smell of the sea.

LASHA BUGADZE
The Round Table

I finished work at eight P.M.

As usual, I was the last person to leave the office. I left the keys with the guard and squelched my way through the rain-soaked streets.

It was cold. The wind scattered clouds across the sky. The streetlights cast trembling reflections onto asphalt that shimmered in the rain.

It was a good thing I'd thought to put on a heavy raincoat, otherwise I'd be shivering to death by now. But even though I'd aired it out for a good ten minutes on the balcony it still smelled of mothballs. This morning I'd put on clothes from the top shelf—winter clothes.

I didn't want to go home. Achille, my cat, would find his own food; he wouldn't start looking for me until the early hours.

Specks of dust from the papers I'd been proofreading since that morning tickled my nostrils, my hair was full of the rye-bread crumbs our director had spat at me from a record distance (he'd called me over to make some pointless comment in the middle of eating his health-food lunch), and my coat stank of mothballs. You can judge for yourself what kind of day I was having, and I couldn't wait to shake it all off.

In my wallet there was slightly more money than I'd budgeted for the day (I'm prudent enough that I'm able to save a bit each month), and I still had four whole hours until bed (midnight on the dot, after I've fed Achille). For some reason—I don't know why—I didn't want this day to end in the usual way, with me sitting in front of the TV. I thought I'd give proper fun a try.

I stood at the intersection, next to the lights. I didn't know which way to go.

I'd already ruled out going home.

A brothel?

I only went there on the last Monday of the month. That was still ten days away.

My little brother's?

For that I needed to call first. I couldn't just turn up out of the blue. Especially with his wife being pregnant.

The pizza boat on the river?

I couldn't stand the way the boat rocked. And it was cold.

The Turkish baths?

That was a good idea—I would get warm—but I couldn't put these dirty clothes back on after a bath. I should have thought about it in the morning, but I didn't have a change of clothes with me.

As a last resort, if I could think of nothing else to do, I could always buy some beer, get a bit drunk, mess around with Achille, and call my ex-wife (she's in the psych ward, but nobody says she can't come to the phone). Talking to her is so much fun. No matter what I say, she believes me. It's a blast.

A sudden gust of wind hit me. I staggered, and grabbed onto a lamp post. I needed to make a decision.

It came to me in a flash. The Round Table!

What a fabulous restaurant that was! My god, why hadn't I thought of it straightaway? I'd last been there a month before and it had done me a world of good. And of course I couldn't stop talking about it.

I needed to go to that restaurant right away.

It would mean changing buses twice, but it still didn't take me long to make my mind up (I'd bought a three-year travel card, after all). I hurried to the nearest bus stop and checked the timetable: my bus would be along in twenty-one minutes.

The Round Table restaurant had opened three years ago. It was an unusual but extremely pleasant establishment and, if I'm not mistaken, this would be my eleventh time there. The first year, I had to stand in line for two weeks to get in—everyone in town was going—but now I could just turn up without a reservation.

What really set this restaurant apart was its staff. They were polite, educated, and amenable. Where they found so many exceptional people—the younger ones were splendid, the older ones equally worthy—I'll never know. It was a positive joy to have them take my order.

The doorman greeted me like an old friend the minute I walked in.

"Monsieur Rostom, do come in!" he called out gleefully, and opened both of the enormous double doors (they only open both doors for their special guests).

The checkroom attendant took my coat from me so carefully, so deferentially, you'd think he was being handed a baby. He gave me a brass token in return. That, too, was a special gesture: they give regular brown tokens to most of their customers, but this was the fourth time they'd given me a brass one.

Before I went to the dining room I went into the bathroom. I had an ugly, black growth on my ring finger from holding my pen—I urgently needed to wash my hands. I needed to wash my work away.

The mirror here is forgiving, unlike the ones at the office or my apartment; when I see my reflection, I always look more presentable than I really am, my features more refined than they actually are. If it could be said that someone else always stared at me through a mirror, then here it was doubly true.

I go into the second dining hall, as always: this room only has tables for one, and when the maître d' recognizes me (because, yes, we know each other by now) I point out *my* table to him. As a rule I sit by the stage, behind the cellist.

But it's taken. An attractive young woman is sitting at my table and chatting to a waiter with red hair.

The maître d' leads me to a table in the center of the room. I take it—what else can I do?—but it's not a bad table.

As soon as I sit down the waiter (a silver-haired man) comes over and hands me a menu with a gold cover.

So far our relationship has been a silent one. We smile at each other.

The musicians on the stage start playing Schubert's Trio in E flat (they always play Schubert here—it was what the restaurant owner's dead wife would have wanted).

I study the menu:

APPETIZERS
Health (Diabetes, Cholesterol, Heart Disease)

DAILY RATIONS
Terrorist Act in New Amsterdam, Goat Flu, War in Turkmenistan

COLD DISHES
City News for Vegetarians
Regional Salad
Literature, Music, & Painting Salad
Sport, Shows, & Cinema Soup

HOT DISHES
Birth Rate
Mortality Rate
Fortunate & Ill-Fated Marriages
Politics
Love
Sulking as an Existentialist Act

Palette of Phobias
Forgetfulness
Past & Future

MENU FOR FASTING
Religion
Apocalypse
Examining & Analyzing the Sins of Self (and Others)

DESSERT
Sex
Mysticism
Pouring out Hostility & Hatred onto Others

LIQUEURS
Pedophilia
Necrophilia
Zoophilia

I wasn't worried by the prices—everything was the same price aside from the main dishes and daily rations, and I wasn't planning on ordering those anyway.

Since first coming here I've tried Fortunate & Ill-Fated Marriages a few times, Love, A Palette of Phobias, Politics, the Literature, Music, & Painting salad (which includes, I suppose, my topics), Examining & Analyzing the Sins of Self and Others and, of course, Love, and I'll admit that these dishes left me very satisfied. As a matter of principle I've never ordered dessert, and tried the liqueurs just once—I tasted them out of curiosity and they haven't passed my lips since.

Last time I came I had the Politics (there were bombs raining down on the Caucasus again and I couldn't really *not* try) but, as you might expect, they were rather hard to digest. Mind you, it was a really good discussion, and we certainly examined every aspect very thoroughly. But today I was in a sentimental mood, and I chose my dishes rather quickly instead of taking forever to choose what to eat.

"Are you ready to order?" the waiter asked me, pulling out his paper and pen.

"Mm . . . Yes." I ran my eye over the menu. "A small portion of City News for Vegetarians—very small—and from the hot dishes I'll take Love. That's it."

"At last someone's ordered something proper," smiled the waiter. "They've been going mad for the Goat Flu all day."

"I can guess why," I grimaced sympathetically. "It's gone cold and people are scared . . . but I'm not!"

"Who do you want to feed you your dishes?"

"Number nine, as usual."

"Wig?"

"Blonde. Blonde, of course. My grandmother had blonde hair. She raised me . . ."

The waiter wrote down my requests carefully, bowed, and left.

After a short time Number Nine appeared: pretty, lively, and rosy-cheeked. She was wearing a blond wig, just as I'd ordered.

"How are you, sir?"

"How kind of you to ask. I'm rather hungry, as you can see."

Number Nine draped a napkin over my chest as a parent would for a child, sat down in front of me and said in a businesslike manner, "If you start to well up, wipe your tears with this."

"Okay, but it's City News first, isn't it?"

"Yes, but there are deaths in it today and I thought—well, I thought what if it was a relative, God forbid, or someone you knew . . ."

I started to wish I hadn't ordered it, but tried not to let it show.

Sometimes you order something and then decide you're not happy with it, or you eat your fill, and don't want to pay for the rest. What can you do? That's human nature.

But this time, it seemed, I'd gotten away with it. Number Nine didn't tell me anything particularly depressing (I didn't react at all to the obituaries—I'd never even heard of the people who'd died), we touched briefly on the city news and then talked at more length about the rather bland rumors that were doing the rounds . . . and none of what we talked about had any real bite.

Number Nine tried to apologize. "It's really not our fault, Mr. Rostom, sir. We've had bad weather, the suppliers had hardly anything decent for us—even the chefs' fantasies didn't help."

Oh, I'm going way too fast, I thought to myself, I shouldn't have ordered this. But maybe they won't charge me! After all, I'm a loyal customer!

"If you want I can change the tone a bit," she suggested, "and say everything a bit more informally—with a more dessert-like tone, if you will. It might enhance the flavor."

What could I say? She was a professional.

"You should have thought of that sooner!" yelled Number Fourteen from the table where he was standing (which wasn't so strange in this place), while his customer looked around with embarrassment and timidly replied, "You're right, you're absolutely right . . ."

It was obviously the customer's first time here.

My feeder turned out to be right. Adopting a more direct style of conversation (with a warmer tone) definitely brought out the flavor of the saucier city rumors. You might even say I got a second wind. And yet, I'd barely started eating.

The waiter I knew came over to our table. "It's time for the hot dishes," he reminded us gently.

"At last." I rubbed my hands together.

The musicians moved on to their next piece.

"Are we in the mood for Love today then, Sir?" Number Nine smiled at me devilishly (just the way I like it).

I smiled back at her. "What other mood is there?"

"A declaration of love?" she asked.

"No . . ."

"First date?"

"Second. No, third . . ."

"Have we had sex yet?"

"No. Actually yes, twice . . ."

"Is it passionate?"

"Oh yes. Very."

"Are you at all jealous?"

"I don't know."

"Do we end up arguing?"

"Oh man . . . I've got no idea! Let's wait and see. Probably just a lovers' tiff. It's not worth breaking up over."

"Any tears?"

"Er, no. A few."

"Let's find out as we go along, shall we?"

"Yeah."

"Have I got a name?"

"Yes, I want you to be called Ana."

Number Nine moved her chair over to me and rested her head on my shoulder. Then, all at once, she started to feed me.

"I'm tired of being here," she said.

"Really? Why?" I asked her, somewhat confused—I always have trouble at first. I feel awkward. I think I even blushed.

But without any warning she shoved in a second rich mouthful: "I want you."

"I want you too." I looked down at her. Under different circumstances I would most definitely have kissed her forehead, but here kissing was not allowed here—who kisses food?

"I just want to touch you," she said to me, "in the street, at work, here . . . But you're so uptight. Are you too shy?"

That morsel made me feel slightly bitter, but I put my hand on hers (that was allowed) and, because I could think of nothing else, whispered to her, "No, I want to do that too."

"No, you're scared." She lifted her head suddenly.

"Of what, for God's sake?"

"You're scared people will see us."

"So what if they see us?"

"I can't keep on hiding all the time. I want to be free to stand by your side, to walk down the street with you, to call you when I want, to come over whenever I feel like it . . ."

This fillet was really tough. I was struggling to swallow.

"You're with me all the time already, aren't you?" I asked her in dismay.

She looked up at me with tears in her eyes. "I'm jealous," she said angrily.

I had thought it was me who was supposed to be jealous, but apparently it was her.

"Who are you jealous of, Ana? I love you, there's no one I want more than you!"

"When I imagine you spending the night with your wife I want to kill you . . . I come this close to deleting your number from my phone."

Ah, so that was the problem. This dish came with a wife on the side. I hadn't agreed to that, but it was no big deal—and I was hardly going to spit it back out, was I?

"Please, let's not talk about my wife today," I said through clenched teeth.

"Do you touch her?"

"Ana, please . . ."

"Do you kiss her?"

"Ana . . ."

"Is she better than me in bed?"

How this child loved to torment herself! I told her as much, too: "You're a masochist."

"Do you kiss her clit?"

I almost choked. Even the pianist looked over.

"Ana, I'm begging you . . ."

"Leave her!" She hit out at me, like a child having a tantrum.

I felt she was feeding me too quickly; the last mouthful had actually burned my tongue. I fought back though.

"Can you really not see that I'm with you all the time already? Have you gone mad?" I should have done better, I'll admit—I could only think of stupid things to say. "I want you, only you, and nobody else. Can't you see that?"

"Yeah, you only *want* me." Tears rolled down her left cheek.

My heart broke.

My God, what hideous torture was I inflicting on this child, my little angel, my little sparrow . .

"You are being so unfair, Ana. Are you saying I don't love you? Me?"

"Do you think I won't put up with you? Do you think because I'm twenty-two years younger than you that I'll just go and get myself a young lover? Do you think I'm that frivolous? What does your wife do that I can't? Tell me what it is that makes you stay with her!"

"Ana, you're making a scene . . . People are looking at us."

"Let them look!" Her voice got louder. "Let them look! I don't give a damn. I've got nothing to hide!"

"What's wrong with you? You've never done anything like this before. Do you want us to go?"

Even I don't even know what I was stammering on about.

"Where to? To the attic room again, hidden away from the whole world? I don't want that, no thank you, not anymore . . ."

"I'll leave her, you'll see," I said to her with absolute sincerity.

"I don't believe you! You've said it so many times before!"

I thought it was the first time I'd said it. Never mind.

"How can I prove I love nobody more than I love you?"

"Come with me—"

"I will come with you, Ana, I will."

"There you go again, repeating yourself! Don't you get tired of it?"

"What did you tell your sister?" Number Fourteen shouted at his panicked customer.

"Just listen, Dad," she mumbled back, "give me time and I'll explain everything . . ."

I didn't have time to listen to them; I had enough on my own plate.

"Maybe I need a bit more self-control, but I just haven't got the strength anymore," Ana covered her face with her hands. "Everyone looks at me like I'm a criminal. My life has become one big mistake—and you never stand up for me. Do I really ask that much of you? It's just, I haven't got anyone but you . . . and I've never had anyone . . ."

"What do you mean, *you've never had anyone*? What about that sergeant?"

(How had I come up with that sergeant?)

"I lied to you . . . I never *had* him, either."

A piece of chili. I started coughing. I could barely get my breath back.

"What, you were a virgin? I'd have realized, surely . . ."

"I'd only been with one man before you—and that was at school. The deputy principal raped me. Since then I've been afraid of men. Well, I was afraid of them till I met you . . ."

She'd killed me, the child had killed me! I didn't know what to say anymore, or whether there was even any point saying anything. I cupped my hand around hers once more and held it to my chest. I wanted to make her some kind of promise, to give her some faith in my words, but I couldn't think of anything, and just gulped down each mouthful without even chewing: "I love you, little one . . . Don't be afraid . . . Everything will be all right . . ."

Ana started to cry. I couldn't restrain myself any longer; I started to cry too (it was a good thing I was wearing that napkin), and soaked her wig with my salty tears.

She stopped suddenly, like a child. She wiped her tears away with her sleeve and said harshly, proudly: "I'm pregnant."

That sound I let out—they call it a belch. I stared at her in dismay. How could she be pregnant?

Ana said nothing, wouldn't even look me in the eye, just stood up and ran toward the exit.

There was nothing left on the plates; they were sparkling.

The last bite had been the best. I needed several minutes to come back to my senses.

Number Fourteen's client brought me back around again—she was rather agitated, and saying that something had been lost in the war. I don't know what, though.

I called the waiter over and asked for the check.

"Did you enjoy your meal, sir?" he asked.

"I'm still licking my lips now. It was so exquisite!" I laughed, fully sated. "Please give Number Nine my sincere thanks."

"Certainly, Sir."

It was very late now.

The doorman opened the door for me and called out, "Please come again!"

Did he even need to say that? I mean, what else was I going to do? Who have I got but them? If they go bankrupt I don't know how I'll carry on.

It was even colder outside now. The trees, with their few remaining yellow leaves, swayed and bent in the strong wind.

I decided to eat out again rather than boil frankfurters at home. Even though I'd gone over my budget for the day I went into McDonald's and dealt with my hunger. Having left the Round Table, I was, as always, starving.

ZAZA BURCHULADZE
The Dubbing

You can't get hold of heroin in Telavi. You can get an automatic gun, a fake passport, a tank, even a Romanian slave or an atomic bomb, but not heroin. The city's a hellhole. And what you really need is a bit of heroin! That's what the unthinking majority doesn't understand. The thinking minority, on the other hand, understands it perfectly well. But that's only one side of the coin. To cut a long story short, it's a complicated situation.

It gets even more complicated when the director is part of the majority, and you're working on his film, and the shoot's in the middle of the desert outside Telavi, and the temperature's 120 degrees, and the film's a costume drama. And even when you're in costume you're so cold . . . Sometimes you just want to scream something meaningless. Something terribly urbane. Something like: "Cut! That's a wrap!" And then proudly take your leave with a bow, leave the film set fully upright (not all that easy) and zoom off to Tbilisi in the nearest taxi. Tbilisi, full of its saints, psychics, poetry, Chinese shops, and heroin. But you can't scream anything and you can't fly off anywhere. Because you've signed a contract. Two weeks ago you signed a piece of paper for the devil who introduced you to the film.

Two weeks ago I would have signed anything you'd asked me to—and never mind the devil, I'd have signed it for a zebra in the zoo if he'd credited my bank account with a thousand-dollar advance. It's a pretty healthy figure, however you look at it. A thousand dollars: that's a few loans paid off, a pressing debt or two, a lot of heroin, and a little bit of spending money too. Although there's one strange thing about heroin: no matter how much you've got, it's never enough. That's especially true when you've got it both in your veins and in your pockets. At times like that you start feeling a bit generous. You want to feed the hungry, shelter the homeless, give water to the thirsty—you're a one-man Red Cross branch office. You only realize that you can't help everyone when it's too late.

When I got to Telavi I had twenty-two grams left. At best that should have been enough to last me forty days. I'd shoot up once before each day's filming and once after. But I got the math wrong. I found myself cooking up the last of my gear after only a month. The next day I realized that even though Telavi is not quite Las Vegas, you get fear and loathing here too. You only grasp the simple truths like that when the hit's wearing off, though. That's when the fear and loathing set in: the endless fear, and the even more endless loathing.

I was on the verge of turning into John the Baptist. Another week of this and if I didn't make it straight into the host of angels, they'd at least let me start as an intern in God's chancery. All month long the wish to somehow understand how our essence subsists on God's daily bread gnawed away at me. So for the whole month I denied myself, shook the postmodern rubbish from my brain, and journeyed further and further back—in other words, I went back to my real roots and origins: the dawn of Christianity. At the same time I followed a strict fast and sang hymns of praise to the Lord. Had I done any more I'd have cured the Canaanite daughter too. After three weeks I was already speaking in spiritual parables and able to understand the language of the birds. I understood the director too; I had thought he was as pure and unspoiled as a dove, whereas in actual fact he turned out to be a vassal of the devil himself. That was in a former life, though, as Frederick the Great's astrologer, soothsayer, and aide.

And so I'm standing in the middle of the desert, and I'll stay standing here until the director calls "It's a wrap!" but there's a long and winding road to go down before we get there, and the cameraman hasn't even framed his shots yet. I suppose though, ladies and gentlemen, I'm not in a hurry to get anywhere, so you can take your time with the shots. I like it here. I like the silence—the symphony of the soul. You only get silence like this in an angels' rest home. I like standing on this coarse sand, this discolored, granulated mass that looks so much like heroin on the spoon before you cook it. That's how my city-dweller's brain works: when I'm eating a strudel I always remember my grandmother, and when I see sand I think of heroin.

But sooner or later my time in the desert will come to an end, too. Because the cameraman is a sly old fox: refined, an aristocrat, a virtuoso of his craft, a veritable László Kovács. So even framing your shots will be over soon. And then we'll film another scene, another extreme wide shot in which I'll appear no bigger than a dot. Under the circumstances it would be perfectly possible to use a double in my place (there's not a single viewer out there who's going to know whether it's me or my psychotherapist there in the barren desert, walking off into the distance) but the director doesn't want to hear about that. He likes everything to be authentic. He can go on for hours about the magic of authentic, one-hundred-percent cinema (it seems he's brought magic-worship, soothsaying, and sorcery with him from his former life). He can go on and on about cake recipes, fitness, and potted plants too. Incidentally, they say he knits great socks. But that's another story.

Every grain of sand around here carries the stamp of the divine. It's always sunny, but I'm still really cold. My flesh itches so much it's like torture in every part of my body, as if there are thousands of maggots crawling under my skin . . . Or maybe it's a divine spark being kindled inside me? It wouldn't be all that surprising. This is sacred ground. You have to walk on it in bare feet. This desert is the kingdom of the Lord. O Jehovah, I like it here a lot, but still I humbly ask you to take me from this world into your vast and blessed kingdom with its rivers of honey and heroin, the kingdom of the Hittites, Amorites, Perizzites, Hivites, and Jebusites. But I know I will never leave this desert. What do you say, Mr. Kovács, will I leave? Maybe I'm not supposed to leave. Maybe my eternal pillow lies buried in these sands.

Anyway, Mr. Kovács, what's going on? What's the hold-up? How has framing a few shots turned into all this? I mean, I like it here, but I really don't want to die here. I like figs too, but that doesn't mean I should hang myself on the first fig tree I come to. And even if I wanted to, can you see any figs around here? There aren't even any brambles. But all the same, I can feel inside me how close my father's God is, the God of Abraham, the God of Isaac, the God of Jacob. It feels as if the eternal light is reflected in me, and shines inside me, as brightly as the sun. That celestial spark which at any moment might kindle fire. So be careful, Mr. Kovács! Don't play with fire. Frame your shots and then let's shoot the next scene and another wide shot where the servant of God is the size of a heroin crystal.

They say that when you work with great directors you'll often hear them shout "Roll!" to tell the crew and actors that filming is starting. These maestros shout out their commands and straight away the entire film crew starts to act as a single organism, dancing the dance of a hundred synchronized movements, and the orchestra starts up, meteorites fall from the sky, and the infantry begins its attack. But ours is not one of the great directors—directors like him are a dime a dozen and their names are legion. So don't wait around for him to shout out a command like that. And I'm not. I'm waiting for something else. Specifically, for the sun to strike me down, knock me out, melt me like a jellyfish washed up on the sandy shore, swallow me up. But it's just an unrealizable dream. Because it's easier for a camel to pass through the eye of a needle than for me to get to the Holy Land, dressed for a costume drama and itching all over. But it's possible that fears like that might just be the byproduct of traumas experienced in childhood. But why would I want to attain the unattainable, the vast, the unbounded? It seems I will never be able to escape. It is a magic circle. It appears that the little legionnaire is not talking about magic in vain. What do you say, Mr. Kovács, will I ever escape, will I ever get out of this circle?

If it was up to me I'd have left a long time ago, flown back to Tbilisi in the first taxi I could find. But, as you can see, for the time being I'm still standing here and I haven't really got the strength for anything else. Because I've signed a deal with the devil according to which I'm due another two thousand dollars. It's a pretty healthy figure, however you look at it. Not a penny more, not a penny less: two thousand dollars. That's heroin, a lot of heroin, and an audience with God. It's one of those exceptional times when you can even put a bit of heroin to one side for a bad day. When you've got heroin put aside for a bad day you feel somehow calm, like a grandmother who's got all her preserves stored for the winter. And at times like that there are two things that fill my heart and soul with new, evolving dreams: my trouser pockets full of heroin crystals and my internal moral code. At times like that you're an empty moral, a walking parable, a spiritual lesson. Your eyes, though, are full of enigmas, just like the Bible.

Do you understand now, at least, why I'm being so patient, Mr. Kovács? So I'm still standing here, and I'll stay standing here for as long as I've got life in me. I've given up hope in the legionnaire. I gave up on him a long time ago. He'd prefer to be knitting socks. Cinema is really not his thing. But I'm surprised at you. What the hell are you playing at with these shots? Can't you tell the world is on fire? I've said my piece. But I need to ask: why the hell are you putting up with this scorching heat? Did the producer talk you around? Is that it? Well, you did the right thing—if you're standing in fire you may as well gradually make friends with hell.

Sorry, but it's a different boundless space that I inhabit. Just imagine that in my pocket there's a one-year subscription to the angels' opera. I'm standing here now and I'll probably stay here, too. The house of God is to be here. And if not the house of God, then at least the house of a man who faithfully respects God. Can you hear the sound of the lyre and pipes in my heart? It's a secret song, a song that heralds the offering of a sacrifice. Which is not really that surprising—this is, after all, a holy place. This desert is the absolute point, the universal dividing line. In modern terms, a dead zone. The threshold between the rotating bodies of heaven and earth, the meeting point of heaven and hell, good and evil.

And if you haven't been taken in completely by its hazy charm, if you haven't yet signed that dubious contract with the producer, then there's still a chance. If that's the case, fight your way out of here. Move, Mr. Kovács, move! You don't need to worry about me—I have my cross. I have to stand. I'm holding onto my God here. And don't be fearful, just have faith in God and believe in me. And you will see that even John Chrysostom and Maxim the Confessor cannot defend the institution of the Pope as selflessly as I will defend the authority of God. And if even after this confession you still think that I am a hypocrite (I have read it several times in your shrewd eyes) then at least it follows that I'm a divine hypocrite. Have you forgotten? Within me shines the reflection of the eternal light, as brightly as the sun.

Don't forget either, that the devil never sleeps. The most important thing to remember is not to sign anything. If he hasn't won you over yet and if you haven't made him any promises, then tear up any contracts you've got. And sober up, get clean, because you don't know what time your Lord will come. If you keep the fast and say your matins prayers too then have faith in me—he will not tarry any longer. Prayer is, in the first instance, the promise of a bright future. Prayer and fasting. But don't worry, if you don't know how to pray I'll teach you. The Savior didn't even know he was the son of God until someone else realized and forced him to see it. But remember, if you're writing in Greek make it sound like Plato, and if you're writing in Latin make it sound like Cicero. Indeed, Mr. Kovács, indeed! I was not born a saint, nor a hermit, nor a confessor of the faith, but the heavens which seek to indulge me put me on the one true path: the stairway to the Lord's penthouse suite. And do you know why? Because I prayed and fasted. And because I stayed clean. True, maybe it is only a spark of that great light, but it's a spark nonetheless, and there is no smoke without fire. So, get clean, Mr. Kovács, and the strength of heaven will come down upon you to help you.

I ask just one thing of you, finish framing those shots soon. And then let's film the scene and move another step forward on the path of truth. But if you believe in God just leave that little legionnaire alone. Can't you see he's fallen asleep? He wants to shoot this film about as much as a pig wants God's blessings on his soul. So, let's take care of our own business. Or, to be more precise, you take care of it, it's you who needs to sort this one out. Even though I'm just standing here. And I'll stay standing here until I fall down. But with my eyes open. Because he has said that he who hears the words of God, and knows the knowledge of the most High must have his eyes open when he falls, so that he might see the star come forth out of Jacob and the scepter rise out of Israel, which shall smite through the corners of Moab and destroy all the children of Sheth.

But don't say a word to anyone, my friend! Let's not forget the wise old saying: the field hath eyes, and the wood hath ears. First and foremost, steer clear of the producer. How much wisdom is incumbent upon you before him, who not only notices and sees the conduct of men but also reads the thoughts they hold in the depths of the soul. Follow my example. As you can see, I am silence itself. It's hard, but I endure. Something much more powerful than me, unbounded and all-encompassing, brings me calm. Maybe the infinite silence of the eternal space? What, you think if you put an ice cube on a hot pan it won't melt? But I endure it nonetheless. And if I don't let anything show on the outside, it is only so I don't create too much suspicion. This is the greatest trial. Now all that is incumbent upon you is endurance and sobriety. You must pass through every level of the dungeon of tears. And if you endure, the daughter of Jerusalem will rejoice greatly, the daughter of Jerusalem will shout aloud, and the Lord will bring you out of hardship into a fertile land, flowing with honey and heroin, the land of the Hittites, Amorites, Hivites, and Jebusites.

Although before then we need to frame those shots. Film that wide shot where the servant of God appears as thin as the tip of a syringe. Say your prayers, Mr. Kovács, say them only in your heart but fervently and with determination, and all your undertakings will be crowned with success and your name will spread far and wide. Prayer has great power. What use is it to follow the example of Prince Alexander of Hohenlohe-Waldenburg-Schillingsfürst, who only used the power of prayer to heal the sick! It would be better if you prayed about framing your shots, and I will pray that my father might have eternal rest.

I often remember my father when I'm here. It only takes the slightest nuance, a distant association, and suddenly my father's there before my eyes. Recently he's been feeling the cold too. With his blanket pulled warmly up to his neck he tugged his woolen hat right down to his eyes, went out onto the balcony and sat in his chair to warm himself in the sun until evening. His thin, aquiline nose was all you could see. If our eyes ever met he would give me a wink to reassure me he was doing okay. It didn't work. He was too tired for anything to work. His body was gradually breaking down, falling apart like an old car. At the same time he was shrinking, as if someone was mercilessly rubbing away at his form and his contours with an invisible eraser. His shoulders were fading without a trace, his muscles, teeth, bones . . . And yet his stomach was swollen beyond all imagination. He looked as if he were pregnant. In the end, apart from his little bird-like head and exhausted eyes, he was just a stomach. A giant fluid-filled ball. But deep inside him something else was lurking, something that was willfully sending its roots throughout his body, like a flower in a pot. But the flower needed the sun, and my father met its needs like a kind gardener, and sat in the sun all day every day wrapped in his blanket.

But that is not the important thing. The important thing is that the sand reminds me of heroin, and heroin makes me think of a syringe, and a syringe of my father. Probably because I had to inject him with morphine, three times a day. The chain of thought is understandable. But what I don't understand at all is why, when I think of my father, it always reminds me of Elvis, the King of Rock and Roll. Even as they were laying him to rest in his coffin I remember thinking that any moment a big fat Elvis in a white leather suit would leap up and start singing. Even now, when I look at the sand I find myself thinking that the coffin is going to coming floating across like a limousine in which a fat and sweaty Elvis will be standing with a guitar in his hands. Maybe this chain of associations leads me to Elvis because he took heroin too? Maybe my brain really does need a hit and that is why my imagination is remembering so indiscriminately everything connected to heroin, directly or indirectly. That's probably it. But I can boogie-woogie till dawn too. When you run out of gear you start dancing around like an frantic Shiite worshiper during Ashura. Or, to put it another way, at such times you'll go to any lengths, do anything. You'd even send Paul the Apostle a text message. But something stops you. Probably the fact that you haven't got Paul the Apostle's number. If you had it nothing could stop you.

And so that's why I am standing here. And also because you still haven't done those shots, Mr. Kovács. Which makes me think seriously that the producer really hasn't got you on his side. If that is the case then I need to ask: what he has promised you? Is it something I don't know about? There's something I don't get. It turns out we are not shooting our film after all, just going through the motions. But why? I am not so naïve as to believe that all this is being done just to deceive me, to make me deny my God and sign a new contract with the producer. It's just that where I am right now I'd agree to anything for the sake of a single shot, I'd even swear Shakespeare is immortal. And then . . . Hallelujah! Then I'll sing hymns of praise to the Lord, I will be master of the lyre and pipe players and choirmaster to the angels . . . When you've just shot up you're somehow capable of anything, even a video conference with John the Baptist. It's no longer even a shot, it's a papal indulgence. A certificate of pardon for my sins. A vein of kindness, a root of love. A universal truce and a memorandum of peace.

Nevertheless, I would like to say right now that whatever happens, I've no intention of changing my confession, and even less intention of denying my God. But one question keeps hounding me. If God sees my torment, why doesn't he do anything to help me? Surely he is not testing my resistance, my stability? Let's suppose he is. Although if that's the case then how the hell do we interpret the actions of the devil—is he giving me money so that soon I'll start singing hymns of praise to the Lord?

You'll blame all this dithering on the heroin, no doubt. In fact I think you're already doing so. The fact is, I'd blame the heroin too. But actually it's the opposite—it's being without heroin that's to blame. Just being without heroin, just that and nothing more. I'm sure that God knows how much I need it, how much I really need it. I'm sure he's appointed me my own personal fairy—a white-gowned and blue-eyed celestial nurse, like a winged syringe, a sleeping child with the smell of milk on its neck, who will fly down to me like a swallow every morning and night, painlessly stab me, and then fly off again.

In spite of all that, for some reason I still believe that the King of Kings knows all about what's going on. He knows even better than I do. I believe that the moment is drawing near when the celestial parliament will vote in a special law that will provide me with a blue-eyed fairy to keep me strong. I believe that the cabinet of Apostles has already discussed this law and approved it with its various articles and sub-articles. In any case, that's what they are saying in the corridors of power. And in the corridors of power they are not wrong. The final word lies with the parliament. So now, lads, the image of heaven both at home and abroad depends on you as never before. The most important thing is not to mess it up! I'm a realist, and accordingly I'm not asking for the impossible. I ask only this, that you don't mess it up. Surely that's not too much to ask?

Just remember, care for the poverty-stricken and homeless now lies with you, just as care for the suckling babes, body-builders, war veterans, and sexual minorities does too. Do you remember the Ephesian slaves and their torment? Anyway, I turn to you now in their name, me, one of those slaves. In particular the last one, a poet and martyr. You should know that I have hope in you. The poverty-stricken have hope in you too, just as the stone masons, malingerers, and fanatics do. We believe deeply that you are sending me a little fairy to bring me strength. Blessed are the faithful.

I would be blessed too, if I had some heroin. I would be blessed even if I didn't have any, but knew where to find some in Telavi. Somehow I'd make it to evening. But you can't find heroin in Telavi. You can find everything but heroin. But oh, how I need a shot right now! I need it not because I'm being demanding; I need it because I need it. Woe to you Telavi! For if the works done in you had been done in Tyre and Sidon, they would have repented long ago in sackcloth and ashes. But I tell you that it will be more bearable on the day of judgment for Tyre and Sidon than for you.

Nevertheless, until the celestial parliament votes in a new law, it would surely be better to explore in more depth the theme put forward above and to get some answers to a few questions. In particular, is the devil paying me so that I can sing hymns of glory to God or not? He is. Did he bring me here to the monastery of the Fathers of the Immaculate Conception or not? He did. Did he give me the chance to return to my true roots and origins, in other words to a belief in Christ, or not? He did. Did he create the best conditions for me to draw closer to my God or not? He did. Did he help me to take a stand as a hermit and a confessor of the faith or not? He did. Does he help me get clean so that the hour of God's coming will not pass me by or not? He does. And finally, if not with the assistance of the devil then with whose assistance was the divine spark within me lit? The divine spark which, incidentally, may at any moment kindle fire. If all this is true, then what is my God doing, testing me? I know that God's ways are unknowable. But I also know that everything is God's will.

I may not know much about dogmatics, exegetics, and apologetics, and I've never heard of a church sermon written in shorthand, and because of this my limited intelligence may not be enough to examine this thesis. But even a child could see that these two propositions are completely incompatible. Truth speaks through the mouth of a child, though. And so we must investigate the topic in a childlike way. We can say that the first proposition is the basis of the second, and conversely, that the second proposition is the basis of the first. However, you can also assert the opposite with the same degree of success, say that the first proposition refutes the second, and conversely that the second refutes the first. These two are mutually exclusive theorems. Thesis and antithesis, as it were.

Because even if God's ways are unknowable, it means that like a grandmaster he's making moves that we can't recognize or which confuse and bewilder us. That is all still possible. But the second part is completely impossible, in other words the part that says that everything is God's will. Christian theodicy in particular asserts outright that evil exists but that God has nothing to do with it. Which completely contradicts the second thesis. If not it follows that although God does not commit evil, evil still exists. Which completely negates the idea of his omnipotence. But if the opposite is true then it follows that the devil is not an important figure at all but a simple puppet, and that he too is merely an actor in God's theater, in the role of a petty insurgent. Which doesn't correspond to the truth. Evil just gets attributed to God in a different way. But God can only be merciful and benevolent, a kind shepherd who lays down his life for his sheep.

Maybe we're overstating it, maybe this is all a bit improper, because asking questions like this will undoubtedly lead us to the devil. Here we are though; we did it, and that's that. Although to be precise, first the devil took you to the Lord, then the Lord gave you back to him again. In other words, it turned out to be a circle. So where are my will and my initiative in that? I'm not really free after all, am I? I'm just a puppet, a bio-robot carrying out somebody else's wishes. Is the best I can hope for that what I have already done, what I am doing now, and what I am yet to do, was, is and will be God's will?

That is why I love my God. However far I wander every path leads to him. You cannot fail. What is more, you don't even want to wander, because you are already in his house—everywhere is his house. Realizing that is the most important thing. Otherwise the path will mislead you so badly, confuse you so much that you start to think that if you don't strew ashes on your head as a matter of urgency, give up meat and fast, and harden the tendons in your knees doing matins prayers, then you will suffer for all eternity and be cast into the dark recesses of hell, where Simon Magus the sorcerer was sent to languish. But I beg your pardon. God would never forsake you like that. Because everything is as he wills it, and he is infinitely benevolent and merciful. And he is everywhere. In heaven and on earth, in fire and in water, in the grass and in the stones, in the sand and in my heroin . . . and that is why I love him. Every path takes you to him. And that is why my brain thinks of everything connected to heroin, directly or indirectly. And that is also why sand makes me think of heroin, and heroin makes me think of a syringe, and a syringe of my father, and my father of Elvis—so that I might close the circle and return from Elvis to God, again and again. Everyone and everything bears God's stamp. Everyone and everything is a synonym of God. Even my father is God, Elvis is God, heroin is God, the devil is God.

I cannot say that I too am God. Instead I'll say that God calls out through me, speaks, sings . . . for some reason that is what I think and feel. It's he who sings, while I just open my mouth as if it's actually me. He has a hand in everything. Everything happens according to his will, even the fact that I'm sick and will soon be better because I'll go to him. And even the fact that I'm standing here and will stay standing here for as long as he wishes it. Now and forever and unto ages of ages. Amen.

DAVID DEPHY

The Chair

As I stand here today, in the same room, observing this familiar space, a strange feeling grips me—a feeling of silent inner pain and boundless sorrow. Because I don't have the strength to forget—not for even a few moments—this story or the part that I played in it; because it will give me no peace till the end of my days.

For a long time, Sandro and I were together. He rented this small room and we lived here for three or four years. He was a strange man; he rarely went out, and spent most of his time sitting here with me. Often I saw him dozing at his table, exhausted after another sleepless night, head bowed senseless above his work. He worked a lot; he wrote incessantly; but I never got the chance to read what he put on paper, because he'd put his writings into a little bag and take them away somewhere. He'd open the door without making a sound, and leave without a backward look. He never noticed that he was leaving me alone there in the room, its air thick with smoke of his cigarettes. He acted as if I had no place in his life, as if he lived alone, never attempting to speak to me, never making a sound.

Everything was done with such indifference. It was as if he were blind, or angry with me. It doesn't really matter anymore. What troubles me—torments me—is something else, the question I ask myself daily: Why me?

Why me, not someone else? Why did he choose me to help him carry out that dreadful, inexplicable, painful deed? I can't find the answer, and as yet I've found no one who can help me even partly understand. Because surely it could have been somebody else that fateful day, couldn't it? Of course it could. But someone, someone more powerful than us—maybe Chance itself—wanted it that way, arranged it so that I was the only one near him at the time, so that, at the crucial moment, he'd see only me. Whereas for all those years he'd never noticed me or spoken to me . . . Me, who almost never left his side, who bore continual witness to his life. I knew everything about him, how he worked, how he suffered, how he loved, how he felt happiness, pain . . . He was especially happy when his book was published, the one still sitting there on the shelf with the others. It wasn't that he shared his sufferings or feelings with me at the time—he never even looked at me, almost as if he were following some established rule; and though he wouldn't leave my side, this too was done with that same indifference. For years I lived like that, and suffered with him.

And how terrible it was when for the first time in his life he truly saw me, felt that I existed, maybe even asked for my help, and I . . . I adapted to the situation, albeit unintentionally, and helped him to do what he did, though it wasn't what I wanted.

One day Sandro came home in a state of great anxiety. Naturally he came into the room as if there was nobody there but himself. He was restless; something was troubling him. He smoked one cigarette after another, paced rapidly back and forth across the room. I watched him closely, and couldn't understand what had him so agitated, so unsettled.

Abruptly he stubbed out his cigarette and turned to me. I stood there, rigid, and felt a stab of fear. For so long he'd paid me no mind, but now he stared at me fixedly . . . Sandro walked slowly towards me, never shifting his gaze, took me in his hands, stood me in the middle of the room, and stepped up onto me.

As he stood on me he seemed to be reaching out to touch the chandelier, to caress it. He stood like that for a while, and I couldn't understand what was happening. Suddenly he gave me a powerful kick, and I fell on my back and slid across the floor.

I can barely describe what I saw a moment later, that horrific scene.

A rope ran taut from the chandelier to Sandro's neck, and he hung from it, gently swinging.

TEONA DOLENJASHVILI
Real Beings

> *I have not enough patience for life.*
> —*Søren Kierkegaard*

He was last here fifteen years ago. Almost nothing has changed; the hotel, eucalyptuses, and lakeside are all the same as they were back then. Time has stopped here, and it almost seems as if it's still that summer, that carefree summer of fifteen years ago.

Maybe it's because everything seems so boring and monotonous to him now. Before he got here he thought differently. Back in the city he had made the deep blue lake, its shoreline, and the summer he'd once spent there sound as attractive as possible for his wife and children, and they had agreed to go, albeit grudgingly. After all, he who pays the piper calls the tune. And so he made his choice—the best room in the hotel. He packed their bags and started up the car and now, suddenly, here he is. He looks at the view from his hotel room and feels a sense of regret. He realizes that spending his time off here will not be pleasant at all—in fact, it will be torture. He felt like this when he first saw the lake and the light green painted façade of the hotel, and when they were unpacking their bags and Lana was throwing a fit about some toiletries she'd left at home, and again when he realized how it actually hurts to revisit the past with a tired heart and an empty future. He tries to rid himself of this oppressive feeling. He leaves his room and walks slowly along the shore. In the distance he sees other people on vacation and hears their voices mixed with happy laughter. He doesn't want to see all those unfamiliar happy faces and sits down where he is. He throws pebbles glumly into the lake. He feels just how tired he is . . . Maybe it's the contrast between the carefreeness he left behind here fifteen years ago and the oppressive weight of the present day. Or maybe it's Lana's neuroses, which tighten around his neck and stop him breathing like a choke chain on a dog, or this landscape, completely unchanged and uncomplaining, with which he's somehow fallen out of step, and which unlike him has not aged or deteriorated at all, and which confirms to him once again that you can never go back and can never go into the same lake twice.

Even recalling the days he spent here in the past doesn't bring him much pleasure. Somehow it feels like flicking through an old album, looking at photos that faded long ago and with which you no longer have any emotional connection, where nothing transports you anymore—not the surroundings, not the people—and the only thing you find in there to like is yourself, just as you were back then, and nothing more.

It would be good if there was some kind of romantic history attached to this place. One of those stories that you later embellish in your mind and repeatedly furnish with new details. In such stories there's always a girl— her face forgotten, but suddenly accessible again. A girl he loved, a girl this place brings to mind. It made his heart beat a bit harder, brought about a slight yearning, yes—a bittersweet yearning, the pleasing thought that one day the girl might come here too and sit on the lake shore, and that his face would suddenly come back to her too.

But that is not how it is, and he ruthlessly casts those days gone by into the water like a handful of pebbles. The pebbles quickly disappear from sight, circles ripple across the surface of the water and he gets to his feet again, straightens himself up, regains his calm and serenity. Mika thinks a person's life is but a slight ripple on the surface of existence. A few faint circles and then—*glup!*—eternal invisibility . . .

He hears footsteps behind him. He doesn't want to look, wants to pretend he isn't even there. He wants solitude. And silence . . . But someone always ruins it. Lana, of course. She has calmed down; her face is like the sky after the clouds have passed. In her fingers she is holding a cigarette. She stands silently by his side. She sniffs, takes her lighter from her jacket pocket. Still saying nothing, she lights her cigarette. She is so sweet, so meek, as if she has offloaded the uncontrolled rage of a few minutes before onto that snail there, crawling toward the lake, hauling its load on its back. Mika finds his wife's sudden metamorphosis irritating. Even more than her senseless anger, it is her radical change in mood that infuriates him. And even more than that, the fact that her good mood is so arbitrary and incomprehensible . . . If one moment Lana was a real tempest—destructive, eyes blazing, screaming at the top of her lungs—then the next moment she could make the whirlwind dissolve into its own turmoil and start dancing around in the middle of the room on shards of crockery she had smashed a few seconds before. And even now, it seems, she is planning to talk about something cheerful. She stubs her cigarette out on the grass and opens her mouth to speak . . .

She has just spotted an old friend, Keta, from the balcony, she says. Apparently she comes here on vacation too. Keta, the one who lived in Germany for a few years, the one she used to talk to on Skype. How can he not remember? Ketato, Keta! Blonde, big boobs? Mika doesn't normally forget women like that, but then he never takes any interest in his wife's friends. Lana's face darkens again. She doesn't think Mika is interested in any part of her life. Actually, it is Lana herself he is not interested in, not this way, not that way, not during the day, not at night, not in the long grass, not in bed . . . She could always dye her hair blonde and get implants. Maybe then she'd attract his attention. Mika feels a sense of dread. He realizes this is the start of round two. The mountain air has clearly filled Lana with new strength and energy.

Thankfully it is dinnertime and their fellow vacationers are hurrying back up toward the hotel restaurant. Mika throws his lit cigarette toward the lake and stands up. Lana's attention shifts to the other people. When it comes to judging others one look is enough for Lana. Generally speaking her judgments are unchanging and unshakeable, a final verdict against which there can be no appeal . . .

Mika and his family sit on the terrace. From here he can see just how varied this group is—teenagers with sunburn from the lake shore, married couples, pensioners convinced of the benefits of mountain air. The view from the terrace is not bad at all, but Mika is the only one who notices. Lana is still busy looking at everyone else, Nia is in her own little world, and Datuna is playing a new game he's discovered on the Blackberry. He is so engrossed that he only occasionally breaks away from his game to chew mindlessly on a mouthful of food.

Datuna really can't stand family dinners, feasts, all the rituals of communal eating and drinking. At times like this his mouth fills with food, his stomach with junk, and his heart with sorrow. He fantasizes about it all being over as soon as possible. Datuna hates this place, and by this place he means reality. He hates all living people, but most of all his parents, because they are the closest to him, the most real. He sees their humanity every day—their hideous, weak, imperfect humanity. Datuna raises his head for a moment and looks with thinly veiled disgust at the array of animated faces all around him. They think they're all different, but they're all made from the same old shit—locked into their petty routines, narrow-minded, mortal. Insatiable pigs who shove down huge portions of food, then noisily void their bowels with relief behind closed doors before lying on the shore satiated, or licking each other clean like dogs.

Datuna feels sick. No, he's not like them. He's a space alien, sent here on a special mission. He realized this when he was a little boy, and set to work planning his escape from this place. He started planning how to carry out his mission. It was in that other world that he grew up, developed, and multiplied, and now he is thirteen, and his real name is David and soon he will replace these pitiful degenerates with new, beautiful, perfect people. People who don't shriek like his mother, who aren't lazy and uninterested like his father, who don't have ugly screwed-up faces like his grandmother, and who don't shuffle back and forth from bedroom to bathroom carrying stinking bedpans full of their own urine like his grandfather. Datuna will replace them all with virtual beings. All he needs to do is work out how to get them here. How to get them here? Surely that's just a utopian fantasy? Not at all. If we can enter their virtual world then they can enter our world too. Datuna is sure the process is reversible and spends many hours shut away in his room, glued to the computer screen, surrounded by his perfect virtual creations, working to complete the mission entrusted to him . . .

"The food's fantastic tonight," says Mika.

"Yes. And you always have such a good appetite in this air. Do you actually *want* to be fatter?" Lana curls her lip and lights another cigarette.

"Is there any dessert?" Nia asks and covers her mouth with her hand. She's yawning. It's boring here, although probably quite not as boring as she first thought. There was the lake, after all. That meant swimming, sunbathing, and boys . . .

"Oh look, there's Keta," says Lana. She stands up and smiles at the woman coming toward her. The woman, wearing a light pink dress with a low neckline, comes swaying between the tables and waves at Lana. "She really has got huge boobs," thinks Mika, and his mind starts making multiple connections: Madame Tussaud's wax women, bowling balls, a juicy peach, Tinto Brass, a hearty evening meal, a female pheasant, belly dancing . . .

The women meet in the middle of the terrace and kiss each other affectedly. Mika watches them and observes how this meeting of erstwhile friends somehow resembles a meeting between boxers in the ring. They look each other up and down, exchange a greeting and—ding ding!—from that point on it all comes down to evasion techniques and the strength of their punches.

The first round goes to Lana. Lana introduces her friend to Mika and her teenage children. Keta finds Lana's family quite delightful. Especially

Nia—already fifteen years old, quite stunning to look at, with fair, honey-colored hair and a gorgeous young body. Keta married later than Lana and she only has one child, five-year-old Barbara. There they were, over there in the hall, Barbara and Keta's husband.

"Bebe!" calls Keta, and Mika sees a small, fair-haired girl. She runs over to her mother. A man follows behind her, striding toward them miserably, unsteadily, like some rum-soaked old sailor. His face is beetroot-red. He is holding a beer. Lana compares her friend's "sailor" to her own husband and feels satisfied. Extremely satisfied . . .

After dinner Datuna shuts himself away in his room. Nia pulls out a series of colorful items of clothing from her bag like a magician and scatters them around on the bed and floor until the room looks as if a band of gypsies has set up camp in it. Eventually she chooses a white pinafore dress. She picks up her book from the bed, walks across the multicolored carpet of clothes and goes outside. First she walks along the tree-lined path that leads to the lake. She walks slowly. She chews her gum determinedly and eyes her surroundings with an inattentiveness typical of a teenage girl. Down by the lake there are bamboo pergolas along the shoreline, a few beach bungalows, and some blue hammocks a short distance from them. Nia sits in an empty hammock, crosses her legs on top of each other like the Buddha, and opens her book. After a few minutes she looks over to the bungalows and catches someone staring at her. Good. The trap is set, the countdown has begun, and in a few minutes the first victim will be well and truly ensnared . . .

Nia blows a bubble with her gum and pops it. As she does so she leafs through her book, giving it a cursory glance. After a while she looks back over to her victim. He must be around forty. Maybe a bit less. A rather ruddy, mature man on the brink of a midlife crisis. Nia looks at him and then goes back to her book. Her victim comes out of the bungalow and sits in a nearby hammock with a can of beer in his hand. Nia chuckles inside. Oh, what a lustful world this is! She may only be fifteen but she already knows a lot. People think she's just like other girls her age: a stupid little girl with her head crammed full of romantic stories. Ha! How ridiculous. She might not know exactly what she wants from life yet, but she knows just what she doesn't want. At least, she knows how she needs to live if she doesn't want to turn out like her mother or those thousands of other desperate housewives . . .

Nia swings her hammock with one foot. The shoulder strap of her dress falls off one shoulder. Engrossed in her reading, she doesn't notice the thin fabric drift downward . . . Nia's flawless young chest is half exposed. The oaf in the hammock salivates. He washes huge mouthfuls of spit down with his beer. Oh, how he stares, and doesn't even seem ashamed—a man of his age!

"Where's Nia gone?" Only now does Mika notice that the number of people wanting to go for a swim is now one less.

"She went off with her book. She's probably gone to sit somewhere. Or maybe she'll meet us down by the lake," replies Lana, standing in front of the mirror. She's finished applying some light make-up and now she's trying to objectively evaluate how she looks in a swimsuit. She can't see the cellulite piling up at the top of her thighs just under her buttocks and thinks that if she covers her flabby stomach with a sarong and sucks every-thing in a bit—yes, like that—then she looks pretty good. Great, even.

"Look over here a minute. Does this look all right?" she calls to her husband.

"Does what look all right?" asks Mika.

"What do you think? What I'm wearing."

"Yeah."

That answer isn't good enough for Lana. What does "yeah" mean? He's supposed to say she looks really nice. Perfect. That she is the most beautiful woman in the world, that she has the ideal body and that no matter what she wears it always suits her.

"And how does it look *on me*?"

"I've already told you, it looks fine."

For Lana that's grounds for a fight, but that would just be a waste of time. While they're arguing the sun will go down and she'll miss the chance for an evening swim. So she locks her anger away inside for now and throws her things into a straw bag with considerable irritation—sunscreen, a comb, her phone . . .

Down by the lake they're putting up parasols and setting out chaise longues. There are boats for hire, the barmen are busy mixing cocktails—in other words, everyone and everything they could possibly want is there waiting for them. Including Keta, it would seem. She is lying face-down on a chaise longue, resting her chin on her hands and watching from behind her dark round sunglasses as people come down from the hotel to the lake. And whom should she see but her long-lost friend, who fate has decreed is now sharing her hotel and getting a tan under the same sun.

As soon as Keta sees Lana and Mika she gets up from her chaise longue. But no—it's not that straightforward. In reality it's a whole sequence of actions, a performance, a blend of movements, mannerisms, and mimicry perfected over many years. Even the timing has been carefully worked out, precisely configured to her audience . . .

First of all, like an aerobics instructor demonstrating a move, Keta supports her weight on her hands and raises her body. Slowly. Deliberately. She stretches her body upward, gracefully, like a cheetah. Gradually she comes up onto her knees, pushes her bottom up and back. In this position her breasts are displayed in all their splendid, captivating glory. Heads begin to turn . . . Keta slowly straightens up from the waist, brings her hands to her chest, sits back on her heels on the chaise longue and adopts the guileless, smiling expression of someone who is ignorant of their own sins, like a rather insipid churchgoer. An unparalleled performance! And now, of course, the eyes of every man at the lakeside are on her. Mika feels rather excited too, but out of fear of his wife keeps it hidden.

Keta gets up off the chaise longue. She slowly brings one leg over, and then the second. Even the soles of her feet are attractive, so she stands on tiptoe on the sand. She knows, too, that this makes her seem taller, more slender. She can't help it if she looks so good: tanned, curvaceous, her figure-hugging black swimsuit highlighting every well-rounded contour . . .

Keta's caused such a stir and now, like a true professional, she fires her warning shot—as a final detail she removes her sunglasses and shakes her hair coquettishly, like Pamela Anderson in *Baywatch*. Many people are in need of rescue, but Lana's first in line. She's been knocked out, brutally, with one clean punch. Second round to Keta.

Mika takes a sideways look at his wife's face. He realizes that later tonight a violent storm will be passing through this sheltered, tranquil spot. That much is clear. Despite this, he feels a strange sense of calm. Over the course of the years he's got used to such sudden changes in the weather and they no longer upset him as much, but in any case right now there are other things helping him to maintain a good mood. On the chaise longue next to his lies Keta, and now she's faceup . . .

Whether to hide her feelings or show off her swimming skills, Lana goes into the lake. Mika watches his wife in the water and tries to remember when it was that Lana's endless series of hysterical outbursts first started. He comes to the conclusion that she's been like that since day one, and blames himself only for not ending their marriage sooner, before she had a chance to give birth to their two children, raise them, and put down such deep roots in his life. He knows deep down, though, that even if Lana were the devil incarnate he still wouldn't be able to replace her. Living with her for so long has made her his reality, and one that has no counterbalance. Better the devil you know than the devil you don't, as he sees it. He just hasn't got the kind of patience, energy or, most importantly, strength that would be needed for changes like that. For new dramas. For a new life.

Lana swims far out into the lake. She is swimming fast. "What if she drowned now?" Mika thinks. "If, say, she pulled a muscle, couldn't call out, and just sank to the bottom. So fast that nobody could save her in time and when they finally got her out onto the shore she just wasn't breathing . . ." Mika keeps thinking about this and as he imagines the scene he is filled with an indescribable bliss. It's not the first time he's had thoughts like this. He's imagined a terrible car crash, for example, in which only Lana is killed and everyone else escapes with superficial injuries. He's thought about a fire when Lana is home on her own, or Lana getting food poisoning from something she bought in the supermarket that morning and which only she has eaten. At first his conscience was haunted by these thoughts and he chased them from his head. Eventually, though, he had trouble resisting the pleasure they brought and gradually they became his sweet, forbidden, hellish bliss and supplanted all the thoughts and fantasies that had existed until then, starting with an adolescent's sexual fantasies and ending with a youth's most daring desires or unrealizable selfish goals.

"I don't suppose you've got a light?" Mika hears and sees Keta leaning over toward him from her chaise longue.

"A light? Sure," laughs Mika. He gets his lighter from his shorts pocket, lights Keta's cigarette and takes another look at her lovely torso. Keta holds the cigarette in one hand and with her other hand sifts sand through her fingers. She smiles an enigmatic smile. Mika's associations become more concrete now, and among them are a hotel room, some enticing Playboy bunnies, the rapid ebb and flow of water, loud moaning . . .

* * *

The waiter brings cold beer in bottles dripping with condensation and a couple of decorated tankards. Tengo upends a bottle into his tankard and firmly grips the outside like a woman's waist. This is already his fourth. He only really needs one tankard to get drunk, but then getting drunk is not what drinking's all about. It is a ritual. An event. Something best done with another person. That's why he has a companion, somebody he met right here, sitting here with him quietly. A pleasant breeze cools their grateful brows and cold beer cools their throats. On the table in front of them is some fish, a few other dishes, and some glasses that, moments before, had contained delicious, neat, wheat vodka, and which had already been emptied.

"We should have gotten a whole bottle to begin with. When I order shot by shot like this I'm sure those bastards are counting how many I've had," Tengo says.

"You're right, and we should order some more," his companion agrees, catches the waiter's eye, and gestures toward the vodka glasses. "Two more doubles, please."

They laugh inanely. The bungalow rocks from side to side and it seems to Tengo that he has been sitting here a very long time. So long, in fact, that time has actually slowed and is no longer counted in seconds and minutes but in shots of vodka poured by the barman.

The sun goes down, the sky turns a beautiful red and then slowly darkens. The people on the shore start coming together. Lights go on in the hotel rooms. Everyone starts getting ready for a new part of the day, new situations, new rituals. Tengo's family are probably among them but by now Tengo can no longer remember what they are called or what they might have been doing—and he doesn't care . . .

They drink some more, smoke a cigarette, and order another glass each. The bungalow rocks from side to side like a boat set loose on a lake and Tengo starts to think that the bungalow is the ark and that only those sitting in it will survive. It is a pleasurable feeling, but suddenly he is troubled by a vague recollection. It's as if the thing he can't quite remember is a splinter that's just lodged itself in his finger and is causing him some pain. He racks his brain. It feels almost as if someone else should be here in this ark with him, someone else should survive, someone important to him, dear to him . . . But he really can't remember who. Uncomprehending, he shakes his head. He's just not in the mood right now for thinking and remembering. He'd need to sober up for that, for a start. He'd need to leave his ark and go back to the pain and the flood . . .

"Did you want to say something?" his fellow ark-dweller asks him.

"Well, I wanted to—Here's to our health!" he stammers and clings on to his vodka glass hanging surreally in the troubling void . . .

Meanwhile that other person, the one he's supposed to rescue, is sitting right there on the shore playing. Five-year-old Barbara. Bebe, who really doesn't want to go to Daddy's ark right now. She's holding a little stick in her hand and tracing strange creatures in the sand. Strange, nonexistent creatures, almost like the ones the clouds make in the sky. The sun's going down. The sky is red and the water in the lake is still blue with some red on the surface. Everything is very beautiful and Bebe feels how big and round the world is. And she is inside it. Just like an embryo in its mother's belly. She is inside it and with her are the birds, butterflies, and clouds in the sky, the ants and tiny worms on the ground, and the jellyfish and fish in the sea.

Bebe is happy to discover this and to realize she is not alone. Even though she can't see her mother anywhere, nor her father, she is not alone. It is getting dark and the lake shore is emptying of people. In the yellow-lit bungalow Tengo is still drinking. He thinks he must have been here a very long time. So long, in fact, that time has actually slowed and is no longer counted in seconds and minutes but in shots of vodka, yes . . . And then that thought again, the thought that he's been left in charge of someone. That he was supposed to be looking after someone. But who, who? He can't remember and feebly casts his eyes around . . .

* * *

Nia comes back up from the lake and lies down on the sand. She likes swimming at twilight like this, when there is hardly anyone around. That oaf on the chaise longue doesn't count. Pitiful creature . . . He looks completely dumbstruck. He is still just sitting there, staring fixedly at her. His family is probably right there in the hotel, waiting for him. Or maybe he's not even married, maybe he's gone on holiday with friends who are single and disappointed just like him. After all, men like that don't even dare approach a woman, let alone ask for her hand.

Nia lies on her stomach and swings her long lower legs back and forth. Her book and dress have been cast aside. Her lustrous hair spreads over her wet back and still-childlike shoulders. Her curvaceous, womanly buttocks are covered with droplets of water. She lifts her head and turns over slowly. Her stomach and chest are coated in golden sand. There's a bit of sand inside her bikini, too. Nia sits up and tries to get it out, tries to pour it out of her bikini. She does this so guilelessly, and yet so brazenly, that as that poor wretch watches his mouth goes dry, his breathing quickens and large beads of sweat form on his brow. Nia is a cruel, cruel girl. She likes playing with people's feelings. She never did like playing with dolls. She has a lot of fun with these newly acquired skills of hers. These are dangerous games, the games of a naughty, immature child who has now developed the passions of a grown woman. Games like this: while emptying the sand out of her bikini she pulls the material to one side and fingers her own pussy. Her victim stares. He is all eyes, two enormous eyes. Nia is the only character in a play, and he the only spectator. She chooses her role beautifully, plays it to perfection. Her time in the school drama club was clearly not wasted. Although she is acting she tries to enjoy herself all the same. She slowly wets her fingers and finds the sand stuck between those small, pink lips, feels it mixing with her juices . . .

The spectator cannot move. He is completely paralyzed. He's on the verge of having a heart attack. Of course he doesn't yet know who he is dealing with, or that this little Lolita who has so completely captivated and bewitched him will make him empty out his pockets and his wallet, that for her he will withdraw an entire year's savings from the cash dispenser in the hotel lobby, and that he won't get anything in return. But for now this scene really is worth any price, even life itself. And it seems to him, on this astonishing evening, that this near-naked young siren lying enveloped in twilight on the shore is the most wonderful vision and dream he has ever laid eyes on.

* * *

He puts his thin legs down off the bed and puts the glasses he'd left on the bedside cabinet back onto his nose. He shuffles off to the toilet. He cannot bear this automated series of actions he has to perform—droplets of urine on a white enamel toilet bowl, cold water on his face, the rhythmic motion of the toothbrush against the surface of his teeth. Outside the sun is shining. He hears the jumbled sounds of vacationers making senseless chitchat as they bustle around pointlessly. This life consists of so many meaningless, empty activities and rituals, he observes, whereas in his world nothing is superfluous, nothing is a waste of time, you only do what is necessary and important. He switches on his notebook.

Colorful 3-D beings appear on screen. Datuna still needs to create another thousand or so, as many as is needed in order for them to be able to multiply and replace human beings. At first Datuna used to take the people he knew and replace them with other characters. His father Mika became that stupid Mickey Mouse, his mom some emaciated troll. Or some wretched failure who's flunked his exams at the school for evil magicians. For constantly oppressing him and yet always managing to justify herself to their parents, he'd turned his particularly loathsome big sister into a blood-sucking vampire that only shows its gruesome face after the sun goes down . . .

As time went on, though, Datuna realized that real beings and images of them should not exist at all and that he should start everything from right back at the beginning, from scratch, from before the point at which God created Adam. If he should leave even one cell then human nature, incomplete and inferior as it was, would still be dominant over the rest, and that single trace would assume power, blossom, multiply like bacteria, devour, and erode the new world just as it has done the present one.

Absorbed in his work, he is startled to hear his mobile phone ring. With his gaze still fixed on the screen he gropes for his phone. After it's rung a few times he locates it and manages to get it to his ear.

On the other end of the line he hears the anxious voice of a woman.

"Datuna!"

"Yes, Mom," he answers grumpily.

"Come down to the lake!" she orders him brusquely.

"I don't want to."

"Come down, or I'll throw that laptop out of a tenth-floor window!"

Datuna really can't work out which tenth floor the sunbathing swamp troll is referring to, but he shuts his notebook down anyway and puts on the shorts he's left on the bed. He's not going to express his dissent though insubordination; he is not some cheap, run-of-the-mill rebel. Datuna is the destroyer of the universe, he is Armageddon, an Armageddon that will not be visited on mankind by fire and by sword but by counterstrike. He is the apocalypse, embodied in a most unexpected form, to be unleashed at the most unexpected moment.

He wanders down to the lake. Blinded by the sunlight, he bows his head. Among the lumps of exposed flesh moving around by the lake he sees several lumps of exposed flesh he recognizes and goes toward them. If he is a lump of flesh too, then he's a skinny, pale one. He takes off his T-shirt and sits down under a parasol. Childlike shoulders, still undeveloped, stick out from his body. He closes his eyes. A thousand jumbled thoughts go through his head.

"The water's lovely! Come on, have a quick swim at least," calls his father.

"Nah, I'll come in a bit later," he answers, eyes still closed. The remaining sunlight makes white circles appear behind his eyelids.

"Nia, where's my sunscreen?" This time it's his mother voice that assaults his ears. He squirms uncomfortably. He opens his eyes, shifts his glasses, and begins the implementation of the first stage of his mission. He holds his virtual weapon at the ready and singles out his first target: a young woman sitting a short distance away and engrossed in licking her ice cream. He puts his finger on the trigger. The woman drops her ice cream and it hits her on the chest. The white, milky ice cream mixes with the blood seeping from her heart, the woman topples over and falls face down into the sand, leaving only her fat little legs and backside visible, sticking up absurdly into the air. Datuna notes his score and moves onto his next victim; he picks out a man talking busily on his mobile phone and dispatches him to the other world forthwith.

Next to come out of the lake is his father, trying to hide his shortness of breath and consolidate the false image of a healthy and athletic man. He gives a youthful wave, showering those around him with water droplets. Datuna looks at his mother lying on the chaise longue, sunburned despite the generous application of sunscreen and now a rather unattractive red color. It's her turn now. Nia is hiding somewhere, but he'll find her too . . . Hell is your family. First and foremost your family, and then other people. Hell is humanity in general. That's why he has to get rid of everyone. Everyone. Without exception. Just like this, one after another . . . By now, Datuna is shooting his victims in quick succession; his deadly weapon is gathering strength and he ruthlessly mows down lumps of flesh of all ages and genders. Many don't even have time to scream. There's no question of escape. The lake shore starts to resemble a battlefield and the corpses pile up. Everything turns red. Datuna's destructive hand fixes on those swimming in the lake and turns its inexhaustible and relentless supply of bullets onto them. Datuna is enthralled. Animated. Everything is in his hands and he feels like the commander of the whole universe. Droplets of blood splatter on the lens of his glasses. Rat-tat-tat . . . rat-tat-tat-tat . . . This is what life really is! This is what really matters!

Immersed in death, he feels someone's hand touch his shoulder and jumps. Not that it startles him that much, though—it feels like a blade of grass or a feather. There's a little girl standing next to him. She looks about five years old and she's handing him something. Datuna slowly turns his weapon and her little blond head appears in his gun's sights. Such a small head, on top of a pretty little body. The girl is looking at him with deep blue eyes that match her dress. He could blow her brains out right this second and add another name to his virtual death toll, but . . . but . . . there's something about this child. She's not like them . . . Datuna stalls, then lowers the gun barrel and asks angrily, "Who are you? What do you want?"

The little girl doesn't answer. She just smiles and extends her little fist. She's got something in her hand, probably something that's only of interest to her, only important to her. She opens her fist and Datuna sees that in the palm of her hand she's got pebbles of all different colors that she's found on the lake shore. The wet stones glisten in the sun and look like nothing that exists in reality. What a silly little child . . .

* * *

"They're beautiful. What kind of flower are they?"

"*Georginus alentus*, with light red coloration. It grows on the mountain slopes. It's especially common near lakes and reservoirs. It consists of the rhizome, pistil, and corolla. Fertilization occurs once a year."

"Really? Are you a botanist?"

"No. To tell you the truth, I've got no idea what flower it is." Mika shrugs his shoulders and smiles at Keta, who laughs alluringly.

"And over here—if you could follow me, please—over here we have the ideal environment for several varieties that can only be found in this area. Shall we go on a little botany walk?" Mika is getting into character.

"Only in this area? Endemic, you say?"

"Yes, we just need to go a bit deeper into the forest." Mika takes Keta's arm. "If your shoes start getting stuck I'll carry you—it's all included in the price."

Keta throws her head back and laughs loudly. Mika looks around. They're quite deep in the forest now. They can't even see the path from here, and not a single voice can be heard . . .

* * *

"Mika, are you there? Where are you? Open the door!" Lana bangs on the door of their room. Nobody answers. Nobody's in. Lana rummages angrily through her bag, but she cannot find her keys. She is hungry and tired, and she wants to get inside, have a shower, have a coffee . . . She's had an awful day. She's spent most of it walking around all by herself. Nobody's seen Nia since the morning, Mika went off somewhere at midday and hasn't been seen since, and as for Datuna—well, it doesn't make much difference if he's there or not. One day that boy will be absorbed into his computer screen and that will be that. She's thought for a while now that Datuna didn't come from her womb—he came out of a microprocessor . . .

For part of the day she had sat alone on the terrace. She'd waited almost an hour for someone to take her order, and all this with terrible sunburn, and then spent ages trying in vain to fend off a swarm of wasps which had flown in from somewhere or other and which insisted on sharing her chocolate ice cream. She really can't stand these bungalows with the ridiculous roofs like splayed birch brooms and this hotel full of self-satisfied reptiles. Essentially, everything is annoying her, getting on her nerves. Standing here in front of a locked door, rummaging in her bag and looking for her keys in vain is making her even more furious. She throws the contents of her bag onto the floor. The keys aren't there. Lana picks up her mobile, speed-dials her husband's number and taps her foot impatiently while she waits for him to answer. "The number you have dialed is switched off or out of range," a recorded message calmly informs her. Lana runs down the stairs, dialing his number over and over again as she does so, but over and over again his phone is switched off. First Lana decides to go down to the lake to look for her husband, but then it occurs to her that she'll have time to yell at him later, too, and that right now it would make a lot more sense to go and find the hotel administrator, who was usually right there on site. Lana asks for a spare set of keys.

Once back inside the room she takes a shower. Standing under the stream of warm water she calms down a little and notices how tired she is. Her sunburned skin hurts so much, though, and her nervous system is still irritated, tense, a tightly coiled spring, bristling like a cat with its fur on end . . . She gets out of the shower and lights a cigarette, then opens her towel, stands in front of the mirror and looks at herself. She doesn't like her appearance this time. Peeling skin on her shoulders, flat, wet, over-dyed hair and a sagging chest. She hears music carried up on the breeze from the bungalows below, where people are having fun, laughing, loving each other. At least they *think* they love each other . . . But Lana feels as if her time is coming to an end. She is worn out. And she never managed to achieve anything, to produce anything, never fulfilled herself or her wishes . . . Suddenly she feels all alone, feels that nobody is interested in her and her sagging chest and sunburned skin . . .

Lana's heart aches. She can't understand why things have turned out this way, why she was never in the right place at the right time, why she only met people who didn't value her and couldn't fulfill her desires. Why didn't they love her? Why didn't they care? Why was nobody devoted to her?

Lana doesn't get it. Maybe its because while she's good at judging how others treat her she never stops to think about how she treats them in return. Does she deserve to be loved? But anyway, for Lana it is all clear. Very clear. And she hasn't got the time or the patience to think, analyze, or discuss anymore. Choking with uncontrolled anger she stubs out her cigarette in the ashtray and dials her husband's number once again . . .

* * *

"Oh my god, a dragonfly!" Keta shrieks. She puts on a frightened face and jumps up and down on the spot like a helpless little girl. As she does so her breasts jiggle so much they almost pop out of her dress like leverets. Without further ado a gallant knight appears at her side to defend her from the deadly insect attack. But the dragonfly has already circled up above their heads and disappeared, and all that is left is for Mika to try and comfort his terrified companion . . .

Keta leans against a pine tree, her face flushed, her breathing quickened. Her red-Lycra-clad bosom heaves turbulently. Mika senses that in a few moments their botany walk will become an erotic tour and that once that wave of pleasurable anticipation has struck the relevant portions of his brain it will quickly travel down to the region below his waistband . . .

* * *

Bebe has got little legs feet and takes little steps. The paving slabs in front of the hotel are big, though, and Bebe can't quite walk with only one step per slab. Daddy could do it really well and together they counted every single slab. But Daddy isn't here. Maybe he's asleep in their room, or maybe he's sitting somewhere, in a bungalow. Bebe carries on walking. Bebe is alone. Bebe is often alone. Sometimes she likes it, sometimes she doesn't. Right now she doesn't like it and wants—really wants—somebody to come and count slabs with her.

Bebe watches people walking by. Everyone is bigger and taller than her. They come, they go, and nobody tries to walk properly, like her, with one foot on each slab. Bebe starts to feel a bit fed up, turns around and sets off for the lake. She can't understand why they say water's dangerous. Not when water is so pretty and blue, and Bebe can see herself in it like a mirror . . .

* * *

His phone is still switched off, but she hears the door open. "He's back!" Lana thinks happily, but the speech she has prepared dries up in her mouth, because it's Nia who comes running in.

"Mom, are you in here?"

"I'm here—where on earth have you been? Where's Datuna? Have you seen your father?"

"I've been swimming. And you know where Datuna will be—on the computer."

"Mika?"

"No idea. Weren't you all going shopping?" Nia grabs all her jeans and T-shirts out of the closet.

"Who?"

"I thought you were going shopping or something. I saw him and Keta sitting in the car and I thought you were there too."

"What?"

"Get off my back, Mom, I don't know, do I?" Nia doesn't bat an eyelid; she's used to Lana's hysterics. She just wants her mother to go away so that she can transfer the money she's got tucked inside her dress into her bag and hide it away somewhere.

* * *

Mika lays one hand on Keta's heaving bosom and puts the other one around her waist. Wrapped in his arms, Keta closes her eyes. The birds are whistling somewhere above them and Mika suddenly notices that Keta's lips taste of pine-flavored gum. Slightly bitter, cool, aromatic . . . It is the taste of sunny meadows, forests at dusk, swings that make you giddy and a childhood lost somewhere in the mists of time. Mika feels happy, but suddenly the taste fades away, and with it the innocent memories of childhood vanish without a trace, without a backward glance, and in their place come totally different images and a haze of passion. Keta moans lustfully, Mika becomes giddy with pleasure and falls onto Keta's bare chest. He slips his hands under her dress . . .

* * *

Lana's head is swarming with wasps, thousands of them, driving their thin, fiery stings into her brain. With shaking hands she lights a cigarette and looks off the balcony. Traitors! Traitors! Murderers! The words are like an assault on Lana's brain and almost drive her insane. She's completely convinced that her husband has forsaken her, betrayed her without a second thought, and with *her* . . . This must be how demons get into people's souls, she thinks, and now she understands the strange feeling that's arisen inside her better than anyone else, that feeling which turns over and over in her intestines and begs to be let out. She can just make out Nia standing by the door. By now Nia has hidden the money that old prune gave her in her little bag, among her notebooks and clothes, changed into a clean T-shirt, and is ready to go out.

"Where are you going?" Lana's own voice sounds strange to her.

"Out. I'm going for a walk."

"Stay here. Please." Lana can't even manage to raise her voice.

"Oh give it a rest, Mom. Why would I want to stay here? There's nothing to do here, is there? I'll be back soon." Nia doesn't wait for her mother to reply, but slams the door and runs down the stairs.

Nia is really quite happy. She finds money—the most important thing in this world—very easy to come by. True, she won't be able to live on her own until she's an adult, but she doesn't mind waiting. In the meantime she'll save up, so that maybe she'll even be able to buy a flat, or a car . . . She goes into the bungalow. She jumps up onto a high stool by the bar. She orders a cocktail. She slurps it down and makes playful faces at the barman. She moves her shoulders and body in time to the music. She sways alluringly from side to side. The guys sitting at the table opposite stare at her as one. Nia looks over at them and laughs . . .

* * *

Bebe has got a new game—stopsies. It's one of those games you can play by yourself. Bebe is sitting on the shore, picking up sand in her cupped hands and letting it run through her hands like an hourglass. It runs through slowly, slowly . . . Then she clenches her fists and stops time. She sits stock-still, dumbstruck, doesn't even sway slightly, enjoys that feeling of holding onto a particular moment in time. She tries to comprehend how both she and the universe that surrounds her are spinning in the middle of this moment, hidden away and hermetically sealed in its cozy interior.

Time stops, and everyone and everything along with it: the tired earth in its orbit, the setting sun in the sky, fish on a fisherman's hook in the water, small boys busy crushing snails with rocks, Mommy and that fat Mickey Mouse deep in the forest, Daddy in a bungalow somewhere, clutching his vodka with trembling hands, the woman busy cutting her wrists in a hotel room, real beings on the earth and virtual ones in Datuna's head . . .

And Bebe is happy because she realizes she has a special talent. That she is the only one who knows how to do this. That she can teach others how to play stopsies too, and that if she does then people will forget about old age and death. Just like at the traffic lights they'll stop, they'll stop in time. They'll stop and wait, for the perfect time, for the perfect moment, for the moment when they'll start to think, to repent, to change . . .

* * *

Lana realizes that slitting her wrists will be too painful. She's not strong enough for that. At first that's just what she wanted, to inflict pain on herself, to leave a horrific scene for them to find when they came back in. But as soon as the razor burns against her skin she stopped . . . She tries to think how else she might do it and remembers the bottle of sleeping pills in the drawer of the bedside cabinet. She opens it. She tips the contents of the bottle into her palm and looks at them. Her eyes fill with tears. She pities herself. But anger has shrouded her mind in darkness, and she cannot think of a better way to have revenge on her husband and children, so she quickly swallows the pills scattered in her palm.

She sits there for a few moments, delights in imagining the revenge she is about to exact. She rises to her feet, takes a pen and paper and gets ready to write her last words, her cruel, despairing, and destructive last words.

* * *

It is only now that Mika realizes that if you lie on spruce and pine needles they leave puncture marks in your back. He needs to get Keta off him, to sit up. He tries to motivate himself, but to no avail. For some reason, things aren't right. At first everything was fine, he hadn't felt embarrassed and on the whole Keta had satisfied him and proved herself to be worth the wait. But in the last few seconds a strange feeling has come over him, as if he's waited and waited for the first bite of some delectable food and then when he finally sinks his teeth in it tastes nasty and rancid . . . So he lies there, flagging, inert. He doesn't even want to see himself. But he can't sleep here, and anyway there's just no escaping all the things that remind you of your own body, of your physical existence. There are pine needles poking him in the back, ants crawling all over his hands, and Keta half naked, fiercely clinging on to him and talking incessant drivel.

"It wouldn't kill her to stay quiet for a minute. Women are all the same," he thinks, scowling, and suddenly thinks of the wife he left by the lake. He's in no doubt about what to expect from her later: an argument, name-calling, a whirlwind of anger . . . His mood deteriorates even further. Keta mentions Lana's name. She appears to be outlining Lana's numerous short-comings. The women's pettiness makes Mika angry. He can no longer bring himself to look at Keta. So he looks up instead. He looks up at the sky and listens to a bird singing its evening song. Suddenly it changes its tune and Mika thinks he hears it calling his name, as if it's looking down at him and taunting him: "Mi-ka, Mi-ka, Mika, Mika, you bored, fat Mickey Mouse . . ."

Mika tilts his head back further still and tries to see the bird, and yes, the other birds too, flapping around in the sky, the most beautiful and perfect of all creatures. There are countless birds' nests large and small among the branches of the tree and Mika is surprised to see that in them are sitting birds with children's heads and children with birds' heads.

* * *

Bebe is still sitting on the shore and looking at the sky. Clouds drift across the sky and wave at Bebe. Bebe thinks you could probably sit on clouds and go for a ride. How lovely that would be. And Bebe imagines she's up in the clouds, Bebe is in the sky . . .

Then Bebe gets bored of staring at the sky and starts collecting pebbles. She collects blue, yellow, and green pebbles. This place has the prettiest pebbles ever. The ones on the shore are pretty too, but the ones in the water are even more colorful and lovely. Bebe puts the pebbles she's found into the pockets of her dress and feels how they drag her dress downward. She takes slow steps. Not even the strongest gust of wind could carry Bebe away now. Because Bebe is on the earth. Bebe is at one with the earth . . .

Somewhere there are frogs croaking. Bebe wonders how frogs stay on the surface of the water. Maybe she could manage it too if she pulled her legs up all funny like frogs do . . . Bebe looks into the water. She sees her face all twisted, and laughs. She knows that water isn't dangerous. Bebe is on the water now. Bebe is at one with the water . . .

* * *

Lana holds the pen in her hand, looks at the sheet of paper lying in front of her, and tries to write her letter. But that first, most powerful wave of despair and wrath has already passed and Lana is struggling to find the words she needs. She looks outside. It's almost evening and the room is filled with soft light from the setting sun. From somewhere a breeze carries on it the smell of freshly cut watermelon and Lana suddenly remembers her watermelon-colored sarong. Her beautiful Gucci sarong! She searches for it. It's not in the wardrobe. It's not in her bag. What a nuisance. Oh, of course—she must have left it at the lakeside . . .

While she's thinking this her anger almost completely disperses, dissipates, and Lana looks at the medicine bottle on the bedside table. "I think I took a lot," she thinks, suddenly very scared. She should probably get her stomach pumped or at least phone the doctor . . .

She dials the number for hotel administration on the hotel phone and asks for a doctor. Then she sees the sheet of paper in front of her and remembers she was supposed to write that farewell letter for her family. "I've left my sarong by the lake," she writes. She sighs deeply, sits on the armchair and folds her legs up like a weary crane.

* * *

Tengo's evenings are as alike as identical twins. People think that nothing ever happens to Tengo. But in fact his heart is full of a thousand things. A thousand thoughts, sorrows, adventures. And he tries every way he can to endure, to resist, to defeat them with drink. Leaving the rest aside, how does it feel to just sit there every evening in his ark, awaiting the inevitable flood? Tengo downs drink after drink, glass after glass, and looks into his own mind with dulled eyes. His drink-soaked worries sink to the bottom of his glass, their razor-sharp edges blunted by inebriation. The ark rocks from side to side, rocks like a cradle . . . Tengo closes his eyes and dozes off peacefully. Oh, it feels so good when the pain is dulled, when the waters subside, when everything that was to be has come to pass . . .

Tengo dozes off. Now time stops for him, but only him. Everything else carries on moving, turning, and his little Barbara carries on too, carries on moving from stone to stone on her little legs. The lake is getting deeper, the water getting darker, and yet the pebbles are still visible.

And a marvelous thing happens. Right there, Bebe sees the most beautiful pebble on the whole shore and probably in the whole world. The most wonderful, smooth, sparkling stone. That thin boy who always has sad eyes would love it. Bebe really wants to get that stone and make that sad boy happy, to make him smile. She can probably reach it quite easily. If she just puts her hand a bit deeper . . . Bebe bends down and sees her distorted little face appear in the water again. Bebe puts her hand into the water, and it turns cloudy, and her face disappears. Because water isn't a mirror, that's why . . . Water really isn't a mirror. Water stretches deep beneath the surface. But the water is warm, and the stones are pretty. The sky is blue. The earth is green. And Bebe is happy. Bebe is everywhere. Bebe is at one with everything . . .

GURAM DOCHANASHVILI
The Happy Hillock

And so it happened that my commander, unreachable and omniscient, wordless and hidden, sent me to this very country. And I, the dust of his feet, ever feeble in the face of his mysterious wisdom, listened submissively to my assignment, and when he turned his back on me I followed the handsome ship as a light breeze, as invisible and watchful as the commander himself, and with my help the ship's sails filled, proud. From the top of the mast I gazed down at the unfamiliar, turbaned people. Knowing what sword lay within the curved scabbard on that gem-studded belt was nothing for me. Why, I even knew how many drops of *sharbat* syrup that arrogant man drank each time he lifted the flagon to his lips, and I knew his name too—Sidi Ben Ijnbal. I do not think he even knew I was there, although the very first word that broke away from his lips was my name: "Truth be told . . ." he said. That is what he said, and I am Truth—I am Truth, who wanders everywhere, roams everywhere, an invisible witness, an all-seeing itinerant. Nothing can astonish me. I was not even surprised when Ben Ijnbal's companion agreed with him using the name of my commander: "Right, right," he said. That is how he agreed with Ben Ijnbal.

Here I was on the boat, and it all seemed so tedious, and I rested gently on the soft silk sail. Here, as on any journey, people seemed unlike their normal selves—in spite of the beautiful weather the travelers held within the far recesses of their hearts a hastily hidden fear of death and felt compelled by it to behave in a better way than they were used to and to chat politely with each other, but the arrogant Ben Ijnbal, known throughout Isfahan for his great wealth, merely commented, as if an ordinary mortal: "Truth be told, it's not all that hot on this boat." That is what he commented. And the company commander, still standing, delighted by the rich man's directness, agreed with him right there and then: "Right, right." How senseless! But then again I, Truth itself, do not recognize that commander.

Then I turned around and started looking at the sky. I gazed, squinting, at the sun and the clouds. Who knows how many times I had looked at that flaming disc before; I knew its size and volume, its intensity and path. Scorched many times and yet invisible, I knew its speed and its trajectory, and it was awful to think that despite all this I still did not know what the sun really was, nor how it was created, nor what had warmed it. Tense and agitated, I stared at it until it dropped majestically into the farthest point on the sea and upon its disappearance I turned my eye away from the red-tinged horizon and looked at the sky. I gazed at the clouds, gradually darkening, becoming one with the encroaching night, but soon they disappeared completely. I found the flickering stars carelessly strewn across the night sky, and their weak radiance brought beauty to my eyes; if I had not been Truth I might have thought the sun had been smashed to smithereens and scattered across the sky, but I was not permitted to think that way; instead I merely marveled at how man had given those distant, radiant, unidentified stars—so different and yet so similar to the Earth—such varied names as Auriga, Virgo, Scorpio . . . And because it was dark, and it was night, I slithered smoothly down the mast, invisible, and went to wander through the ship's tiny rooms. I love to watch people as they have just fallen asleep. I gazed at the weary sailor, his face flush with fatigue, and floated around by his bed, bewitched by his sleep. I filled the air. Then I stood next to Sidi Ben Ijnbal, whose only son was the reason my commander sent me after this ship, then I looked in disgust at the company commander lying with his mouth gaping open, and his unpleasant expression made me yearn once more for people who were awake; I gently touched the shoulder of the sailor standing stiffly at the creaking helm, stubbornly staring out into the darkness. Then, irritated by the heavy breathing and numbed faces of the ship's passengers, I threw myself down into the silenced sea and for the whole night chased an enormous, mischievous fish, which cleaved the enormous waves with vigorous movements of its greased tail and whose smooth back flashed brilliantly as it jumped.

* * *

The great city of Isfahan welcomed the hero of heroes.

I flew freely around the city of many mosques and swooped down at moments to be among the people thronging the streets. Young and old, I could hear them glorifying the hero as if with one voice. His name was on everyone's lips. Sometimes I flew upward and looked down on them, and from that height they appeared so small, so uniform, and then I saw them spread out colorful mats and start to pray, and as a breeze I touched the mullah who stood looking down from the highest point of the mosque, and whose sweet and chilling wail permeated deep into the heat of the midday sun. Everyone stood still and silent, as if they could remember nothing, and even I could not wait to see the hero of heroes—even I, who knew what he was like. I could so easily have rushed to meet him where he was, and yet it was here that I wanted to see him, here among these people. Agitated, impatient, I passed the time by blowing specks of dust up to the clouds. And when in the distance dust rose up on the road, I saw the hero of heroes himself, the man who was to be given the title of Khan just two days later—Areb Khan himself came along the dusty road in a beautiful chariot. He stood on a chariot drawn by white oxen brought over from India who trotted daintily like stallions. With heads bowed, they stretched their red-painted horns out before them, and woe to anyone who stood in that chariot's path.

The capital city, Isfahan, welcomed the hero of heroes: at the very moment the chariot came into view the musicians raised their long horns skyward and sounded them and even I, Truth itself, had never heard such an awful din. In an instant, tambourines, bugles, and kettle-drums joined in the unimaginable cacophony. Amid the noise I somehow made out a melody that seemed exotic and wild. The sound must have reached Areb Khan, because he straightened up even more where he stood. He was entering the city from the Mount Damavand side and five thousand richly dressed horsemen had lined the route. The wind was blowing dust into their faces, but who would turn their head away? The hero of heroes was coming to the city of many mosques. The whole city had gathered in an enormous throng along the main road and all stood there enraptured, gazing at Areb Khan—painters and traders, soldiers in awe, weavers amazed by the scale of the rejoicing, veiled women whose eyes flashed with excitement, and unemployed men from the town square who threw their turbans into the air. Even the eyes of the imperturbable Sidi Ben Ijnbal twinkled with a tear of joy. "Friendship," Ben Ijnbal would sometimes say, "true friendship, is all a man has in life." That is what Ben Ijnbal would say, and Areb Khan was his friend. Had I had a moment to spare I would have taken a better look at his only son, standing there, mouth wide open as if he had been struck dumb, as if he was in the middle of a thought. At that moment, though, my eyes rested solely upon Areb Khan, even though it was precisely because of Ben Ijnbal's only son that my commander had sent me to this country in the first place. But I merely gave him a cursory glance and was met with great surprise.

Had it really been worth coming all this way for this unfortunate creature? But my commander understands everything better than I, and with the hope that I would have other chances to see this boy with all his white brocade finery, I hurried back to Areb Khan. Squinting to avoid the sun and dust and dripping with sweat, he gazed languidly at the delighted crowds and when he suddenly caught sight of the shah's gift a look of satisfaction snaked its way into his darkened eyes. It was without question a gift fit for a king: thirty splendid steeds were galloping toward Areb Khan, lynx skins spread across their backs, with golden bridles and bits and diamond-set saddles, and at the reins of each horse was a beautiful woman. Areb Khan watched the riders come floating through the heat haze like an apparition; unveiled, in tight-fitting velvet trousers and transparent silk tops, they were themselves gifts, and with joyful cries they spurred their horses on, the gold around their necks flashing under the sun as they moved. At this hint of the pleasures that were yet to come the hero of heroes's face darkened further and, very slowly, his tongue ran across his bottom lip with delight. The horsewomen drew closer and skillfully brought the horses to a halt, and as the rising heat haze gathered, they showed their respect for their new master and fell into line behind the chariot. At the main gate to the city stood a resplendently bedecked and rather sedate camel. A short servant lightly tapped its knee with a stick and the obedient animal dropped to its knees, the bells on its bridle jingling. Areb Khan stepped down from his chariot and settled himself proudly in between the camel's two humps on a beautiful swan-down cushion, before the camel stood up and moved off, swaying from side to side, and carried Areb Khan into the city. The musicians sounded their horns loudly again and banged their tambourines, and into the city, sitting proudly atop a jingling camel, rode the hero of—but no, enough! I cannot go on with a pretentious term like "hero of heroes." What I should say is this: into the city of many mosques came that provincial miscreant, Areb Khan.

I will no longer listen to any more of this enthusiastic shouting and applause. I will no longer watch the glittering turbans thrown skyward. I will instead look at the village where you grew up, Areb Khan, oh dear Areb, you miscreant. You were born in a marshy, stagnant village called Mordof. The soil and water were poor and your livestock starved to death. Hungry and thirsty, dressed in rags, and sleeping in damp mud huts, you were taught early on by life's suffering and hardship not to think. The people in your village, though, huddled stiffly around the fire on those cold nights, were not even able to think. If the naïve inhabitants of your village were fortunate enough to have hot food to eat, they would not even blow it to cool it down; I do not know why, other than that it was their ignorant custom to let the food they so longed to eat cool down by itself, and while they were waiting they tried harder and harder not to think about anything. That was your people: hungry, cold, suffering, half sleeping. But flowing inside you, the miscreant, was the blood of the whole world and you headed for the big city, Isfahan, the city which now welcomed you with ecstatic shouts and cheers, where people stood atop square houses with flat roofs and hurled roses and poppies at you, at you, a miscreant from a village in the marshes. When you first came to the big city you spent some time taking everything in with great interest, and very quickly you learned all you needed to learn—you learned to use a bow and arrow, you knew where to put the knife into the enemy, you became adept at flattery, you mastered the difficult skill of always seeming naïve, and you learned how to play the raging youth, just to frighten other people. You traveled a difficult path, yes, and a strange one at that, and one that was fraught with dangers; you beat many men and even killed one. On your head, where now a diamond-studded turban sits, there remains a diagonal scar from that very time when you shed blood . . . And at times you were even afraid, as is right, as is right, and then suddenly everything started going your way and now you find yourself right outside the door of the shah himself, with the crowd roaring, and it is you they are cheering, Areb Khan, hero of heroes . . .

At first they gave you small jobs to do: keeping close watch on dubious individuals, taking secret orders back and forth, and then once you had shown yourself to be reliable, they made you part of the shah's retinue. You had a silver tongue, Areb Khan, but your unpleasant, grayish eyes clearly displeased the young shah and he gave you an unusual, extraordinary task with which to win his favor: a conspiracy. You knew Rustam Beg very well: he had a hearty laugh, and was gullible and trusting, but he was also amazingly proud and daring. And once, after the shah had easily beaten him while drunk, you stared at him mockingly and then, just when you felt he was about to blow his top, you glanced all around, adopted a sympathetic expression and suggested he kill the shah at the next session of the court. You also said that you would stand with him as he did so, because in fact the shah wanted every single khan put to death. You told him you knew that for a fact, having seen the secret order for this hidden in the pocket of the shah's gown. And then of course, you said, the outraged khans would flock to Rustam Beg's side as the person who had saved their lives, and choose instead of the young shah somebody else who after this event (you were still staring at him mockingly) nobody would dare to attack again. Rustam Beg sat there stunned, flushed beetroot-red, for a long time, then turned his dumbfounded face toward yours and nodded silently, and when at the next court session, in the presence of all the great figures of Isfahan, you and your accomplice stood behind the shah's back, you waited until you sensed they were slightly drunk, then glanced at Rustam Beg, full of anticipation, and gave a slight nod of your head. He leaped forward brandishing a gleaming dagger and prepared to bring it down, but you leaped forward too, grabbed his wrist with your left hand, and with your right hand you brought out your long, fine knife and jabbed into his neck, and twisted it three times. Then you put your arm around his waist, rose up onto the balls of your feet and looked into the eyes of your victim. His head had fallen to one side, he stared up at you with a look of faint surprise and before that surprise could become astonishment or outrage he breathed his last. The shah, pale with rage, glanced over at you, then looked at you, looked at you, while you put on your most naïve, loyal expression once more and stood there in front of a stunned court, your clothes and hands stained with blood, like some inoffensive dye merchant.

But now the great city has put on a festival in honor of you, Areb Khan, the man who saved the shah, and you entered proudly into the roaring streets of Isfahan! Along the way acrobats somersaulted in front of your camel, jesters worked their way among the crowds, tricksters and magicians showed you their skills, dancing Indian women made their bodies shake and writhe, and roses rained down onto your sloping shoulders, oh hero of heroes. When you drew near to the palace they brought you an Arab steed so skittish that two servants could barely hold it still while you climbed on. The horse was famed throughout Persia; the shah's stablemen gave it water from an enormous gold chalice. The horse tried to bolt, but you had a strong hand and walked it forward slowly step by step. You dismounted by the shah's palace and walked calmly through the magnificent gardens, with their almond and pomegranate trees and cooling fountains, marble basins filled to the brim with lemon, peach, and melon in abundance, and the walls painted with scarlet birds and flowers . . . And when you entered the shah's palace you prostrated yourself on the shining floor, until he ordered you up again and let you have the honor of kissing his knee.

And while musicians played the lyre and viol in the background, the shah gazed affectionately at the hero of heroes and then asked him, smiling, "Do you love me, Areb Khan?"

Without giving it much thought the hero of heroes answered, "With a love that will last forever, Your Excellency, and that must be kept hidden like a pearl sealed inside its shell on the ocean floor."

Then he lifted his head and gazed snake-like at the shah's face and, seeing the shah's satisfaction, bowed his head again and added, "Forgive me if I failed to adequately express the extent of my love for you, Your Excellency."

But the shah started clapping and said to his ever-attentive servant, "Bring me that sapphire."

I rushed out of the city toward the fields. I had no wish to stay in that palace anymore. I could no longer stand so much sycophancy and falseness, and anyway I knew how it would all end—first they would offer the guests some sweets, then they would set out gold plates on the table and lay out a thousand different kinds of food, drink large amounts of red wine until they were drunk, and then the servants would remove the tables so that they could carry on their party rolling drunkenly around on the floor. Why on earth would I want to be there? I had nothing to gain from watching that drunken noise and chaos. I preferred to sweep like a wave across that grassy meadow once again, and if I came across a hillock in my path

I would swoop lightly up and over it. I like those little hillocks with the colorful flowers growing on them—happy hillocks, I call them. I have seen many bare, lifeless hillocks in my time, but here, near Isfahan, there were many happy hillocks to gladden my eyes. And I could feel him, too, with the whole of my invisible body, I could feel the person I had gone to look for, the one I was to meet here. I gasped for breath.

It was him. Not the one the commander had ordered me to observe, but one who nonetheless I had followed to the city of many mosques. Until that moment I had been disillusioned, but now there you were, and I was staring at you, Mahmoud Ali, standing proudly on a cheerful hillock.

I remember your pale face, your muscular arms and long fingers, your face and its every feature, your brilliant greenish-gray eyes, now squinting slightly in the sun, the slight frown on your brow. I remember your nostrils, which flared when you were thinking, your proudly chiseled cheekbones and chin, the way your eyebrows twitched at the slightest noise and your face, slightly surprised, doubting, a feeble smile flickering across it. Dressed in a simple gray turban and wide robes, nobody looking at you would think that you had such a narrow waist, although occasionally, once in a blue moon, if you put your hands on your hips your body fanned out from your waist to your shoulders, oh my chosen one, Mahmoud Ali!

I would rather gaze at you than do anything else, wherever you went I would follow behind and circle around you. You could not see me but I knew how you loved me and when I saw you I too was seized by love, Truth itself, wearied by my indifference to these brightly clothed people. I would rather gaze at you than do anything else—but I knew that from somewhere up there my commander was watching me angrily.

* * *

Sidi Ben Ijnbal was known throughout the kingdom for his wealth and intelligence. What a man he was: money, rest assured, he had plenty; his herd of horses grazed from the slopes of Mount Damavand down to the hillocks on the plain below; the handiwork of Ben Ijnbal's weavers was taken to faraway kingdoms by camel, and he had gold and gems and pearls in abundance; but all this was nothing as compared to his wisdom and prescience—in his place who else would have befriended Areb Khan when he was still just a miscreant from the provinces? The very same day he looked into those horrible eyes he gave Areb Khan a horse and a saber and promised him his assistance. Areb would visit him regularly and Ben Ijnbal always rewarded him generously. But it was not generosity that made him do so, it was fear. Fear. Until then he had never given gifts to anybody other than the shah and the khans, and to them—oh! to them he sent truly magnificent gifts. "May Allah grant long life to our shah, who shines like the sun, and may Allah make his every day equivalent to a thousand years," Sidi Ben Ijnbal always added to his gifts. That is what Ben Ijnbal said, but in his heart he thought, "Insurance and peace of mind are all a man has in life."

Ben Ijnbal liked to wander around the palace at first light. He took small steps as he walked through the sparkling halls and surveyed his many riches. He paid close attention to the gold, the precious gems, the imported crystal, and the soft animal hides. "Possessions," thought Ben Ijnbal, "are all a man has in life." But the eye is a strange creature and Ben Ijnbal looked sometimes this way and sometimes that, dissatisfied, and finally he tired of looking at his immovable property and hurried off to the silk-decked room which housed his movable property, namely his only wife, Soraya Khanum. Oh! how deeply she was sleeping. Now that she was breathing rather heavily she was barely movable property, but in general when she was up and about . . . And although I am Truth and so do not really have the right to make comparisons like this, at the same time Truth compels me to say that Soraya Khanum was a woman like a melon: cool, sweet and, like the plant it grows on, able to be trained in a particular direction. And at first light when the miserly and reserved Ben Ijnbal looked at his wife, his heart was strangely moved, and he lay down some distance from her, stretched out his neck and gently lay his cheek against her naked arm. He lay there like that, saying nothing, and the feeble Ben Ijnbal thought to himself, "This is a real woman, yes, and a real woman is all a man has in life." As a rule, a man of his wealth should have had numerous wives, but Soraya Khanum always warned him in the strongest possible terms: "If you take another wife you will never see me alive again." "No, no," Ben Ijnbal would reassure her, "I want nobody but you." Soraya would stretch out her arms in front of her and Ben Ijnbal would quickly open his short arms too and then they would embrace. "The blind love of a beautiful woman toward her man," Ben Ijnbal thought with bated breath, "is all a man has . . ." But Soraya Khanum was staring at the richly decked rooms and boasting inside, "What, let another woman swan around this palace doing whatever she wants? As if I would!"

But Sidi Ben Ijnbal was not always so meek and kind. His servants and craftsmen would pale when they saw him and regarded him with the deepest respect—Ben Ijnbal knew how to behave anywhere. He would examine his weavers' handiwork with an arrogant, unsmiling face, furrow his brow and go again. The anxious craftsmen would glance at each other and resolve to apply themselves more assiduously to their work, thinking, "No, he's right, we really can work harder."

Not a day went by without new purchases being brought in for Ben Ijnbal—gold was piled atop gold, diamonds onto diamonds. A wealthy man is never short of friends, but Ben Ijnbal chose four worthy citizens and talked only to them. They would sit cross-legged on the rug, slowly counting their beautiful prayer beads and attaching appropriate words to each bead: "May Allah—" Ben Ijnbal would say, counting a bead, and then another bead "—protect—" and another bead "—the shah." His friends' prayer beads clinked their beads in time: "*Inshallah.*" Then they sat for a long time in silence and after they had counted through many more beads their host broke the silence: "Words," said Ben Ijnbal, "should be few, but as clear as a cloudless day and as uncompromising as steel." The guests nodded their approval and took great sips of their *sharbat* syrup drinks, eyes closed.

"Why don't you come and visit anymore?" Ben Ijnbal's scar-faced friend said, "Do come over and I will give you the sight of both my eyes as a path."

"So beautifully expressed," said a rather plump guest whose turban sat at an angle—one of his ears had been cut off during childhood. He counted a bead. "*Masha'Allah*, that was beautifully said. Only true friends can give voice to beautiful words like that."

"Oh, true friendship," the third man agreed. He had a collapsed jaw and moved his lips in a strange way. "Oh, true friendship warms us and lights our way along the path of life like the sun."

"Of course," said the fourth, a handsome man. "The betrayal of true friendship is the most heinous of all mortal sins."

"Betraying a true friendship," proclaimed Sidi Ben Ijnbal, in the most arresting and horrific way possible, "is like raping your own mother on Mohammed's grave."

"Oh!" The guests were stunned. They raised their eyes to the ceiling. "May Allah protect us, Allah protect us!"

"All power to Allah our protector!" said Sidi Ben Ijnbal and clapped his hands together. "Bring us some horse meat."

In the meantime a veiled Soraya Khanum came boldly into the room and all at once Sidi Ben Ijnbal was thrown into turmoil. Sitting as he was next to the most handsome guest, he felt his position would not put him in the best light, and so he rose as if to stretch out his legs and started walking around, while enunciating with affected clarity, "Do you like the meat, Babut Khan?"

"Yes," nodded the guest, "it's absolutely delicious."

And Sidi Ben Ijnbal stood as straight and tall as he could.

But it was when his son was born that Sidi Ben Ijnbal became most arrogant. He could not wait to see the child, even though in the city of many mosques there was a strange local custom which dictated that wealthy men were not allowed to see their child until the age of five. Ben Ijnbal waited several months, and waited some more, and finally he crept into the room. The nanny was asleep, but the child, wrapped in silk brocade, was staring at the ceiling, and when he saw the unfamiliar face leaning over him he fell asleep in an instant. And Sidi Ben Ijnbal was overjoyed, and crept stealthily out of the room again, and was finally sure that it really was his child—he had the same attentive gaze, and short arms, and his face seemed to glisten like an expensive mask in just the same way his father's did. For a long time afterward he felt so reassured that in fact he had no desire to see the child again—even if not for another ten years. Once in a blue moon, though, a strange sense of doubt would take hold of him: "Did I just imagine it?" But no, no, the child really did look like him. "Thank you, beautiful Soraya Khanum, you faithful woman, *barakallah*," Ben Ijnbal said over and over in his heart.

And the child ate, drank, and grew, and time passed uneventfully, although sometimes if a fly landed on him he would furrow his brow. When he learned to walk they dressed him in pretty gold-threaded robes and put a sparkling turban on his head. And when finally he appeared before his father for the first time with a beautiful toy dagger on his belt, Sidi Ben Ijnbal called him over. But the child stayed where he was, and instead Ben Ijnbal went to the child, looked at him for a while and didn't know what to do, then tickled his chest with two fingers and said, "Tickle tickle!" The child stared at him and Ben Ijnbal was pleased. "He's looking at me, he's looking at me!" he thought. The nanny slapped the little boy's wrist a few times, as if to compel him to do something, and for a while he resisted, but finally he said, "May the all-powerful shah be Allah's protector." Ben Ijnbal put his head on one side and peered at the child, and the very next day he appointed a great teacher to help the boy with his oratorical skills. And as for a name for the boy, which should have been simple enough, Ben Ijnbal had great difficulty choosing. He tried saying names out loud for the whole day: Maheb, Maheb, no, that's no good, maybe Hassan, Hassan? Hassan . . . No, no good. Kenja? Kenja, Kenja . . . but still he could not choose, and then finally his eyes alighted on a decanter filled with sweet *sharbat* syrup and suddenly it came to him, he felt that now he really had a name, and he rushed into the child's room and stared at his small, soft features, his sweet, sweet face and named him . . . Sharbat. The name seemed somehow wrong to Soraya Khanum but then she grew to like it, and let her voice sing as she called him: "Sharbat, Shaaaarbat!"

News of this spread throughout the whole of Isfahan, and many others copied Ben Ijnbal in naming their children Sharbat too, although none were wealthy, it must be said.

The great teacher started with the basics: "Look, Sharbat, is that the sun?"

"Uh?"

"It's a sunny day, Sharbat. Go on, say 'May our praise of the shahs be as radiant as the sun.'"

But Sharbat just grabbed a silver drinking bowl and asked, "What's this?"

"Sharbat, Sharbat." The great teacher shook his head, "First tell me what you say when it's a sunny day and then I'll tell you."

But Sharbat thought and thought and finally said, "No, you tell me first."

"Ahh, Sharbat, Sharbat . . ."

"Boy," Sidi Ben Ijnbal said that same evening, "We have rules in this country. Young men are expected to know three things: how to ride a horse well, how to handle a bow and arrow, and how to speak the truth. But as your father I'm telling you this: a man needs to know how to ride a horse, use a bow and arrow well, speak the truth, and be erudite, do you understand? If not, well . . ." Here Ben Ijnbal lost his self-control, because Sharbat simply lifted a pear from the table and sank his teeth into it with complete indifference. "If not, my boy, I'll take you and beat you so badly that not even the mirror will recognize you. Now put that pear down!"

The great teacher continued with his lessons. "What could possibly be deeper than the ocean and more vast than the skies across which the smallest birds fly? What else but my immeasurable love for you, oh Shah, oh Sun, oh everlasting beauty of Isfahan."

"Be bold, be bold, wrap your feet around tightly so he can feel there's someone riding him. Be bold, don't be scared," the horse-riding teacher encouraged him. "Now ease off the reins a bit, give him a few slaps on the back—no, no, not like that, hold on, pull back on the reins! Whoa! Whoa! Are you hurt, Sharbat?"

"Bend it, bend it, and at the same time hold it more upright, more, more, yes, like that. Now look carefully over there; there's an effigy of an infidel. Imagine it's alive and aim for the heart, draw your arrow back a bit more, now let go and watch it fly, let go! What, you can't open your fingers any more? Point it over there—over there!—or it'll go wherever you're facing, won't it. Don't kill me—over there I said! What's wrong with you? Oh! Oh! Well, thank heavens it hit the saddle . . ."

"Who does the Almighty raise up? Oh Almighty Allah, who do you raise up, and who do you commit to the dark grave? You raise up those who love the shah, and to the man who does not love the shah you bring death and damnation. Now, I'll start at the beginning and you repeat after me. Who does the Almighty raise up?"

"Pull, pull, now let it go, let go or it won't shoot. Open your fingers, pretend it's burning hot and let go! Oh, well done."

"Hasn't he grown!" Soraya Khanum said. "When he was born he was so little."

In the mosque, the mullah sat facing a semicircle of children. The row of children resembled a bow pulled taut, while the mullah sat a short distance away like the feathers on the arrow and shot strange ideas toward an invisible, sharpened arrowhead that lay somewhere beyond the children. "To Allah belongs the East and the West, wherever you turn there is the face of Allah. Indeed, Allah is all-encompassing and all-knowing; may he grant us victory over the heathens."

"May he grant us victory over the heathens."

"And if someone oppresses you, you should oppress him as he has oppressed you." The mullah pulled himself up angrily; the bow became more taut.

"Real friendship," Sidi Ben Ijnbal often repeated to the child, when he became Areb Khan's most trusted servant, "is all a man has in life."

And Sharbat seemed to learn a lot, and yet while he was thinking he always just stared, raised his round, wide eyes to the ceiling and when

I—invisible—approached him and stared into those eyes, it seemed to me almost as if I was looking into a big, round pool from high above, a pool of still water with a faded old barrel floating about in it. Oh, how I hated him. When I saw him I wanted nothing more than to disappear again, but I remembered the task my commander had given me and had no other choice but to follow him like a decrepit old man; I followed him to his lessons, to the mosque, and loped joylessly toward Areb Khan's palace while Sharbat carried the most valuable presents. I didn't hate the great miscreant as much as I hated this magnificently dressed child. In fact, Ben Ijnbal, famed for his wisdom, did not have much understanding at all: what sensible father would dress a child who looked like Sharbat in such expensive, eye-catching clothes? It would have been better to veil him like a woman. And because I am Truth I could see that he did in fact have the right features: eyebrows, nose, forehead, and lips, but those eyes, those eyes, and that blank expression—when he was thinking he would actually start to sweat and his mask-like face would shimmer even more.

But then whose child was this? This was the child of a craven miser, who always painted false pride on his face even when he did not have the cheek of his melon-like wife pressed against his arm. And I could have tolerated it all, but for the fact that when I looked at him—how he ate, how he slept, how he looked at himself in his gilded mirrors, how fussily he chose his various turbans—I remembered that everything, absolutely everything—the way he looked, moved, thought—had been taught to him by his teachers and his father. And even though he knew what to say in a given situation, could gallop on a horse and knew how to use a bow and arrow, he was still just an oversized puppet who only aspired to two things: wealth and security. Although wealth came at a price, and while he took pleasure from eating delicious food, gazing out onto his fountains, receiving gifts, from his exquisite clothes, the dazzling smoothness of gold, from a rare pearl, the doubts that accompanied them were not pleasant, nor was the fear of robbery, nor the giving of gifts in return. And even as he sat astride his galloping Arab steed, flying like the wind, when any man's blood should surely stir in his veins, that idiot just sat there in a stupor. He was a puppet, however much they dressed him up in fancy clothes—his face still shimmered, and then there was his name, hmm . . . Sharbat. Oh Mahmoud Ali! I used to follow you when I was bored of him and shaking with rage, I would catch sight of you and follow you everywhere; how I loved looking at you, at your face with that flicker of a smile, sometimes sad, sometimes fearful. I would follow you through the dusty streets and into the mosque, you would stare pensively at the jobless men who congregated in the square, and at the children, and then walk, your arms by your sides, stepping proudly, your head raised proudly. In the market among the chattering crowds, clamoring to be heard, your body and calm, sad face stood out so much. Although in the city of many mosques the market was everywhere—everybody was selling something, everybody was trying to cheat somebody else. And if you turned away from the noise of the bellowing instruments, then I loved to look at you from behind. That faint, blue vein on your temple, which disappeared above your cheek and then was barely visible again on your neck, your doubting gaze, your gentle sculpted cheekbones, your long neck, powerful and fair . . . Mahmoud Ali! Your thoughts, your doubts—you could not tell them to anyone, but I knew everything, after all. And just your gaze, your gaze, eloquent, true and direct . . . I watched the way you looked at that man who so valued his silk brocade, that caravan leader who had packed too great a load onto his camel and then plunged his knife into its throat in two places when it fell, the man who spoke with honeyed words, the man who looked at everything with such indifference . . . Mahmoud Ali! For you nothing was insignificant, you knew the value of treasures worn out through use—the water you drank, the air you breathed, the sun that warmed you. And once when Sharbat took a peach and sank his teeth into it, I rushed over to you and was amazed, for in your fingers you were holding high another of the same fruit and gazing, gazing at it. For Sharbat it was nothing, he took it and ate it, but you looked at this soft, downy fruit in wonder and from the mullah's thick book—where there were things you did not like—you remembered this sentence and repeated it slowly and with delight: "From the heavens he sends forth rain, with it we make each seed become a growing plant. With these we fill our meadows, which yield the cereal crops laid out in rows, and date trees, whose branches put on vast brushy leaves, and orchards covered in vines, and olives and pomegranates, which resemble each other and yet are different from each other. Behold the fruits of these plants, consider their yield and their ripeness—all of these miracles are with 'those who understand.'"

Mahmoud Ali! I have seen too, how as soon as you leaped onto your horse it would rear up its hind legs, it would stiffen in an instant when it sensed a real horseman on its back and happily gallop off with long strides across the meadow. You sat straight-backed on your galloping horse, the wind streaming past your ears, sometimes you looked down at the ground rushing beneath you, and sometimes you looked toward Mount Damavand, wrathfully dancing its way ever closer.

And of course I also knew why the citizens of Isfahan did not like you: what did they want with your proud, mistrustful gaze? They avoided meeting your eye, they were filled with anger and hatred toward you—you, who walked around their dusty city, smiling, doubting, like their conscience, oh chosen one, Mahmoud Ali!

But I was forced to go back once again to Ben Ijnbal's brightly sparkling palace, to pace up and down by the singing fountains, to squeeze under that table on which were piled various delicious foods and where he sat tapping his feet carelessly right in front of me. What on earth did I want in this place?

But my commander, unreachable and omniscient, understands these things better than me.

* * *

The head cook looked around for a short time, rather bewildered, and having seen there was nobody around he greeted Ben Ijnbal respectfully and relayed his terrible tale in a low voice.

"Who, Soraya?" Ben Ijnbal gasped and sat down, as white as a sheet.

"Yes."

"Do you know this for a fact?"

"Yes." The cook seemed deeply troubled.

"Did you see it with your own eyes?"

"I did."

"The whole thing?"

"Absolutely everything."

"And you couldn't put your saber through her?"

"I didn't have it on me." The cook shrugged. "Should I have killed them both?"

Ben Ijnbal was lost in thought, ignored what the cook said and laid his prayer beads down on the rug. He went over to the window to recover, but the beauty of the front gardens only served to irritate him further. "Bah!" He should never have started stirring things up in the first place, he knew that. "Self-control, self-control . . ." He absorbed this thought, and interlaced his trembling fingers. Then he raised his head proudly and said to the cook, "Go and find out exactly what happened for me."

"I already know, your Excellency." The cook put his hand on his heart. "What do you want me to find out, exactly, when I already know, and saw it with my own eyes?"

Ben Ijnbal flung his hand out toward the door. "I said go and find out!"

"Oh Soraya, you pauper, I'll make you sorry you were ever born!" he thought, and tried to rip at his robes, but they were woven so well he could not. "And you! You dare to do this to me, you wretched creature! . . ."

But he was not a wretched creature at all, he was a very healthy baker, with big, white arms.

Up until this point I had been standing in the corner, bored and listless. But when I saw how unsettled and confused Ben Ijnbal was I found myself wanting to find out what he was thinking and wrapped myself like a turban around his shaven head. "Calm, calm . . ." I heard a quiet, tense voice say. "Calm, calm, the most important thing is calm." But from inside his robe his heart began to flutter: "Cut them up, cut them to pieces." "Calm down, calm down, the most important thing is to stay rational," his shaven head stubbornly repeated to him. "Be rational. Being rational is all a man—" "Cut her up!" His heart paced up and down restlessly, and managed to win his fingers over too. They clenched into a fist. "Cut her, or get someone else to." "Let's get someone else to do it," his head suddenly—unexpectedly—agreed, and just when nearly everything had been decided his mouth chipped in: "No, no," it pleaded, "If you have her cut up she'll surely die!"

"What choice do I have?" Ben Ijnbal thought to himself, "If I let her live the news will spread all over Isfahan. Ah, if only Areb Khan was in the city . . ."

But Areb Khan was standing silently in front of the sultan. He knew that a tense silence would make the sultan lose his self-control, and when he felt it was necessary he looked the sultan in the eye and slowly articulated, "The almighty and most beauteous shah of the great city of Isfahan has entrusted me with ensuring that you shackle Suhak and surrender him to me."

"I wish long life to the wise and astute shah of Isfahan, and I swear to you that Suhak is not here."

"Everyone says that you have him."

"I swear to Allah, he is not on my land," the sultan said and placed his hand on the Koran, "May Suhak eat pork on a feast day if he is on my land!"

It was a terrible oath, and they stared at each other for a long time, each sure of the truth of what they were saying. The miscreant knew for certain that the sultan was sheltering the fugitive, whereas the sultan could quite brazenly swear, "He is not on my land," because he had put Suhak in a large wicker basket with some food and drink, given him his reassurances, told him to keep completely quiet for a couple of days and had two of his most loyal servants hang the basket from a tree deep within the forest.

"If he were on your land would you let me kill him?" Areb Khan asked him gravely.

"I would let you kill him."

"Even though he is your brother?"

"To his faithful servants, the glorious ruler of Isfahan is more dear even than a brother or a father."

"Very good."

Despite the sultan's invitation, Areb Khan did not stay in the palace but pitched his tent in a field, intending to spend the night there. To get into his low tent he had to bow his head. Far away in Isfahan the cook bowed his head too as he entered Ben Ijnbal's room, even though the doorway was high enough for him to pass through easily.

"What happened? Did you find out?" Ben Ijnbal asked him slyly.

"I thought a lot, Excellency, and asked myself whether I might have been mistaken about anything, but things really happened just as I told you first time around: Soraya Khanum was standing in her room by the window and when you left the baker came out into the yard with his sleeves rolled up and Soraya Khanum wagged her finger at him and . . ."

"Go on, away with you!" Ben Ijnbal berated him. "I told you to find out exactly what happened, didn't I?" He gave the cook an evil look.

"Yes, Excellency."

He didn't sleep all night, and at dawn the thick darkness stretched itself thin and turned pale. Areb Khan dusted off his clothes, carefully washed his hands and face and arrived at the sultan's before first light.

"I'm going now," he said and pulled back hard on his whinnying horse's reins. "I'll tell the shah he wasn't here, as you told me."

"Tell him the oath I swore and the beauteous ruler of Isfahan will believe everything."

"I'll also tell him that if Suhak had been here you would have let me kill him."

"Yes, tell him. And may Allah protect the shah!"

Areb Khan calmly turned his horse around and walked it out of the palace grounds. The agitated sultan summoned his servant and ordered him to follow, unnoticed, and not to take his eyes off Areb Khan until he passed the furthest hillock. He waited until dusk for his servant to return and all the while a doubt gnawed away at him—supposing they turned back? And when the servant came galloping into the courtyard on his exhausted steed and told him that Areb Khan had passed the hillock, the overjoyed sultan went to the forest unnoticed, with no torch and no servant. He rode his white horse and took the black one with him too. It was a moonless night, and so dark that he could hardly make out the black wicker basket. He arrived at the tree, wrapped the rope ladder around his waist, stood on the saddle, and grabbed onto a branch. He carefully, noiselessly crawled along the branch, groping his way in the darkness with his strong arms, feeling for the next branch. Then he unwrapped the rope ladder, tied it firmly around a thick branch and carefully, carefully climbed down the rungs. He felt around for a while with his outstretched foot, and when he could find no more rungs he jumped cautiously down next to his brother. The basket rocked, and the exhausted man could no longer hold his balance and fell on top of his brother. "Suhak, wake up," the sultan whispered, "I've brought you a horse, mount it and go . . ." He shook his brother by the shoulders, then ran his fingers quickly over his brother's chest and touched something cold, something unpleasant. He jumped backward, breathed in sharply and then, wide-eyed and unable to breathe, he looked down and saw a knife sticking out of his heart.

Oh, Areb Khan, Areb, you miscreant . . . When you got to the furthest hillock you galloped mercilessly onward on your horse and by evening you were close to your native village, Mordof. Resplendent, adorned with gemstones and pearls, you stopped to stare mockingly at the people in their dirty rags, and they stared back at you in surprise and needless to say did not recognize you; and when you were ready to leave one man with disheveled hair showed you the palm of his hand to signal that you should wait. You were surprised too, but waited, still staring mockingly as the man flapped his way through the marshes, disappeared into a mud hut and then came back out slowly. He came carefully toward you and when he was near you he raised his hands high in the air to reach up to where you sat high on your horse, and handed you a bowl filled to the brim with milk. The smile dried up on your face and suddenly you were at a loss for what to do. You felt an overwhelming urge to hack him to pieces, because in his eyes you saw the thing you hated the most: selfless kindness. But you could not kill him, and not because you did not dare to—no, you knew only too well you would get off scot-free, but you still could not do it. In fact, you could not even accept the milk—it would be like poison in your throat. Confused, you turned your horse around, looked down at the disheveled man one last time, mercilessly whipped your trusty thoroughbred with rage and galloped off into the darkness. In the villages you passed through sleeping peasants turned over in their beds, roused by the clattering of hooves; there were no lights at all, everyone was sleeping, exhausted peasants sprawled out supine on their beds and thrashed about senselessly in a world that I, ever-vigilant Truth, had never seen, while wealthy Ben Ijnbal did not sleep at all, and at first light his servant saw him sitting on the mat and ran into the room.

"I found out everything, Your Lordship."

"What?" Ben Ijnbal reached down for his prayer beads and avoided looking at his servant. "What did you find out?"

"Everything! I made him talk all night long. I sidled up and reminded him we were like brothers, that nothing could come between a baker and a cook, and told him to tell me everything, because after all, I'd seen him with my own eyes, hadn't I? And he told me he'd never met a woman like Soraya Khanum before in his life and that her husband was a lucky man . . ."

"Get the hell out of here!" Ben Ijnbal shrieked at him, "Get out and if you haven't found out everything by this evening—and beyond doubt—I'll cut off your head!"

And in the evening the exhausted cook hesitantly approached Ben Ijnbal, kissed his feet and said, "Forgive me, Lordship, it seems it was a lie."

Ben Ijnbal straightened himself up proudly and gave the cook his pardon, and the next morning, still out of sorts, he went to visit Areb Khan. At midday the head cook and baker were beheaded in the main square, as traitors of the shah. Ben Ijnbal went back home quite satisfied, but suddenly an agitated Soraya Khanum came rushing into the room and said something very strange indeed: "Why did you have them killed, Sidi Ben, why? I made the head cook say it!"

"What do you mean, made him? Why?" Ben Ijnbal was confused.

"I wanted to see if you would believe it or not. You did believe it, didn't you? You did believe it, Sidi Ben . . ." And Soraya Khanum wept so bitterly—and yet so beautifully—that Sidi Ben Ijnbal was unable to fully grasp whether the head cook and the white-armed baker had betrayed the shah or not.

But that same evening, when Soraya Khanum was dancing and singing so mischievously, Sidi Ben Ijnbal pinched her very hard on the arm, almost affectionately, right where every morning he would gently lay his cheek.

* * *

Once again I was bored of this rich house, my eyes had grown accustomed to their beautiful gardens and I had had enough of everything.

As before, great teachers still came to educate Sharbat and I found the one who taught oration particularly irritating. Then they engaged the Arab astronomer Khalil Menajem and he was just what I had been missing—on moonlit nights they would go out into the gardens in front of the palace, a servant would bring out a crystal bowl filled with fruit, the great Menajem would stretch out his finger toward the sky and start teaching—there, look, that star up there is called such and such, this one over here is called such and such, and so on—and the young child lying there on the ground on his side would help himself to a grape that he'd cooled at the base of the fountain and then dry his hands on a piece of thin bread. Things were going very well for Ben Ijnbal—he had many horses, large amounts of gold, and his acquaintances still valued him as much as they ever had. In addition, as a friend of Areb Khan he was relatively well protected, and Sharbat had even mastered the art of eloquent speech, although he still delivered his beautiful words rather indifferently. There was nobody in all of Isfahan who could teach him to look delighted, though, so Ben Ijnbal sat the boy next to him in front of a large mirror and taught him himself: "Pull your cheeks up to your ears, like this . . ." And the boy tried—he tensed his face, but no, it seemed that smiling was beyond his capabilities. "Try stretching your lips, like this, and now screw your eyes up . . . Really stretch those lips, come on, as far as you can . . ." And Sharbat did everything he was told, but simply could not learn how to smile with sincerity. And so instead of smiling Ben Ijnbal tried to teach him the most extreme form of deference—he crossed his short arms over his chest and bowed his head to the floor. And even though Sharbat could not copy this either, Sidi Ben Ijnbal was pleased nonetheless: "This boy will not be subjugated—he is a real man," he thought.

These great friends went around together as they had done before, and once when Areb Khan himself came to visit a delighted Ben Ijnbal ordered a rich feast to be set out. But his guest was feeling out of sorts and suggested they go for a walk through the streets instead. Ben Ijnbal took advantage of this fortuitous event and took Sharbat with him too. They went from street to street, and people stared in delight at the three of them strolling along in their finest robes. The miscreant walked in silence, and if people threw flowers onto the road for him he didn't even acknowledge it. From left and right people offered humble greetings to Ben Ijnbal too; they touched their fingers to their chest, lips, and forehead, and smiled affectionately at Sharbat, and the three men took great pleasure from so much obvious respect. Finally Areb Khan shook off his bad mood, and it was then that, unexpectedly, in the middle of the street, they came across a Persian stranger and froze. All three of them stared at him, while he looked at each of the three faces in turn: one had the face of a puppet, the second that of a prudent miser, while the third had the face of a covetous, repellent miscreant; the Persian stranger looked at each face equally calmly. Each of the three men, though, was troubled by something different: Sharbat was unsettled by the Persian stranger's evident sense of superiority, reflected clearly on his face and in his body; Ben Ijnbal was so surprised by his stare that he bowed his head and started there and then to doubt Soraya's honor; only Areb Khan continued to hold his gaze, and now the Persian was looking only at him. He seemed so familiar! Areb Khan felt it too, although it wasn't the stranger's face he recognized—there was something about his eyes that Areb Khan didn't like, and he knew that someone had stared at him like that somewhere before, and recently . . . And then he remembered: yes, he looked like the man who had brought him the milk back in his village of Mordof—well, he didn't look like him exactly, but Mahmoud Ali stared at Areb Khan in the same brazen way as the man in the village. Infuriated, Areb Khan put his hand to his dagger, but as killing an innocent man like this, in broad daylight in the middle of the city was not acceptable, the miscreant chose the next shortest route instead.

"Do you love the shah?"

And I, Truth itself, agitated and fearful, rushed to his ear and fed him a whispered falsehood: "Say that you love him, say you love him very much, what harm will it do?"

But without batting an eyelid Mahmoud Ali answered, "I cannot say— I've never seen him."

"What? What!" Areb Khan licked his lip and I realized that by being here I was making matters worse for Mahmoud Ali—because I am Truth, after all—so I fled from there as quickly as I could; I leaped lightly over the houses and came to the happy field of flowers, but I had no time for them now. Tormented and troubled by doubts, I crept for a long while through the grasses, and then I flew up high again and made my way slowly across toward Mount Damavand, just to kill time. Then I came back again, at a leisurely pace, but halfway back I ran out of patience and I shot back to the city like a thunderbolt. But there was nobody left in the street. I rushed straight to the shah's palace and was stunned to find everyone there, and Sharbat, lying spread out on the floor, was finishing a long sentence with the words ". . . of Isfahan, that everlasting sun!"

And by some miracle, he was laughing cheerfully.

"You see how he loves you?" Areb Khan said to the shah and waited for Sharbat to kiss the shah's knee before nodding his head slightly toward Mahmoud Ali and saying, "Now ask him, Excellency."

The musicians carried on playing the viol and lute. The shah looked my chosen one up and down and, satisfied, asked him, "What is your name?"

"Mahmoud Ali."

He should have added, "Your Excellency!" I dashed myself against the wall.

The shah furrowed his brow, but then asked affectionately, "Do you love me, Mahmoud Ali?"

And suppressing a smile he looked at the shah and said, "I don't hate you."

"And what about love? Do you love me?"

"I said I don't hate you."

And the shah clenched his lips and wielded his staff. Mahmoud Ali, my chosen one, clutched at his split eyebrow, then calmly cleaned the blood from his eye socket, looked at his palm, stared into the young shah's eyes and gave just the kind of smile I liked and said, "I still don't hate you."

But what, what was happening? The servants were carrying a long stake toward the square and no matter how hard I tried to get in their way and wrap myself under their feet, I just couldn't manage it and I was trampled down, crushed, and I went among the people rushing down to see the spectacle and looked into everyone's eyes, caressed them, begged them to unsheathe their swords, pleaded with them to stage a revolt, but none obeyed me—they couldn't even hear what I asked of them, and some even rubbed their hands together eagerly while waiting for the spectacle to start. But I, invisible, weak, soundless, I blew up under the hems of their clothes— what more could I do? Furious, I hurled stones and whispered to myself and just when I had lost all hope of making them take heed the muscular musicians sounded their horrible horns: the shah had appeared. He was coming toward the square, a bow and arrow in his hand, and all of his retinue held bows and arrows too, and in the middle of the square, tied like a target to the top of the long stake, was my chosen one, Mahmoud Ali! The shah marched proudly in with his retinue in attendance—the miscreant with his sloping shoulders, the short-armed Sidi Ben Ijnbal, the khan with his cut ear and lopsided turban, the company commanders he had trained like dogs, even the man with the collapsed jaw, I noticed, who now put his bow to his shoulder as proof of his loyalty to the shah—even the idiot puppet boy was there admiring the sharpened arrow tips. If only I had had a voice, if only I were visible! My chosen one, abandoned to his fate, stuck there on top of the stake, was also looking at the retinue, and I could not look anymore, no, I couldn't! And when the young shah stopped his horse and I looked closely—ferociously—at his face, they sounded their horns even more loudly and then the bells and tambourines and bugles too. And in that awful senseless cacophony there was still some kind of wild melody, and when the shah took an arrow I finally battled against him and, though enfeebled, threw myself against his face, but he found the breeze pleasant, satisfying, and pushed his face toward me, and took out an arrow, and when he stretched his bow taut I flew angrily up into the air, wrapped myself around it and at that very moment felt the arrow come whistling outward and split me in two, and it pierced my chosen one, the Persian stranger, in the throat—in that barely visible, light blue vein. I did not look at him, but I knew that he was flapping weakly and I did not want to see it or hear it, but in an instant the musical instruments fell silent, the shah looked over his retinue and declared with a smile on his face, "All those who love me, shoot your arrows!" and a hail of arrows flew past me and surrounded my chosen one. Shaking with rage, I flew toward them and with deep loathing looked once more into the eyes of everyone, everyone who had shot an arrow. Then I looked up at the stake from afar and was lost for words—nobody was even visible behind the halo of a thousand arrows that encircled the top of the stake. I wanted to see him and so, trembling, I went in among them, those arrows of which some were dripping blood, and with a silent roar I wrapped myself around him, and although weak and grieving I found one consolation—he had died in the air.

Before night fell properly I took shelter in the hollow of a fallen tree and mourned, and then, carried along by revenge and anger, I flew over the sleeping kingdom and the sea that flickered in the moonlight and now, sprawled at my commander's feet, with the thirst for revenge kindled inside me, I stubbornly implored him, "Have somebody plunge a saber into him, or even an arrow, or let him contract a terrible illness that will have him moaning and gnashing his teeth as he dies. Choose whatever punishment you want; if you wish just bring your wrath down onto the miscreant, or the miser, or his son, or all three of them together—I'll make do with one, I beg you for one, I am but the dust at your feet, loyal, humble, and mercilessly ravaged. They killed my chosen one, taught by Mother Nature herself, and if you only could have seen how he walked, how he—"

I looked up and could no longer find the words. He knew everything.

He gazed at me sorrowfully, pensively, sadly. He knew something I could never even have imagined, looked at me for a long time, and when I started to become fearful he said to me in a clear voice, "Poor, pitiful Sharbat!"

He said it with a clarity I had never heard before; my mind went cloudy and I, the outraged servant, answered my omniscient and mysterious commander, so rudely: "Who is pitiful, who? That idiot puppet? The one who never lifts a finger but eats exquisite foods, dresses in the finest clothes, walks around his fountains all day? . . ."

But my commander just smiled faintly and said, "So what?"

What more did he want? I was confused, and then I remembered everything and started rambling. "They only give that mindless idiot so much respect because of his greedy father's wealth!"

But my commander didn't bat an eyelid. "So what?"

I remembered the most important thing: "He's been brought up since childhood on flattery by a cowardly father and learned teachers! My chosen one, unfamiliar with all of this, has just been shot to death by thousands of arrows on top of a stake which now resembles some kind of enormous dandelion in the main square—although no amount of blowing will make those arrows fly away—whereas he, poisoned by his teachers, just stood there spouting his honeyed words!"

The commander quietly, sadly repeated: "Poor, pitiful Sharbat!"

He was saying it to himself. I probably hadn't explained things to him clearly:

"What does he have to be pitied for? Everybody envies his property, his gold, gems, and pearls, his thoroughbreds, crystal, and sapphire, and he has one diamond so amazing that—"

But the commander cut me off harshly. "All those things will go," he said and gave me a look that hypnotized me in an instant, and I shrank back. "Know this: all those things will go, and even if they lay him in his vast grave with all his wealth and possessions he cannot take any of it with him to heaven. Of that you can be sure—" he said, and added affectionately, "—my most loyal helper."

I looked at him in dismay, but he was staring angrily into the distance. "Don't think for one moment that this Ben Ijnbal is happy, that he chose to be a provincial miscreant, and do not hate that poor wretch Sharbat, who has spent his entire life sitting in a palace. Make sure you pay heed to who is really happy . . ."

He thought I had understood everything and stopped talking, but curled up into a little ball, I asked hungrily, "Who?"

"Those who are left behind."

A thought flashed across my mind and I began to have my suspicions. "Who was left behind?"

And he, my commander, looked at me and smiled, and said, "The people who were loved."

And then I almost understood it all and yet still I asked, hungrily, impatiently, "Who was loved?"

And he, my commander, hidden, unreachable and omniscient, looked at me tenderly, nodded his head seriously and gravely, and told me, "Mahmoud Ali, on the happy hillock."

When my joy had passed, I stretched my unsettled, pensive self out across the night sky as a mist over the sea. I remembered the words of my commander and yet, ever feeble in the face of his mysterious wisdom, felt I could not be completely certain of anything and so it was all the better that, blinded by the invisibility of my body, I felt the truth of his words. I floated about in a fine, translucent mist above the nighttime sea, gazed at the waves swelling gently in the moonlight and felt my eyes calm. Then I looked out at the sea and realized why they called it boundless, although I knew all too well where its coast lay and turned over onto my back. And there in the sky hung countless stars and I—who could not go beyond the clouds—gazed up calmly at the mysterious distant brightness and merely marveled at how man had given those radiant stars that were so similar to the Earth such varied names as Auriga, Virgo, and Scorpio . . .

REZO GABRIADZE
The White Bridge

I'm standing on the bridge, spitting into the river—
It doesn't rhyme, but it's a fact.
—V. V. Mayakovski

I was a mama's boy. I read books, always had a clean collar, was so good to beat up that it was rare for people to pass up on the opportunity to do so unless they were going on a business trip with a suitcase in each hand, or a mourner busy carrying a coffin. The war had just finished, life was hard, and people had little to give them pleasure and keep them entertained.

I was Library No. 6's most avid reader. I had to be careful when I went to the library. If anyone saw me they would beat me up, and so I was careful: first I would casually cross to the other side of the road, then I would equally casually spit off the bridge, and when I was sure nobody was watching I would quickly walk into the library.

I was sitting in the library that day too. Suddenly I became aware of the noise of the river Rioni. I guessed that somebody had opened the door. I looked up at the librarians: two unmarried women with nothing left to tell each other. The woman in front was standing over a kerosene heater with her legs apart and staring at the doors, white as a sheet. A flowery red heat rash spread up the inside of her legs. Keto Pavidloian seemed unable to close her mouth and slowly waved her backside from side to side behind her in search of a chair. Fear had spread through the library like mold across a damp wall.

At first I thought they'd seen Ipolite. Back then in our town there lived a rat they called Ipolite, because apparently the actor Ipolite Khvichia had thrown boiling water over him at some point. Ipolite was everywhere you went, at the Kutaisi traders' association, the pawnshop, the market, the bank—bald, pink, and with a long green tail. He was a really unpleasant sight.

Ipolite and I were the only ones who ever went to Library No. 6. Back then we were both obsessed with the classics: Ipolite with the book bindings and me with the rest, and I still remember how I miss those days. The noise of the Rioni faded again; the doors had closed. I looked behind me cautiously.

In the doorway stood Adrakhnia.

Adrakhnia was a solitary man. He only ever appeared in profile, and his face bore a variety of old scars. One of these scars was more prominent than the others: it began above his hairline, cut across his forehead in a diagonal line, and then across his eyebrow, before skirting along the side of his nose, showing somewhat fainter where it crossed his dry lips, deepening on his chin and fading completely underneath it. He was especially dangerous at nightfall, in the fog, and while watching the film *El Dorado*. At the very sight of him even the road would shy away beneath his feet and try to escape.

And this was the man whose eyes were now looking at me.

Adrakhnia sat down at my table and took a black bound notebook from his pocket. He put it in front of me, looked at me, said, "You're going to write me a letter," and pointed at the notebook with an index finger that wasn't there. "I can't write," he said, and again he showed me the index finger that wasn't there. "No one must ever know," he said, waving at me the finger that wasn't there.

"I swear on my mother's life," I mouthed, but no sound came out.

"On your mother's life," Adrakhnia voiced on my behalf. He started dictating. "Write this. 'Dear Margalita, they douse me down, but still I burn for you.'" Margalita was the widow of Rafael, the commodities expert. Two years previously Rafael had gone in front of the auditors . . . It was the second year Margalita had dressed only in black. The second year she spent her days sitting by the windows she cleaned with vinegar, looking out at her dead husband's car, which she refused to sell and which stood there on bricks, buried under yellow flowers, a monument to their love. She would sit there, mourning his loss, pick up a cherry on the point of a needle, clean the needle with a handkerchief, and then press it to her nose as a sign of her sadness.

I don't remember how long I was writing for. A lot of what I wrote was borrowed from the classics, but a lot was my own work. I can still remember saying something about them meeting at the wrong time and in the wrong place, like in the middle of having your blood pressure taken, or during the border crossing between East Germany and Poland, and things like "Oh, yellow chrysanthemum, painted on a fan," or "My love, why did we meet in a tapestry?"

There are parts of that letter that I struggle to understand even to this day. "It is you that makes each of my eyes so jealous of the other! When they compete to see where your gaze falls theirs is a wakeful sleep, and in place of pillows they lay eyelashes underneath their heads! Sometimes the first eye falls asleep before the second, and sometimes the second before the first; each strives to make the other wait to glimpse the fount of beauty, the flame of mercy!"

Adrakhnia spent a long time reading what I'd written in the notebook. His lips mouthed the words silently. He looked out of the window to read the town clock, again mouthing silently, then raised his lower eyelids to close his eyes and said, "You're going to get a beating." My heart stopped. My finger twitched rapidly in its place.

Adrakhnia stood up. "But if anyone beats you up I'll rip their arms off, and then I'll rip their legs off and walk you to school on them," he said, and left.

Almost twenty years have passed since that day. I was back in Kutaisi recently; I wandered through the streets and said to myself, "I'm back in my hometown. Shouldn't I be feeling sadness, heartache, affection? Shouldn't I feel its beauty?" I went one way, but felt nothing, I went another way, but felt nothing. I sniffed a leather cap (like one I had bought) and still felt nothing. Desperate for nostalgia, I went to the white bridge. "I'll spit off it, and maybe that will spur some affection and tenderness in my heart," I thought, but even this didn't work. Every time I tried to spit it came out too slowly, and twisted back under itself. "Spitting off the white bridge is completely different when you're a child," I said, with a spurious sense of distress.

In Kutaisi the air moves in a particular way, when it is already more than a breeze but not yet a wind. It smells of glycerin, it is warm, lazy, and very well-mannered, and if I had my way I would call it Liziko Gabunia and enroll it in the Faculty of French at the Kutaisi Pedagogical Institute. The breeze came along and I doffed my cap, but it passed by me as if it didn't recognize me, and at the corner of the road it adjusted its earring, probably caught sight of me, and vanished.

I sat down on a lemonade crate. Somebody set a low-heeled boot down on the pavement in front of me. I looked up at him, and stood in his way. It was Adrakhnia. He had aged well, had not put on any weight, and his profile was now as transparent as thin paper. He didn't recognize me. I reminded him about Margalita's letter. He looked off to one side and offered me a cigarette. The next day, it turned out, was the fifth anniversary of her death. He invited me to come to the grave.

The next day I went up to the cemetery. Under a trident-shaped lime tree I met Margalita and Adrakhnia's two children. The girl was like her father, thin and silent. The boy had Margalita's tear-filled eyes and voice, peach-colored lips, and stood shyly in the shade.

A white stone lay on Margalita's grave. Above it there was a colored photograph. The stone turned turquoise in the gentle drizzle.

And standing by that stone I learned with a sense of gratitude that buried deep within the earth were those first words of mine, laid on beautiful Margalita's chest. It seems it was her final wish.

KOTE JANDIERI
Cinderella's Night

"Arepsta, Pshegisha, Atsetuki."

Suddenly, one by one, these strange words floated to the surface of the exhausted woman's mind like some pagan incantation. How many times had those same words come to her during her darkest hours as she stood, exhausted, on the sandy shores of despair?

"Arepsta, Pshegisha, Atsetuki." The clock struck half past something. The woman cast her eyes around her. In the ashtray in front of her a thin column of smoke rose from the nub of an abandoned cigarette and all around her everything—the soft armchair, the tapestry, those corner cupboards from Bohemia or God knows where filled with crockery and books, the expensive glass chandelier—everything was caked in a thin, indifferent layer of dust. Everything in this house had been bought by her father. Apart from the books.

Settled in on the ottoman sofa in front of the flickering screen, legs tucked up under her, she listened to the noises coming from the street and carried on her waiting game. A child's tuneless song drifted in from another room. "He'll get tired soon and fall asleep," the woman thought. Every now and then he abandoned his song and in its place came endless mumblings, incomprehensible, monotonous, made more audible by the woman's expectant waiting. The bright light from the chandeliers in every room only served to highlight more mercilessly the emptiness that surrounded her. Only in the child's room had dusk been allowed to fall, a tranquil dusk filled with disparate, unfamiliar, and mysterious sounds.

"Arepsta, Pshegisha, Atsetuki." The names of these mountains had first been told to her by her father. They were sitting in a restaurant, eating fried trout and gazing out of a vast window at the shimmering green lake. The tourist season was nearly over. Far below them the last few suntanned vacationers lingered on the lake shore, but high up where they sat nothing broke the silence of the densely forested mountains and the lake, perilous and cold as the eye of some prehistoric reptile.

"The most stunning feature of this landscape is that lake," her father said, "but you know if it weren't for these mountains—Arepsta, Pshegisha, and Atsetuki—it wouldn't even be here. It's the mountains that hold back the clouds, make them release their rain onto the slopes, give source to the streams, establish which way they will flow, then stem them, block their path, make them pool, provide underneath them a bed on which to form a lake . . ."

This charming man, well into his sixties, always spoke in such short, razor-sharp sentences to his colleagues at the construction department; even he was surprised to find that when speaking to his daughter he used such an affected tone and highly literary vocabulary. In his daughter's opinion it was all a bit bland and mediocre. Her father, an engineer by training, harbored a secret wish to be somewhere else and an unfulfilled love for refined language and beautiful art that made his more erudite daughter smile wryly . . . The father lit a cigarette and gazed out at the black cloud that had appeared over Mount Atsetuki. It was clear that the weather was worsening.

"I don't know whether you realize it, but you and I are of that stock. Our people are the kind that that dam rivers . . ."

The black cloud now covered half the sky and on the far shore of the lake the pretty government dachas were shrouded in a cold, heavy mist.

"If you don't know what I mean by that, then I've brought you up wrong. I wanted you to be surrounded by great books, art, and music. But those poets, those opera singers and artists who I still feed and clothe to this day, whose pockets I sometimes even line directly, they come from a lower order, I'm sure of it. They're dairy cattle . . ."

Sitting cross-legged on the ottoman, the woman recalled her father's eyes, tired, all-knowing, devoid of hope, and that bottle of plum sauce, accidentally knocked over, its contents spilled across the white tablecloth like spots of blood, and the sound of her own increasingly exasperated voice, full of thinly veiled irritation.

"I never asked you for any of it. Just the opposite, in fact."

It was an unguarded comment and an unfair one at that. This man—pragmatic, sometimes severe—could not be blamed for the fact that at one point she had taken full advantage of his generous charity. To her amazement, her father said, quite calmly and without a hint of irritation, "See? You're talking like them now too."

And at that very moment a storm blew up outside. Amid the blackness of the tempest the wind tore through the clouds of mist that hung low over the surface of the lake, ripped them to shreds, spun them, mixed them, roused the steely waves and sent them roaring and crashing against the shore.

"People like that think that God created the entire universe and everyone in it to serve their needs!"

And with a sudden thunderous clap it seemed the sky had split in two, the heavens opened, and her father's voice now fought against the roaring of the wind and rain and the scraping sound of metal against metal from the sheet-iron roofs.

"And now it will be us, not them, my dear, who'll build the ports, the railways and embankments, and the wind belts. Without us they wouldn't even have their lovely glass houses, crammed full of food and drink, built to withstand even storms like this! And yet we don't ask them to flatter *our* egos, or applaud *us*, or declare *us* Fathers of the Nation. Why have you gone so quiet?"

"What do you want me to say? Piffle!"

"What do you mean, piffle? Just tell me what you think!"

"I think Lear hath gone mad . . ."

This snobbish jibe was lost, lost in the roar of the storm that raged on the other side of the restaurant's vast window.

Then later, staring out of the window of the car as they drove along the wet, deserted road, staring at the mountain slopes under a sky now clear again her father said, "I haven't gone mad. Some of them are normal, but most of them can't even eat their bread without bragging and boasting and flattering. Listening to them talk always made my head hurt, their compliments made me sick, their laughter was like poison to me."

Eucalyptus and oleanders flashed past the window where before there had been spruce trees. On the surface of the sea, now turned deep indigo, the golden sun's reflections made fiery bands across the water.

"I can feel a sea change coming. They'll ruin this country if they're given the chance, God forbid."

His words were interrupted by his daughter's laughter.

"Who? Poets and artists? Ha!"

Many years have passed since then, but she can still remember how her father took a cigarette in his hand, lit it and glanced over at her. In his eyes she saw no hurt or anger, but rather loneliness and fatigue.

"Your mother has been dead a long time and you'll be nineteen in three days. I don't know how to tell you the things mothers tell their daughters."

"Just tell me straight."

"Well, basically, don't let men like that fool you with pretentious talk and fancy manners, and then expect you to feel you owe them something."

Was this really what was happening? Or had some withered former lover, some stupid woman with an ax to grind told him that his precious daughter was having steamy trysts right there in his house with an esteemed and promising young art lover? It was interesting to think what this powerful, steely nerved man would say if faced with the sight of his own child, stripped of the protection of clothes and culture, naked in the arms of a stranger, moaning with animal passion.

"Explain again how embankments and wind breaks come into this, will you?"

"I'll say it again, we're not like them. You won't be able to put up with it, their pride, their meddling, their weak will and countless little lies and eccentricities, their fake enthusiasm and conceit."

"If that's what you really think then, yes, you did bring me up wrong."

"What do you mean?"

"I mean that the door of our house was only ever open to the very people you now dislike. Ordinary people—engineers, builders, workers—only ever existed in that other bit of your life, the side you kept hidden from me and shrouded in darkness."

"What do you mean? What dark side?"

"Money, the ruthlessness you need if you want to get it, the endless dealings with prosecutors and investigators if you want to keep it, the law of the jungle that applies in a world that is hidden from the sight of ordinary people. In short, everything you hid from me so deliberately."

"And who opened your eyes to it? Or is that something you're going to hide from me?"

"It's not time for that yet. I'll tell you when it is."

The car went gliding down the rain-soaked, tree-lined avenue. The rays from the sun, half sunk into the sea, gave the magnolia flowers a stunning blood-red hue. Flowers of death, thought the girl. For some time the two of them stayed silent. Then her father broke the silence once again.

"Maybe you're right. Maybe it was a mistake, all of it. Absolutely all of it. Anyway, an old man's warnings count for nothing, I realize that only too well."

"You never talked to me about life. And you brought other people in to talk about books and pictures."

"I didn't want you to see the 'dark side' of my life, as you call it. I just wanted you to have a different path in life, a different fate," her father said and stopped the car by the main gates to the vacation resort. "But when you can do almost anything and have almost everything, and others cannot, and do not, then you remain alone. People greet you with false smiles and well-rehearsed hospitality, they make long toasts in your honor, praise you, entertain you, joke with you—but really they're only thinking one thing, and that's how to get you."

"You've only just realized that?"

"No, I always knew, but it never really bothered me until you grew up. Now I see how they circle around you, these poets, artists, and painters, how they stick to you like butterflies to a lilac tree, how they try to intoxicate you . . ."

"But they live on the light side, don't they? Is that why you don't see them as the same as you?"

"It's all just a charming fairy tale. The dark side and light side don't really exist. Life would be much easier if they did. Sometimes well-lit living rooms are much darker and more dangerous than a prison cell, and sometimes, even in a rat-infested dungeon, there's a shining light that only you can see. Experience teaches you how to perceive it. But a lot of water's got to flow under the bridge before then, and I won't be by your side anymore. That scares me."

"Maybe it would have been better if you hadn't raised me in this hothouse."

"Maybe."

"What's that, a belated apology?"

"No, I'm not apologizing. But the doctors say I haven't got long. Not long enough to change anything, anyway."

That was September twenty-fifth, 1980. They went back to their government dacha and in the orange light of the setting sun her father no longer looked anything like King Lear, alone and raving in the storm. It was one year, four months, and three days until he died. The young man came to his father-in-law's funeral with a white-flecked burgundy silk scarf wrapped around his neck in place of a tie. He was an expert in eighteenth-century French art.

* * *

The woman stared blankly at the wall opposite. There, above the television, where the Mondrian reproduction now hung, there had once been a picture of her father. The picture showed him sitting on the back seat of the car, looking out of the window, a lit cigarette in his mouth and a full glass of wine in his hand. She didn't know why they'd taken it down. There had never been much warmth between the two of them; the conversation they had on September twenty-fifth, 1980 was, in fact, the only one the woman could even recall. Maybe it was because of the man she now sat waiting for—and not for the first time—chewing her lips till blood came, the man who owned nothing in this house but for the Antoine Watteau, Boucher, and Fragonard books, a few novels, and a razor . . .

The woman stared blankly at the fuzzy image on the television screen. "The antenna needs adjusting," she thought, and suddenly realized that something had changed, unexpectedly, and broken the sluggish torpor of her waiting: the child had fallen silent. The woman got up and headed to the darkened room.

Looking through the glazed door all she could see was two gleaming dots. The boy, she realized, was not asleep at all; he was staring wide-eyed at the ceiling.

"Aren't you asleep?" she asked him from the doorway.

The child did not answer. The woman went over to the bed.

"Are you still thinking about it?"

"What?"

"The fight you and Zuriko had at the cinema."

"I can't believe Nana told you. I'm not going anywhere with one of your friends ever again. I don't want her to take me out anymore."

"Were you fighting over a girl?"

"No."

"Come on, we're friends, aren't we? Tell me what happened."

The child scrunched up the corner of the blanket in his hand and said nothing.

"Aren't you going to tell me?"

"No."

"Okay. Then go to sleep, it's past eleven," the woman said, and closed the door.

The harsh light of the chandelier dazzled her. In the middle of the room the television flickered pointlessly. All the programs had finished. The woman looked at the clock. It was half past twelve. How had she missed midnight? Surely that old clock hadn't stopped? She turned off the television and went over to the window. Everywhere the lights were off, only in the house opposite could she see one light in a window and, against this illuminated square backdrop, the dark, clearly defined silhouette of a woman, as if her own image was being reflected in the mirror of the pitch-black night. Somebody was waiting there, too.

The woman came away from the window and went over to the mirror hanging in the corridor. For no good reason she opened the box in which she kept her many pieces of jewelry. For a long while she stared intently at herself, as if she didn't recognize the thin, disheveled creature peering out at her from the mirror. Slowly her face changed: the look of expectation was replaced by one of disgust. A man would not have deemed her unattractive, but still the woman was slowly seized by anger, about the endless waiting, her unkempt appearance, the woman in the neighboring house who was waiting just like her, and more besides. She could not take much more—any longer and she would probably have reached for the first thing she could lay her numbed hand on and thrown it at the mirror—but at that precise moment she heard her child calling.

"Mom!"

The woman could not speak. It took her a moment to quell the fire kindling in the depths of her soul and that flashed in her eyes, the fire that augured evil. Without thinking she picked up the antique enameled brooch with the coral-colored stones and clasped it to her chest.

The cry came a second time: "Mom!"

"What? What do you want? Go to sleep, right now—I don't want to hear another peep!"

"I'm not sleepy!"

The woman straightened her hair, raised her hand to her face and then headed for her child's room.

"Why aren't you asleep?"

"I'm just not sleepy."

"Close your eyes and you'll fall asleep."

"I want a story!"

"You've been watching cartoons all day long, what on earth do you need a story for?"

"Oh, go on. Please?"

"Why should I? You never tell me anything."

"Oh, please. Tell me a story."

The woman smiled. She sensed that talking to him was helping him settle.

"Okay, but only if you close your eyes."

"Okay."

"Which one do you want?"

"A boys' story. One where the main people are boys."

"A boys' story? I'm not sure I can think of any . . . Come on, let me tell you one with girls in. Don't you want to know what girls get up to?"

"Which one is it?"

"The one with the widower and his daughter, Cinderella. You know, where he takes a new wife and she gets a new stepmother. Remember?"

"No."

"Well, as soon as they got married the poor girl's life became miserable, because although the stepmother never made her own daughters do anything, she made Cinderella work day and night and only gave her old rags to wear."

"She sounds wicked."

"Yes, she was very bad. Anyway, one day there was an announcement: every girl in the kingdom was invited to the palace! But only if they dressed up in the finest, most exquisite clothes."

"Why?"

"Because nobody wants people wearing horrible clothes with their hair all over the place, do they? That wouldn't look nice at all! And who'd get any kind of pleasure from seeing something ugly and unattractive like that in a palace, eh? Anyway, the stepmother was crazy with excitement. She bought her daughters expensive dresses and took them off to the palace."

"How much did they cost?"

"Five thousand. And close your eyes—we had a deal."

"What happened next?"

"Poor Cinderella was left behind. She sat at home and started to cry."

"And was that when the fairy godmother appeared?"

"Yes. See, you do know this story!"

"No, no, I just guessed. What happened next?"

"Well, the fairy godmother pointed her wand at the girl's tatty old dress and it turned into a beautiful gown. There was nobody else in the whole kingdom who had a dress like it, because no seamstress could ever sew anything that beautiful."

"Was Cinderella beautiful?"

"Yes, she was very beautiful—but when she was dressed in rags with her hair all tangled nobody ever noticed. Then the fairy godmother turned a pumpkin into a carriage and some mice into horses and sent Cinderella off to the palace . . ."

Suddenly the woman heard the sound of a car coming into the courtyard. Engrossed until a moment before in her storytelling, absorbed in the half-light of the child's room, she suddenly found herself back on the deserted shore where she waited, waited . . . In the depths of her soul something sinister and nameless began to stir once more. She heard a car door slam and—briefly—the sound of a car alarm. Then everything went quiet. The woman wiped the beads of sweat from her brow with her hand . . . Their Peugeot had a different alarm.

"Mom, keep going!"

The woman looked at the boy. "Surely," she thought, "he'll never say the kind of pathetic things to a girl that his father said to me? Like 'The eighteenth century brought freedom to man, liberated him from religion, morality, the tyranny of his own past. Without that I would never have dared to embrace you so boldly and kiss you on the lips.' Or 'Eighteenth-century art rescued pleasure from a forest of hazy prohibitions and created an atmosphere of free thought and action that can be seen in the paintings of Watteau and Fragonard, and the writings of the Marquis de Sade and Choderlos de Laclos. It is thanks to this that you are able to close your eyes and calmly surrender to the pleasure of a man's hand caressing your breast . . .'"

"Okay, where were we?"

"The bit where Cinderella's waiting for the prince."

"Ah yes. Well, Cinderella waited and waited, endlessly waited. The waiting almost drove her insane."

"What do you mean?"

"Well, when somebody does the same thing over and over again for a very long time it can drive them crazy."

"So when you spend all day cooking it might drive you crazy?"

"I suppose it *might*—but then again I don't make the same food all the time, do I?"

"Oh yeah. Then what happened?"

"The prince fell deeply in love with Cinderella and searched far and wide for her."

"How much did he love her?"

"He was head over heels."

"What does that mean?"

"Well, you know, he loved her very, very much. He didn't even sleep at night."

"Why didn't he want to sleep?"

"Well, he wanted to but he couldn't—he just kept thinking about Cinderella."

"What kind of things was he thinking?"

"Things like 'If only she could be mine! . . .'"

"Oh."

"Look, are you not sleeping at all tonight? Close your eyes like we agreed! That's right. Anyway, as I was saying, the prince searched far and wide for Cinderella. He carried the small glass slipper with him wherever he went because that glass slipper would fit no girl in the whole wide world but Cinderella . . ."

The telephone rang briefly and then fell silent. The woman jumped. It didn't ring again. She felt the winds of anger begin to rage somewhere on the edges of her exhausted consciousness; soon these winds would gather force and unsettle her mind, stir up the searing dusts of outrage and cloud her understanding. Maybe it would better not to put them up this time, those rickety wind-breaks torn to shreds by countless previous storms. She had been given an opportunity to harness her own hellish raging, to blast through the protective levies she had so carefully constructed around her own mind over time, to finally uncover and investigate what lay beyond. And maybe that really would have been better—but right at that moment her child lay there in front of her, tired and confused by the day's events . . .

The woman lifted her fingers, long and pale from waiting, to her face again, then straightened the child's blanket and continued with her story: "Cinderella waited for the prince who loved her so much to come for her, to turn her rags into beautiful dresses and to carry her off to the palace . . . See, you're feeling sleepy."

"No, keep going."

"Do you know what time it is?"

"So? Keep going, keep going!"

"Keep going, indeed! Don't you know how it ends? Cinderella finally made it to the palace, but it wasn't the prince who came to get her as she'd been expecting. Instead it was a servant who came with the glass slipper, tried it on her, and took her to the palace. They put Cinderella in a beautiful dress instead of her rags and, true, it wasn't as beautiful as the one the fairy godmother had lent her, but Cinderella liked it all the same. And from then they lived there in the palace, and that was the end. Now go to sleep. Sweet dreams."

"But Mom, what was their life like?"

"Normal."

"Normal how?" the boy asked, mumbling, fighting sleep.

"Normal: the prince spent the rest of his life looking for other Cinderellas and Cinderella spent the rest of her life sitting in the palace waiting for the prince. Now go to sleep. It's three in the morning!"

The boy was already asleep, and in his dreams he was bringing a glass slipper to a little girl jumping about in an empty cinema foyer . . .

* * *

The car drove into the courtyard at the precise moment that the woman was tucking the child's arms in under his blanket and straightening his pillow. The sound of the front door slamming brought her around, and the fire that augurs evil and that had flashed behind her eyes a while before was kindled once again. She could already hear his footsteps. She could see his polished

Spanish shoes and crisp, long-sleeved shirt. A man was coming up the steps. It was as if she could already hear him breathing . . . Her mind clouded over, somewhere on the edges of her consciousness a storm was brewing, the surface of the waters turned cloudy, waves formed on the boundless seas of her patience. The woman felt not a moment's fear—she surrendered to the winds of anger, which filled her swollen lungs with fresh air and let her feel some happiness again. The flames of revenge spread across her face and a strange light flashed in her eyes. The woman was ready. She stood in the corridor with her hands on her hips and waited for the door to open so that, finally, she might tell him what she was thinking . . .

The keys turned twice in the lock, the door opened, and a man walked in. He walked in as only he could, his movements somehow free and elegant, then no less elegantly placed his folder on top of the cupboard and said, "Oh, you're not asleep yet, then?"

He walked over to her, looked at her brooch and said, "That suits you, you know. Where have you had that hidden away all this time?"

The woman's hands hung down by her sides. The man went down the corridor with lively, unfettered steps and went into the bathroom without closing the door.

"You'll never guess where I've just been! I really will have to take you one day. I've discovered a new painter, you know, really fantastic . . ."

He washed his hands, then took a towel and dried them, hung the towel back up, and headed toward the kitchen.

"Have we got anything quick to eat?"

The woman barely managed to move her flagging body from the spot. She went to the kitchen and said, "Piffle."

"What did you say?"

"Yes, we have. Hold on and I'll cut you some bread."

"What's the boy been up to today? Did Nana take him to the cinema?"

"Yes, and he had a fight with Zuriko over a girl," replied the woman and smiled . . .

And finally there were only three hours left till dawn. A starry sky hung over Arepsta, Pshegisha, and Atsetuki, and the moon that protects the world from the demons of revenge dipped slowly into the drowsy, perilous waters of the lake . . .

IRAKLI JAVAKHADZE
Kolya

"I met Nikolai Subotin on the fifth of August at a resort on the Black Sea coast. I knew him for two days. On the seventh of August, at midday, Kolya killed himself. He jumped from the roof of a twelve-story hotel with his arms outstretched, and smashed head- and chest-first into the marble steps that ran from the first floor of the hotel out into the courtyard and went up to the second floor of the restaurant. The same steps where I had met Kolya two days before and where, the previous night, Kolya had introduced me to Sveta. According to witnesses, Kolya stood on the roof for several minutes, seemingly oblivious to the shouts of the people gathered in the hotel courtyard below. Then he shouted, 'I'm through with it!' and leaped off as if he was diving, and as he fell threw the air he called out . . ."

I'd kept that entry in my drawer for several years. I can't even remember why I started writing about Kolya, nor when I wrote that passage. Nor can I remember whether or not I planned to carry on writing that entry at some point; I would probably never have gone back to it had I not received a letter from Murmansk a couple of days ago . . .

It was on the fifth of August that I arrived at the coastal town. I caught a taxi from the railway station and went straight to the resort. The driver asked me for seven rubles and told me if I rounded it up to ten he'd carry my bags to my room. I gave him eight rubles and carried the bags up myself. I had reserved the room from Tbilisi, but still had some trouble at reception: the hotel administrator tried to put me in a single room. I smiled as politely as I could and said, "My friend is arriving from Moscow tomorrow morning. And I can see you've got 'room with twin beds' written next to my name in the register."

"Everyone says that. They get a twin and then nobody else shows up: no friend, no wife, no cousin. It's only ever temporary wives here, sometimes several in one day."

Still smiling, I answered, "As you'll see for yourself tomorrow, my friend couldn't really be anyone's temporary wife, for the simple reason that he's a man."

"Well, if he really does come we'll transfer you to a twin room tomorrow."

"So you're saying that what's written in the register doesn't matter?"

"That's right."

I sighed. "Okay, fine. But remember one thing: Georgian men never go on holiday alone."

"As I said," replied the woman, slightly nervously, "if your friend does arrive we'll transfer you to another room. That's the best I can do."

How can I put it? I think that woman jinxed me—when I was coming back from the beach at midday she waved me over just as I was about to get into the elevator and said rather humbly, "Your friend's named Dato, isn't he?"

"Yes."

"He phoned from Moscow ten minutes ago. I put him through to your room but you weren't in. He spoke to me instead . . ."

My heart skipped a beat. "What did he say?"

"He said he can't come just yet; apparently he's got hepatitis. He said he was sorry, and that you'd still see loads of people you know and that he'll be here in a week or so. He'll ring you at four and try and catch you in your room. What a funny guy—kept me talking for ages . . ."

"Oh, he's got a knack for that," I smiled, and remembered that when I'd spoken to him from Tbilisi the day before he'd said he wasn't feeling well.

"So, er, how old is he?" the woman asked, out of the blue.

"Who?"

"Who? Dato."

I looked her in the eye. Then I looked her up and down and said through clenched teeth, "About your son's age? And anyway, people with hepatitis can't have relations—of any kind—for several months." I muttered under my breath, "That's all you lot ever think about."

"I'll thank you to watch your language. I haven't got a son."

"That's your problem," I tossed back, and went back over to the elevator.

At four o'clock Dato rang. He was in a jovial mood. He told me that he'd been admitted to the hospital but that he hadn't told his parents.

"They think I'm coming home tomorrow. Let them think that—I don't want to worry them unnecessarily. If my dad phones tell him I'm there with you."

Then he remembered the hotel administrator. "And what's the story with her?" he laughed loudly. "I just flirted with her a bit because I was drunk and the next thing you know she's practically jumping on a plane to Moscow. She gave me the number of a couple of friends of hers here. You should talk to her. I reckon you'd have her within ten minutes—I'd even put money on it."

"I've already talked to her, for half an hour."

"And?"

"And nothing, we just argued."

"You're unbelievable. I've never understood how it is you lot always manage to fight with women. Vakho was here for two days, and in that time he managed to hit six women and swore at four of them. Then he swore at us too and buggered off to Tallinn to see his Kristina. He's probably swearing at her by now, even though he doesn't know Estonian and she doesn't know Russian . . . Of course, that's probably how they've stayed together so long. So how old's this administrator, anyway?"

I smiled bitterly. "What, have you two got the hots for each other? She asked me how old you were, too."

"No, man! I'm just trying to work out how old her friends would be. About thirty-five to forty, would you say?"

He was spot-on, but I lied shamelessly: "Davit, have you lost it? She's fifty if she's a day!"

"No kidding."

"I'm telling you! Don't believe me if you don't want to."

"Well, fuck it! She didn't sound that old . . ."

Then he told me about the hepatitis. He said the doctors had told him it was a mild form and that he'd be discharged in a week. He begged me to hang on until he could get there. We couldn't decide what to do.

"The place will be packed! Of course you'll see people you know!" He wasn't about to back down on the trip. "And there'll be loads of girls there too. Worse comes to worst, you can make nice with the administrator. I mean, you're not going to come back tomorrow, are you? There's nobody left in Tbilisi! I'm stuck in hospital all week—are you telling me you can't put up with a week by the sea? Have you lost your mind?"

I promised to stay for three days, then he would ring me on the seventh at six and we'd decide then what to do about the rest of the week.

"Look, joking aside," he eventually said to me, "buy the administrator some flowers from me, would you? Seriously."

"Yeah, whatever," I said, and hung up.

Then I went to the beach again. I swam for half an hour, then went up to my room, got changed and went to the bar on the second floor of the restaurant to have a few beers.

That was the night I met Kolya.

I came out of the bar and stood on the steps. I couldn't decide whether to go into town to see friends or leave it till the next day. I knew for a fact that Zaza and Tamuna were staying somewhere in the same resort, but I wasn't in the mood for traipsing around hotels. Anyway, I thought, I wasn't going to find them in their room during the evening, so I decided to go to the beach the next morning and find them down there. I leaned against the railings and lit a cigarette. Kolya was coming up the stairs. He stopped suddenly.

"Have you got a light?" He smiled.

I gave him a match and looked out to the sea. I assumed he'd light his cigarette, give me the matches back, and go on his way.

"You're new, aren't you?" he smiled again. "I got here five days ago and by now I recognize nearly everyone in our hotel."

I nodded, took my matches, and put them back in my pocket.

He held out his right hand and said, still with the same smile on his lips, "Nikolai Subotin. I'm twenty-seven, I live in Murmansk, and I'm here for two weeks." Then, with more of a grimace, he added, "I've got previous convictions, for hooliganism. I was inside for two years. They let me out six months ago."

I shook his hand and told him my name.

"Oh, you're Georgian, are you? You don't look it, I thought you were one of us."

"No, I'm not one of you," I said. That comment irritated me.

"What does it matter, anyway? We're all human, aren't we?" He hadn't even noticed I was angry. "I like everyone, especially Georgians. Although your women aren't that great."

I felt the blood rush to my brain.

"Is that right? Well, you can just get lost!"

"Have I offended you? My apologies." He seemed genuinely upset. "I didn't think you'd be upset by that. It's just that I've never really seen a pretty Georgian woman . . ."

"And how many Georgian women have you seen, then?" I moved away from the railings, moved my feet apart slightly, and tensed my shoulders.

Just one more wrong word and I was ready to hit him. Physically, he looked much stronger than me. Anyway, he must have read my mind—he put an arm around me and said gently, "That's the other bad thing about Georgians, you're way too volatile."

"Leave me alone." I shrugged him off and left him on the steps.

He came after me, followed me, called my name. He pronounced my name in such a strange way that I burst out laughing, stopped and turned around. He was still smiling.

"Look, I've said I was sorry. If I'd thought you'd be offended I wouldn't have said anything. Do you think I was put on this earth to apologize to you? I've backed off, I've said I'm sorry, what more can I do? I mean, when it comes down to it I'm at least five years older than you, aren't I? So let's just be friends."

He was like a little child. A child who knows he's done something wrong but can't quite work out what. I couldn't help but smile too. There was a spark of happiness in Kolya's eyes.

"Come on, I'm going to the bar, let's go and have a drink."

I followed him. The bar was slowly filling up. Kolya bought us a bottle of vodka and two beers. He wouldn't hear of letting me pay. "I invited you," he said. After a while, Dima from Leningrad came to join us; he'd met Kolya the day before. Dima had an unusual way of drinking. He didn't ask the waiter for a glass. Each time we took a drink he'd pick up the bottle, toast whatever it was we were toasting, lift his arm, bend it in the air, and pour vodka into his mouth from half a meter up—at least a shot every time. Kolya was very taken with Dima's approach: "Look, look at what he's doing!"

"He'll be sorry in ten minutes," I said. For some reason the guy was really getting on my nerves.

Then Dima brought a second bottle of vodka and a Pepsi. "Pepsi for the ladies. If you want we can mix a bit of vodka in; they'll get so drunk they won't recognize each other."

"What ladies? Where can you see ladies?" I asked in surprise.

Dima spread his arms open. "We've got to have girls! I was just about to get us some," he said, and staggered off in the direction of one of the other tables.

"He's had enough," Kolya decided. He stood up and walked over to Dima with that trademark smile still on his face. He stopped him on his way toward a table at which two young Slavonic-looking women were sitting, and turned him around.

Dima didn't give in, turned around and carried on.

"Come with us," he shouted at the women. "If you want we can go to the restaurant, Dima will pay! Come on!"

The women didn't look particularly alarmed; they were, it seemed, used to drunk men approaching them. They laughed and whispered to each other. Kolya finally managed to get Dima back to our table. As soon as he sat down I was proved right—he was in trouble: he tipped his head over to one side, put his chin to his chest and started snoring.

"Shall we leave him?" Kolya asked me.

"Well, what else are we going to do with him?"

Kolya Subotin called the waiter over, slipped ten rubles into his pocket and told him to take Dima back up to his room. No sooner had they hauled him off than we were caught off guard by two Armenians: "Were you bothering our girls?"

"No," Kolya said firmly, without even looking up.

"Well if it wasn't you, who was it?"

Kolya poured some vodka into the glasses, clinked his glass against mine and knocked back his drink. I downed mine too.

"We're talking to you," protested one of the Armenians.

"What's the problem, guys?" He didn't look at them this time, either.

"We were gone for ten minutes. We just went downstairs to reserve a table in the restaurant. Did you give our girls any trouble while we were gone?"

Kolya pushed his chair back, spread himself out a bit in his chair, lifted his head and looked the man in the eye.

"I've already given you an answer."

The other guy chipped in. "We were in the restaurant, booking a table. If you guys can't afford the restaurant just sit here quietly in the bar and don't bother other people's women, got it?"

Kolya and I glanced at each other. We both started laughing out loud.

"Come here, son." Kolya pointed at the second guy. "Is this the first time you've been out with a woman or what? Why are you acting all macho? You want to talk about money? What's the most you've ever seen at one time, eh? Five thousand rubles? Ten thousand? A hundred thousand? Have you made sure you've got enough to be able to leave the waiter a three-ruble tip? I can tell from looking at you that you're not going to be able to leave any more than that." Then he looked at me. "You and me managed to sort things out, but the whole country is full of idiots like him."

He was still smiling, and I started to wonder whether it was possible for someone to just smile all the time, whatever the situation.

"Do you smile in your sleep, too?" I asked Kolya, slightly irritated. I turned toward the Armenians. "What do you think, does he smile in his sleep too? Or does he think about money like you and have nightmares?"

I didn't get a reply. The Armenians stood there, eyes blazing, motionless.

"On my way into the bar," Kolya said to one of them, "I didn't see a sign saying 'Please feel free to act like an idiot in here.' Did you?"

The Armenians said nothing.

Kolya wouldn't let it go. "I asked you a question."

"I didn't see, no."

"That's because it's not okay to act like an idiot in here. Now get lost. Go and take care of your lovely ladies."

"Let's go and talk about this outside," the Armenian said at last.

"You want to go outside and fight?" Kolya adopted a mock serious expression.

"Are you coming?" the Armenian said, pulling himself up to look as big as possible.

"Yeah, okay, give it a rest," said Kolya. "You go on out and we'll be there in a minute."

The Armenians left the bar.

"Stay where you are." He was still smiling. "I'm not about to ruin my evening for those two idiots." He called over to the two women, "Come over here and sit with us! It'll be a nice little scene for your boyfriends to come back to."

The women discussed it for a minute among themselves and then turned away.

"Oh, come on!" Kolya raised his voice, "So you don't have dinner with those losers, big deal! I'll give you fifty rubles each and won't expect a thing in return—neither of you are my type." Then he turned to me and said, "I don't suppose you fancy either of them, do you? It'd be worth a hundred rubles just to piss those idiots off, don't you think?"

"Do I fancy either of them?" I wondered, looked over to the women and then called over to the one who was looking straight at me, loudly enough so that the whole bar could hear: "You slut!" I said it in Georgian.

Kolya guffawed. "What did you say to her? I think she's guessed you said something bad to her. What an insult!"

"Couldn't they just bite their tongues? Would it have killed them not to say anything?" I was getting gradually angrier.

"What are you worrying for?" Subotin leaned toward me.

"They're pissing me off. I can't stand girls who talk all the time."

"Come on, man, let's have a drink." Kolya refilled our glasses.

I can't really remember what happened next. I know that after a while the two women left and the Armenians never came back. I got horribly drunk. I remember Kolya saying something about having had enough of it all, telling me that the sea had been right up to his neck and that if he hadn't met me he'd just end it all. I told him he needed to find himself a woman. I was right, he said, and reassured me that he would. Then we bought another bottle of vodka and a beer each and sat there until very late. Afterward we took a short walk in the fresh air and when we finally went our separate ways it was well past midnight.

Needless to say, I didn't wake up until late the next day. I lay in bed for a long time, unable even to open my eyes. I really wished I'd brought a beer home with me from the bar. When I finally looked at the clock I leaped up in shock—it was five to three. I took a quick shower and went down to the restaurant. I had some breakfast, drank a beer, went back to the hotel lobby and settled myself into an armchair. I decided against going to the beach for a swim or into town to see Zaza and Tamuna—I really didn't feel like doing anything. I don't remember how long I sat there, half-dead. In the end, Kolya's voice brought me around.

"Wake up, my Georgian friend!" He was standing over me and grinning from ear to ear.

"What are you laughing for?" I could barely speak. "Aren't you hungover?"

"My hangover only lasted till eight this morning."

"Till when?" I almost shrieked.

"Eight. I went down to the beach. Then I had a shot of vodka. Now I feel fresh as a daisy." Kolya sank down into the chair next to me.

"Bravo, my friend. Now tell me, what was it they put you inside for again?"

He obviously didn't like that. He started to look rather uncomfortable, but answered me anyway. "Hooliganism. I told you, I beat some idiot up."

"What, and he made a complaint against you?"

"All he ever does is make complaints; he's been doing it my whole life and he still is now. He's really not worth talking about, but anyway, for some reason so long as there's breath in our bodies we can't leave each other alone."

"Why? Who is this person?"

"He *wants* me to leave him alone, and he fixed it so that for two years I'd have to, but beyond that . . . I won't leave him alone. I can't tell you how much I loathe him. We can't break free of each other, because something binds us together . . ."

"What?"

"My life, my whole world, my being . . ."

"You're not making any sense." I got up from the armchair. "What do you mean, your life? Tell me."

"Let's not talk about it now. I'll tell you some other time."

In a more cheerful voice he told me he'd taken my advice on board. "I'm going to sort it out today. In an hour or two I'll introduce you to my lady friend."

"Have you found someone?"

"No, but I will. Two hours is plenty."

"Yes, but would you have thought about it if I hadn't say anything?"

"What, about getting a woman? I don't take women too seriously. If they're there, fine, if they're not there, even better."

"You're a strange guy," I said, with my eyes closed.

"Come on, we should go for a swim in the sea, it'll sort you out in no time."

"Have you lost you mind? I can't move. If I even see the sea I'll throw up."

Kolya stood up. "Okay, but I'm going. Don't spend your whole life in this armchair," he said, and went out of the lobby.

I lit a cigarette but didn't like the taste and threw it away. At that moment I wanted a glass of orange juice more than anything, but I really didn't feel like going outside and walking all the way up to the second-floor bar. I lay there half dead until I noticed a Russian girl coming toward me. She had a devilish smile on her face and was holding a wristwatch.

"Excuse me, what does your watch say? Mine's stopped, so . . ."

She looked about seventeen or eighteen and she wasn't bad-looking. I sobered up as quickly as I could, glanced down at my watch and answered, "It's half past four now. I don't suppose you'd mind meeting up with a certain young man outside the restaurant at seven, would you?"

She laughed, adjusted her watch, put it back on her wrist. What she said next almost made me fall out of my chair.

"Why would I mind? But seven's still a while off so . . . Do you fancy meeting a young lady in the bar at five?"

"Let's go now!" Hangover? What hangover? I was soaring like a bird!

"Calm down, there's no hurry; the bar doesn't open till five."

"Oh, what a shame," I said. "In that case sit yourself down, we can wait here."

We settled ourselves down in the armchairs. I found myself liking her more and more.

"So, is he nice then, this guy?" she asked me.

"What's your name?"

"Lena."

"You know what, Lena, how should I put it? He may not be quite what you deserve, but he's not all that bad. He's from Tbilisi and he looks a lot like me . . ."

"And his Russian is really, really bad," added Lena.

"That's true," I smiled, "but his Russian's hardly the most important thing, is it?"

"It's not? What *is* the most important thing then?" She stared at me with those devilish eyes again.

"What, you're saying his Russian *is* the most important thing?" I was really confused.

"Well what then?"

"Oh I don't know, everything else?" I couldn't think of anything better to say. I think it was obvious from my face that I was confused. Lena threw me a lifeline.

"Of course his command of foreign tongues isn't the most important thing; the most important thing is his command of his *own* tongue."

That was so ambiguous it confused me a bit, but I was still not nearly as confused as I'd been a moment before.

"Oh, he's highly skilled with his own his tongue, don't you worry," I said daringly, "but only at certain times and in certain places . . ." I thought maybe I'd gone too far so I changed the subject quickly. "Tell me honestly, was your watch really broken, or . . . ?"

"Or what?"

I was starting to get irritated now. Why did pretty girls always have to be so silly, I asked myself for the hundredth time. Then I went on the attack. "Or did you see me and use the watch thing as an excuse to meet me and get to know me?"

"It was just an excuse, really. I did want to meet you. I'm still deciding whether I want to get to know you. Is that a good enough reply for you?"

"Yes," I said, as decisively as possible.

"What's this young man's name, then?" the girl said, and looked at me alluringly.

"Oh, let's forget all these games. This young man, this young man . . . Just ask me my name and I'll tell you. I don't want to hear about "this young man" anymore."

"Are you always this rude?" She seemed angry with me.

"No, only between four-thirty and five. After that I repent of my sins."

"What sins?"

"Whatever sins I commit during that half hour."

Now Lena was confused. "But you haven't committed any sins yet . . ." Then she asked me my name and I told her. We went up to the bar and ordered some orange juice; the waiter wouldn't bring us champagne, saying he couldn't serve us alcohol. Then we had a coffee and she told me that she lived in Zagorsk, that it was a small town near Moscow and full of churches and monasteries. Then I offered to read her fortune from the coffee grounds. I turned her coffee cup upside down, looked into it and made up some nonsense or other. She liked it, and laughed at everything I said. Finally I furrowed my brow, narrowed my eyes, stared into the bottom of the cup and said to her slowly, as if I really was reading the grounds, "In a few seconds a young man will kiss you."

That made her laugh. Really laugh. She laughed non-stop for five minutes while I sat there like an idiot holding the coffee cup.

"What's the matter? What's wrong with you?" I asked her every so often, but it turned out getting Lena to calm down was no easy matter.

Finally she stopped laughing, wiped her tears away with her handkerchief, leaned over toward me and told me in a near-whisper, "Which young man would that be, then? The one from Tbilisi who looks a lot like you?"

"Yes," I whispered back.

"What happened to 'I don't want to hear about 'this young man' anymore?'" She lowered her voice even more, closed her eyes and parted her lips slightly in anticipation of my kiss.

I kissed her, but pulled away again quickly; there were quite a few people in the bar. Then I kissed her again, for slightly longer. And then again.

"What are you doing now," she said suddenly, "repenting of your sins?"

"What sins?" I didn't get it.

"It was you that said it in the first place!"

"Oh yeah." I remembered. "Well of course! This is the preparation stage, where I reflect on my sins. Actually repenting is a longer, more pleasurable process."

"That's good," she replied and took a sip of her juice.

She told me she'd come on holiday with her parents and her oldest friend. Her parents were on the fourth floor, Lena and Olya on the sixth. "Where's your friend at the moment?" I asked and she said she had a local admirer and had gone off somewhere with him. Then she asked me to dance but I said no, and we left the bar.

As Lena and I went down the steps we saw Subotin and a young woman coming up. As we drew level I looked away to avoid catching his eye. But he stopped and said in a loud voice, "First there were two of us, now there are four. Even better, don't you think?"

The women were confused. Lena looked at me, and Subotin's companion looked at him.

"Sveta, let me introduce you," Kolya said to his companion, and pointed at me. He told her my name. "He's my very best friend."

I was very surprised to be introduced as such, but I didn't say anything. I introduced Lena to Subotin and asked what his plans were.

"You see?" He was in a jovial mood and started speaking very quickly, without thinking. "It didn't even take me two hours. And Sveta's from Murmansk too, but we met here! That's how it goes, isn't it? And as for plans, we thought we'd go to the bar."

I told him Lena and I were going to the restaurant and invited them to join us.

"When your best friend asks you to do something, you can't refuse. And if you want to spend the evening in the company of three amazing people, and in a restaurant to boot, then all the better!" Kolya declared jubilantly and the four of us headed downstairs.

I had known Subotin for one day and I had yet to see him in a bad mood. But that evening he was even more cheerful than usual. As soon as we went in he called the waiter over, ordered almost the entire menu and then turned to Sveta and Lena. "Right, ladies, what are you drinking?"

"I'll have champagne," said Sveta.

"Me too," Lena said quietly and I realized that even though she would have preferred to, she couldn't refuse Kolya.

I followed the waiter to the kitchens and told him to work out how much it was going to cost so that I could pay up front. I knew that at the end of the night there was no way Kolya would let me pay.

"We'll drink vodka, shall we?" Subotin asked me when I got back to the table.

"I'd rather have wine," I answered.

"Four bottles of champagne, one of vodka, and three bottles of wine," he called out to the waiter.

Several toasts later, I went back into the kitchens and paid for the drinks, too. When I got back Kolya seemed upset.

"Who do you think I am, eh?"

"What is it? Has something happened?" I tried to look bewildered.

"Okay, fine," he said, suddenly cheerful again, "Today it's on you, but don't even think about doing that again. When all's said and done I'm your big brother, aren't I?"

Dinner was lovely. I knew one thing for sure though: if I drank three bottles of wine they'd have to carry me out. So I paced myself. Kolya was drinking large amounts of vodka and after a while he ordered a second bottle. Even so, he didn't seem to be getting any more drunk. I was both surprised and delighted to see Lena working her way down the bottle of champagne with Sveta.

"I don't really drink. But today's been such a nice day," Lena whispered to me and then said something I really wasn't expecting: "You used your tongue so beautifully back there in the bar. I can't wait till you start repenting."

"Oh God, she's really drunk," I thought to myself and smiled at her. "Lena, my dear," I said, "don't drink too much. You don't need to drain your glass every time."

"I'd like to propose a toast to Georgian women," Kolya said, getting to his feet. "The ladies present will forgive me, I'm sure. You asked me earlier how many Georgian women I'd seen. Well, I had a think and I realized it's been very few. And also, most of them were on television and, well, I've already apologized and I'm not going to do it again. So, a toast: to Georgian women!"

Sveta and Lena were confused, but did their best to hide it and echoed the toast enthusiastically.

Kolya put his glass back down on the table and sat down to get his breath back. Then he glanced around at the other tables, until one caught his eye. "Look," he said cheerily. "Look who's out having fun."

Sitting at the table were our Armenian friends. They were with different women this time and were making a lot of noise. One of them was down on one knee in front of one of the women, holding a champagne glass in his right hand and beating himself on the chest with his left. Kolya called the waiter over and asked him to send over three bottles of champagne.

"That's how they do it in the Caucasus, right?" he asked me, rather pensively. "Was three bottles enough?"

"They're not even going to get through one bottle now! Just look at them, they're practically under the table already!" I laughed. "After yesterday I hope they don't take it as an insult."

But the Armenians were so drunk they wouldn't have recognized an insult if it slapped them in the face—I don't think they even recognized us. They stood up, raised their glasses into the air and thanked us in Russian and Armenian. Then they went back to their women.

My plans for the evening started looking more and more unlikely with every toast we drank. Lena kept draining her glass and by ten o'clock couldn't even get her tongue back in her mouth. Then Kolya and Sveta got up to dance. Lena really wanted us to dance too, but I couldn't be persuaded. I thought I'd ask her room number before she got too drunk to tell me—after all I'd have to take her up there later. "614," she said. Kolya and Lena didn't look as if they were planning to come back to the table—they were already on their third dance. I stood up, went over and told them Lena wasn't feeling well and that I was going to take her back to her room. Kolya told me to come back down if I wanted as they'd be there for a while yet. I said I didn't think I would, wished them goodnight, stood Lena up and off we went. All the way back she kept calling me "young man, young man." I stopped by the entrance to the hotel and tried my luck. "Do you fancy staying with me tonight?"

"Of course. Why would I want to go back to Olya when I've got you here?" She clung to my neck. She was staggering, and speaking in fragments.

Just then I realized that I'd done something really stupid—Lena was going to fall asleep straight away. So I took her back to 614 and knocked rather timidly. A woman in her mid-twenties opened the door. When she saw Lena she went pale.

"What's happened to her?" she asked in a shrill voice.

"She's had a bit too much."

"What?" She turned to look at me. "What did you say? She doesn't even drink. What have you done to her?"

Olya pressed herself against the wall to let us through. I put Lena on the bed and turned to her friend. "Make sure she stays like that. If she rolls onto her back, put her on her side again. Call me if you have any problems—I'm in 505. There's nothing really wrong with her, she's just drunk two bottles of champagne."

I ran back to the fifth floor, went into my room and put the television on. Jean-Paul Belmondo appeared on the screen. It was some famous detective film or other. I lit a cigarette and lay on the bed. I'd seen the film a few times before and I'd had a few drinks, so I really wasn't all that interested in it. After a few minutes I fell asleep. Half an hour later the telephone woke me. It was Olya.

"Sorry, I was a bit rude to you before," she said, and used my name. "Lena told me what your name is. This is her friend Olya."

"I recognized your voice."

"Lena's a bit upset. She wants to know why you left."

"What, she's not asleep?"

"No, but she's very drunk. I have to go out for an hour to meet a friend and, well . . ."

"Okay, I'll be over in five minutes." I hung up and looked at the clock; it was a quarter to twelve.

I turned off the TV, splashed some water on my face, put my cigarettes and matches in my pocket, and left the room.

Then I saw Kolya for the last time. I bumped into him in the sixth-floor corridor. He was coming in with Sveta. He seemed really pleased, told me his room was on this floor too—number 604—and invited me in for a drink. He was holding a bottle of champagne. I declined his invitation and said I hoped he'd enjoy the rest of the evening. He patted my shoulder, said something to me with that trademark smile on his face, pulled Sveta closer to him and went off down the corridor. I watched Sveta as they walked away and for the life of me couldn't work out which foreign movie star she reminded me of. She had short blonde hair, green eyes, and long legs, with a longish body in between and arms that swayed elegantly from side to side.

"Kolya," I called out to my friend.

Subotin turned around but the woman didn't look back. I gave him the thumbs-up and gestured at Sveta with my chin as if to show I approved. Kolya gave such a broad smile I could see his teeth.

"Absolutely."

I knocked on Lena's door but nobody answered. I waited a moment and knocked again. Eventually I heard Olya's voice say, "I'm coming, I'm coming," and the door opened. "Come in," she said. She seemed agitated and scared. "She's not right. She's feeling sick. She's in the bathroom."

I went in and stood in the middle of the room.

"What should I do now?" Lena's friend seemed confused. "If her parents find out they'll kill me. They told me to look after her. Her mom could come in at any moment." She turned around and went into the bathroom.

I sat down on a chair and looked around the room. Lena's clothes were lying all over the bed. Suddenly there was a knock at the door.

"Can you get that?" Olya called.

"You go," I called back and went out onto the balcony.

A few moments later Olya came out too.

"Don't worry, it was just someone from the next room looking for matches."

"Why should I be worried?" I asked in surprise.

"Come on, come and give me a hand." She grabbed my arm.

"What do you need a hand for?" I pulled my arm free. There was no way I was going into that bathroom. "She'll throw up and then feel better."

"But I've got to go out," Olya said, "I've really got to meet a friend, I need to give him something. I'll try to be back soon."

"Who is this friend? The local?" I asked casually.

Olya was momentarily lost for words, but then recovered and smiled at me. "Lena never could stop talking. I'll be back in half an hour."

"I'd love to know what it is you're going to be giving him at twelve o'clock at night." I looked her straight in the eye. "Although I think I've got a pretty good idea . . ."

"This is no time for wisecracks," she said, spun around and went back inside. I followed her in. "Don't open the door to anyone, and don't answer the phone; I'd rather her mom thought nobody was in than see her like this. I'll knock three times when I get back."

In the meantime Lena had staggered out of the bathroom. She had a towel wrapped around her. When she saw me she just lay down on the bed and turned her back to me.

"She's upset with you," explained Olya.

"No, I'm not upset," Lena turned over and pulled her towel out from under the blanket. "It's nothing to do with him, is it? It's all my fault."

I settled myself into the armchair. Olya stood in front of the mirror combing her hair.

"Are you off to repent of your sins?" Lena asked her friend.

"What?" Olya wasn't really paying attention.

"Yes, that's just what's doing," Lena looked at me and laughed.

Lena stopped posing in front of the mirror. "What are you two laughing for? I don't get it," she said, and closed the door as she went out.

"We should introduce Olya to Kolya," I said.

"You're right." Lena seemed to like that idea. "Olya and Kolya—you could write a poem about that."

Then Lena started to apologize. It was the first time she'd ever got drunk, she said, and she'd put me to so much trouble; why on earth Olya had phoned me she didn't know, it was all Olya's idea. But then she changed tack: "You're a nice guy, why didn't you stop me drinking so much?" I stopped listening, pushed myself right down into the armchair and started thinking about myself. How stupid was I? Right now Kolya was rolling around in bed with Sveta and Olya was getting it on with that local guy. Even my woman from hotel administration was probably spreading her legs for someone, and here I was sitting like some nanny with this silly tart. And Lena looked so awful, you'd really have to be completely sex-crazed to try it with her right now. "If she wants to do it she'll let me know," I thought, and picked up the phone.

"Who are you calling?" Lena asked.

I found the number for the bar in the telephone directory, rang down, and ordered an orange juice and a beer. They told me rather contemptuously that they didn't do room service. I told him I'd pay ten rubles and five minutes later the waiter came running up with our beer and juice. Lena asked me to turn around so she could put on a T-shirt. I smiled and said no.

"Fine. Then I won't put it on, I'll just lie here like this." She said it so indifferently and apathetically that I gave in and turned around. Lena put the T-shirt on and sat on the bed. I poured her some juice and gave it to her. Then I sat back down in the armchair, opened my beer, and put it to my lips. Lena sipped her juice, licked her lips clean, and stared into her glass. "You know, I feel awful. That champagne nearly killed me. I'm sorry about today. I'm here for another week, so . . ."

I felt really ashamed. "Yeah, it's fine," I interrupted. "No big deal. I still like being with you."

Then she started telling me about her first love, some guy called Anatoly, who, from what Lena was saying, sounded really stupid. Not that I was that interested, of course; I just slurped my beer and nodded my head every now and then. Then she asked me to come and sit on the bed with her. I put the bottle on the table, went over to the bed, and sat down. She took my hand in hers and held it there as she carried on with her story. Anatoly was followed by Boris, Boris by Victor, and I realized that any moment now she'd be talking about me. I stood up and went back to the armchair.

Olya didn't come back in half an hour; she didn't come back in an hour either. She came back at four o'clock, just as Lena and I were falling asleep. She banged on the door for ages and finally managed to wake Lena up. When she came in and saw me fully dressed and half asleep in the armchair she was clearly surprised, but tried not to show it.

"Olya, my dear, where have you been all this time?" I stretched. "You said you had something for him, but how many times did you give it to him, eh?"

She laughed and put her bag on the sofa.

"And what about you two? Have you been discussing what love means all this time?"

"Yes." I stood up and took a sip of the warm beer left in the bottle. "And you got back just as I was getting ready to go out into the courtyard and pick Lena some roses."

"Oh yes, of course." Olya kicked off her shoes. "You were fast asleep. I've been knocking on that door for half an hour. But anyway, thanks for your help, and I'm sorry for putting you out."

"I'll be off then," I said, and headed for the door. "I'll go down to the courtyard, pick some roses, and bring them up to you in the morning." I opened the door and went to leave, but then I remembered something and stopped. "Olya, tomorrow I'm going to introduce you to Kolya."

"Who the hell's Kolya?"

"Just someone. You can give him something too," I laughed, and left. As I closed the door behind me I heard Olya call out, "You idiot, stop talking trash."

I went back to my room and went to sleep. Outside it was nearly dawn, on the seventh of August . . .

At first I couldn't work out whether I'd woken up by myself or been woken by the shouts of the people gathered in the courtyard below. When I opened my eyes I remembered—I'd heard shouting and commotion in my head even as I slept, until finally a woman's scream woke me properly. It was obvious something had happened. I looked at the clock: nearly one in the afternoon. I got up and went out onto the balcony. A group of men were standing by the restaurant steps, some of them were kneeling down, shouting for somebody to call an ambulance and a doctor. The women were running around in a panic. "Someone's fallen," I thought to myself and just then I caught sight of Sveta. She was on her knees by the hotel entrance, hiding her face in her hands and shaking all over. "Kolya!" I thought, and ran inside. I don't remember how I got dressed or got down to the courtyard. I ran over to the group of men and pushed them aside. Kolya was lying on the steps. I turned away again quickly and walked about ten steps away from them, and then my knees gave way. I grabbed onto a tree and slowly sat down. The rest I can only remember in fragments. A man called out, "Don't touch him, he might be alive. We shouldn't move him," then another man said Kolya had shouted something as he fell. A third man said he didn't think he was shouting but singing, and a fourth said he had definitely jumped, that it wasn't a fall—everyone had seen how long he'd stood there getting ready. Then the ambulance rolled in. The men moved aside to let the doctors through. I stood up and walked slowly toward the steps. One of the doctors, wearing a white coat, turned Kolya over. I didn't want to see his face and turned away. Nikolai Subotin was sprawled across the steps. I saw his body, tall, firm, and strong and a very strange thought came to me: "Tonight they'll be ringing Murmansk and making another beautiful woman cry, a beautiful woman who loves Kolya." Because somebody must have loved Kolya, with his ever-present smile and his eyes full of life, his broad shoulders and fearless expression. Then an even stranger thought came to me: "Maybe nobody loved him and that's why he jumped!" And then I left. I'd only gone a couple of steps when someone caught up with me and threw their arms around my shoulders. I turned around and there was Sveta.

"What happened? What happened? Tell me what happened!" She was hysterical.

"Go back to your room." I put my arm around her.

"What happened? Tell me! Why won't you tell me? Is he dead? What happened? Tell me what happened." She kept repeating herself, over and over.

"Go back to your room," I shouted at her at the top of my voice.

Sveta turned and ran.

"Maybe nobody loved him!" I couldn't get the words out of my head. I walked along and the same thing went around and around in my head: "Maybe nobody loved him!" Dusk started to fall. I sat for a long time thinking the same thing. It began to get really dark and I sat there some more. Then it was night and I got up.

I went up to my room. I found the door half open. I went in, got some money, locked the door and went down to the restaurant. I asked the waiter to wrap up some cheese, smoked meat, and bread, bought a bottle of vodka, and left.

When I got to the hotel lobby I saw something that made me happy for the first time that day—there was a different woman on the administration desk. I told her there was a woman called Sveta staying in the hotel and asked for her room number.

"Do you know her last name?" the woman asked me.

"No," I said, and slipped her a five-ruble note across the counter. She spent a long time looking through the guest list and said, "There are two Svetas. One is in 205, the other's in 818."

"Which one is here on her own?"

She went back to her list and answered, "The one on the second floor is here with her husband and children, the one on eight is here with another woman."

"Thanks." I nodded to the administrator and got into the elevator.

The elevator went straight up the eighth floor. I found the room and knocked. A young woman opened the door.

"Is Sveta in?" I asked.

"Come in," she invited me.

It was dark in the room and I stopped in the doorway.

"You're so-and-so, aren't you?"—she used my name—"Sveta's asleep, she's nodded off just now."

"I need to wake her up," I said, apologetically. "I'm leaving in the morning and—"

"Okay." She nodded and went toward the room.

"I'll go." I stopped her. I left the vodka and the food on the table, went over to Sveta's bed, knelt down, and called her name quietly. She woke up, got to her feet and introduced me to Oksana.

"I'll go for a walk," Oksana said to us and went toward the door.

"You really don't need to," I said, and blocked her way.

"I know everything," she smiled. "You probably want to talk about Kolya and I'll really just be in the way."

I was uncharacteristically forthright. "You know what? If it's no bother, I'll give you my keys and you can stay in my room for the rest of the night. We'll probably be talking for a long time . . . But don't get the wrong idea."

"Why would I?" Oksana smiled at me again. "Give me your keys."

When Oksana had gone I went back to Sveta.

"Have you eaten anything today?"

She shook her head and sighed. I brought the food and drink through on a plate, took some glasses from the cupboard, opened the bottle of vodka, and poured. Then I cut the bread, put slices of meat on top, and gave it to Sveta. We sat in silence for a while. Sveta slowly picked at the food and stared down at the floor.

"You should eat too," she said to me at last.

"I will," I nodded, raised my glass to my lips and drank.

"Give me some too," she said quietly.

I passed her the glass and she drained it without a word.

"I don't understand what happened," she said, as if she was talking to herself. "He was in a really good mood this morning. He left me by my door at five A.M. and arranged to meet me at ten. We met up and went to the restaurant. There didn't seem to be anything wrong. He just drank quite a lot. He talked about you, said what a nice guy you were, but said it was strange that you'd been here two days and still hadn't been for a swim in the sea. He said he'd just get another bottle of vodka and then he'd go down to the beach because if he didn't go for a swim every morning he'd go crazy. He even drank a toast to you. He said he'd only met you the day before yesterday but that you were his best friend . . . He was in a fantastic mood, really affectionate, he kept giving me compliments. We left at eleven thirty. I went to the hairdressers to get a manicure,"—Sveta looked down at her nails—"and I think he went down to the sea. Then someone came running into the hairdresser's and said there was a man on the roof threatening to jump. They all rushed outside. I was left on my own, so I stood up and went outside too. I didn't recognize him at first. The courtyard was suddenly full of people. They were shouting at him to get back, not to jump. He stood there and just ignored them. He was looking straight ahead. Then he took a step forward and I recognized him. I recognized him and I almost passed out. I already knew nothing was going to make him change his mind. I watched him, and I was just numb. He spread his arms out and walked forward as if he was going to dive into water. I didn't see him fall. I just stood there, frozen, staring up at the roof. I heard his voice and it will stay with me for the rest of my life. Yes, before he jumped he shouted, "I'm through with it!" They say he was shouting something as he fell, too. I didn't hear anything."

There was silence again.

"Pour me some more," she said finally, and gave me her glass.

We drank. I knelt at Sveta's feet and placed my hands on her knees, looked her in the eye and asked, "So you were in Kolya's room till five A.M.?"

"Yes," she nodded.

"And everything was all right?"

"Yes." She looked away. "Three times."

It annoyed me a bit that she felt the need to specify, but I didn't let it show.

"What else did he talk to you about?"

"Nothing in particular. The kind of things men talk about with young women. He told me stuff . . ."

"You seem very familiar with what men say to young women." I touched her arm and stood up.

"This is no time for that!" Sveta said crossly.

I went to the table and refilled the glasses with vodka.

"By the way, it turns out I went to school with Kolya's sister Vika," Sveta said. "We were never really friends, but I'll definitely go and see her when I get back to Murmansk. I didn't even know she had a brother. Her parents died in an accident a long time ago."

"When did you last see each other?"

"This morning, when we came out of the restaurant."

"I meant you and Vika."

"I haven't seen her since we left school."

"When was that?"

"Seven years ago." She looked at me in surprise. "Why does that matter?"

"I'm just asking. Did Kolya tell you why he served time?"

"He served time?" Sveta jumped to her feet.

"Yeah, calm down. For something stupid. A fight or something like that."

"He never said." She sat down and knocked back her vodka. Then she asked me, "What are you going to do? Are you going to stay?"

"I'm flying tomorrow morning," I replied and remembered that Dato was going to ring at six.

"I'll probably leave too. I can't stand being here anymore."

She wrote down my address and gave me hers.

"I'll write to you. Make sure you write back."

"Of course," I promised.

Then we talked for long while about Kolya and about the hours we'd spent together in the restaurant the night before. Sveta asked after Lena.

"I haven't seen her today. She's probably heard about Kolya too," I said.

"How could she not have? They probably know about it in Murmansk by now."

"Yes." I bowed my head.

We drank a few more glasses in silence and it was dawn again.

"I'm going to go," I said, and got to my feet. "I'm going for a walk on the beach. Oksana will probably wake up around nine and then I'll go back up to my room. I need to leave for the airport early tomorrow—there's only one flight to Tbilisi and if I miss my plane I'll have to wait until evening for the train."

I said good-bye to Sveta and left.

I sat on the seashore for two hours smoking cigarettes and once again the thought ran through my mind: "Maybe nobody loved him!" At nine o'clock I went up to my room. Oksana had already gone; the door was unlocked. I flung my bag over my shoulder, got my passport back from hotel administration, flagged down a taxi and was at the airport by ten. The flight to Tbilisi was at one. I bought a ticket, then went down to the nearest beach for a swim. The flight left at one and landed at Tbilisi airport at two. For that whole hour we were in the air the same thought went around and around in my head: "Maybe nobody loved him!"

Seven years after that day I received a latter from Murmansk. I'll translate it word for word:

> Hello. You are probably surprised to be getting this letter. I thought long and hard about writing it and only finally made up my mind to yesterday. I am Nikolai Subotin's daughter Anastasia. I've been thinking about you a lot for the past two months. Sveta told me you were Kolya's best friend. She'd never mentioned you before. She gave me your address there and then—she said you wouldn't even know that Kolya had a child and that you'd be very pleased if I wrote to you. So I'm writing to you, and hoping your address hasn't changed. It's been seven years. Please write back to me as soon as you get this. I'm thirteen years old now. I was six when my father killed himself, but they didn't tell me until I was ten. If Auntie Sveta hadn't turned up I probably still wouldn't

know. I know this letter's very confused; I'm sure it's confusing you too. So I'll start at the beginning and tell you everything I can remember.

I grew up with my grandparents. I don't remember my mother. I remember pictures of a beautiful woman on the wall. They'd tell me she was my mom, that she worked in another city and that she'd be coming back one day soon. I used to wake up in the mornings and ask my grandmother or grandfather whether she was back yet. They always told me she'd been back during the night, that she'd given me many, many kisses and then gone again because she was in such a hurry. That was when I was three or four years old and easy to fool. I never even thought about my father. I'd never seen a picture of him and I never heard anything about him either. At three I didn't even know there needed to be a father. I started to think about him later on. I must have been about six. I was playing in the yard and the neighbor's boy told me my dad was in prison. It made me think for a while, but when I got home I forgot all about it. A few days later I remembered and asked my grandpa where my father was. His face changed and he shouted at me not to ask anything about him, and said it was all my father's fault that my mother wasn't with us. I thought about that for a long time. Sometimes my mother's face would come to me, sometimes the face of a stranger, a man that must have been my father, and I felt that something connected the two of them to each other. But my grandparents never said anything about him. I turned seven and started school. When they read out the class register for the first time they read my name out as Anastasia Borisovna Vasileva. I knew that Boris Vasilev was my grandfather and was surprised that they'd given me his name instead of my father's. That was when I first realized that I didn't even know my father's name. I didn't say anything about it at home, I'd learned that much.

When I went back to school after the New Year break there was a man waiting for me outside my classroom. He saw me, came over, squatted down, hugged me tight, and gave me lots of kisses. He was hugging me and crying. I knew straightaway the man was my father. It was as if I remembered him from somewhere. He looked exactly like I'd imagined him. I put my arms around him and clung to him. Then my dad had a word with the teacher and spent a long time explaining something to her. I stood some distance away, paying close attention to every movement he made. Dad kissed Ludmila Mikhailovna's hand, thanked her, came back over to me and said, "Let's go, you've got the day off school." We walked through the streets holding hands for ages, not even talking to each other. Every now and then Dad would look down at me. I pretended not to notice and just looked straight ahead. We went into the park and sat on a bench. He asked me whether I remembered him at all. I lied, and said no. I remembered him—otherwise how would I have recognized him at school—but I didn't admit it. Actually, I didn't remember him until he turned up there, but as soon as I saw him I knew who he was. He was the man who used to come over when I was about two or three. My grandma and grandpa wouldn't even let him in the house; they'd just stand with the door half open and talk to him through the gap. His face must have stayed in my memory. I asked him why he'd been in prison. He laughed for a long time and I can't remember what his answer was. When we came out of the park he bought me some pastries and sweets and then took me to a café. I remember feeling really relaxed with him. We talked a lot and I told him about school and my dolls. He listened really closely and laughed a lot. Then I asked him why he hadn't brought Mom with him. He fell deep into thought, looked down at his watch, took me outside, and flagged down a taxi. He took me to the cemetery. He led me over to one of the graves and told me I was a big girl and that it was time I found out that this was my mother's grave. I didn't cry or anything. It was as if I was finding out something I'd already known for a long time but had just been reminded of. He cried, though. He tried not to let me see but I did, I saw the tears rolling down his cheeks. He said when I got home I shouldn't tell them he'd come and taken me out or that anyone had told me about my mom's grave. He said he'd asked Ludmila Mikhailovna and she'd agreed not to say anything either. He took me back to school and watched from a distance as my grandfather's driver came to get me and I got into the car. Even now I'm surprised that he trusted a six-year-old so much. I could so easily have told them everything when I got home. I'm not sure he even cared. Just imagine, we carried on meeting like that for two months, and nobody else knew apart from Ludmila Mikhailovna. He would come to my classroom once every four or five days, clear it with the teacher and take me out of school. For me, my dad showing up was the best thing ever. We'd go here, there and everywhere. He did whatever I wished for, most of which, I now realize, was pretty much impossible. In those three hours I should have been in school I would ask him to take me to four or five different places. Sometimes I fancied the zoo, sometimes the circus, sometimes even a show, and even now I'm amazed at how he managed to fit everything in. One time I saw a doll with messy hair in a shop window and asked Dad to buy it for me. He didn't have any money and promised he'd buy it for me the next day and bring it with him next time he saw me. For some reason I didn't believe him and my eyes filled with tears. When he saw, he took off his watch right there in the street and sold it to a passer-by and then bought me the doll. I remembering telling my grandparents a friend had given it to me. Then I lost it somewhere and I'm still heartbroken about it to this day. He took me to the cemetery almost every time I saw him. We'd sit there and he'd tell me about my mom. He'd tell me about how they'd met and how he'd fallen in love. I realize now it wasn't really me he was telling—he was saying it as a way to remember it himself. When he talked about her he'd sometimes forget I was even there. He'd look somewhere into the distance while he was talking. Dad loved my mother very much. It made no difference that she wasn't with us anymore. You could tell from everything my father said and did that he still loved her. Once when we were at the cemetery I was playing a little game to entertain him: I gathered sand into a little pile, stuck wild flowers in, and arranged colored pebbles and bits of glass around the outside. Suddenly I asked Dad anxiously whether Mom would be cross that I was playing. He laughed and said no, just the opposite, she'd be really glad. Then I asked him why we never brought flowers— surely you were supposed to bring flowers to the cemetery? He said we couldn't because my grandfather would see them. I couldn't understand why he was so keen to steer clear of my grandpa, but I didn't ask. On our next visit he bought flowers and took them to the grave. It is what it is, he said, and Grandfather would find out anyway that he was out of prison. The next day Grandpa came home from work really angry. I guessed that he'd been to the cemetery. He grabbed my grandmother and started talking anxiously at her. Then they turned toward me and said that if a man I didn't know came to school and tried to talk to me I should go straight to the teacher. I blurted everything out. It was probably my own little protest. For two months I'd said nothing and in ten minutes flat I told them everything from start to finish. I clearly remember my final words: "It was me and Dad who took those flowers to Mom's grave yesterday. I love my mom and dad very much. Dad's made me love Mom more than I did before and I will never, never lose him." Their eyes nearly popped out of their heads. I started to cry and hugged my grandmother close. That was the worst day of my life. I didn't get to sleep for ages. I just lay there thinking about Mom and Dad.

From that day on my grandmother took me to school. They didn't trust the driver with me anymore. Every day I thought my father would come, and if not that day the next, but he never appeared. Gradually he faded from my memory again, although not completely; from time to time I remembered him and felt a terrible sorrow. It's only now that I realize my grandpa probably called him or saw him and threatened to get him sent back to prison. Grandpa held the kind of position where he could easily do that. Especially as Dad had been in prison before. The last time I saw him was in the summer. I pestered Grandpa to take me to my mom's grave and I saw him just as we were getting out of the car. He was standing with his back to us and didn't notice us. I ran over and threw my arms around his legs. He turned around, crouched down and kissed me. Then Grandpa came over to us. I don't know what they talked about but I remember Dad saying he'd be going to the coast in a week's time and that he wanted to have me for one day so that he could introduce me to his sister. He said he'd bring me back the next morning. But Grandpa wouldn't let me go. That was the last time my father and I saw each other.

That made me think about my aunt, although I soon forgot all about her again. A week later Dad went to the coast, where he met you and Sveta and where he died. As I've said, I only found out about this four years later. After that when I asked Grandma and Grandpa about Dad their answers were less aggressive. They said he'd stayed on the coast, and that he was working on a ship. I was always scared that Grandpa had got him sent back to prison and once I even asked him outright. He swore he hadn't and I stopped worrying so much. Then, when I was about eight—I don't remember exactly—I found out from Grandma that Mom died in childbirth. By then I'd already been through quite a lot and so not even that discovery really shocked me. It just reminded me of my mother once again and broke my heart. A few years went by and my grandfather retired. He just sat at home all day. He became warmer and more sensitive, and started taking me to my mother's grave. One day, when I got home from school, I found two women I didn't know sitting there. I found out later they were my aunt and Sveta. I was ten years old. Grandma took me into the other room. I somehow knew that my grandfather was talking to the women about me. He called me in and introduced me to them. After that Vika and Sveta used to sometimes pick me up from school and take me to another house for a couple of days. Vika lives on her own and I used to love being there. Sveta used to come over quite often to stay the night. They even took me to my dad's grave. Sveta told me how my dad killed himself, but she didn't say a thing about you for three years. She tells me now that she'd forgotten about you, and then just by chance after seven years she'd found your address. My aunt told me all about my mom and dad's relationship. Apparently my grandfather was strongly opposed to their marriage. When I was born and Mom died, Grandpa took me home, gave me his name and wouldn't let my father come near me. Then, when I was four, my father burst into Grandpa's office when he was drunk and beat him up. That's why he went to prison.

There. I've nearly told you everything I know about my life. Because you used to be a close friend of my father and everything connected with my father is dear to me. I only knew my father for two months. I probably only met him ten times in all, but there's no end to how much I love him and his name—Nikolai Subotin. I love my grandfather a lot too. The grandfather who was so strict while he was working and who changed so much once he'd retired; the grandfather who made my aunt and Sveta too scared to come and tell me about my father for four years; the grandfather whose presence made my mother's pregnancy and labor so hard she died in childbirth; my father lost my mother, went to prison, couldn't see his own child and saw his life go so wrong that finally he killed himself; my aunt didn't see me until I was ten years old. The grandfather because of whom I didn't meet my father until I was six and only knew him for two months. How Ludmila Mikhailovna had the courage to keep my father's visits a secret from Grandpa I do not know.

Now I spend part of the time at Vika's and part of it at my grandparents'. But basically I live with my grandparents. After all, I grew up here and can't imagine life without them. I probably need to grow up a bit more before I'll understand it all. Before I'll understand why Dad killed himself. Why he didn't think of me and Vika at the last moment. But he probably just couldn't bear it anymore—I'm not blaming him for anything. I've been thinking and thinking about him my whole life. You might laugh, but at night Mom and Dad are with me, in my thoughts and in my dreams, and we're all together: me, Mom, Dad, Grandma, Grandpa, Vika, and Sveta. Sometimes when I see families together in the street or on the television it makes me so sad I almost cry. There are so many happy families around, and all I have is my parents' graves. But then again, I often think about the fact that I had a very beautiful mom, and a very kind and charming dad, and then I'm happy too.

But I'm not going to read this letter to Sveta. She's a great friend, but still. I'm sorry to have bothered you, although I'm sure you'll be pleased to find out about me. I hope to receive a reply from you very soon.

With kind regards,
Anastasia Vasileva-Subotina.

DAVIT KARTVELISHVILI
The Squirrel

I

I was eighteen months old when I first started talking. Of course I only know that from what people have told me—I don't remember the momentous day myself. There is, though, a second momentous day that I remember very well indeed. Yesterday. The day I fell silent. Yesterday I realized that my wife Natia and my best friend and business partner Levan were lovers and the power of speech deserted me. My wife Natia once said that she would fall in love with Levan, not me. Wives like to spout annoying things like that—it's how they pay us back for always being late and getting drunk and all the rest. Natia and I have been together for three years. Three years of marriage. Three years of sleeping together: moaning, groaning, heavy panting, a scream and then, covered in sweat, we collapse side by side on the bed. But we haven't got any children yet. We want some, but we haven't got any. This is the major problem in out relationship. Levan is my best friend (disregarding the fact that he's having an affair with Natia, I have no better friend than him—and that is my misfortune) and my business partner, and so of course he knows about our big, big problem. Sometimes we talk about it over lunch. Levan always tells me I should go and see this doctor or that doctor. Once Levan even gave me a list of doctors he'd printed out. Levan doesn't know that Natia and I went to see those doctors long ago and that they found out I was the problem, that the problem's in me . . . although as Levan and Natia are having an affair, Levan probably knows everything after all. Natia probably puts her head on Levan's chest and blurts stuff out. She probably blurts everything out. Until yesterday I was taking special pills and following a special diet. Now I've stopped bothering—what on earth's the point? Levan and Natia are having an affair. Levan and I have known each other since we were children. We used to play soccer and war together; in soccer he was the goalie and in war he was always a Red. In soccer I was a forward and in war I was a German. Sometimes I'd score against Levan and sometimes I couldn't get the ball past him, sometimes in war I killed Levan and sometimes he killed me. Me and Levan were in the same class at school, and after we left Levan went to America and I went to England. We both studied law. While we were away Georgia had its civil wars and a period of reflection, and then heroin, cocaine, and hash arrived, along with nightclubs and saunas. Levan and I came back to Tbilisi at the same time and celebrated our return in a fancy sauna—we drank champagne, wrapped ourselves in dazzling white towels, and walked about like the Romans we'd seen in the movies. We watched naked women dance for us, and then the same women showed us a bit of affection, and whispered sweet nothings to us as we left. The next day we started work. Levan and I agreed to start a business together. And because we'd followed parallel paths when we started working—Levan in America, me in England—the only real difference was that Levan got paid in dollars and I got paid in pounds. Dollars and pounds. Both easily convertible currencies, and with our savings we opened a law firm. It was right there in the law firm that one fortuitous day I met Natia. She brought her problem along just like anyone else. Levan was out having talks with a major client. Natia told me about her problem, and I said it was something we could sort out for her and told her how much we charged. Natia said our rates were okay and we drew up a contract, shook hands, and smiled at each other. Natia had a lovely smile and so I asked, "Shall we go to the cinema?"

Natia looked slightly confused, slightly cross, slightly embarrassed. "Why?"

I was feeling bold. "Because I really like you."

Natia smiled. Natia had a lovely smile. "Well, okay then, seeing as you've got such a good reason. You've got my number—call me and we can fix a time, draw up a contract if you like. . ." And after a perfectly timed and charmingly executed pause, Natia said, "What kind of films do you like?"

I like British detective series, but didn't think that would strike the right tone, so I lied: "I like art-house."

"Looks like we have similar taste then," Natia said. After we got to know each other better it turned out that Natia doesn't like art-house cinema at all. Natia watches American melodramas.

Just then Levan came back to the office. Nothing much happened. Levan said hello to Natia and sat down at the computer. I walked Natia to the lift. When I got back to the office Levan told me we'd got the major client, and I told Levan that I liked Natia and we were going to the cinema. Levan gave me a few words of advice, as best friends should. Then we went and got drunk.

Three days later Natia and I met up. Natia was late, of course. I was nervous, of course. We saw a really tedious Michelangelo Antonioni film, *Red Desert*, and I caught myself thinking it would have been better to watch modern rubbish rather than this classical nonsense, but I didn't say that to Natia. After the film we went to the nearest café. We ordered coffee, cake, and cognac and talked about various things, some serious and some less so. And then I answered one of her questions with a lie, and because of that my life changed for two months. For two months I was in a state of panic. "Sandro," Natia asked me, and I knew from the fact she started with my name that she was going to say something serious. I braced myself. "Do you believe in God?"

And I reasoned to myself that desire is the most important thing in a relationship, and that religious people, because their conduct is restricted by the Ten Commandments, experience greater desire than atheists, who are enthusiastic rather than desirous. And because enthusiasm is so ephemeral, and because I wanted a long relationship with Natia, and because the fundamental basis of a long relationship is desire (this being the rather pathetic train of thought I had back then), I said, "Yes, I do!"

In actual fact I'm neither a believer nor an atheist. I realize that something much more powerful and more perfect than human beings created the universe, of course—I just don't really think about that stuff anymore. I don't ask myself who that being is and what he's asking of me. I've got my own problems. I want our law firm to be famous throughout the world, I want shares in our firm sold on the international financial markets, I want to be a famous global expert, and I want Levan as my highly skilled deputy. I'll ask myself who that being is and what he's asking of me the minute he starts sorting out my problems for me. I'm not holding my breath.

"Would you like us to start going to church on Sundays?" Natia offered.

I nodded. It was another opportunity to see her. "Let's do that."

People who work six days a week need their Sundays for sleep. That lie I answered Natia with robbed me of my Sundays and I started to feel a sense of constant panic. Every Sunday for two months we got up before daybreak so that we wouldn't be late for church. We were late a few times all the same. But anyway, two months is enough time for a couple to grow really close, so after two months I told Natia I wasn't going to church anymore.

Natia's reaction was not what I expected; she shrugged her shoulders and said, "Don't go then."

And I stopped going to church. Natia didn't.

In those two months I learned that the soul exists and that the soul is immortal, that by nature the soul is light, but that with his sins man makes it heavy, and the soul becomes troubled and tormented. At the same time you have routine, and this routine drags you along so forcefully and turns you and turns you and turns you so much that you forget the soul exists. And you turn and turn and turn and think that you are moving forward. My dream about the international market, my dream about the global financial markets, my dream about becoming known worldwide—apparently it's all nonsense. Well, I don't like that way of thinking. I like a different way of thinking. When I lived in England I made friends with an Indian girl. I was a foreigner there and she was too, both of us representatives of very ancient countries and cultures. The girl was called Estay and one day, when we were sitting in the park watching squirrels run about in the trees, Estay told me that these squirrels might be our ancestors, and we talked for a while about transmigration of the soul. That really appeals to me. I realize that while one lifetime might be enough for me to realize my dreams I won't have time to enjoy them too. I want my soul to transmigrate and for me to be born again, although I don't suppose it's really possible and even thinking about it confuses me.

Then, one fine day, they told us that I was the problem and Natia said to me, "It's because you're a nonbeliever. You're being punished."

"You really think that—"

Natia didn't let me finish. "Yes, I think that—"

Now I didn't let Natia finish. "You really think that God is judge, jury, and executioner, even for something like this?"

Natia shook her head.

"No, I don't think that, I think that God gives man a sign and if man chooses to be blind and stupid then it's his own fault."

"What, so we punish ourselves?"

"Yes." Natia put her arms around my neck. "Just think about it, will you? Please, just think about it."

"I'll think about it," I promised.

And since that day I've thought about it a lot and rather unexpectedly I came to the conclusion that my wife Natia and my best friend and business partner Levan are having an affair. In spite of that I still haven't changed my opinion that something much more powerful and perfect than humans created the universe. Last night I registered a handgun. A Beretta, sixteen rounds.

II

Suspicions always need to be confirmed, whereas if you see something with your own eyes . . . I need to see Natia and Levan together with my own eyes. And so I am forced to break my day-long silence. I say to Natia, "Nati, I'm going to Batumi," and wait for Natia to ask, "What do you want to go to Batumi for?" so that I can joke, "Well, I can't go to Sokhumi 'cause we lost it in the war!" But Natia asks me something completely different: "Is Levan going too?"

"No."

"When will you be back?"

"In three days."

I look into Natia's eyes. "It's worked out just right for you, hasn't it?" I think. "You're happy now, aren't you? I'm going, Levan's staying. I'll be back in three days. Knock yourselves out for three days, why don't you . . ." And suddenly I see that right before my eyes, them knocking themselves out—they're doing it, they're doing it all, pleasuring themselves and each other in every way possible. No. No, those three days aren't going to happen.

I call Levan. I'm going to Batumi, I tell him, and wait for him to ask me what Natia asked me, only about Natia: Is Natia coming? I answer: no. He's pleased. Delighted. He asks me when I'm coming back. Three days, I tell him. Quick as a flash, Levan plans those three days in his head. And suddenly Levan's plans appear right before my eyes. They're doing it, they're doing it all, pleasuring themselves and each other in every way possible. No. No, Levan's plans aren't going to happen. But Levan asks me something completely different: "What on earth do you want to go to Batumi for?"

Aha, are professional suspicions eating you up, friend? Are they?

"Do you remember the Turks?" I ask.

Levan remembers.

"They're coming to Batumi and I want to meet up with them, see if I can tie up some kind of international deal." And after a short pause I ask, "Do you want to come along?"

"No, I've got some people here I need to look after. When are you back?"

"Three days."

The blood rushes around my head and my heart. I repeat Levan's words to myself—I've got some people here I need to look after—and I see those horrors before me once more: they're doing it, they're doing it all, pleasuring themselves and each other in every way possible . . . but no, those three days aren't going to happen.

"Are you going by train?" Levan asks.

"No, I'm flying," I answer automatically.

"Well, have a good flight."

"Thank you." I hang up.

Then I pack my bag, kiss Natia on the forehead, tell her to be good and say good-bye for three days. I go out into the yard and sit in the car. Natia stands on the balcony to wave me off. I put the gun under the seat. You might say I'm sitting on a powder keg. I start the car and actually set off on the road to the airport. I start thinking maybe it's better if my suspicions remain just that, that I don't really need to confirm anything or see anything for myself. There's a voice in my head telling me my suspicions are nonsense. There's another voice in my head telling me they're not nonsense at all.

I wander around the airport concourse. I smoke a cigarette and think, and think, and voices in my head tell me different things and I just can't make a final decision. Should I get on the plane? Should I stay here? Maybe it would be better if I went to Batumi. I could have a three-day break, walk along the seashore, listen to the sound of the waves. I look out to sea and the sea calms me, looking out to sea calms me, brings me to my own sea of calm. I go to the ticket desk.

"Are there any tickets left for the Batumi flight?"

"There are, yes."

"I want one ticket." And suddenly those three days with me not there flash in front of my eyes again. They're doing it, they're doing it all, pleasuring themselves and each other in every possible way. "Sorry, sorry, sorry, I've changed my mind," I say to the girl on the desk, "I'm not flying anymore."

I leave the ticket in her outstretched hand. She mutters something at me. She probably thinks I'm crazy, that the country's full of crazy people just like me. But no matter what she thinks, those three days with me not there just aren't going to happen. I go out of the airport concourse, I get into the car, I'm sitting on a powder keg, I put the key in the ignition and then I freeze. I start to wonder, wonder whether I'd be able to kill somebody if my suspicions were confirmed. I'm surprised by how quickly my two best friends have gone from being my wife Natia and my best friend and business partner Levan into just some generic "somebodies." I'm not wondering whether I'll be able to kill Natia and Levan, I'm wondering whether I'll be able to kill "somebody." I don't know. I'll find out when I get there. I turn the key, start the engine, and set off back home. On the way I phone Natia and tell her I'm already on the plane, everything's fine and that she should be good while I'm gone. Then I phone Levan and tell him the same, I'm already on the plane, everything's fine, and that he should—I change the last bit—take care. Then I put the phone on the car seat next to me and think and think. If my suspicions are confirmed will I be able to kill? And in one ear I hear Natia's voice, and in the other I hear Levan's. Then, quite unexpectedly, I remember something else. I remember a beautiful day when Estay and I were sitting in a café drinking tea and Estay suddenly asked, as women are prone to do, "Do you love me?"

I sipped my tea, put the cup back on the saucer, smiled, and said, "Yes, I love you," lifted the cup back up and started moving it toward my lips again.

"Aren't you going to ask me?"

"What?" I stopped with the cup right in front of my mouth. The steam from the tea tickled my nose.

"Whether I love you or not."

"I'm asking now: do you love me?" I sipped my tea. Then I put the cup back on the saucer and tried to look serious, because I guessed from Estay's expression that she was about to give a serious and thorough answer to that four-word question.

And Estay said, "I've got nobody here. I look left and I'm scared, I look right and I'm scared, I look straight ahead and I'm scared, I don't look behind me but it always feels like there's something there. And when I look up I'm really, really scared. Because there's something really strange up there." I looked up, instinctively—above me the ceiling had painted patterns all over it. Estay carried on with what she was saying. "I'm talking about heaven. That's pretty much why I go around with my head bowed all the time, but going around with your head bowed is really stupid . . ."

I interrupted. "Then lift your head up and look around and don't be scared. What are you scared of?"

"There are people all around me I don't know and I'm scared. I'm scared they'll attack me, hurt me, maybe even kill me."

I tried to make a joke. "So what if they do? You'll come back to life as a squirrel and spend all your time running around in the treetops."

Estay smiled. "You don't even believe in reincarnation. And anyway, what I'm talking about is something completely different. I've got no one here apart from you. Can't you see how much I love you?"

I kissed Estay. On the neck, for some reason—and then later when they found Estay on top of the rubbish dump with her throat cut I thought back to that kiss and it felt as if my lips were on fire. The police questioned me because my number was the only one on Estay's phone and she had all my messages saved. In the end the police decided some invisible serial killer was responsible for Estay's murder. It was only after her murder that I first seriously considered the possibility that someone in that country might kill me too, and that I too had nobody looking out for me, nobody on my side, nobody to call a friend. The opposite, in fact. Any wistful citizens dreaming of the British Empire's former glory might even say it's what I deserve. Why did I come—uninvited—to their glorious empire when I should have stayed in my own country, when the empire was already full of freeloaders, when their patience had already run out, and so on? But none of that matters anymore, because I'm back in my own country now, and I have a wife, Natia, and a best friend and business partner, Levan, and they're having an affair. I pick up the phone and call home. Natia answers, I don't speak, I hang up, I ring the office, Levan answers, I don't speak, I hang up. So that means they haven't met up with each other yet. I put my foot on the accelerator. A patrol car stops me, and I remember I'm sitting on a powder keg—I'm licensed to own a gun but not to carry it, and definitely not to sit on it, and I get nervous. But after a few seconds everything becomes a bit clearer: they've stopped me for speeding and our relationship never goes beyond them issuing me with a twenty-lari fine. I put the receipt in my pocket and the patrol car goes on its way. And then, finally, I get home. I park the car well away from the house and open my bag. In my bag along with my clothes, razor, and essential documents there's a telescope. I take out the telescope and start watching the house. Either Levan will come here or Natia will go out. After an hour Natia comes out of the main entrance. And just where do you think you're going, my dear? Natia crosses over the road at the lights and goes into the supermarket. That's when dark thoughts start to appear. I know now what will happen, and that she'll leave by the back door. But there is no back door. There's a staff entrance, for the supermarket's employees—she'll ask them, I should think, and they'll let her out that way. What should I do? What should I do? After a couple of minutes Natia comes back out of the supermarket, and I can relax again. Natia's carrying bags, she's bought some things, she hails a taxi, agrees on a price with the driver, and gets in. The taxi drives off. I'm following you, Natia, my love . . .

III

We're in Natia's old neighborhood and I suddenly realize where it is that Natia and Levan meet up. In the attic of Natia's old house. Before, when we—Natia and I—were in love, we would often meet up in that attic. We'd kiss, we'd talk, we'd dream, and then we'd kiss again. I park the car some distance away, stick the gun into my waistband, and think about how to get up to the attic without Natia noticing me. I'm in luck: they're obviously meeting here for the first time and Levan doesn't know the exact address. Levan is my best friend and business partner, but I've never taken him to Natia's house or up to her attic. That's just how it is, there's no particular reason for it, significant or otherwise. Natia stands at the side of the road near the entrance, but luckily there's a second way into the lobby that goes off the yard, so I run in that way. Natia's building is five stories high. I run up five flights of stairs. I go up into the attic. I feel at home in here. It all seems so familiar, every little nook and cranny, even the smell. I hide myself safely away, hold the gun in my hand and wait for them to appear . . . It hurts so much to think that my suspicions are confirmed, that my wife Natia and my best friend and business partner Levan are having an affair.

After a little while they come up to the attic. I'm watching and listening, my dears.

"This isn't an attic, it's a whole apartment," Levan says.

I said that the first time too. Natia and I had stood there facing each other, both nervous.

Natia puts the bag onto the table.

"My dad fixed it up. He used to joke to me and my mom that he couldn't stand living with us anymore and that he'd fix up the attic and then come and live up here. At least I think he was joking. Maybe he was being serious, I don't know. Anyway, when he'd finished renovating it he died, just like that." Natia takes a bottle of brandy out of the bag, and some sweets, and lays them out on the table. "Whenever anything important happens in my life I come up here."

Levan sits at the table.

"Are we having a party or something?"

"Yes," says Natia, "we're having a party."

And what am I doing all this time? Just waiting to see what will happen.

Levan opens the brandy. Here we go. They'll have a brandy each, then Levan will sit by Natia's side, kiss her neck, caress her ear, tug playfully on her ear lobe, and then Natia will heave that first sigh and close her eyes, and then everything will happen so quickly . . . I'm drowning in sweat. I know I could kill. When should I kill them? Should I wait? Should I do it now?

Levan pours the brandy into plastic cups. He raises his and says, "What shall we drink to?"

"I'm pregnant!"

"Oh my God! When did you find out?"

"Yesterday."

My head starts to spin. Natia is pregnant, Natia is going to have a child. In no time at all Levan has managed what I have failed to do for three years. Levan and Natia are going to have a child. I think about killing myself and raise the gun to my temple. The gun barrel feels cold. If I kill myself now it will be a protest suicide. The first consequence will be that I no longer exist, the second will be that I'll ruin Natia and Levan's happy day, the third will be the same as the first—I will no longer exist. The barrel of the gun cools my temple, and I stay like that, gun barrel pressed against temple. I hear my name.

"Have you told Sandro?" She'll lie, she'll lie, I'm sure she'll lie to Levan. She'll tell him she's told me, that I went crazy, out of my mind, slapped her, swore at her, threatened her, tried to kick her in the stomach, but that somehow she fended off every blow. She'll do everything she can, she'll say everything she can to drive Levan mad.

I hear Natia's reply. "No, I haven't told him."

"Why not?" Levan seems surprised. I'm surprised too. "The man's going to become a father and you haven't told him?"

Levan's such a snake. He's going to run out on her. The woman's pregnant and he's going to run out on her. Natia's going to fall into a blind panic, God help her. I pity Levan, my best friend and business partner and I'm glad I'm here to witness this. Go on, Nati, go on, jump onto the table and hurl things at Levan, hurl angry words, cakes, plastic cups, go on, Nati, go onnnnnn . . . But Natia doesn't jump onto the table. Natia sits down on a chair. Oh, this is no good at all! Now Natia will start crying, and begging, and pleading, Levan, don't abandon me, Levan, don't leave me with that beast Sandro, Levan, dear Levan, I love you, and all that kind of thing. Natia's already crying. Levan sits down next to Natia and strokes her head.

"Calm down, don't cry. You're having a baby—you should be happy," Levan says and after a short pause he asks Natia again, "The man's going to be a father; why haven't you told him?"

Ah yes, that'll do it. Natia won't be able to bear it anymore. Yes, now she really will jump up onto the table and hurl, hurl, hurl things at Levan, hurl angry words, cakes, plastic cups. Go on, Nati, go on, can't you see, can't you hear, don't you understand that he's dumping you, leaving you, running out on you? But Natia doesn't move. Natia says, "I'm not going to tell him till he works it out for himself."

Levan stands up, puts his hands into his pockets and asks Natia, "Why? The man's going to be a father—why won't you tell him?"

And suddenly I start thinking that maybe it really is me, maybe Natia's pregnant by me, and my heart starts to pound and I'm so happy I don't know what to do with myself—should I shout out, should I dance, or should I curl up in a ball with my head tucked in, put my fingers in my ears and stay there curled up with my head tucked in and my fingers in my ears so that I don't see or hear anything and stay happy till I die, albeit curled up with my head tucked in and my fingers in my ears? I can't decide, so I just remain in that pitiful position, hidden away, with the gun still pressed to my temple. I hear Natia's voice. "If I tell Sandro that I'm pregnant now, he'll put it all down to those stupid pills and that stupid diet . . ."

Levan interrupts her. "What pills? What diet?"

My whole body's on fire.

"Didn't he tell you? He must have been too embarrassed—we went to see a doctor and it turned out Sandro was the reason I couldn't get pregnant, so the doctor put him on pills and a special diet."

I can feel my cheeks burning.

"So what I'm saying is, he'll put it all down to that, the pills and the diet. But I want him to see it as miracle, to realize it *was* a miracle. I want

Sandro to believe in something transcendent, something immaterial. I want Sandro to realize that his stupid empty life is actually causing Jesus pain. I kept pleading with Jesus to give Sandro and me a child, and the very day I gave up and let myself doubt it all was the day I got pregnant. I knew I was pregnant—I felt it with my whole being, my whole heart. Levan, you are Sandro's best friend, he'll listen to you. Do you understand what I'm saying?"

"I see."

She's getting ready to hit me with the I-told-you-sos, I think to myself.

"If you don't know what to say to him we can carry on meeting up here and I'll tell you."

"I do know, of course I know."

He's getting ready with the I-told-you-sos too, I think to myself.

"So, what are you going to say to him when he gets back from Batumi?"

"Hello, how are you, and everything's fine at the office."

"No, no, no . . ."

"Ah, I've got it: your wife's pregnant."

"No, no . . ."

"Well then?"

"Tell him you believe in Jesus."

"Lie to him?"

"Lie to him. The most important thing is for Sandro to believe in Jesus, and then Sandro and I will help you to believe in him too."

"All right, I'll tell him." And after a pause Levan says to Natia, "Come on, let's go to a café. There's something about this place I don't like anymore. I feel like we're trapped. Let's go to a nice café and talk about Jesus."

"Okay, let's go," says Natia. She looks at the table. "I'll come back this evening and tidy up then."

Natia and Levan leave. I come out from my hiding place. I eat a cake and drink some brandy. I feel so happy. I go up onto the roof and fire all sixteen rounds into the air.

IV

I'm back. I'm back on the ground. I don't want to sit in a car—I need space, so I go straight to the public gardens opposite Natia's old house. I sit under a spruce tree, and come to a decision: I'll go back home tonight, I'll tell Natia that the meeting with the Turks fell through and in the morning Natia and I will go to Batumi for a relaxing break. We'll walk along the shore next to the sea and bathe in our sea of love . . . I hear a chattering sound and I see it coming toward me, chatter-chatter-chatter, and it chatters some more and sits by my side, a squirrel and we look at each other . . .

And I say, "Hello, Estay."

BESIK KHARANAULI
Ladies and Gentlemen!

When we got to the cemetery I got out of the car to open the gate. I was tired. The sun, the tired old sun, was setting. But I had no time for tiredness. There was no sign of anyone, even though I had hoped to find the gravediggers there. After all, I knew it would take four men to get the stone down. Sometimes people are there, sometimes they are not—just as now, when I'd hoped there would be someone but ended up alone.

"What about us, don't we exist anymore?"

"What's your name, boy?"

"8–10."

"You?"

"I'm 14–15."

"Then let's get started!"

"First let's get the tip to the edge of the trunk. For that, 8–10 needs to be in the trunk to put the support underneath and make sure it doesn't roll back onto us. I'll find something wooden and stand the front wheels on it so that the edge of the trunk drops down, and then we can get started."

"Don't get your hands caught!"

Sometimes you can't move, you just can't summon any strength, as if strength is irrelevant, as if it would be redundant in the situation you are in—in short, as if having any strength would be futile. We thought about the ancestors of modern man who moved much larger stones than this, and managed to get the tip to the edge of the trunk. But our joy was premature—the stone was too heavy and rolled back inside the trunk again. 8–10 escaped unscathed but on his own was just not strong enough, and the stone swiveled around and fell back down toward us, heavy end first. We started again from the beginning: 14–15 grabbed me around the waist so that my legs were anchored to the ground and I put my upper body into the trunk, lay down, grabbed onto the stone with both hands, joked about whether I would be able to move it, given that normally I cannot lift anything heavier than a glass. I threw myself on top of the stone and started shifting it toward me. 14–15 held me firmly on the ground, 8–10 breathed heavily, the triangular tip of the stone pointed down toward the earth and 8–10 hastily shoved a piece of wood in underneath as a support. After that it was time for brute force. We paused for a second to rest, and then gave it our all. We lifted, lifted, and, as agreed, 14–15 put into position the plank we planned to slide it down, wedged it firmly into the earth and when there was nothing left to do but actually lift the stone out of the trunk we all worked together to raise the bottom of the stone and set it on the ground. It settled so well that the grass around it did not even sway, and you would think it had no weight at all—it seemed to fly down, to find its proper place at last . . . And for the whole of this time—four hours, maybe five—we could feel an outpouring of sympathy from all around us, as if our surroundings were breathing with us, the graveyard's chest rising and falling with the grave stones.

As soon as we had set the stone down we heard the sound of rain, like applause, and the skies thundered, and the shingle-covered cemetery slopes, the surrounding forest and the electricity cables all had their own means by which to echo our feelings, our roaring, our screaming, whether through the sound of rain or the sensation of hail striking skin.

As often as not, what starts out as a serious mission descends into farce; in practical terms, lifting that stone, bringing it here and then putting it in place was as impossible as any large undertaking could conceivably be.

The sunshine always seems so strange in cemeteries. Squinting in the sunlight I looked for 8–10, who was nowhere to be found, and 14–15, who was likewise nowhere to be found. To the west of the sun two small flecks of cloud drifted across the sky. I was alone.

"Alooooooooone . . ." I howled like a beast.

The author had been home for an hour, a day, a year, or maybe no time at all when, while looking for a cigarette, he discovered this piece of writing. He recognized his own scrawl and started to read, but then gave up and put it back where he had found it.

"If I really had written that book," he thought, "I would win that international prize and proudly hold open the door to my native village. I'd be arrogant, mock the whole world except for my part of it, stir things up as much as I liked. I'd get drunk on plum vodka and although I'm too old (people always get the chance to do what they wish when it's too late), I might even have a bit of 'this and that' with that star of the world stage Nina Amoradze, one of the last remaining members of the Amoradze clan, who would, of course, fly in from some far-flung corner of the world with various other important people. She would cut her concert tour short for me, and in doing so would make the whole world turn its head to look at me but also at its own whims. It would prove to the world that heroes exist where women are able to sacrifice themselves. And that would be the fulfillment of my dreams—the rest is nonsense! 'This is your world too! We've fooled the world!' Nina would tell me during one of our tender moments: Nina Amoradze, the youngest of the youngest of the young. The quintessence of every Nina—whether in one village or the whole world—and the main thing is to love 'this and that' and to die while you're doing it.

"At the award ceremony for this international prize, for which every writer is even now preparing a badly worded opening line and which—Well, I've had that line ready inside me for forty years. I shall say, 'Ladies and gentlemen! You shouldn't find it too hard to imagine the scene: a writer, armed in advance with suspicions and counter-suspicions, sits at his table and reads the changes he's made to his poems, and is amazed to find that it is not literature that jumps out at him but life, the life he has led. Everything is a path, a labyrinth . . .'"

And so the boy of 14–15 years of age takes his notebook filled with poems and goes to meet the famous poet. Just then he sees his beloved, but is only as happy to see her as he is to leave her again, because today is the day he sets off down the path toward changing himself.

In childhood, though, the writer does not just think—he also starts living his real life. He sees himself at the ages of 8–10 and 14–15 and starts to get involved in their lives and in their passions . . .

The most important event in the writer's childhood happens when 8–10 nearly drowns and is saved by 14–15 while the writer runs away.

After the rescue, 8–10, 14–15, and the writer go to their abandoned house in the village. At night the rain comes, as if to clear the charged air of all that is transcendent and make reality visible again; the rain pours down off the roof tiles, smashing through the gate in a torrent and flooding into the yard. The writer is feeble in the face of the elements; he is alone once again . . .

The next morning, as usual, the sun shines brightly. The writer starts repairing his storm-damaged house and its grounds—the hedge, the roof tiles, the branches that have been brought down, and he fixes the gate and cuts the waist-high grass . . .

After this spiritual event the writer returns to town and tries to fit back into the rhythm of his normal daily life; he tries to write, but instead of poems something else flows from his pen. The writer is shaken by these visions he cannot shift from his mind and which for a long time had escaped his memory, so shaken that he tries to cure himself with a method he tried once before, when he drank so much that not only did he forget he was a writer, but tried to obliterate the final vestiges of humanity within him.

The writer tries in vain to turn his spiritual metamorphosis into a book, tries to compose something, but he is unable to produce anything at all. "You see?" he says. "You see what poetry is? It is the only truth which is a total lie . . ."

Why is the Creator not satisfied with his genius and why will he not build on it? Why is genius so bad, so impossible to bear?
"They don't know how bad it is!"

One day, 8–10 and 14–15 visit the drink-weary writer and tell him about the time the cross on their mother's grave fell over during a storm. The writer never goes to tend his mother's grave . . .

The writer goes to the mountain that the locals call the ogres' field and to the source of the river. He needs to choose from the many stones strewn like soccer balls across the ogres' field one that he can lay on his mother's grave. But the stone he likes most is too heavy to put in the car. The writer struggles, drips with sweat. At the same time, though, he had never imagined he would have so many sympathizers around him: the morning sun, the midday sun, the sky, the stars, the moon. He has never before felt that anybody supported him in his struggle.

He collapses, exhausted, by the stone. The only thing that keeps him from wishing for death is the thought that an insignificant death like this would be so cowardly. He lies facedown by the stone in a half-sleep, devoid of strength and hope. This is his secret, and nobody may help him; he must do this himself, he must lay that stone by himself, alone . . . Then 8–10 puts his hand on the writer's back: "Come on, I know a way to do it." He holds in his hand a length of driftwood washed clean by the river over time, and says to him, "We need to roll the stone along with this until we reach the slope, and after that we'll wedge a smaller stone underneath to stop it rolling back on us every time we turn it over." But the stone just starts spinning on the spot and they realize they will need another lever. They find one. It's a shame Rostia and Obola are not yoked—they are good, strong buffalo.

Just then 14–15 comes thundering out of the forest like a centaur . . . and the three of them manage to move the stone and take it to their mother's grave.

The sunshine in cemeteries always seems so strange.

In the morning the sound of the birds and cattle herders wakes the writer. Now he can do everything: he sees the hawthorn and dog rose which have grown in this very spot. Everything brings him joy and he feels that the taste of happiness may even be enhanced by despair . . .

This book has three authors and three characters who, as has been established, really come to life for the writer . . .

Along with 8–10 and 14–15, the writer also brings to life his village, his region, the people whose ancestors God once sowed like rye seeds at the feet of the Caucasus mountains and who grew to be the country's warrior guardians. The writer gives 14–15's pathetic existence a reality, and will in the same way depict this world of twenty or so village households, squatting on a little clod of earth . . .

Should we be surprised that under the Creator's own gaze some quite unremarkable writer might have the power to create his own universe and decide its rules and order? Maybe the Creator had himself drawn up just such a plan for the village and the district beyond it and stuck it up on the sky? Maybe somebody once made him think, "I wonder whether one day I should become man?" and as soon as he had thought it he started controlling that carefree writer once again:

"I swear that in what I write no fresh blood—the most terrible color in art—will bubble forth and make the reader lick his tongue in it. We will not kill, nor will we torture, and not a single teardrop will be on our conscience—in short, we will not give the reader more to think about than he can bear, but will instead fly lightly from page to page. People kill each other for a morsel of bread and a crooked-handled frying pan, but are too ashamed to admit it; they conceal their ideas, their peoples, their past, and their future . . . We will extend an invitation to an honorable man who cannot bear to be alone, because it is dangerous for an honorable man to go out among the people. 'Come!' we will say."

"Come on," he'll say, "let's unite in tragedy-sincerity-deceit, come on, let's make our writing rapid and fluid. This piece of writing won't work unless we give it its own, unique character . . ."

"Come on, let's get our reader used to these fragments. Nothing happens in a continuous flow in real life. It's all a series of fragments. Come on, let's make him fall in love with them, let's get him accustomed to them, come on, let's give him faith in fragments. Who cries one tear after another? Tears are shed in a continuous flow. Today everything has an arrow and an eye aimed at it. Only the wind doesn't know its own name."

"Only children are honest, ruthless, and alert, with their willies sticking up and their eyes never at rest. And yet the universe never gets angry with them and they are forgiven everything . . ."

"Let's hide death from our children! People die all around us, and how shameful that is: the beautiful die, the intelligent die, the foolish die, everyone dies . . . I do not want it to be that way! Surely somebody deserves to not die? Let it be so, and may God give us a sign, and choose from us one who will not die, even if it is someone who is lame, or a fool. May minutes not die, nor seconds, nor days . . . It is so good to be able to say something like this, something nobody will answer because what you have said is neither wisdom nor madness. That is the only reason they listen to you and the only reason you speak!"

"Ladies and gentlemen! When the word veers off in search of artistic merit it forgets itself and not its goal. Tell the whole world this, so that it might avoid bloodshed. May every nation and every language live long, so that the earth does not suddenly tilt sideways. May the larger nations refrain from swallowing up the smaller ones, lest some turn out to be like precious jewels . . . Oh languages of the many, do not belittle the languages of the few, lest some of them be pleasing to God . . . Our most difficult task is to retain our humanity. Come, let us embrace our humanity! Our most difficult task is to love. Let us try to love!"

"Long live love, the only feeling to which man wholly devotes himself. Long live the island of love, where those with eyes wide open are also blind, and devote themselves to the art of 'this and that,' the ancient art." That is what I will say, and what I will get in return is the knowledge that my listeners will not comprehend why the writer has this sadistic, base wish for his reader not to understand him.

The essence of man and the life of man are in a state of incessant and mutual blundering and this is probably another of the foundations that underpins the creation of literature, even though to this day, just as in mythical Colchis, we still sing simple songs full of faith and lyricism: the sun is my mother, the moon my father, these many small stars my brothers and sisters . . .

"Ladies and gentlemen! The human race has inhabited the earth since time immemorial and will continue to do so to the end of time itself. But each individual human is merely a guest for twenty-four hours. This too may be worthy of song—a guest does not forget his host's house nor the dreams he had there."

"And now," says Nina, overcome by drink, "I will go and will piss on this country, and then you can come and piss on it too if you want, if I've left any parts of it dry, and I'll raise the lantern and I'll light up the whole of the earth's surface."

And Nina pissed and pissed . . . and she pissed so much that the squatting earth pointed its head at her, right where the dust and dirt snow down unceasingly. . .

And I stood on the high mountain, the ogres' field, from where the thawing glaciers send down torrents of water and make the rivers swell. And it seemed to me that the world had bathed itself, maybe even purified itself too, but I had nothing to add . . .

The earth was already so softened and drenched that I just turned on a fast-running tap and poured water and more water onto my face. My head felt almost clear again, just as the earth felt clean after Nina had washed it . . .

I stood on the ogres' field . . . I lit a lamp for Nina . . . I looked at the thawing glaciers, at the water flowing down the mountain crevices, at the distant, blooming mother earth.

Man loses so many talents in the search for absurdity! How funny that he then searches for those talents elsewhere. When we woke in the morning there was a book on the table, already written; we were amazed, we read it, we liked it, and we decided to share it with others too. We drew lots to decide on the author; the name on the cover now is the name of the person who won. The book itself is not really anyone's. It is not mine, nor does it belong to the children—either of them—nor is it our mother's. It is simply a book, which we found open on our table.

It was page fifty-eight:

> Having returned from the city he decided to secretly visit 14–15's house. And so he slowly opened the gate to the yard and inspected his surroundings, and in doing so he glimpsed 8–10 sitting on the grass by the apple tree. He was sitting in the very spot where his mother had measured him for his shoes, and he hadn't moved in case anything changed. How long had he had to wait, I wonder, how long had he had to be so patient? His mother would come back very soon, and bring him one shoe and the other, but if he had moved, then who knows! . . . Had he gone for a stroll down that path or gone into the house to get some bread, everything might have changed. But that story had taken place here and it was here he had to wait for her. He had to stay still, not move, so that nothing would change. He was scratching around at the ground between his sprawled-out legs and all his attention was directed toward that—he was piling up earth to kill time waiting for his mother. He felt sorry for 14–15; it was as if he were sitting next to an orphan. For an orphan is surely always waiting for someone to come back, for something miraculous to happen, and so you have to go into his yard secretly, quietly, because you can't perform a miracle and you're not carrying red boots. 8–10 started thinking about the shoes and watched 14–15 rather sadly, as if he was wondering whether he could trust him or not . . .

All this made 14–15's heart sink; he clasped 8–10 to his chest and because he trusted him he clutched him close, entwined their necks together, and moved closer toward their mother's smell . . . He clasped him, clasped him, and when tears fell from his eye and hit 8–10 like tiles off a roof he could no longer stand being alone, absorbed him into his soul, and then noticed me too, leaning against the balcony pillar . . .

14–15 needed neither affection nor for somebody to clasp him to their heart—he came walking up the steps with total awareness, came over to me, stood in front of me, nestled his neck into my neck, his chin into my chin and said, "You're me!"

I felt like howling, but pulled myself together and spoke as human beings speak and said, "I am!"

MAMUKA KHERKHEULIDZE
A Caucasian Chronicle

And these clans know of blood feuds, and if one clan kills,
the other will not rest from generation to generation for all
eternity until it kills in return, and the one who seeks re-
venge calls down to his murdered clansman in his grave,
saying, "I have killed your killer," and believes that in doing
so he earns blessings for himself.

—Vakhushti Batonishvili, historian,
eighteenth century.

In the hamlet where this story takes place, vengeance is one of the oldest traditions and is considered to be one of the community's most important values. A worthy man is one who has avenged the killing of his clan member. According to local custom, he should throw his hat onto the grave and call down into it, saying, "I have killed your killer!" There is a certain strange, brutal sense of honor in making the killer's family suffer; all the more so in the Caucasus, and in the mountains at that. Laws were brought into this region with fire and sword by an invading nation, but the people of the mountains refused to submit to these laws that the Russians imposed on them. They sought to live by their own traditional customs and laws, and to obtain justice the way their forefathers did: "If you should kill another then you too shall be killed; the clan will always make the killer pay," wrote Vazha-Pshavela. They may not cut off their enemy's hand and hang it on the door of the house any more, as in his poem, but . . .

Even for me, the number of women who go around these parts dressed in the black of mourning with photos of the dead pinned to their chests like flowers seems remarkable.

I say even for me because the hamlet is part of me—or rather, I am part of the hamlet. Batka was an artist—a wood carver. He carved figurines, fretwork, crosses, bowls . . . He was very skilled, able to turn his hand to anything. But I especially loved the delightful little characters he carved; they were so accurate, so realistic. We were the same age and from the moment we met we were friends—and straight away it felt as if I'd known him for a very long time. He was a tall, thin boy with a melancholic smile and the sophisticated moral code and principles of an adult man. The year the events of this story took place he was working on a sculpture of Don Quixote, and had decided that he himself would live like Don Quixote, against the backdrop of the Caucasus mountains.

Batka's father had been killed by the famous outlaw Stalin Petre, who had earned this moniker thanks to both his ruthlessness and his appearance (a mustache, military tunic and boots). This devil of a man was responsible for the deaths of several others too and, needless to say, killing Stalin Petre was the primary goal of all the young men of the clan—apart from Batka. Before I understood what was going on I was always very surprised to find that people living in the hamlet would say hello to me but not Batka.

"I'm not surprised at all," Batka once said to me. "I used to be in love with a girl in my class, but she gave in to pressure from her family and left me. They said if I wasn't even thinking about avenging my father's death then what kind of man would I grow into?" I knew the girl he meant; never could I have imagined that a blue-eyed, rosy-cheeked slip of a thing like her could be caught up in a blood feud. And yet it was because of that very tradition that Batka's classmate refused to turn her back on her family. By the time I met Batka his father had already been dead a long time, and his mother was seriously ill and relied on him for help getting about. They lived in the center of the hamlet, almost right on the main square itself. The square was bordered by a crooked line of ugly administration buildings, severe-looking fortresses which several times a day discharged streams of people who crisscrossed their way across their beloved town square, and whose aimless wanderings always ended up by the bubbling spring. In the evenings, though, the setting sun cast its light onto the peaks of the Caucasus with their ever-present covering of snow, giving them a reddish glow, and when dusk fell the throaty voices of people talking in the square became more distinct. Batka didn't like to talk about his father and Stalin Petre; it irritated him. I didn't insist, either—you could easily find out the truth anyway; among this strict people there are plenty with smooth tongues who love to tell stories.

Stalin Petre had killed one of Batka's relatives, a peasant, over an ox. Apparently he loved oxen as much as he disliked people, and it was said he was almost affectionate toward them. The peasant refused to give Stalin Petre his favorite ox—why would he?—and what is more he went for his dagger, stubbornly stood his ground, got more and more angry . . . and before he could act on his anger three bullets hit him in the head. "His teeth were blown right back into his head"—that was the detail everyone emphasized. It was at the keening for this very man that Batka's father met his end. Because of heavy snowfall he went to the upper village at night. A long table had been set out in the yard, and weary guests who had traveled from far and wide were sharing Lenten food and vodka. Batka's father drank three glasses and poured one into the ground in memory of the deceased—"May my blood be spilled like this if I fail to avenge this good man's honor!"—and suddenly, almost as if they had been waiting for his words, he heard shooting and screaming coming from the house where mourners had gathered to lament over the body. Everybody leaped up, scattered in all directions, making all manner of excuses as to why they had to go. But Batka's father went toward the house with his gun in his hand. He began shooting from the veranda itself, although it was unclear why—whether he was just girding his loins or actually shooting at a specific target. Inside the room he found nobody but female mourners and the deceased himself. It later transpired that the women had tried to give him a warning sign but had not managed to do so in time—Stalin Petre crept up on him from behind. "Aha, got you!" he cried and fired three rounds from his Mauser. Batka's father fell face down onto the deceased's divan and died right there. Stalin Petre turned around, leaped onto his horse and galloped off, and nobody dared follow him, nor did it even occur to them to do so. "Who on earth would follow the devil in the dark?" they said, and told terrible tales of Petre's speed . . .

The next day they brought Batka's father back down to the hamlet on a sledge. Batka, who was eleven years old at that time, kissed his father's frozen, rigid face and split chin for the last time and committed the feel of his coarse mustache to memory. He could still remember the armed policemen who had spent the night in vigil over the deceased so that Petre wouldn't come (this awful man would burst into the funerals of his victims and shoot at the women's feet, shouting, "Dance!"). He also remembered the sound of stone and frozen earth raining down on the lid of the coffin, "almost as if it was being scattered onto my brain," he told me.

After that Stalin Petre vanished from sight. That was what people had been waiting for—they were free to say what they liked: "They've seen Petre all over the place! They've even seen him in Dagestan and Kabardia!" . . . Batka was the only one who joked, "I don't know about Kabardia, but I did see him crossing the boundless skies astride an ox, like Europa crossing the seas . . ."

Petre committed his first murder because of his sister. She was married and lived in a village some distance away, but one day arrived back at her brother's house badly beaten and with a black eye (in such situations the woman is always both beautiful and morally faultless) and said she would not go back to live with him anymore. At the time, Petre was building something out in the yard and right there and then he threw down his trowel, set square, and hammer, flung on a rifle, mounted his horse and rode to his brother-in-law's village. It was morning. When Petre's brother-in-law came out for his morning wash expecting to feel the sun on his face, he instead felt the barrel of a rifle against his jaw. A shot rang out and the man fell face down into a pool of soapy water. Petre fled and on reaching the mountain pass realized he was now an outlaw. He hid in the forest and never went back home again. Time passed, and then the brother-in-law's relatives burned Petre's house down; by the time his neighbors got to it the wooden skeleton had completely collapsed. Among the glowing embers lay Petre's sister, unconscious and with badly burned legs. They pulled her out, tended to her, and revived her, but she never regained use of her legs and never spoke again.

Now it was Petre's turn. He set up camp in the forest near the village where his brother-in-law's brother lived. From there he watched. He knew a man from the village would have to come into the forest sooner or later. And so it was that two weeks later the man came to check on his livestock—he stroked his beloved oxen, scratched the neck of his favorite white ox, whispered enigmatically in its ear. Petre knew how to choose his moment—his rifle roared, boulders thundered, the bloody-headed man collapsed over the neck of his favorite ox, soiled it with his blood and fell at the startled beast's feet. Stalin Petre rolled the corpse away with his foot, led the beast to water, and washed it clean of blood.

From there he went back to his native village and to his sister, who was mostly recovered. He wrapped her in a thick felt cloak, tied her to the saddle with rope and took her away with him. From then on he moved from one hiding place to the next, taking with him his severely injured sister, who had either lost the power of speech or pledged to God a vow of silence, nobody knows; but she certainly could not move her legs . . .

Batka could even remember his room, a scene of eternal mourning. In a lifeless, gray-white room hung an enlarged black-and-white photograph of his father. In the photo you could see the father's regret for crimes he had not had time to commit. Batka spent the whole of his childhood with this photograph and an iron bed. His father's belt, dagger, and pistol had been specially laid out on the bed right next to his ironed clothes. Only after his killing had been avenged would these items be put away and kept with the deceased's other effects in the coffin-like sideboard. As soon as he grew up the boy brought this room to life, put more things in it, dismantled the iron bed and took it and the sideboard downstairs to the large room where his mother slept. He decorated the room with drawings, figurines, book-shelves, and an old rug. His mother never berated him for it, she just said to him, "You'll find it hard without our traditions . . ."

Not all traditions are necessarily good, Batka had told her. A mother is a mother, of course, the one person who understands everything, but their relatives and neighbors no longer paid him any attention unless they needed something from him, they no longer really acknowledged him at all or even exchanged greetings with him. But he could turn his hand to anything and was an industrious worker. His artist friend from Tbilisi first took his wood carvings back to the city with him after he had visited the boy's house and found his handiwork to be to his liking. Foreign tourists, mountaineers, artists, and craftsmen from the city who visited the hamlet would stay with him. Guests also made good use of Batka's books; he had a very good library, which was unusual in that region . . .

Early that morning he woke before sunrise. It was spring, and it was cold. He quickly put on his winter clothes and went outside. The roosters were already strutting around and he could hear the sound of hatchets striking wood—the village was waking up. He went downstairs to the first floor, picked up some wood in one hand from the pile by the stairs, reached down for the hatchet with the other hand, and opened the door with his foot. It was dark in the one-window room and the only light came from the candle flickering by his mother's bed. He could just about make out his mother's dried-up, veiny hand, like a fragment of a fresco.

"Good morning," his mother greeted him; she probably smiled at him too, but her face was not visible through the darkness and it seemed as if her hand were talking.

"How are you today?" he said, and squatted by the fire.

"How am I today? What a question. I want to get up . . ." said the hand.

"I'm just lighting the fire now," he said, and skillfully and silently chopped the firewood with the hatchet into fine pieces. He arranged it in the rusty, cold stove, lit the fire and put the iron bolt across. Then he blew on it from below and the ancient stove roared to life (in all my travels I've never seen anyone light a fire in such a spellbinding way). "Stand up," he said, and held his hand out to his mother. The woman leaned on her own emaciated arm and stood up groaning. "Now she'll start," the boy thought. And she did: "May their people become as thin as this arm . . ." Batka had been hearing this one-woman lament for twenty years. The script never changed—it was carved in stone. Unavenged blood, a man to carry on the family line, that accursed Stalin Petre . . . Batka didn't even listen anymore, he knew the whole lament off by heart, and every possible variation on the curses. But sometimes he got a lump in his throat nonetheless, and was overcome by grief at his mother's words and the tears that were shed during his childhood, that he had not been able to stem by getting revenge. At such times even he felt these blood feud killings were justified, although these moments of weakness were fleeting, and he would then feel ashamed of his own thinking and feel afraid—"I haven't gone mad, have I?" Such instances were very rare, though, because in truth he knew he could not kill a man.

The sunlight was already filtering into the room. Batka sat his mother in the armchair by the stove, took his unfinished carvings off the table, and went outside. Once in the yard he settled himself down in the shade on his usual tree stump and set to work. "Batka, you mournful knight, this will be your self-portrait, at least Kherkheulidze will say it looks like you . . ." he laughed.

The church bell tolled. The square filled with people, on their own or in groups. Suddenly, there was a rumbling noise in the distance. A truck pulled in and everyone rushed toward the police station—something important was happening. Batka put his carving down onto the tree stump and joined the crowd. A policeman in military uniform was struggling to open up the back of the truck—the rusty lock would not give. There was silence in the square, only broken by the sound of the scraping lock and the policeman's grunting. Finally the lock opened and the truck's wooden hatch fell open with a terrible clatter. In the back of the truck lay an unshaven corpse. The onlookers became agitated, crowded around and pushed forward. A second policeman got up onto the back of the truck, and the two of them grabbed the corpse, dressed in a military tunic, and threw it straight onto the ground. Batka didn't understand what was happening, he forced his way through the crowd and stared at the dead man. Stalin Petre was not wearing boots; blowflies swarmed around his muddy, blood-caked legs; and he was dressed in filthy old clothes. His toothless mouth hung open and blowflies swarmed around that, too. His matted white hair was caked with blood and soil. Somebody had closed the corpse's eyes so that none could now read what was frozen within them for all eternity, what was hidden behind his eyelids—fear, curses, or repentance. It was Stalin Petre, elusive bandit and murderer made legend. Mothers used this man's name to scare their children, he brought misery to numerous families and re-awakened the desire for revenge in so many young people, turning them into frustrated would-be killers . . .

The policemen carried the body toward the building and left it by the wall. This was an old custom—it would lie there until it started to decompose, so that everyone would see with their own eyes what happened to outlaws and criminals. All at once Batka hated this community and his Dulcinea—everyone, in fact, who had asked for or wanted this man to be put in this position.

The crowd started to disperse; Petre had been killed, the bloody comedy was over. Batka went back home, tired, drained, called out to his mother—"They've killed Petre!"—and sat down next to the carvings he'd left on the tree stump.

"The man must have relatives . . . May they steal him in the night and bury him quietly—or I will myself. If people see where he's buried they'll dig him up and leave him for the pigs to eat. And whatever happened to that girl, I wonder? Where does all this leave the poor cripple?" thought the young man who lived in one of the highest, most traditional regions of the Caucasus, where they do not cut off the murderer's right hand anymore, but . . .

ARCHIL KIKODZE
The Drunks

Number One—Swaying and Yearning

Number One couldn't think of a single widely accepted criterion by which to measure a woman's beauty. He had his own particular yearning, though, or rather an image which he cherished, hidden away in his heart from the sight of others: gymnasts in denim jackets, who had thin under-dresses, diamond-patterned knee-length socks over pretty, bare legs, and playfulness in their honey-colored eyes, who told loud, obscene jokes so as to seem more sexually experienced and more debauched to older boys. It worked, too . . .

At one time Number One had been that older boy himself, and maybe he wasn't yearning for those young, foolish girls at all, but rather for the boy he was back then, in an unfamiliar neighborhood, a resentful new arrival at an unwelcoming school, who would herd the prettiest girls in school past his immature classmates, pile them into the car he'd taken from his father (things were still going well for his father back then) and drive them all over the place. But he would always bring them back untouched, and to this day he remained unmarried.

But it can't just have been the yearning for days gone by that made those diamond-patterned maidens come to him in his sleep from time to time.

And what were dreams, anyway? Fears and wishes, fears lying in wait and wishes hidden away, and while in a dream you could sometimes defeat your fears, you could never defeat your wishes . . .

Sometimes, though, his days were colorful, beautiful, and dream-like. Today felt like a dream, and it felt like a film too. A Japanese film.

The sun was shining. It was hara-kiri weather.

Number One didn't see the resemblance straight away, but after he'd sat thinking on the frozen bench for a long time he realized his surroundings were making him think about Japanese films more than anything else. He loved the cinema.

That morning was far from ordinary. Autumn had ended overnight. A sudden frost had struck, and it was a heavy frost at that, and yellow leaves had started falling from the trees. There was no wind, not even the slightest breeze, and the leaves fell from the sky as lightly as snow, spinning slowly before spreading out over the frozen and frost-covered ground. In the silence he could even hear them breaking off the trees. It was beautiful here. He sat there, silent in the middle of this yellow snowfall and although he was too hungover to even reach for a cigarette from his pocket, he nonetheless retained his sense of style. Yes, on that morning which marked autumn's sudden end he was as refined as ever: a velvet hat and trousers, a warm coat and scarf, a clean-shaven face, and a melancholic yearning in his eyes, even though in this beautiful, quasi-Japanese sunshine there was nobody here to see or appreciate it. But what kind of Japan was this? There were no colorful fish in the filthy River Vere, running through its concrete channels—you'd be lucky to see so much as a sprat—and the alders didn't look like Japanese trees at all, and as for women dressed in patterned kimonos with painted faces and parasols, all he could see around him was a few pensioners pretending to exercise. They trotted about, sluggishly waved their arms around, and sometimes even their legs, and alongside all these withered old pensioners who trotted out so infrequently onto the yellow leaf-carpet he could not see a single pert silver-Lycra-clad bottom to console him.

The leaf-fall was still pretty, though and Number One thought that he would sit there for a while longer, away from onlookers and spectators, and he pondered over the fact that nothing happens by chance in this world, nor was it by chance that he had wandered into this park, hungover and penniless (but with his sense of style preserved to the end). He couldn't even remember the last time he'd been here. Seeing all this made everything worthwhile . . .

Number One was not a bitter man. He considered this one of his greatest qualities; even while toasting he often said, "The most important thing in life is not to become bitter." He had once seen a film about birds on the Discovery Channel which said that large birds of prey conserve energy by only rarely flapping their wings; instead they spread their wings out and glide up and down on the air's ever-flowing updrafts and downdrafts. He liked this comparison very much. He was not a predator himself, but all the same he rarely flapped his wings. Although, yesterday he had wanted to, just as he always did once every year on that day.

Once a year there was the kind of lavish birthday party people rarely bother with anymore, and among the many acquaintances and friends who attended there were always two guests who only served to irritate him: one was a particular woman he found himself desiring every year on that night, the other was a young lad he knew he was supposed to beat up at some point. He couldn't even remember why anymore—he wasn't a bitter or vengeful man, after all—but he knew he was supposed to give him a thrashing.

This year the woman looked more beautiful than she had two years ago, but not nearly as lovely as she had last year. Last year she had looked simply amazing. Unique. As for the lad, in the space of a year he had become a man. The boyish features that had irritated and repulsed Number One in previous years had become rougher and more coarse. It seemed, too, that during the year he had not managed to preserve his strength and had seen fit to flap his wings on numerous occasions. Number One decided that if the opportunity presented itself he would hit him—well, box his ears—but only after saying to him, "You look like a man now, so people can hit you back." In previous years he could have got away without hitting him and still have preserved his style, his style . . . But the young man survived—he got away by leaving very early, and on the way out he passed by so close to Number One that he actually knocked him with his shoulder in such a way that made it obvious he had no idea how many times he'd escaped a beating.

And the woman? She left even earlier. She spent a long time trying to leave, politely saying good-bye to many people whose hearts were probably breaking like his, and with the words "No, I can't stay, my ride's waiting for me," she did not interrupt them so much as kill them. She was leaving, and she left in her wake a string of yearning gazes shot at her by other partygoers from over somebody's shoulder, or under somebody's arm . . . And if Number One could do nothing more than that himself, then never mind—even though he had been getting ready for this since last year. Because he believed that everything happens in its own good time, and that every dream will eventually come true, and that the most important thing is not to become embittered . . . At the same time, over the years the woman had noticed him so little that she probably did not even realize the effect she had on him. Number One could find no other reason for her snubbing him so decisively.

"It's better out in the fresh air, isn't it? Goes down more quickly, doesn't it?" One of the pensioners was standing over him, pointing at the cigarette between his fingers. God knows when he'd lit it.

Number One just nodded, he wasn't in the mood for talking and anyway, what was there to say?

"I gave up twenty-five years ago. On my birthday one year I just decided to give up, and gave up. It was like a present to myself."

Number One nodded his head in awe, as if to show just how admirable he thought the man was.

"The boys told me I'd never be able to quit. I was on two packs a day, but I just picked them up and threw them away. I recommend you do the same. You're a young man—why would you want to kill yourself with those?"

He nodded again, even more humbly, with even more awe, as if to show just how impressed he was by the man's determination.

The old man looked him up and down with pity, realized he wasn't going to get anywhere, gave up, did some kind of breathing exercise that sounded like deep sighing and went on his way. In an instant he was gone, lost among the leafy snowfall, as if he had never existed.

Yesterday though, Number One exceeded the limits of his own potential. Having discovered a bottle of whiskey on the shelf, he drank almost the entire thing by himself and then followed it with some wine. He got very drunk, but as usual managed to hold it together and in fact it was only now that he was reaping the consequences—he felt very ill. And yet once again he began to think with an almost innocent yearning about the woman who once a year took possession of his mind. About the woman who at that moment was probably still asleep and who would be neither a spectator to nor partner in his torment, and who for another year at least would not remedy it either. But all the same, Number One spent some time diving under the surface of those hazy dream-like fantasies in which he and the woman were caught up in a blissful, turbulent maelstrom from which they could never escape . . .

Of course when you're hungover you experience these yearnings differently. He recalled a line from some Russian film or other which had stuck in his mind: the body of a hungover man exists in a pre-heart-attack state; it senses death close at hand and feels the instinct to procreate stir within it. Surely this was not all it was? No, for Number One a hangover was a deeply moving spiritual state, whereas coming out of the hangover was like withdrawing consent for any kind of association with such a state, and the shift into the new, different, more perfect phase (death and reincarnation) was no less than craftsmanship. He could quite easily have written a treatise about it. He had actually considered it: he would have started it with something prosaic and trivial—albeit universally effective—like hot stew and grappa, and ended it with a mug of brandy followed by freshly picked fig, cooled by the dew of a summer's night. If he had written it then no doubt it would have done very well, but he had no time for such things. In today's reality the thing that was most thought provoking, troubling even, was that a man with so much theoretical knowledge was sitting here with empty pockets, staring at falling leaves, and thinking. Hungover thinking is like no other thinking, though: it's all betrayal and yearning, yearning and betrayal, with an occasional bit of good cheer if you suddenly recall something especially stupid you or one of your friends did the day before, and then there's the wish, the wish to have that unattainable real woman, and even this is tinged with melancholy . . . and betrayal, which looms over you like a bad dream and weighs heavy on your heart . . .

He pulled his jacket around himself more tightly and tried to fight his instincts and his wish for revenge by thinking about something else. He did not get very far, though—he was still circling with open wings over yesterday's events.

The most amazing thing was that Number One had had a really good time yesterday, and even when the irritating guests left he remained in a good mood. He was pleasant and affectionate to everyone. He raised his glass with everyone too . . .

He raised his glass with one particular girl he had never seen before. That was unusual in itself. Something about both her appearance and her speech seemed rather foreign. Number One clinked glasses with her and she said, "Tell me what good qualities Georgians have! Or have you already told me?" She asked so forcefully. Somebody else had apparently extricated themselves from the debate, so she'd now hooked Number One instead. "And don't give me any of this singing and dancing nonsense!" she warned him ahead of time. "I want present-day qualities!" Clearly she was either a foreigner, or had been living in Europe for longer than necessary or not long enough, and now that she was back on Georgian soil she'd found various things about us that she didn't like. So here she was now, drawing nervously on a long cigarette and asking him to list the positive qualities of the Georgian people for her. It was not an easy situation.

"I'll give you the answer to that question in just as long as it takes me to drink this," Number One promised her, and poured himself a large tumbler of whiskey. But the girl gave up, just like the pensioner he'd seen earlier that day, walked off, and left him standing there . . .

Number One started the exhausting but pleasurable process of circulating and mingling once again. He had great faith in himself. He clinked his whiskey tumbler against the cut-crystal glasses of the chattering guests, spoke admiringly to them of tradition and family . . . He'd known everybody here for many years and loved each of them for who they were.

After clinking his tumbler against a martini glass, its owner explained to him that while she couldn't stand conformism, she preferred apathy to fanaticism of any sort. She compared herself to a little seahorse in the ocean, taking refuge in a dark crevice. She preferred it in the depths, in the darkness—she felt more protected there. Number One nodded. He, like the Georgian people at large, had a lot of good qualities, and one of them was being able to listen attentively to women. While he was talking to Miss Martini he made good use of not only both his upper limbs but also every curve and protuberance in his entire body. She looked less like a seahorse and more like a mixed-blood mare and even though she seemed like a pretty safe bet, Number One was by now already clinking his whiskey tumbler against the vodka glasses of the social misfits dotted about the various corners of the room.

He himself was never wary and shy like that—he swayed much too freely to be scared. He knew every one of them and could read their thoughts and sometimes even calm their fears. More often though, he would make them worse, and then he would blame others, others whose ill-considered words—blurted out through stupidity, meddling or, more rarely, a wish to deceive—could in an instant transport those misfits back to the very battlefields where they suffered their defeat, to those places of sadness and yearning, and then in the next instant bring them back again, full of spite and anger. Vodka would do that to you. There was no point trying to teach upstarts how to control their aggression—they were already hauling those misfits outside and even though Number One followed right behind them he already knew he wouldn't be able to change what was about to happen because, although their hands were not yet clenched in a fist, their arms, right or left, from their shoulders to their fingertips, were already twitching, restlessly rocking, dancing a dance that was even more impatient than its owner, and which was imperceptible to all but the most skilled eye . . .

The ephemeral diamond-patterned knee-high sock clique was seated right here, still in their exclusive little group, barely mixing but gossiping about others as usual. He couldn't come to this party and not have a drink with them, could he? So he did, and told them they were gorgeous as he always did—although it was clear their young beauty had been fleeting. He noted with regret that childbirth had ruined some of them, and that for others what had once been delightful silliness had now become embarrassing, brazen, wide-eyed foolishness. The only thing that hadn't changed was their voices—ingratiating, honeyed, metropolitan drawls, real telephone voices . . .

Number One loved life and so he loved these people, because they were his life and his city—they were the people he knew, for better or worse . . .

And just as he decided that he hadn't given each of them enough attention first time around and was about to circle the room for a second time, culminating in a deadly swoop onto that she-mare seahorse, he found himself face to face again with the strange creature who had asked him to list the positive qualities of the Georgian people.

"Friendship," he said, without thinking. He had drunk much, *much* more than that one glass of whiskey.

"Eh?" She seemed to have no recollection of any of it.

"We're great at real proper friendship. That's a good quality, surely."

"You know what, you're right," the strange creature said, looking him up and down as if through different eyes. She took a drag on her thin cigarette. "It is a good quality, and we really are great at friendship. Do you want me to tell you one?"

"Go on, then." He readied himself. When it came to looking attentive he really was a master.

"Well, I might be saying something really bad or really stupid so don't laugh but, well, I think we're pretty good at family, too . . ."

"Family, hmm," Number One said, nodding his head very seriously and frowning. He was really good at this.

"Yes, I mean, the Georgian family can be such a source of stress—sometimes it's like a cage, or a prison, because of all the things you can't do out of respect for your family. But it's also good, and sometimes it's even wonderful—a refuge, you could even say. Don't you agree?"

Yes, that was the strange creature from yesterday—she had clearly given it a lot of thought, and yet she was afraid to talk about family in case it made her seem pathetic in his eyes, less independent, less emancipated, and less principled. She was stuck somewhere between enlightened Europe and the still-dark Caucasus and could not bear to turn her back on either. In that moment she was wonderful (to him) and much more beautiful than Mzia, that first European woman from Dmanisi . . . Yes, she really was a great girl.

And amid that Japanese-cinema yellow-leaf snowfall that he had chanced upon so fortuitously, Number One smiled—just a moment earlier his phone had silently vibrated in his pocket and brought him a message which, though unexpected, was nonetheless uplifting. Almost dead from his hangover, he had suddenly felt that something good was about to happen (he was good at intuition, premonitions, and that kind of thing), smiled to himself and was not at all surprised to see the message come in; he looked at the screen without batting an eyelid and took what he read there as a given, and all this while always upholding his style.

"Do you want to go for some food? Some *khinkali*,[1] perhaps?" his mobile was asking him, and this question was like another silent confirmation, of

---

1 Boiled pockets of dough filled with meat and spiced and sealed with drawstring-type folds at the top.

friendship, of that best of Georgian qualities, which he would revere for as long as he lived.

He got up slowly off the bench and started his ascent. He held his phone in his hand and composed his reply as he went. Walking wasn't too hard—he had caught hold of an updraft. He left his sadness and betrayal behind him in that park, filled with so many hideous bodies, but into which he had decided to return once he had arrived at the Tbilisi-Japan border. He looked down from above at the trees, already almost leafless, at the wretched yellow earth and at the shrunken figures of those exercising pensioners, and in his head he played with words: "*hara kiri—khinkali, khinkali—hara kiri.*" It sounded almost poetic.

It was great, and the day was only just beginning.

NUMBER TWO—ANGUISH AND MELANCHOLY

When Number Two received exactly the same message he was sitting in a café, his usual shot of cognac in front of him on the table and, rather unsurprisingly, was staring dumbfounded at the telephone lying on the table right next to it.

In the whole of his neighborhood this was the only café which opened at nine A.M. and so every morning as soon as he dropped his child off at school he quickly made his way here. This little café had one more distinguishing feature, which probably set it apart from all the other cafés in Tbilisi. Beautiful women never set foot in it. Hard to believe, maybe, but that's how it was. He had often thought that, had he been a writer, he would start his short story, or maybe his novel, like this:

"He was sitting in that café where beautiful women never set foot. . ."

He liked the opening, but hadn't been able to think of anything else. He was not a writer, just someone who read what others had written—and avidly at that—but nothing more, and in reality he struggled to imagine that even an experienced wordsmith could create a decent story from all this. It was boring and steady here, and that's what he liked most of all.

"You would never see a beautiful woman here . . ."

Maybe that was a better opening line, but the main issue lay elsewhere. Number Two really thought that downing cognac in a "café that beautiful women avoided" was confirmation of his great love and gratitude for his own wife, and clear proof of the infinite devotion he felt for her. Of course, he wouldn't say that out loud to anyone, especially his wife. As a rule Number Two rarely said out loud what was most important and essential to him. He had tried a few times and it didn't go well. After all, as well as reading books he loved to think, and some of his thoughts and observations seemed important to him, but to air them out (as foolish politicians and imbecilic journalists would) involved great risk. Number Two occasionally—rarely—had outbursts of frankness, usually in wholly inappropriate places, and more rarely still he would start to float his own theories; but somehow, once uttered out loud, his ideas and opinions floated completely unconvincingly. He soon learned his lesson and nowadays preferred to keep quiet rather than sound inane. He thought it very unlikely he would come across the kind of person who would not be scared off by his disclosing his own ideas more than once in a blue moon. He thought he had met one such man at a dinner the previous year, and although he didn't manage to tell him the most important thing, he did not really regret that. Who knows, it might even have been for the best . . .

He wondered how many years older than him that man had been. Probably at least fifteen, if not more. He loved books just like Number Two did. Not texts, but books. Seated face to face at a dinner quite by chance, they identified each other as book-lovers, so the difference in their ages never seemed relevant. The stranger loved his childhood books for their illustrations—and in fact remembered them by those illustrations too—and Number Two was only too happy to reminisce with him. It was the pictures they started talking about.

Who was it, they wondered, who illustrated those thick adventure books with beautiful pictures, which you would start looking at well before you set about reading those long, unforgettable tales of love, loyalty, self-sacrifice, and courage? Under each illustration there was always a short caption, a quotation from the text (pfff, from the book!). They started with these captions. First they would recall the quotations and then the illustrations themselves. I think he started first—the older man, the stranger, as kindly and reliable as the old books themselves:

"'I saw Milady last night . . .'" He looked out devilishly from beneath the strangely formed wrinkles of his furrowed brow.

He remembered, of course he remembered, Number Two remembered everything: the Bastion Saint-Gervais, Athos with his glass raised, d'Artagnan in profile, Grimaud's frightened face, Porthos from behind; he couldn't picture Aramis anymore but remembered he was there . . .

"'To his surprise D'Artagnan perceived that Athos staggered . . .'" He came back at him with another illustration: Athos, so drunk he could barely stand, leaning heavily on his sword, with hair disheveled but still so handsome, and at his side, supporting him like a walking stick, the rakish d'Artagnan . . .

And off they went. All around them there was toasting, talking, debate. They were still drinking, of course, with happiness at having found each other. From time to time they clinked their glasses together, but they drank quickly and without stopping for breath, as if time was too precious to spend on making toasts.

"Do you remember this one? 'Down the road came a ghostly figure, enveloped from head to foot in a hooded white robe . . .'"

Of course he did. The stranger recognized the good-for-nothing English nobleman, creeping away from the battlefield disguised as a leper and carrying a crossbow in his hand, and the two boys, frightened and dumbfounded, one of whom was in fact a beautiful lady in disguise.

"Joanna?"

"Joanna Sedley."

"I was scared of that picture."

"Me too, really scared, until I read the story." And they slapped their hands on the table as if to say, "Of course!"

They drank some more.

"'The mustanger, anticipating this action, had armed himself with a similar weapon and stood ready to return the fire of his antagonist—shot for shot.'"

"Colt's six-shooter!"

They filled their glasses.

"'Unclasp your loathsome arm from the waist of my sister. Louise! Stand aside, and give me the chance of killing him!'"

They laughed, and drank.

All around them the talk was of politics, local and international, but in truth the standard of Georgian political analysis was roughly on a par with that of two old codgers from the village. America wanted something from Russia, Russia was putting pressure on Europe, Germany was Russia's lap-dog, France was talking out of its arse, China was lying in wait like a tiger waiting to pounce, Iran was building the bomb, and Georgia, the tiny pearl with aspirations of joining NATO, was getting squashed in the middle of it all . . . And the two men protected themselves from all of this foolishness, almost as if they were sitting not face to face but back to back, all-seeing, experienced, and so able to thwart any attempts to ambush them. Each in his own time had accepted the title of warrior from the vainglorious hunchback prince, an old elephant had conferred the blessings of the jungle on them and they had complete insight into the meaninglessness of the people's debate—during the period in which they were held captive in a cage by the future king of Indapur both of them had come to know mankind very well . . .

Mowgli, Mowgli . . . They stayed with you the longest, made themselves at home with you, were welcomed in by Kipling. And when the politics got dangerously heated and the dinner party was nearing crisis point because the loudest mouths accused the quietest mouths of secretly backing the government, and it almost descended into violence, the stranger said, "The meat is very near the bone," and winked.

They drank more. The government supporters really were pathetic (the bone cracked) and sulked for ages, as was their custom ("Eowawa! *Thus* do we do in the Jungle!"). That's how it is brother—they don't let the weak creatures stay outside after the howling starts . . .

And then everybody at the table moved to sit in front of the television—each one of them so *engagé* (what a vile word!) that they just had to watch the latest news, be comforted or irritated, and afterward return to the table even more enraged; and the two men sat almost forehead to forehead, and gave a muffled mumbled rendition of the melancholic song of the old pirate:

> "Fifteen men on a dead man's chest—
> . . . Yo-ho-ho and a bottle of rum
> Drink and the devil had done for the rest—
> . . . Yo-ho-ho and a bottle of rum."

And finished up with:

> "But one man of her crew alive
> What put to sea with seventy-five."

They drank some more.

> "Ho, Darby, fetch aft the rum!"

And then his wife phoned (also a bad portent!). She had fallen ill, a cold had come on since she got to work that morning and by now she could already feel it spreading through her body. She asked him to pick up their child from a birthday party ("I am taken, d'Artagnan!") and Number Two quickly sobered up. His started looking for his jacket under the pile of coats in the hallway.

"Cry your trail, Little Brother," the stranger said sadly when he saw Number Two with his coat on. Number Two could not hold back any longer and embraced the stranger, taking his big paw in his own hand for a while. "Maybe your lips are still burning from the passionate kiss of Doña

Isidora Covarubio de los Llanos?" But no, he was going back to his wife and child and when he got outside a single tear rolled down his cheek. Yes, after a few weeks of constant drinking Number Two had become sentimental. As he understood it, it was something to do with the nerves.

In the taxi he thought about the nobleman Avtandil's testament on the importance of friendship and Jean Valjean's candlesticks—no more, no less. He thought again about kingdoms created by mortal creatures like himself, powerful, impregnable ramparts that surrounded them and the demigods that inhabited them and were capable of such excessive love and hatred. It was not only countries that disappeared; whole peoples were swallowed up and lost, and yet these kingdoms stood firm to this day: Homer's Greece was still there, Dostoyevsky's Russia, Dickens's England, Hamsun's North, Faulkner's South, the Orient of the courageous white colonialist sahib . . . Today's texts, bloated like drowning victims, would not be able to take anything away from them. That is what he believed, at least.

Yes, new states were being born all the time, and until today the freest citizen of this newest-born—and therefore truly free—country floated around on a raft on an enormous river and everywhere was his home, whatever shore he should choose to disembark on. But on the other side of the world a vast empire was crumbling and a frightened doctor stupefied by morphine, locked away, sheltering in his own house, his last fragile refuge, stood at the sealed window with the officers he himself had created and looked out onto the senseless and bloody rebellion . . .

Yes, there was fear . . . and out of this fear and the useless and selfless search for the forgotten God so many great things were created. On the shores of Algeria some poor sun-struck soul riddled the Arab with bullets for no good reason, and a dreamy aviator stared down at that same Saharan sand and the war-weary earth from his reconnaissance plane in search of the tiny figure of the monarch's child, in a boat lost in the Caribbean Sea a man wrestled with an enormous fish, on the grasslands of Kyrgyzstan a tribesman driven mad by passion went looking for his camel, and on the other side of the world a thief, smuggler and murderer, sick with leprosy, swam along trustingly in the gentle waves toward his own death, and while he had more than enough time to think over his life, now so near its end, he still could not reconcile himself to what had befallen him . . .

He arrived at the building, went up to the apartment, and went in to the birthday party, a noisy confusion of children and balloons. The women greeted him, asked after his wife's health and shook their heads so sympathetically that he felt as if he were himself the very bacterium that had invaded their friend so mercilessly and made her so ill. The husbands invited him into the kitchen, where they'd set the table up for a little party of their own. They were sitting around a television which blasted the news so loudly that it threatened the well-being of those in the room. Number Two drank only one glass, standing up. He didn't stay any longer. He didn't even let the child stay; he anxiously helped him into his coat, pulled his hat down over his brow, and almost dragged him outside.

They set off striding down the street; their house was neither near nor far. The child, walking slightly behind, sulked and whined because he'd had to leave the party early. But then, quite fortuitously, Number Two's wife rang him and asked him to buy her some painkillers. Her head was hurting now too and from her voice it was clear that she really wasn't well.

When they came out of the pharmacy he explained to the child, who was somewhat calmer now, that his mother was ill and she needed medicine urgently, and that was why he had been in a hurry and had taken him home from the party early.

"Give it to me, then, and I'll give it to her." This was a ritual, a step toward reconciliation. On the rare occasions that Number Two bought a present for his wife, it was the child who liked to give it to her, and it seemed that he counted medicine as a present. Number Two acquiesced without saying a word, but told the child to put the medicine right into his pocket so that it wouldn't fall out.

The sulking child caught up with him and grabbed it. They were still walking in silence, but it seemed now as if everything was back to normal between them. The boy was taking his sick mother her medicine. And why not? And then suddenly Number Two remembered a favorite childhood book of his—how had forgotten it?—a lovely journey through the Georgian alphabet, written as a kind of Enlightenment for Georgia's youth. Back then Georgia was just as small as it is today, of course, and yet it somehow seemed bigger, indeed the world itself was bigger then too, more interesting, more unknown. And this luminary used his book to smuggle stories out to children learning to read and write, a series of lovely little stories written by him and other like-minded people, one by one, like pearls threaded onto a necklace. This enlightenment introduced the reader not only to his own country but the world at large, told tales of states and continents where he had never been and would most likely never go, but it told him anyway, told him that in France, whose capital is Paris and which has three million inhabitants, the main crop is wheat, that the number of states in the United States of America is rising to fifty, that Africa is on the whole populated by black-skinned Negroes and that the arrogance displayed by the British, and through which the Englishman preserves his dignity and self-respect, is called, "being a gentleman."

Who were these people? What century was this? They came out of the depths of the nation, speaking the language of the people and bringing enlightenment to the people, and yet the very people they sought to enlighten were apparently preparing Berdenki's bullet for them. Did they really not want this enlightenment? Did they not want us to become like the West, despite not even really knowing what the West was like? And yet they tried to tell that "arrogant" gentleman—outwardly proper and inwardly refined—so many things about his own country.

Walking back home with his son along a street lit by a single streetlight, Number Two felt drunk and tired, and also felt the loss of that stranger with the furrowed brow who was as kindly and reliable as those childhood books, and whose address he didn't know and whom he would probably never see again.

"I'm scared." The child looked up at him, almost as an answer to Number Two's own thoughts.

Number Two stopped. He was surprised to see a bat fly right by their heads and then turn against the cloudless sky and come back toward them.

Sitting in the plain, woman-free café the next morning, he remembered that bat from the night before and decided to phone his friend the zoologist to ask him whether bats hibernated in winter. Or do they rush off to countries that never get cold?—in which case the one from the night before must just have been lost and looking for shelter. It was still early and—who knows?—the zoologist might still be in bed. He couldn't decide whether to phone or not and just gazed dumbfounded at the telephone lying on the table next to his glass of brandy . . .

He knelt down so his head was level with his child's and explained to him that bats were not dangerous at all and that when he was little he also believed they would fly into his hair and other silly things like that, but that actually all that stuff had been made up by somebody very cowardly and stupid . . .

They carried on walking. He was already holding his child's hand very tightly.

"But I'm still scared. I'm not scared of bats anymore, but I still feel scared of something."

They stopped again and Number Two felt that he too was scared because in the same way that the boy who stood before him was a child of his own flesh, right at that moment he felt that he was a child of this land and this country, of this country where people demonstrated both awful hatred and oppressive love, where faith and tradition had become commodities to be traded and where false enlightenment had declared inertia a religion. The bringers of enlightenment were huddled under a red lamp and did not rule out the use of force in the interests of the country, even though they themselves had never landed a real punch in their lives, while their enemies stood talking to the people stirring in the streets about self-respect and worth, and giving them false promises. Frank disclosure challenged injustice, sharpened its sword against the kind of immorality that hid behind legality, and everyone—absolutely everyone—swore in the name of a luminary killed before the turn of the century by his own peasants with a Berdan rifle and claimed it was they who would take his work forward . . .

He was scared because the father and son who had stopped in this empty street under the solitary light were children not just of this country but of this shrinking, polarized planet too, this planet where one half faces interminable poverty, famine, and bloodshed, while the other half faces the scourge of peace, pampering, and inertia. It was all so fragile, so fragile that on that quiet autumn evening the planet had not a single child, a single being, a single child who felt it was a place of safety . . .

"I'm scared that the days will come to an end . . ."

And when he clutched his child close to him and kissed his face and hands, and found gripped tightly in his fist the painkillers they had bought for the boy's mother, he followed the child's logic like a unraveled ball of string found in the pitch-dark—no, not his logic, for the child was still too tender and too good for this well-worn word. He just intuited, and understood the little person, his own flesh and blood, who had suddenly taken fright because of his mother's illness, the cloudless autumn night sky, the red sunset, the solitary streetlight and the disoriented bat flying around their heads, and had suddenly become fearful about the ephemeral nature of things—a primeval fear, as old as mankind itself, which from birth has haunted man and with which only a small group of people had managed to coexist peacefully, while the rest started wars, massacred each other and destroyed, recreated, and demolished what others had created before them, fell in love and then betrayed each other, but never said a word about this fear, for nobody dared to but the children . . .

They set off for home again and he told the child that he should not be afraid of anything so long as he had his father by his side and that their days would never end—and he was not deceiving him. He also said that he himself was not scared of anything when he was holding his son's hand and they were walking along together like this, and he wasn't lying then either; on the contrary, he couldn't even remember ever having been so honest . . . And he thought more about the fact that really they too were part of a book. A book which had already been written many times before and would be written many times again . . . But what of it? Who knows how many fathers and sons had already walked down here holding hands and how many more would do so in a moment they would never forget, that many years later would come back to them—when the time came to look back over their life and reconcile themselves with it—and they would try to summon up the courage to think about the other person too but would not quite remember . . .

It didn't matter. They were together now, and nearly home, and they would finally bring the child's mother her medicine . . .

Did Number Two derive any pleasure, though, from the message that came through on his phone, which first fluttered restlessly on the table and then bellowed at full volume? He was staring at the phone with his eyes opened wide so as to better hold back the tears on his lashes. It was all to do with his nerves . . .

Yes, he was pleased. Even though he had promised his wife—who had rallied a little—that he would not drink today so many times that he almost believed it himself, he was still pleased.

He drained his glass of brandy, beckoned the waitress over and left as quickly as he could. Not once did he look back toward the café where the only beautiful women were in pictures on the walls.

Number Three—Doubt and Futility

There is a fly buzzing about. Forever circling around us, like fate. More than any other creature, flies are our constant companions. But we loathe this busy, bustling fly because we never know where it has flown in from, what filth it was sitting on before it came to land on our food and rub its little legs together in that self-satisfied manner . . .

But all of sudden here it is, to put us off our food; it swoops down greedily onto our *mtsvadi* and *khachapuri*, our kebabs and pickles, our cheese and bread. The only thing it dares not sit on is the bowl of steaming-hot *khinkali*; maybe it is fearful of those sacred, spiraling folds of dough, or their spell-binding aroma. *Khinkali* are sacred, as sacred as the bonds of true friendship between men, and when futility and doubt take hold of you there is nothing better than to invite a couple of friends you haven't seen for a while to come for *khinkali* with you. Rub each other's numbed limbs, reassure each other that you are still alive, still love each other, still have something in common, something to talk about. It is always better to invite your childhood friends for *khinkali* than to bump into them unexpectedly in the street and then bump into them again a few months later . . . And who knows what your friends might say and how they might console you?

He no longer believed anything like that. But still he sat there and waited. He sat by the window and waited for his friends. He had already ordered *khinkali*. He had already had a drink, too.

He was in bed when he decided to call his friends. His ears were still ringing from the sound of the front door that had slammed shut just a short time ago. Alone with the emptiness, he didn't feel anything yet. He had not yet decided how to meet the solitude that had returned once again to his house like the prodigal son.

He met it head-on. He dressed and got out of the apartment as quickly as he could. He spent the whole morning wandering through streets that were filled with leaves newly fallen from the trees. When the *khinkali* restaurant opened he went in and sent his message. Then he sat down and waited . . .

Number Three had seen his wife the previous day.

Once, several years earlier, he had seen a true wonder of nature. It was back when he was working on laying the pipeline. He had no particularly interesting memories of that portion of his life, and he didn't refer to it in that way because he was especially proud of his contribution to the nation's development. No, personally he had never believed in any of those artificially created legends with which they tried to bewitch the populace: the Eurasian corridor, the Silk Road, and all that kind of rubbish. But if needed, he could bewitch people himself by starting his stories with "Back when I was laying the pipeline . . ." and by that he was referring to the period in his life when he felt most alive, and which he now yearned for more than any other . . .

That night, somewhere between Tabatskuri and Bakuriani, his car broke down on the mountain pass. It was like a little island suspended between heaven and the earth. Below it there were forests, and below that the flickering lights of villages and hamlets, while they themselves had stopped at the edge of a bare, despondent-looking field and had only the star-filled sky above their heads. He had always been too busy to notice all this before. But he had more than enough time that night. They had been breaking the rules by driving at night. Driving at night in an oil company jeep was forbidden, so they could not call out a rescuer until morning.

The driver, whom he had personally trained, got out the twice-distilled vodka made from his own plums and some disposable cups. It was bitterly cold outside and every now and then they had to turn on the heat in the cab. Soon boredom set in. The driver went to sleep, but Number Three had difficulty doing so, and as he sat there with his forehead pressed against the car window, staring up at the sky, he witnessed an extraordinary meteor shower.

Because he never really looked at the sky he could not say whether what he was witnessing was a normal occurrence for this time of year, or whether the sight of him had made the celestial bodies go crazy. But shooting stars were raining down one after the other and so quickly that Number Three didn't even have time to think of a wish. He didn't manage to make a single wish and in frustration decided to adopt a different strategy. He would think of a name in advance, the name of somebody he felt deserved health, longevity, money, and happiness, and then would say the name at the precise moment he saw a shooting star fall. It worked, and the stars were still falling . . .

When he'd run out of family members he moved onto friends, then quietly mentioned a couple of women, and finally the most distant relatives he had. Even the driver snoring next to him got a star. It was a magical night, and every time he remembered it he felt sure that he was not a bad man. If he were he would not have been able to remember so many people so quickly or to bestow those starry blessings so ungrudgingly. Simply, he was a very busy man—running up and down the entire length of yet another long, snaking gash inflicted by mankind onto the earth to accommodate a huge and as yet still unlaid pipeline, in a worn-out jeep, and everywhere he looked he had jobs dumped on him. There was only one oil pipeline but apparently many different Georgias, and each and every one necessitated a different approach. One day he'd be dealing with rebel Tatars—a few times he even found himself dealing directly with a brandished pitchfork—and the next he'd be trying (and sometimes managing) to read the hidden intents of those Svans who had settled in the barren neighboring lands and who stood there watching everything, hostile and suspiciously quiet. Then they took the pipeline deeper and deeper into the mountains and he tried to allay the suspicions of the ever suspicious Armenians (always in vain), he consoled the impoverished Greeks, and if necessary even lied to them. He translated Georgian into English, Russian into Georgian, English into Russian. He even learned a few phrases in Azeri and Armenian, and he grew tired but still he ran about and still he found it all very interesting. But it turned out that while he was doing all that running about and negotiating he had forgotten that he loved so many people, and that he was himself a good person . . .

And by the time the sky started to grow pale again it was already very cold inside the jeep, and the driver woke up, stretched and told him with some satisfaction that he'd dreamed about the village whore, "the Golden Buffalo." Having witnessed the meteor shower Number Three looked at the driver rather more warmly than usual, he felt somehow closer to him and so asked him to describe the Golden Buffalo. She was apparently a very fine, full-bodied woman with breasts like the pistons on a '67 Mustang. This picture of the village beauty was far from perfect and even though Number Three didn't ask what kind of pistons a '67 Mustang had, as he sat here now in the *khinkali* restaurant he had a very clear picture of what the Golden Buffalo looked like—not just full-bodied, but huge, carrying not only the sins of all womanhood from Eve onward but also the depravity of the entire world . . .

Yesterday he saw his wife. She was crossing in front of them at the lights and he told his coworker behind the wheel to toot the horn at her. He had suddenly decided to ask her to come with them. Maybe it would work . . . They were going to Mtskheta for a party.

His coworker dutifully gave a long toot on the horn. The woman—she seemed so different, he thought, she was almost like a stranger to him—was right in front of the car. She looked around and actually failed to recognize her own husband through the steamed-up windshield. She ran coquettishly and affectedly in front of the car like a little girl. The coworker behind the wheel was the first person Number Three began to hate, because he witnessed Number Three become suddenly engulfed by an enormous sense of shame, the reasons for which he did not yet fully understand.

He would never have expected behavior like that from his second star (he remembered very clearly that on the night of the meteor shower the first name he uttered was that of his little girl, who had just started to walk, and the second was his wife's), even though it had been over a year since they'd stopped living together, since she had just up and left with his child one day and gone back to live with her family. She gave up everything, threw it all away. "I want to feel human," she said, and left.

At first Number Three didn't believe it. It was a whim, he thought, that would last one, maybe two weeks, but after failing to persuade her to come back on several occasions he started having doubts. But it was a long time before he really accepted it. Then when he did, he found himself wanting to kill someone. He just couldn't work out who. He started getting drunk and spent whole nights raging in an armchair. He was dangerous, there was no doubt about it, and the gun he gripped in his hand was even more dangerous and sinister than him. Then gradually he got used to being without her and he reaped the sweet fruits of living alone. But other women simply could not combat the solitude that reigned in his apartment, whether he let them stay for weeks (if they didn't ask too many questions) or only a single night (if they bored him with questions about his wife and child) before he started cursing them and then threw them out.

But she was different . . . Although the woman he saw was not the one he'd known; she crossed over in front of them so lightly, so enchantingly . . . She was so unfamiliar, so unsettling, so available, that Number Three felt as if everything he'd had been standing on until now was crumbling beneath him. She seemed so available—and yet, for him, so unattainable. He had felt ready for anything, but that turned out not to be true. Until yesterday he had held onto the hope that she might come back to him. If he had seen her with someone else then he might not have felt so bitter, but she was alone, beautiful, and so free . . .

"She was a looker, wasn't she?" said the coworker about his wife, and Number Three finally made his choice: he would kill his coworker. The woman, in the meantime, had crossed over the road and blended into the crowd on the other side . . .

In the end he didn't kill anyone that day. He didn't do anything else particularly remarkable either. He felt confused and spent the rest of the day on autopilot: he got drunk, brought a woman home for the night, threw her out in the morning—and now here he sat, waiting for his childhood friends, as if he was waiting to tell them about it and see what useful or comforting words the two drunks might offer in return . . .

He wanted something. Not to destroy, or beat, or smash—he was thinking about murder. This thought alone consoled him and entertained him and, perhaps unsurprisingly, today as always when he thought about murder it was still that man's face that he saw. The face that poisoned everything and reminded him of his own feebleness. No, it was not enough to just see the face. You needed to see the whole man, you needed to stand in front of him and look up at him from below to feel the full extent of your feebleness and ineptitude. The man was a killer he'd met in a village near Borjomi one snowy winter. That was back when he was working on the pipeline . . . And back when Penelope, his wife back home, still seemed devoted and desirable.

Ah, Penelope, who always reminded him of his friends' birthdays, of his friends' existence, even, and who organized for them to come over for beautiful dinners when he was back from the pipeline at weekends. Penelope, a good mother, a kind wife, and a loving daughter-in-law, about whom his mother would proudly say, "She's like a cat: so quiet and lovely, you'd never even know she was there." Penelope, who ran off, even though she had her own home, the security of her own family, and all the conditions necessary for a decent life, and who despite all that just wanted to feel human . . . And now it seemed that feeling human meant swaying your hips in the street.

He preferred to think about that than remember the face of that man and remember his other shame. He had also realized a long time ago that he remembered the man from Borjomi—along with everything else connected with "laying the pipeline"—with a kind of warmth and nostalgia. The two years he had spent on the pipeline were already in the distant past, and the killer he had seen for no more than five minutes was one of the oldest parts of the legend. Who knows, maybe he wasn't even alive anymore, maybe he had been destined to die at the hands of some masked special-forces marksman, although Number Three had trouble believing that.

He had run out of drink and after asking around in the village as to where he could get some vodka, he'd ended up at the man's door. The local peasants had told him the man would definitely have vodka, and wine too—although whether he'd be willing to sell it was a different matter.

How could he not sell it? Number Three was an expert in facilitating relationships between people, frightening them, flattering them, appeasing them—it was both what he got paid for and how he managed his own affairs. He knocked boldly on the high iron gate he'd been directed to and was greeted by the sound of dogs going wild. From inside he heard the sound of scraping metal as somebody removed the iron beam that reinforced the locked gate and when the vodka seller appeared Number Three found himself looking not at a peasant ("Uncle, they told me in the village you've got good vodka. Is that right?") but a highway robber ("Your money or your life!").

What was he like? Hairy, with a full beard. He was probably quite old, but there was not a single gray hair in his black beard. He would have suited a huge shaggy surplice or a Mauser, or even possibly both together. His eyes practically devoured you, yet they calmed you at the same time. No, he would not be satisfied with your money alone—he would take your soul too, and bury you right there in his yard.

Number Three knew how to recognize a killer. He'd been born in the kind of town where killers really weren't that hard to find. What is more, there didn't seem to be anyone around who hadn't thought about killing someone else at least once. He'd thought about that a lot back then and he himself had felt ready for anything. He reckoned that if the moment came he would have the strength to face the barrel of any gun pointing toward him, or indeed to calmly squeeze the trigger himself. It seemed that others had thought a lot about this too; some had even written beautiful words on the subject. Number Three knew some of these words by heart: "If you want peace, prepare for war" (inscription on the German Parabellum pistol), "Shoot, but without hatred" (the orders of a Spanish general to his troops), "Readiness is all" (Shakespeare), "If you don't have love you will not be able to kill" (anon.). But all of this, all of these beautiful words paled and faded away as if they had never even existed, vanished like soap bubbles in front of that bandit, who had no idea these words even existed and no interest at all in the people who had written them.

"I won't sell you any vodka. I'm a hunter and I need it in the forest"—not *can't* sell but *won't* sell—"but I'll sell you some wine. How much do you want?"

He really was a creature of the forest—dark and dense. Number Three didn't dare refuse him, even though he knew that the wine in this area was no good. The bandit left him by the gate and disappeared into the snow-covered yard. From the dark yard all he could hear was the sound of clanking chains and dogs snarling ferociously. He fobbed Number Three off with a dusty plastic container full of wine, took his money and sent him on his way . . . As he walked back to this rented apartment that snowy night he kept thinking about the highwayman who wouldn't sell him any vodka. He made some more cautious inquiries in the village and it turned out he really was a killer, burdened by many sins. He had even been punished for some of them. And there were other crimes that had never been proven, even though everyone knew he was responsible . . .

He often remembered the bandit from Borjomi, and he always imagined that it was winter, and that the bandit was deep in the forest, in heavy snow, and with his vicious hounds. He was alone. He was lighting a fire and cut a large piece of rubber from the leg of his own boot with his dagger and used that to light the fire; working unhurriedly, he broke up dry branches and threw them onto the newly kindled flames. Then he took the vodka from his shoulder bag and drank it from a small ram's horn. Who was he toasting, wishing long life to, glorifying? It was hard to imagine. His ancestors, at least: the god of beasts and game, or one of the evil spirits of the forest. Although tethered around the fire, his dogs were shivering violently, they strained to look at their master, waiting for him to throw them a crust of bread, and still they shivered. But it was not from the cold—it was fear and anticipation.

They were shaking in front of their master and waiting for that moment of joy and freedom, when that same master would untether them and use them to track a deer or a wild boar. Along with fear and terror, that call to hunt had made dogs tremble even when they were still wolves and called each other with a hunting howl. Still vicious and still merciless, but now mere half-predators nonetheless—they were now just the slaves of a more dangerous and merciless predator, who carved up his kill—whether four-legged or two-legged—into little pieces with his dagger and who would saw off his own limb without a second thought if it were caught in a trap.

Number Three had always imagined the man all alone in a snow-covered forest but today for the first time he wondered whether the man had a wife. Were there children on the other side of that iron gate, starving away in that dingy lair and waiting for their father to bring home the kill. If not, what would have been the result of the forest creature and the Golden Buffalo cross-breeding? What kind of unique being would they have conceived and sent forth into this most amazing country?

It was then that he saw his friends through the window. Number One and Number Two had bumped into each other somewhere en route and were now coming down the street arm in arm. He smiled—they were real vagabonds. The clean-shaven, smarter vagabond was telling the unshaven, scruffy one something as they walked along. These are your fallen stars too, that came down from the sky on that mountain pass all those years ago. Both of them had bloated faces and Number Three was happy that he had got to them in time, that he had seen them . . .

But what would they say to each other after a couple of restorative glasses? He would probably tell them about the meteor shower and the Golden Buffalo. He wasn't ashamed to talk about the man of the woods from Borjomi anymore. With them he could. He wouldn't mention the other thing, though, the main thing. He wouldn't lower the mood, he would just let them eat their *khinkali*. And just what would he say about his wife, anyway? About the woman he now loved and wanted as never before . . . Maybe it was not too late to put things right?

They spotted him from the street too and raised their hands to greet him. They weren't in the mood for smiling. They would probably have a story to tell, too. They would listen in silence to whoever was speaking, but afterward they would have something to say, and that was important too, wasn't it?

And the *khinkali* came just at the right moment, just as the men pulled open the door. It was a wonderful sight, those piping-hot pockets of dough, with their little topknots and their perfectly formed symmetrical folds . . .

ANA KORDZAIA-SAMADASHVILI
Rain

I live here. From now on I will always live here. It's always raining here. They say it's always rained here and it always will. At first I couldn't stand it, but now I know how good it is for you. See, the skin on my face looks so clear now, just like all the other women here. It's not all because of the rain, though. I don't smoke anymore, because it's always raining here, and everything's damp and it makes the cigarettes taste funny. I don't drink anymore either, because it costs too much and if my boss found out he'd fire me. And so my face looks clear and I'm very white, just like the walls of my apartment. The walls of my apartment are all white too, just like at work. At first I thought I might hang some paintings on them, but then I changed my mind about going to buy them, because it's always raining. I'm not home much anyway: in the morning I go to work, from work to the cafeteria, from the cafeteria back home. I wear rain boots outside, and they're red ones too, so that I don't get sad and so that every day feels like a holiday.

I don't wear my boots at work. We always leave our outdoor shoes with the concierge. It's a good system. I bought one pair of shoes and they still haven't worn out to this day. When I'm at work I don't have to walk around much. I'm a secretary, I sit at the entrance, answer the phone when it rings, and put people through to whoever they ask for. There are only three men I have to put them through to. I work in a small company.

The company I work for belongs to Russian émigrés and makes bottles. What kind of bottles I don't know. It's none of my business, I'm a secretary, I sit at the entrance and answer the phone when it rings, and put people through to whoever they ask for.

Generally speaking I live very healthily and very cheaply.

True, at first I found it hard. Now I know I found it hard because I thought I would only be here for a while. Now I know I'll always live here, and I feel much calmer.

At first I found it hard to get on with the woman next door, because she hates me. She hates me because I have black hair and don't speak her language very well. If I left my washing in the dryer too long she'd throw it on the floor and in the morning I'd end up drying my panties with a hair-dryer. Because of that at first I kept being late for work. But now I get my washing out in time and I get up not thirty minutes but a full hour before work starts. That way I have time to get everything done, and as a rule I wash my panties straight away so they always seem dry to me.

Rainer taught me to do it that way. Rainer's a very organized man. He meets up with me on Friday nights. Or, to be precise, he comes to my place because it's always raining. It's better, anyway, drinking tea at home—you don't have to go out in the rain afterward and it works out cheaper too.

Rainer stays at my place on Fridays because on Saturday mornings we always have sex. Sex is as essential as bread and water, that's what Rainer said. I don't think that for me having sex with Rainer is essential at all, because I don't really care either way. But Rainer said that when a person doesn't have sex they turn bad. And so on Saturday mornings we always have sex, before Rainer goes to sleep and I make breakfast.

We normally go to Rainer's parents once a month for dinner. Rainer's mother makes dinner specially for me. Before we go Rainer always checks what I'm wearing. He wants me to be dressed just right.

Rainer's mother always cooks fabulous steak. I don't eat meat so I just have salad leaves. Rainer's mother says a woman who doesn't eat meat can't possibly give birth to healthy children. I won't be having any children, anyway, because Rainer insists on safe sex. But I'll never tell Rainer's parents that, because Rainer said they mustn't know.

Apart from the steak, Rainer's mother gives us hot chocolate to drink. I don't like milk, but it would be rude to say no to everything. So I drink the hot chocolate and look at photos with Rainer's parents—they spent one summer in Brazil and tell me all about their trip and make me look at photos.

I've been living like this for a long time now.

One time Rainer's father told me that in Brazil it never rains and it's great, and Rainer's mother didn't like that. Rainer's mother doesn't like me. She hates me. She hates me because I have black hair and don't speak her language very well, and I'm three months older than Rainer. She just can't understand what it is Rainer sees in me. He doesn't see anything in me, but I'll never tell Rainer's parents that, because Rainer said they mustn't know.

It was a Friday that day too, because Rainer spent the night with me and in the morning we had sex. When Rainer turned over I reached my hand under the bed. I was sure there was a big stone under there. I picked up the stone and hit Rainer in the head with it.

Then I threw my boots out of the window and went out into the street. It was raining. I bought cigarettes and a bottle of Russian vodka. I opened the cigarettes and the bottle while I was still in the shop, and by the time I got home I was really drunk.

I got undressed and sat on the floor, in front of the mirror on the floor, and carried on drinking. I thought about the high pass on Mount Kazbeg, and how everything up there is unchanged, and how when I go up there— soon very soon—I'll see my dear friend Vatche and our old, soot-covered teapot. Then I threw the bottle out of the window and went to sleep.

Rainer woke up first. He wasn't dead. He lodged a complaint with the police about me. Nobody defended me because Rainer had physical evidence: his smashed head and the stone I smashed it with.

Then the doctor said I wasn't a murderer, I was mad. They sent me to the madhouse.

Nothing has changed. Just like the walls in my flat and at work, the walls of my room here are all white. They cook fabulous steak here too. I don't eat meat so I just have salad leaves. The only difference is that I don't have sex anymore and now I'm just waiting to turn bad. I sit by the window and look outside. It's always raining.

ZURAB LEZHAVA

Love in a Prison Cell

The two men walked into the transit cell in Kharkov prison.

They greeted its inhabitants: "*Privyet!*"

The inmates were drinking *chefir*. Every Soviet citizen would probably know how they came to be drinking *chefir* in a Soviet prison, because at one time or another practically every one of them has been in prison themselves, and anyone who hasn't almost certainly will. There are several ways to boil *chefir*, and a few regional differences in how it is drunk, but basically you sit in a circle, pass the cup around and take a couple of gulps each: *chefir* is a highly concentrated, bitter tea drunk without sugar. Few people like it at first, but they soon get used to it and often end up unable to function without it. And you'll get used to it, too, when you're in prison.

"Where are you lot from then, boys?" asked one old prisoner after he'd greeted the new arrivals.

"Moscow."

"What, you're from Moscow?" A second, relatively young man stuck his head out, and smiled menacingly. In prison, you see, they don't really like people from Moscow; they say they're a bit strange.

"No, we're not actually *from* Moscow. He's from Nikolayev, and I'm from near Rostov," said the taller one, whose name was Pasha. "We were in Moscow for tests."

"What kind of tests?"

"Medical tests for the court, at the Serbsky Institute."

"Is that right?" a younger man called out. "They don't send just any old madmen to the Serbsky. You must be very special madmen!"

"Yes, we are indeed mad," Pasha answered with false pride. "I, for example, have a bilateral brain fracture. And he has a mild case of mental retardation." He burst out laughing, quite cheerfully.

Everyone smiled. Prisoners like cheerful people; they say that they don't have to put their hands in their pockets to pull out a word.

"Come on, boys, let's have a drink—you've had a long journey," said the old man to the newcomers.

The old man was Vitsya Chetvertak. Chetvertak was a nickname meaning "quarter" because his first sentence was for twenty-five years. Since then he'd served several stretches and received terms of various lengths, but that first nickname had stayed with him. He loved two things: playing cards and tea. Yet while scholars, as everyone knows, often travel to villages to collect interesting proverbs, poems, and fairy tales, nobody had ever traveled to meet Chetvertak and write down what he said, more's the pity. Oh, he knew some poems, that man, some real epics—poems from the Gulag. His speech was peppered with—how shall I put it?—"choice language" and oh! he could make them laugh when he was in the mood. And yet none of these poems and witticisms will ever be printed in any collection or almanac. Will they be lost, then, forever?

The main theme of this story is love, so I will introduce you to only some of those in the cell, and only as and when necessary in the course of the narrative. You will get to know the others when you yourself get to prison. But now, before we turn to matters of love, I want to introduce you to one more man, because were it not for him it is likely this story would never have happened, nor would love ever have blossomed in this place.

This man lay some distance away from the others and kept running back and forth to the toilet. He was sick. The poor soul was suffering from cold sweats and bloody diarrhea. He bore it heroically, not even seeking help from the prison administration, and this because cells where dysentery is discovered are placed under quarantine. Every prisoner in a quarantine cell has to stay there in transit for a month, and the transit cell is not a place anyone wishes to be. No cigarettes, no tea, no blankets, no sheets, and almost all those around you are strangers, from every corner of the country. On top of that you have the heat in summer, the cold in winter, cramped conditions, bedbugs, and more besides. That is why everyone tries to get to their destination—the Gulag—as quickly as possible. So they ask prisoners who are sick to just put up with it, to bear it for a while. And they put up with it. But transit prisoners come and go. The old ones are replaced by new ones, and then the new ones ask the prisoners who are sick to wait, just a bit longer, until they've left. At times like this prisoners forget themselves and the solidarity they once extolled. At times like this they think only of themselves.

It's when they take you from remand, stick you in a prisoner transport train, and bring you here that you fully appreciate what architectural monstrosities Soviet prisons are. In this complex, one block was built in the time of Tsarina Ekaterina, a second block was added at the turn of the century when Stolypin was prime minister, and the third block is from the present day. Yet all of these blocks are stuck there together, interlocked in such an unattractive way . . . What an eyesore.

The cell I referred to above was situated at the end of one of these blocks, and in the corner of a second block that ran perpendicular to it was one of the women's cells. It was a small cell housing four inmates. Women in Kharkov prison were usually housed in larger cells, but this one was set aside for women with venereal disease. The women in it were being treated for gonorrhea—the clap. Of course having a relationship, especially an intimate one, with a woman carrying a disease like that isn't really all that pleasant, but when everyone's locked in their cells and there's no danger of catching anything, well then, what does it matter? In fact, it's quite nice having a relationship with a woman, even if her nose *is* falling off; women are still women, after all. Chetvertak had a girlfriend in that cell called Lena. He was constantly climbing up to the window and shouting all manner of compliments to his clap-ridden beloved. But more often he would swear at her. Why did her swear at her? I'll tell you why. There were four women in her cell: Chetvertak's beloved, Lena, and then Nadia, Sveta, and Natasha. Housed in the cell one floor above them was a former police major. He had his own cell. Former policemen are not housed communally; they have their own cells so that the other prisoners don't give them any trouble. The major had a sweetheart in that cell too, just like Chetvertak. It was bold, reckless Nadia. Nadia was a former section manager in a shop and was, it seems, used to attracting the attention of policemen. It was much easier for the major to conduct a relationship with the women's cell because of the proximity of their cells. Without any trouble at all he would lower down to their cell a string onto which he had tied his romantic love letter—but also cigarettes and other things. Nadia had ulterior motives in befriending him. The major was a rich man, and Nadia loved rich men. Both Chetvertak and the major were very jealous. Moreover, you might say they hated each other on a spiritual—in other words ideological—level.

"Lena, Lena!" Chetvertak would call.

"What is it?" the major would reply.

"You're not Lena, you stinking dog!" Chetvertak would explode. "You come down here to my cell for a bit and I'll bloody well show you reeducation! With my fists!"

I'm no more prudish than the next man, but I still can't bring myself to write even a fraction of the things that tripped off Chetvertak's tireless tongue at such times. He swore at everyone. Everyone: the major, Nadia, Lena, the prison guards (who, he said, deserved a reeducation all of their own simply for not letting him get his hands on the major); in a word, everyone.

The major, for his part, complained in every correspondence to Nadia and the other girls about why they kept up their relationship with such a degenerate. Nadia and Lena blamed each other for everything, and there was plenty of drama all around . . .

The fact that he could not write to Lena broke Chetvertak's heart. Whenever he saw the string descending from the major's cell with a letter tied on, he almost gnawed through the bars. He tried so hard to send her a letter, but to no avail; he even made a little arrow, and a catapult, but try as he might he just couldn't get a letter to Lena. The grill always got in the way. That was until Pasha arrived . . .

The very first day his batch of transit prisoners arrived, Pasha improvised an air gun. He rolled up a newspaper to make a tube. He glued it securely together. Then he made a special bullet out of paper, in a similar shape to a badminton shuttlecock. The point of the bullet was made of bread softened to be like dough. Bullets like that always fly point first. Pasha wound thread onto the conical paper tail in a particular way, then inserted the bullet into the newspaper tube, stuck the tube out of the window, aimed it at the women's cell, and blew hard. He hit his target first time. None of them had thought it would work, because the women's cell had a different, modern kind of grill fixed onto it. The grill consisted of iron sheets welded at an angle onto the bars. This made it look like the bellows on a Russian accordion, from where the grill it took its name— they called the grill a *bayan*.

"Lena, Lena," called Pasha.

"What?" Lena called back.

"Lenushka, I've shot a paper bullet at your cell, pick it up and pull it through carefully. There's a very fine thread tied to the bullet, and tied to that fine thread is a thicker thread; when you get to the thicker thread tie it to the grill and let me know when you've done it, okay?"

"Okay!"

Lena understood what was required of her and did everything just as Pasha had told her to.

"Right," Pasha told Chetvertak, "the line's up; you can write your letter!"

Prisoners used to call those kind of string set-ups "lines."

Chetvertak wrote his letter:

> My dear Lenushka, at last I have been given the means by which to write you this little letter. I want to tell you that I love you very,

very much. Lena, there are two guys in here who want to start writing to Sveta and Natasha. They are called Sanya and Vanya. They come from Ukraine, so please ask the girls to be sure to write. Sveta and Natasha can decide between themselves which guy they want. That's all for now, so I'll say good-bye. My heart pounds in anticipation of your reply, while Sanya and Vanya eagerly await their replies from Natasha and Sveta. I kiss your lips many times. Your Chetvertak."

But I am rather perplexed. There are some Russian words I just do not know how to translate. These are the words Russians use when they're indulging in flirting and sweet talk. It's the little diminutive forms they use to make their words sound softer, more delightful. A plain old nose—*nos*—becomes a *nosik*, your eyes—*glaza*—become your *glazki*. But unfortunately other languages don't always let us do this. Although actually no, it's not down to the language. Sometimes it's just that national characteristics—whether that's Georgian candor or English reserve—prevent us from speaking to women in the way Russians do. But how can I properly represent their flirtations if I don't soften my language as they do? I can't write "nose" when they say *nosik* or "eyes" when they say "*glazki*." That would be sacrilege. So in this story don't laugh if you read, "nosey-wose" instead of nose, or "itty-bitty cheeklets" instead of cheeks. Everything new feels strange. If you can get used to speaking to women like this you'll be on your way to becoming a real gentlemen.

The women's cell, of course, took no time in replying. Three letters arrived at once: Lena wrote to Chetvertak, Natasha to Sanya, and Sveta to Vanya. It was the start of a spirited correspondence. Lena, Natasha, Sveta, Chetvertak, Sanya, and Vanya wrote letters back and forth and swore their love for each other. The women liked the fact that their sweethearts were hardened criminals. The gentlemen, for their part, were satisfied too—although not with their beloveds' venereal status. But after all, it was only the clap. People see things differently in prison. I mean, you're not going to find the Queen of England in prison, are you? And anyway, it's not leprosy and it's not AIDS. It's the STD version of a head cold, and there's enough medicine to treat everyone: Tanya, Lena, Sveta, Natasha, and the Queen of England herself, if necessary. Nothing stands in the way of love, because love knows no boundaries!

I forgot one vital detail. Do you remember the prisoner with dysentery? He became very ill—in fact he was dying—and the prisoners themselves called for a doctor. The patient was taken off somewhere. A number of rather beefy nurses, in white gowns discolored by excessive washing, and large guards came down to the cell. They lined the inmates up in the corridor and then inserted a special wire swab into the rectum of each and every one in turn, so as to establish whether they had dysentery. To be precise, it was one of the nurses, a plump Ukrainian woman, who stuck the swab in. The guards just stood and glared. Their presence made it impossible for the prisoners to put up any resistance. The guards in Kharkov prison aren't big fans of discussion, and like it or not you have to do what the administration deems necessary, and that's that.

"Gently! Gently, woman!" cried one prisoner with his pants down. "Ow!"

"Next!" boomed the woman.

"Give it here, I'll do it myself!" groaned the next one.

"Bend over!" replied the woman.

"Oh, I should screw your mother, you—" he cursed.

"Screw your own mother, it'll be cheaper," the woman replied, impassive.

There was no anger or hysteria while this was going on. There was no sense of animosity; on the contrary, everyone found it entertaining in their own way; for the prisoners, nurses and guards it was an excuse to joke about for a bit.

I want to share this with you, dear reader, and to warn you so that when the time comes for you to have dealings with a woman like this you'll know what to do. And I beg you, do exactly what I advise, just as is laid out in the rules below.

How to deal with your nurse during insertion of a wire swab:

1. Smile as warmly as you can at the nurse and look into her eyes. A few sweet words are also advisable.

2. Drop your pants, squat, relax and open up the muscles in your posterior as widely as you can. But be quick! Remember: if you don't relax and open up in good time, you can expect to feel a degree of pain.

3. You should in no way reveal any dissatisfaction, and under no circumstances, oh-no-no-no-no-no, should you put up any resistance to the white-coated nurses. Remember: irresponsible actions like that will result in intervention by those rather large guards.

And then . . .

There was one proud young man who talked back to the nurse. In fact, he put up a bit of a fight. For his trouble, those rather large guards bent him over quite mercilessly while the outraged nurse rammed the wire swab into his tensed body with as much force as she could muster. The result? One hell of a pain in the ass.

The testers took the swabs and cultivated them in the laboratory. It took no time for the swabs to yield a result. They came up positive for a few men, who turned out to have dysentery. They took the sick men to the prison hospital, needless to say, and quarantined the cell.

"Pfft!" Chetvertak spat onto the floor. "I knew we'd get stuck in this damned Kharkov transit center! I felt it in my bones! They eat their porridge with dirty hands, like pigs. Then they get sick and make everyone else sick too. But anyway, I should sit down and write to my beloved!"

So Chetvertak writes Lena a letter:

My dear Lenushka, I want to let you know that something very unfortunate has happened in our cell. We've been quarantined because some of the cellmates turned out to have dysentery. But when they eat their porridge from their bowls like pigs, well, what do you expect to happen? Now wait, wait until this quarantine is lifted. The one thing that brings me comfort is knowing that you love me, my lover, my beauty, my pride, and it is only your letters that dispel my heartache! That is my situation. I kiss your cheeklets, your itty-bitty eyes, your lovely lips and your nosey-wose a thousand times!

Your Chetvertak.

Lena wrote this reply:

My dear Vitsinka! You will probably be angry with me, but I shall tell you nonetheless: I am immeasurably happy that you are still here! Quarantine is good, my little bunny! Just imagine if you had gone with the last batch to the Gulag; whatever would I have done? You know, surely, that I cannot live without you? You are the first man in my life to have left an indelible mark, to have lit the fire of love in my heart. I don't know why—probably because I just sit here and because I've had very few men in my life—but I can't live without you anymore. When I get out of here I won't steal again; I'll wait for you, and when you get out we'll steal things together! But for now I kiss your lips a million times,

Yours alone, Lenka.

That's all well and good, but let's get to the point. As I have already told you, there were a great number of romantic letters flying back and forth between the cells. And these letters were all the same. I kiss you, you kiss me, I love you, you love me, and so on. So I won't bore you with them anymore, we'll read just one more important letter that Nadia sent—as it happens, just around the time they moved the major to a different cell.

And this was Nadia's letter:

> Hello boys, this is Nadia! I want to ask you something: how come you're always sending letters and swearing undying love for Sveta, Lena, and Natasha but don't write to me, eh? What, am I not as good as the other girls? Don't I want love too, eh? Get that tall blond guy to write to me, quick, the one with the blue eyes. I saw him in the corridor when I was coming back from the lawyer's and you lot were on your way to the baths. He must write to me, he absolutely must, do you understand? And make sure it's him, I don't need any old guys or their letters!
>
> Yours, Nadia.

Chetvertak wrote back to Nadia himself:

> Nadia, you whore! Nobody in our cell needs your love, do you understand? You're that policeman's bitch—give your love to the major and kiss *his* ass! And I'm not writing to you anymore!
>
> Chetvertak.

Nadia wasted no time in replying.

> Chetvertak, that's how you always talk to women? I'm a policeman's bitch, am I? Aren't you ashamed writing stuff like that? So what if I've said the odd sweet word or two to a policeman? You saw how many cigarettes and sweets he sent us! I was taking him for a ride—I didn't really love him! I'm a respectable prisoner, you know, and I'm not breaking the prisoner's code for any policeman,

even if he is a general! And as far as the major's concerned you can kiss his ass yourself!

Yours, Nadia.

When Chetvertak read that he was furious. He jumped up to the window and started swearing a blue streak at Nadia. To everyone's surprise Nadia gave as good as she got and started swearing right back at Chetvertak. She didn't back down at all—I actually think she outdid him.

Nadia was in prison for the first time but, as I said before, she was very bold. Despite the fact that everyone else in her cell had been in prison before, it was Nadia who had the most connections. The Russians called women like her "women with balls."

Chetvertak and Nadia's feud carried on for several days. Each was as stubborn as the other, and neither wanted to back down. In the end, though, Chetvertak was forced to give in. Nadia won through. All the feuding and screaming and shouting was getting in the way of letter-writing; it had attracted the guards' attention, so . . .

"Just write a few words to that cow, would you, before she screws everything up for us?" Chetvertak asked Pasha.

At first Pasha tried to stay out of the whole business with Nadia, but in the end he was forced to give in and write her a letter.

Pasha's letter to Nadia read as follows:

> Hello, Nadia, this is Pasha. I've been told you would like us to start writing to each other. I'm from the Rostov area. I'm twenty-two years old. This is my second conviction. I'm three years from release. I don't know what else to write. I kiss your lips.
>
> Your Pasha.

Nadia sent this reply:

> Dear Pashinka, I received your letter and to be honest you really piqued my interest, but the thing is, I'm eleven years older than

you. To me you're just a boy. Also, you have three years left on your sentence. You've still got some growing up to do but soon you'll be a man. You'll be twenty-five when you get out, and girls will be throwing themselves at you. You'll find yourself a nice young wife. So what do you want an old woman like me for? Pashinka, my dearest, let's just be friends and have a sincere relationship on those terms. Okay? Believe me, it's better this way, my child, and in response to your innocent kiss I send you a kiss on each of your lovely little cheeks, as a sister would to her brother.

Nadia.

Pasha read the letter, cleared his throat and started to pace up and down.

"Well? What does it say?" Chetvertak asked.

"She says she doesn't want love, she wants friendship!" Pasha replied.

"She doesn't want love, she wants friendship? She causes all that havoc, tells me to get the young guy to write to her—no old guys, mind—and then she turns you down? Show me!"

Pasha handed him the letter, and Chetvertak read it. "She's bullshitting."

"Do you think?" Pasha asked him.

"The stupid cow's bullshitting us! Write back, tell her to stop all this 'If it's love let it be love, and if it's lovely little cheeks let it be lovely little cheeks' crap. I'll give her lovely little cheeks! She must have lost her mind last week. She'd be better off just writing letters and keeping her head down, to give our ears a break for a bit, our poor little itty-bitty ears." Chetvertak laughed. "Oh, ladies, ladies, just what is it you're doing in our prison anyway? Prison is for us, for men! Prison's no place for women, is it? I'm right though, Pasha, aren't I?"

Pasha reassured him he was, and sat down at the greasy table with a pen and paper.

Nadia, I got your letter. You wrote that you were an old woman. You are not an old woman at all; you are just the age I like. So what if you're eleven years older than me? You're a woman in juice

(Russians always say "a woman in juice." Why, what it means, and what this juice is, even I, the author, do not know)

and you have your whole life ahead of you. I know that you're here on charges of embezzlement and that you're worried you'll be given a harsh sentence. But I'm sure you'll be freed very soon and then we'll be able to meet. They might change your charge and give you a lighter sentence, or they might grant you amnesty. You're a woman—they're bound to release you first. So stop this nonsense and write me a letter! I want you to know, though, that friendship isn't enough for me; I need your love like I need air to breathe. And if you won't let yourself love me I'll slit my wrists. Write to me, will you? I await your reply.

   With much love, Pasha.

Dear Pashinka, thank you for your letter which, if I'm honest, really moved me. Surely you are not really prepared to slit your wrists for my love? That was unexpected! It is such a shame that there are so few men willing to make a sacrifice like that for the love of a woman. Oh, if only men could show love like that on the outside too—but you have no time for us then. No, on the outside all you want to do is eat, drink, and hang around with your friends . . .

   Pasha, I was unfair to you! It's nothing to do with you, my little one; you are still so young and naïve, my little bird. I've held it in for so long but I can't hold it in anymore. Do I love you? Yes, I love you! I kiss your eyes, the top of your sweet head, your lovely little cheeks and your baby lips.

   Ever yours, Nadia."

When Nadia had finished writing the letter she smeared on some lip-stick, kissed the page several times so that Pasha would see the trace of her passionate lips, and then, for good measure, sprinkled on a few drops of perfume she'd stashed away.

Nadia's fragrant, lipstick-smeared letter had a great effect on Pasha and he gave it to Chetvertak rather proudly.

"Hm, those lips of hers aren't work-shy then!" Chetvertak's laugh was tinged with spite.

"Don't say such insulting things about a lady—that's the object of my desire you're talking about there!" Pasha replied, only half joking.

Pasha replied:

> Dear Nadia, thank you very much for loving me! I love you too, but please, don't call me your little bird anymore. Where on earth did that come from? The thing is, I might be transferred out of here soon with the next batch. You know I'm only here in transit. So wouldn't it be better if we got straight down to love and started writing each other more intimate letters? For a long time now I've wanted to write a letter in which we're really together. Let's dream a bit, in other words. If you agree then write to me and we'll dream together.
>
> With love from your Pasha.

And Nadia wrote back:

> Pashinka, first of all I need to tell you off for not letting me call you my little bird. Are you saying you're *not* my little bird? If you want my love remember everything must be as I want it to be, every-thing must be as I wish—and if not then I'll sulk, my little bird, my chick, my kitten, my little hatchling!
>
> As for the most intimate side of our relationship, I've been wait-ing for ages with a pounding heart for you to send me one of those letters. Write one, of course; you didn't need to ask. After all, we

love each other; whatever is natural is acceptable. I will say good-bye for now and kiss you—but I am sulking, so it'll only be on your little cheeks!

Your Nadia.

Pasha liked this a lot. He wrote back to his beloved one of the letters she wanted:

My dear Nadzinka, first of all let me tell you that you are my lady! You are my queen and my goddess! And so you can see me how-ever you like, my beautiful girl! You are so sensitive, you carry each little thing so close to your heart! So I beg your forgiveness. And now here I am, writing you that letter in which I dream we're together. You are my wife, we have a four-room apartment, a tele-vision, a refrigerator, a record player and even a washing machine. You are still sulking about the little bird thing. You glare at me, go into the bedroom, and shut the door behind you. My hearts starts to pound as I see your shadow under the door. You take off your dress and the rest of your clothes, then put on the nightgown and lie on the bed. I walk up and down the room for about fifteen minutes, then I open the refrigerator and eat some salad and drink a shot of vodka. After that I feel quite a bit braver and decide to come in to you, and open the door. And then there I am, lying next to you. You are lying on your side, with your back toward me, and of course you are not asleep, just pretending to be. Oh, how I want to hold you close, to make you forgive me, but I'm scared of you. Or rather, I'm not really scared of you, I just dare not. So I gently take my hand and lay it on your shoulder. Actually, I brush your shoulder very lightly with my fingertips, but you shrug me off. That means you're cross with me. You're punishing me. I've been found guilty. But I lay my hand on your shoulder a second time. This time more boldly, and I also pull you toward me, and very gently—and yet masterfully—hold you close. You stop resisting and surrender to me. I gently turn you over and lay you on your back. Then I start to caress you, to kiss you and to pull up your nightdress. Under your nightdress you've got nothing on. And then after that we do what Auntie Akulina and Uncle Kuzma do every night.

Your Pasha."

Nadia read this letter out loud to the other girls. They laughed for a very long time, and so loudly that the whole prison could hear them.

Nadia's reply:

My little Pashinka, it gave me great pleasure to read your letter, but there is one thing I don't understand. Why are we living in a four-room apartment but haven't got a car? And you write about us having a washing machine as if that means we've got a lot of possessions. Pasha, if you want me to be happy, build me a big two-story house, with a garage underneath. In the garage there should be two foreign cars, one for you and one for me. You're from Rostov, I know, so build the house on the banks of the Don. It's a good river, the Don. And look, dear Pashinka, we need a little pleasure boat. I love going down the river in a little boat, cutting through the waves! Waves . . . waves . . . Now let me tell you exactly what our house should be like. Our house should be very large, and along a hill. There should be something a bit unusual about everything—the shape of the rooms, the texture of the walls. There should be a balcony running around the outside that we can get to from any room in the house. There should also be a spiral staircase inside the house. On the first floor there'll be a drawing room where we'll entertain guests, and a kitchen, a bathroom, and a boiler room for heating the house. On the second floor there'll be bedrooms, a bar, a billiards room, and so on. Pashinka, I'm going to describe our bedroom in particular detail, especially the bed we're going to sleep on. It's a large room with a high ceiling and there should be a round bed taking up almost the whole room. As for the pillows, blankets, and bed linen in general, I'll sort that out. You don't need to worry yourself about that. Then, dear Pasha, you need to find a leopard skin from somewhere, because in the morning when I wake up and put my feet on the floor I must find a leopard skin under my feet. As for the rest of the furniture, I'll worry about that. You can leave all the crockery and linens to me too. Then I also need two maids, but old and unattractive obviously, because I'm a very jealous person and I know very well what men are like. You're all cheats, Don Juans. And also we should go traveling a lot . . .

I have decided to interrupt Nadia's letter here. Not just Nadia's letter but Nadia and Pasha's correspondence in general. Let me just tell you that in the course of this joke, this game, Nadia and Pasha really did fall in love. Unexpectedly, that naïve boy Pasha, who'd been in prison since his adolescence, fell in love with Nadia, considerably older, beautiful, and fiery. And this experienced woman fell in love with this naïve boy. It probably wouldn't happen like that on the outside, but the conditions inside prison are different from those outside. Prison puts people on equal terms. Several times a day they would send letters to each other, several times a day they would fight and make up again. Nadia was the more fanciful of the two. Sometimes she'd ask why he hadn't found her that leopard skin, sometimes why he wasn't wearing the fashionable clothes she'd bought him . . . Yes, that's how they lived; in fact, in that short time I think they even had children in their imaginary world.

Then the time came and they read Pasha's name out from the list of those being sent out with the next batch. He said good-bye to Nadia, to the other girls, to Chetvertak, to his cellmates, and went to the Gulag to serve the rest of his time. He took with him Nadia's letters, carefully wrapped, and the warmth they contained. And the line he'd put up remained in use by the prisoners for a very long time afterward.

MAKA MIKELADZE
A Story of Sex

Whoever you are, it wasn't you who told me I looked tired, told me I should go and have a break somewhere, get better, get my strength back. But one way or another, when seven million tourists visited Romania in nineteen sixty-something (if you don't believe me look it up), and the seven millionth tourist was me, you played your part, whoever you are.

Whoever you are, it wasn't you who turned up your nose, called Romania the most boring country in the whole of Europe, and said that if the tour wasn't passing through this godforsaken place you'd be having a much more relaxing time.

But the tour wasn't only passing through; we had five whole days in the country I'd so unfairly slandered. Our guide was Irina, patriotic and infectiously enthusiastic. One day the members of our tour group were having a chat with some locals.

"*Baia-mare, copșa-mică?*" (Would you like a coffee?)

"*Arad.*" (Don't go to any trouble.)

"*Gheorghe gheorghiu dej.*" (Where is my group?)

"*Tîrgu jiu?*" (How should I know?)

"*Călărași dragalina iași cerna babadag?*" (Are our red wines expensive?)

"*Pitești!*" (What a question!)

"*Oradea mogoşoaia mangalia rîmnicu-vîlcea turnu măgurele?*" (I mean, how can they not know how to speak Mingrelian in Romania?)

Whoever you are, you point out that these are names of Romanian towns, and you ask what kind of fool I take you for. It's true, I admit, but it's all we heard, day in, day out while we were stuck with Irina so we pretty much absorbed it all. We Georgians are clever like that, my friend. You have to admit it, whoever you are.

I was traveling on my own! For the first time in my life! I felt as if I was finding myself for the first time, I was a gypsy, roaming free. Dak-dak-dak, sang the wheels of the bus. Bessarabia–Transylvania, sang Irina. Dak-dak-dak, said the wheels. Sku-sku-sku, said Irina. I was traveling on my own! And even though there were constant reminders of home—the maize, wheat and rye, the sunflowers, the grapes of course, the sheep on the Carpathians and fish in the Danube, the churches—there was no sadness, no longing to go back. (What? What's wrong with that, whoever you are, for a short time at least?) I felt great. Fan*tas*tic, even.

I went a bit crazy—well, what do you expect? On the final day, in the final restaurant, as a final surprise they brought out a Romanian gypsy band. We were over the moon—what a party! The lone violinist raised his fiddle to his shoulder and gave it his all; we raised our arms to his fiddle and gave it *our* all. We stamped our heels, shouted, "Opa, hey!" and threw ourselves around the restaurant dance floor. We finished with a massive Romano-Georgian gypsy-esque circle dance and felt truly exhilarated as we sat in our seats back on the bus, on our way to our last Romanian hotel.

And that's where it started, and that's where it finished, the thing you say is beyond belief, whoever you are, the thing that could never *actually* happen, not really—and I would agree with you, if such a "thing" had not happened to me.

My heart first stopped, then skipped, then when I looked to see that person watching me I trembled. I couldn't breathe. I could barely take my eyes off them: it was a Romanian I'd seen earlier that day, standing dumbfounded, open-mouthed, pale, and wide-eyed—and wearing the uniform of the hotel.

I looked around for assistance. It was a plain lobby with armchairs dotted around to give it a cozy feel. I hid in one of them while I tried to compose myself. I had come over all dizzy, so don't reproach me, whoever you are, if I avoided looking at the wonderful creature who stood by the door. I tried to get myself together but just then, believe it or not, whoever you are, the group leader called me over.

"You're going to have a room to yourself tonight!"

"Me? Why?" It was a sign, and it scared me.

"Because you're traveling alone."

"Hold on, haven't I been traveling alone all along?" I tried to protect myself.

"Oh dear, had a bit too much to drink, have we?" the group leader said affectionately. "Look, in this hotel they've only got twin rooms and singles. Everywhere else they had twins and triples. Up till now we've been able to divide the group up with none left over; this time we can't. Do you get it? There's a remainder, isn't there? One left over." The way she explained it to me you'd think she was scolding a schoolchild.

The Romanian was still watching from afar, then came over purposefully and asked us in English if there was a problem. "You've put the difficult one in the single," the group leader said, handing me over like a package before disappearing.

"On your own?" the Romanian inquired, as if to ask what on earth was wrong with that—but with a voice that made my skin tingle as if an army of tiny ants was marching from my head to my toes and back again, and I never stopped pulsing, pulsing, all the time we were walking to my room. And don't ask me how, whoever you are, but I know it's not just me who felt that way. We arrived in silence at the scene of the crime, opened the door and . . . I was left alone. I was cleft in two. Alone again, I thought.

In that wine-colored single room stood a cream-colored bed—clearly a double—buried under a pile of pillows. I dropped my bags, went out onto the balcony and filled my lungs with the aroma of the summer-turned-to-autumn and looked up at the sky, seeing in it all too clearly a portent of the night's inevitable events to come: the creamy full moon hung there like a nomad in the burgundy night and next to it, barely visible in the haze of my focus, a second nomad-moon. One moon hung there like a spider, ready with its tender, tortuous web of yearning. The second, the spider-moon that permits no sleep but only that which should not be permitted, has not descended but stays higher, swinging in the sky. I went back in, sat on the edge of the bed and because I couldn't think of anything better to do blew cigarette smoke toward those amorous moons, a drifting fog of tenderness and yearning. I was no longer thinking about the Romanian; doing so would be about as worthwhile as sticking my fingers in an electrical socket.

We do not want didactic motifs in our creative works. Do not dare reproach me, whoever you are—I managed to wait until half past three (in the morning, of course) before I went out into the corridor which, if you are a pessimist, was plunged into a dark blue gloom or, if you're an optimist, was illuminated to a light blue, and there, sitting in the very same armchair I had hidden in earlier on, was . . .

By chance.

Yes, just by chance. And just by chance also staring up at the sky with an otherworldly stare, trying to disentangle the moon from a tree-branch web of tenderness and yearning. And holding the key to my room.

We were not surprised to see each other, nor were we particularly glad. This was just how it was supposed to happen.

"What do you want that for?" I nodded my head toward the key.

I got only a shrug in response.

"The door's already open . . ."

And then a strange reaction: I saw a tear well up, and then I saw a nod. It did the trick—I felt us come closer together and my heart flooded with the desire for even more intimacy.

Why was this Romanian so familiar? Why so familiar? I replayed the day in my mind.

It was not I who opened the door, it was unrestrained happiness, of the grapes-piled-high-on-a-platter variety. The giggling full moons fixed their eyes on me and I did something very silly. I didn't make it clear what I wanted. I didn't make it clear my door was open. I didn't dare. I just breathed in and stood there.

We suddenly felt so aware of our difference.

First we could not agree on a language. I went along with the suggestion that we shouldn't use Russian. Definitely not, whoever you are; if you drag me into some political polemic who the hell's going to finish the job?

We realized there wasn't a single language or dialect we could converse in properly (apparently Romanians really *don't* know Mingrelian).

Through fragmented foreign languages we just about worked out who had studied or taught at which university, who did what to make ends meet and who was providing for their parents. We had to switch to our only common tongue, but nothing came good of that either: our kisses were somehow shy and confused; stunned, we stared fixedly at each other across the blackened coffee table that formed a neutral zone between us. The air buzzed with tension.

"This isn't good," I thought to myself, "a pause in proceedings like this can't possibly be a good sign."

The telephone came to our rescue.

"Excuse me, may I speak to the solitary ghost of sleep?" somebody shouted down the phone in Georgian at me. "Are they in? Give 'em the phone, they're needed in Room 17. There's a great party in danger of ending early if they don't get here soon!"

"Drunks!" I called into the receiver, trying to sound as sleepy as I could. "Can't you let me sleep?" I hung up.

"What a beautiful language!" the Romanian said. I held my breath. Once again I sensed the presence of the moon spider. I turned my phone off. I went to the fridge and took out a bottle of wine I'd put there earlier with remarkable foresight.

"I've drunk this wine somewhere before," my guest noted.

"So have I." It was nonsense, but somehow it sounded like wisdom dictated by heaven.

It went quiet. We needed to kiss, I decided. I held a grape between my teeth, then bit down, pop! The sweet liquid flows into my mouth, warmed by my fingers and lips. The moons giggle and melt onto my tongue. Again, again. I sip some wine. We are silent, we are together, we feel good . . .

And then the door. Bang, bang, bang!

"Arise, accursed one, you land of thirsty slaves!" Half the group started hammering on the locked door.

"It's an invasion!"

"Invaders!" I shouted at the same time, outraged.

I mean, what kind of time was this for a history trip, whoever you are?

A hasty gesture: "Don't open it!" I signaled back: "I'll send them away." I wrapped a towel around my head and threw on a dressing gown. I half-stuck my body through the half-opened door as if to say, "I've just had a shower, leave me alone." They wrestled with the door a bit and swore at me a bit. They took my photograph, and said, "Ah, you traitor!" They left, sure I'd enjoyed their jollity as much as they had, and disappeared down the corridor.

Whoever you are, you will surely have heard how tension can heighten the madness of love. As I was locking the door I suddenly became filled with such burning desire that I could already feel deep within my bones the sensation of those flame-red lips meeting and moistening mine, and those blazing chestnut eyes. My mouth went dry. My breathing quickened, my heart started thumping, was this it? . . . This, was this it? . . . Right now? But it was a cigarette the Romanian reached for.

What else could I do? I went into the bathroom and surrendered my randy flesh and hot head to the water.

Braila, Blaj, Deva, Tekuchi, Barlad, Zalau, Hundoara, Siret, Bistrita, Dodenlt, Brodina, the water caressed me and, whoever you are, you must at least admit that I know my geography, especially the names of Romania's rivers. Between you and me, you're not bad either—nobody can get anything past you.

The first warm drop fell onto my chest, the second ran from my neck down my back and disappeared in between two mounds. The water flowed through my jet-black hair, burbled as it washed my body clean, and my flesh, my nerves and muscles, tense and taut with expectation, did not slacken but suddenly tightened further. I washed myself down, purring, groaning weakly, and submitted to the flowing water.

The door opened. I jumped and turned my back. I don't like people seeing me from the front when I'm naked. I remembered too late that I don't like people seeing from behind either, and even less so with the lights on. I was angry. I turned the jet of cool water on the Romanian, trying in vain to put the fire out, drenching, drenching from head to foot. A laugh, and then the door was closed again. And so, I turned the water off. We'd both be undressed now, at least.

Now, though, whoever you are, ohhhhhh, don't let me hear a peep out of you!

Waiting for me on the cream-colored bed was an equally sun-starved body. The cream bedspread had fallen onto the floor and made a cream-colored path to flesh-colored-wine-colored bliss.

And oh, how waiting seems to intensify desire, to make it almost tangible! The most important touch is the very first . . . The nightshirt dropped onto the floor, and then the towel. I pulled my legs up onto the bed. We lay back, stretched ourselves out. And now to feel the skin . . . While we enjoyed each other's nakedness the moon gave itself over to contemplation (unlike certain people) and sought the favor of the clouds. Finally we were alone . . . (unless you count certain people).

Passionate hands roamed as if totally free over the other's flesh from earlobe down to fingertips. The other's blazing lips plunged deep into the cleft between my collarbones. It was exactly what we were supposed to do . . . Somewhere something clicked into place, everything lit up, darkened, united, separated, and became a haze of cream and wine.

And so it began.

No, it was not wild, raw sex. Yet. It was us becoming acquainted, cautiously, ardently.

Ohhh, oh oh, a lip. And ohhhh, an ear lobe, a shoulder, and ah, ahhh, a neck. And here, oh, the spine, the first vertebra, the second, the seventh, the eleventh, twenty-fourth—oh and the small of the back. It's warm, it's so warm, sweet pain, and yes, and again. Eyes, oh, and temples and ohhhhhh-hhhhhh that tongue . . . And going inside feels like achieving great insight, it feels like knowing . . . Gently, gently, gently . . . and again . . . again, yes, yes! . . . Hold on . . . Hold on . . . I think . . . I think . . . Yes . . . I . . . I'm . . . Ah—ah—ahhhhhhhhhhhh!

The first time for those two hot, blind, deaf-mute teenagers. Mutual consolation for Adam and Eve after their expulsion from heaven. At the end of this introduction to passion I breathed a sigh of relief. Nothing had gone wrong.

I carefully opened my eyes. Under the tree branches, which spread their shadows out across the wine-colored walls, the triangular roofs of the houses and the pointed cupola had turned a deeper hue. The bed was bathed in light. The shameless moons—but no, it was now one moon—stared at us with its single eye, filled with fine, translucent joy by our union. The separation of our bodies-become-one-in-soul-and-body still remained undone. For a while we carried on our explorations, our "Oh, oh, your cheek, your shoulder, the tip of your nose." We laughed. And both of us had light and warmth in our eyes.

Ah, it's been so long since I last thought of you, whoever you are. Don't be upset, though, all right? Do you know how good I felt? Oh, if you only knew, if you only knew . . .

I fell asleep, content. In the last years of the nineteen sixties I had the forbidden dream. Even as I slept I became fearful that the secret police would call me in for questioning, that is if the group leader managed to jot down my dream in time, if I didn't throw water on this vision.

It was as if the streets of Tbilisi were full of Rambos, Nikitas, and Ninja Turtles. Faces full of anger, they raised their clenched fists skyward. They were waving flags with slogans I couldn't make out and shouting out things I couldn't understand.

As soon as I opened my eyes I heard the Romanian whispering about a dream where people gathered in front of the parliament, faces full of anger, raising their fists skyward and shouting, "Ceauşescu! Ceauşescu!"

"I dreamed exactly the same!" I said, rather alarmed.

"What were your lot doing that for? What were they shouting?"

You should have seen the confusion on my face, whoever you are, when I remembered that "my lot" were shouting "Ceauşescu, Ceauşescu" too— and anyway, things worked out well for your lot, just as we saw in our dream . . . But we agreed, didn't we, not to talk politics? And let's not make those wasted words, come on; let's go back to bed.

"It's pointless having this many pillows," I decided and placed one affectionately over the Romanian's straw-colored face. Revenge came quickly— a pillow fight and yelling.

"*Dinu dilanu dani amadace tataru!*" Cream-colored pillows flew all over the room.

Whoever you are, you must have guessed by now how it finished, this passion-fueled, breathless, laughter-filled duel. But better to hear it from a witness than merely speculate.

"*Mocanu reducanu lucescu lupescu dumitru!*" With this battle cry my partner pounced on my lips, enraged.

Oy! You're just waiting to catch me out, whoever you are! So what if I'm just naming Romanian soccer players? Nobody can even tell a little lie anymore out of fear of you? Have I missed something?

In short, all hell broke loose.

We laughed, made dirty jokes, wrestled. One of us would leap on the other's back and shoulders, the other would perform a thigh throw. If at first we nipped and clawed like prancing puppies, gradually our play became more ruthless, more heated. We became vicious and merciless. An embrace came to resemble a choke, instead of caressing we clawed at flesh. But entering, penetrating, was like reaching in, reaching to the heart of the matter, demolishing, breaching, ruining, destroying. I could hear the gnashing and grinding of teeth and bones, arms thrown down. I wanted to cry out—Osmali! Barbarossa!—but was ambushed, torn at by that red-hot, inhuman groaning that welled up in my throat behind my writhing tongue. Bang-bang-bang-bang!—we banged, the headboard banged. In my mouth I tasted steel, honey, beer, and blood. I wanted to break free and struggled and fought, the other wanted to break free too, and struggled and fought. War, again! Defeat and temporary victory, again. We tore at the arms that clutched at us, tore at them as if they were manacles. Both of us ravaged and destroyed. Thr-thr-thr-thrace . . . bl-bl-bl-blockade . . . thirst . . . blizzard . . . Goths, Huns, Avars . . . Again defeat, again victory . . . War again, again? We'd had enough, we were tired. We were in chaos, disheveled, fragmented, united, ravaged . . . And when the light finally came spilling into this black abyss—Ahhhh!—my eye again escaped toward the wall. The shadows of our bodies, drained of all vitality, bore a passing resemblance to slaughtered lions piled on top of each other. As one we threw ourselves onto our backs and died.

As soon as I got my strength back I reached for the wine. "Well, I *am* Georgian!" I said. The Romanian was lying with eyes closed and smiling. "Dacia!" I suddenly realized, and faded into infinity in a cloud of dust and ashes.

It was worth giving up one's life for a death like that. Even if we had no weapons in our hands at least we met our deaths on the battlefield, and were joined together for eternity. Imagine, whoever you are, if I had listened to teachers, and actually learned my history, geography, music, and the D major arpeggio properly. But if I had listened to Irina properly what monumental visions I would have seen in those moments of passion.

What is the function of intellect? Shame on you, whoever you are, could you not guess? Or do you think this story is about the friction between human bodies and not sex at all? It's an arguable question! But let's not argue and I'll tell you everything.

I was very cold. I wrapped myself up in my blanket and my thoughts.

During a restless night I witnessed a kind of mystical return from the depths—the Romanian began to sing with closed eyes, and in that voice the reed pipe and folk flute began to give out plaintive groans. The *chimpoi* and *bechumi* buzzed with life. The smoldering tune of a ballad, or a shepherds' song, or a song from times of drought or rain flooded like warmth into my heart—the earth was breathing. The mandolin, cymbal, and zither brought the strings to life and when the violin broke free too, the shadows cast on the wall by the trees started up a circle dance, turned into those Romanian wine-growers and put their calloused arms around each other like branches. Their calloused feet, like roots, squeezed out the grapes in the wine press with dancing and shouting. The *hora* turned into the *sirba*. Everything became life and noise. The shadows, ghosts, thoughts, breath began to sway. My blood was set on fire, it twitched and fitted with exotic rhythms, turned into exotic wine. Soon the strangely familiar sun gave us the first sign that it was rising. The moon paled against the moon-colored sky.

"You and me and you and me and you and me and the dispossessed moon!" Noticing me bid farewell to my nocturnal witness, the Romanian seemed to be singing me a lyrical song.

In fairness I should have sung it too: "You are good, I am good, the moon is good too," but I came to my senses at just the right time. I linked our hands together and kept my silence.

"Now you sing." The Romanian smiled at me.

I should mention that I, a little Georgian child of the Caucasus mountains, cannot tell one song from another. How that can be I do not know.

I stayed where I was. Rather than risk humiliation for the sake of my country I simply said, "I don't know." Then I opened my mouth to say, "I'll sing later," and . . .

I couldn't believe my ears. I was singing an old Mingrelian folk song. I stood up in surprise and started to sing more loudly. The wetness of the swamp and wild honey flowed out of my throat in a torrent. I saw two slate-gray oxen hauling off a cart carrying the pitch-black night back toward its home among the woodrush at Tutarchela, three daughters standing heads held proud and singing with their well-tuned voices, cradling a Georgian lute like a newborn child. A lullaby. The smell of fresh fish and yearning carried in on the breeze and oh, hush, lullay lullay . . . And woe to you if you doubt for a second that I sang with a voice as sweet as a nightingale's, with my eyes shut tight like a warbler and how I wished—yes, this is wishing too—oh, how I wished this bliss would never end . . . Suddenly I started singing words and a tune I did not even know. I sang, "Your church is made of wood and mine of mortared stone," I sang, "The stallion and the dark gray horse," I sang, "Both are from a golden breed," I sang, "Where no one exists," "A boy and girl go a-humming." And tears started flooding out. I was crying!

As quickly as the song had come, it disappeared.

That's exactly what I was telling you about, whoever you are. That is the "thing" I never thought could really happen. Wait—what did you think I meant?

With deep regret I opened my eyes and found the Romanian no longer in my room. I was surprised that I hadn't heard the door. I probably felt that by then we were tangled within a single web. For a long time I watched how the heavens turned to rose, how the roofs turned slate-gray, how the cupolas began to shine bright gold. How a porcelain town edged with lace rose up from lace-edged clouds. In the porcelain bell tower porcelain bells were ringing. The weathervane spun in the flame-colored rays . . .

I went out onto the balcony in my birthday suit. It must have rained. The wet pavement was a burnished red. In front of the hotel a red fountain danced and red roses smoldered. The Romanian! Oh God, oh almighty God . . . The Romanian was standing naked in the fountain wearing a crown of red roses, and was weaving me a crown too.

The warbling of birds and the ringing of bells pierced the sky.

I had thought that rushing out naked onto my balcony was heroic, but what my Romanian was daring to do—it was like Kantaria raising the banner of victory over the Reichstag or the daring of the anti-Hitler patriotic front! . . . The penetrating stare of our hotel administrator would have melted steel—we were probably only saved by the fact that even alert owls doze at dawn.

With light still in my heart I looked over to the rose harvest and when my Romanian looked at me my soul flew up to the heavens. If I ever become skilled enough in narrative to be able to describe those eyes I'll be born again, I know it.

The red rose crown sat on my head. The red fountain took us higher, higher, and higher still. When everything was as hot as bubbling lava, our lips began to buzz and hum, our bodies turned to wax. They merged together. The breast of one, the chest of the other, the lips of one and the tooth of another, the eye of one and the eyelash of the other, the heart of one and the ear of the other—our gaze, our feelings, our thoughts—each and every kiss began to speak and there were no limits anymore. A dying, a destruction. Every exhalation became a hymn, every inhalation a holy Eucharist. The horizon took on the blue-green hue of Georgian and Romanian icons, and a figure with a white beard and robes appeared to me, the scent of incense wafted over me and with a slight Romanian accent he said to me in Georgian, "He took me to the house of wine and hoisted his flag as a sign of love." Anthim the Iberian! I was immeasurably happy. "I am also mortal, like everyone else, descended from man, flesh of earthly offspring, sculpted in a mother's womb." He wagged his finger at me. He smiled at me and vanished.

On my return the entering and the penetration resembled escape. Taking leave. Again, maybe . . . I don't think so . . . When, pray? . . . I want to be with you again . . . Maybe, who knows? . . . But how? . . . From where, and why? . . . Let's not let it end . . . I'll always love you, I'll love you always. Alas, never again.

You said it: it's a good thing I wasn't led astray by a Russian or we would never have managed to get through all the leaders, poet-kings and king-poets we have in common.

It was time to leave.

We got dressed in silence, packed in silence, sat on the edge of the bed in silence . . .

As the Romanian turned to go out of the door an idea came to me. I got to my feet. The Romanian was startled. And so was I . . . and the two of us each put a finger to the other's lips. Well, would it have been as beautiful if we had got out our notebooks and started exchanging addresses?

Because of the way the bus pulled out, we didn't see each other again.

"*Abrud brad*"—come back, come back—the Romanian shouted silently.

"*Rigișoara, timișoara!*" My ribcage almost burst apart. "Out of sight, out of mind. And the farther you are, the farther, the farther you are . . ."

Now, whoever you are, you ask me this: "Why is this story about sex and not love? Am I not present there too?" Well, it's for commercial reasons.

Yes, really. And because I know your story I even told you that this tale was untranslatable. Of course, it's not worth the paper it's written on if the language betrays with the first *he* or *she* which of us was the woman and which was the man. In fact, how do you even know it *was* a man and a woman, anyway?

Is all this too much? How many times should I say it: let's not argue, eh? We love each other very much, don't we? You, and whoever I am.

AKA MORCHILADZE
Once Upon a Time in Georgia

I. SERGIO

One day, a rumor started—Sergio Leone was doing a remake of *Gone with the Wind* and had said he'd be filming part of it in Georgia.

I can't remember whether it was in the newspapers or not, but the rumor started going around nonetheless.

I can't remember what year it was either; there was so much in the papers back then it would be impossible to remember a detail like that.

Broadly speaking, it was a time when people were more interested in what the papers had to say about the old news—perestroika and things like that.

Although maybe we didn't actually call it perestroika until a bit later on.

In any case, it can't have been any later than 1989. Because that was the year that Sergio Leone died. In other words, the story took place back when everything was just beginning, before the upheaval, the misfortune, and the chaos.

So anyway, word got around that Sergio Leone was remaking *Gone with the Wind*.

We'd already come across Margaret Mitchell's two-part saga by that point; you could buy it at the Kirov Park book stalls, along with hundreds of other Russian books. And even before that we'd seen the movie—I don't remember the year—which was already out on video by the time they showed it on TV, rather pointlessly, right in the middle of all the events of perestroika. Clark Gable, Vivien Leigh, and all that other stuff.

In short, Sergio Leone had decided do a remake. Rumor had it he was going to pull out all the stops and he'd chosen Georgia as the setting for some of the scenes.

How and why he came to that decision I do not know.

I don't even think he had ever been to the Soviet Union.

That autumn two English men had come to Tbilisi and taken a load of photos all over the old part of town, Sololaki. They were saying something about filming the Paris scenes from Somerset Maugham's *The Moon and Sixpence* there, and they were going through reels like you wouldn't believe. Leone, on the other hand, made his decision just like that, with barely a second thought. Come on, let's film it there—and that was that. But back then any positive news about Georgia was greeted universally with the same kind of joy you get from a fairy-tale happy ending. In other words, nobody was all that surprised.

Because Sergio Leone was already our uncle, brother, teacher, and many, many more things he could never have imagined, and since he had decided to film *Gone with the Wind* it seemed obvious that he'd have to use Georgia, because Georgia's scenery was an absolute godsend for filmmakers.

Quite why it was a godsend I don't know. One thing I've heard is that cinematographers don't like shooting in summer because the green floods the screen. I don't really know what it means for green to flood the screen—probably that the background gets in the way of the shot, or something like that.

To tell you the truth, I'd never seen a photo of Sergio Leone. They'd never printed one in the papers. Back then it was difficult to find photos of foreigners. But for some reason I thought he must be quite a big guy. I'd seen Sam Peckinpah's photo, but not Leone's. I wouldn't be surprised if I was getting the two of them mixed up in this story.

We didn't realize it back then, but our perception of the outside world was very interesting. Well, not really our perception of the outside world—I didn't even have one—but the perception some Georgian people had of it, which is something we can really only guess at.

To be honest, I only had a very vague idea of what they thought of us abroad and what we thought of them. Those were difficult days for Borjomi—the mineral water, not the spa town. Personally, I had high hopes for it, because perestroika was starting and somehow we were going to free ourselves from the Russians. People were coming out with all sorts of things.

Some wondered how we would ever protect ourselves without the Russians, and said we would die of hunger; others said we could sell Borjomi to foreign countries to sell in their pharmacies. Some people mentioned exporting mandarin oranges. One guy even told me there were arsenic deposits in Racha and gold in Kazreti. And that turned out to be true . . . But even though I've never once seen Borjomi in a pharmacy abroad, back then I really believed that foreigners were taking curative spoonfuls of something we drank by the gallon everyday.

In fact, if people had heard of us at all it was because of the Sukhishvili Ballet, who traveled all over the world. They were especially well-known among the Japanese, probably because the Japanese are also a unique people with a love of ancient culture. When glasnost began you couldn't buy any alcohol other than beer before two P.M. This was strictly controlled and taken very seriously. A waitress once told my friend and me how she used to pour champagne from plain carafes—after all, it was only apple juice, she said—but one man and his lady friend recorded it for evidence anyway. That's the kind of country it was—champagne in carafes.

I really don't remember the exact year, but it was around the time that everyone was talking about Bob Dylan and De Niro. I can't remember which one came to Georgia first, either.

Bob Dylan came as a guest of the Writers' Union. There was a youth festival taking place in Moscow at the time and apparently he'd gone to that, but then they sent him here and because he was a poet the local writers sent a representative to meet him. At the Writers' Union he read them a piece about homosexuality, half-jokingly.

I think this was probably just a twist on that story they used to tell in the old days about the group of beatniks who came to Tbilisi, also as guests of the Writers' Union; they also read out something obscene, and it was up to Irakli Abashidze to respond to it with great wit and skill.

To be honest I don't really know about either of those things, and I don't actually believe that Ginsberg and his friends were ever here at all. Although practically everyone's been to Tbilisi, so what do I know? Even when it only had a hundred thousand inhabitants you could search for days for the most famous people in the whole country and still not find them—it's just that kind of city. So as it got bigger and bigger you simply couldn't be sure who had or hadn't been here, especially as the newspapers never reported anything and when you switched on the TV all you would see was concerts in honor of Soviet workers, where such-and-such a piece had been requested by so-and-so from Chumlaki Collective Farm.

In other words, Tbilisi is more a city of legend and stories than concrete things like meetings, even though in fact everybody's always bumping into everybody else.

The news about Bob Dylan was nothing but positive: he liked it here, he'd been to the hilltop church at Jvari, looked down and admired the site where the Mtkvari and Aragvi rivers meet, bought a few cassettes . . .

Cassettes of folk songs were a vital component of any story about a foreigner who'd liked it here. Even B. B. King had taken a selection of Georgian folk music back with him.

God, that was wonderful news. We thought it was a sign of something that didn't happen anywhere else.

Stalin loved Georgian folk songs and sometimes Ukrainian folk songs too.

People were less complimentary about De Niro. Apparently he'd given a bad interview about us after he left. People said he didn't like it here. They said he got upset about a calf being killed for him. I always thought it was a calf, anyway, although others said it was something to do with them skinning a sheep.

Could that story be true? I really don't know. They also said a couple of unknown—probably nonexistent—socialites had tried to entice, nay, drag him into bed but that he'd refused and then complained about it in an interview . . . Well, what can I tell you? I wasn't there.

I know one thing though, and that is how one girl managed to get De Niro's autograph.

She got him to autograph a video cassette. Back then if you saw De Niro it was always on video; his movies weren't being shown in theaters yet. The cassette belonged to my friend, and it was the very video on which I first saw De Niro. At the time the girl was working at the art museum and knew De Niro was due to visit. A crowd had gathered outside and as they cleared a temporary path to the car for De Niro the crowd roared, and right at that moment my friend thrust the cassette and a pen at him. He looked down at the cassette, rather surprised, looked at the girl, thought for a moment, and wrote, "Hello, Robert De Niro," as they ushered him into the car.

The most important thing was the cassette and, as a general rule, if there's one thing we Georgians know how to do properly it's the unexpected.

Some people think it's feasting and singing that flow through our veins but what we're actually best at is the unexpected. That is how it seems to foreigners, anyway, because we are a nation that revels in transformation and change.

And the cassette was the most important thing because it had *The Deer Hunter* written on it. That was Michael Cimino's movie about the Vietnam War, about young American mineworkers of Russian descent. It starred De Niro himself, Meryl Streep, Christopher Walken and John Cazale.

At the time, I think I watched that movie more than anything Soviet-made. As they said back then, it was a great anti-Soviet movie, but not in a crude, clumsy way—the subject matter alone made it so. Anyway, De Niro must have known that, right? Surely you can't think that this young man and woman did what they did and that De Niro didn't know? They said he looked shocked, and would have been even more shocked if the situation hadn't been so tense and he hadn't had to get into the car. Maybe he wanted to write something different, they said, but just couldn't decide on the spot.

That's what the country was like. No information at all, and so our understanding and our mindset rested on fictions.

Something like that De Niro autograph, the American flag, a Lennon poster, or I don't know what else represented something authentic and good: nobody really gave it much thought beyond that.

My father's friend arrived from Paris with a thousand things to tell us.

What had surprised him, he said, was that there were some sort of buns all over the streets (probably half-eaten hamburgers, which still hadn't reached us at that point) and one smartly dressed man had come along, picked one up, cleaned it and put it in his pocket. I was so surprised, because we still had some standards with regard to this kind of thing. The man said that as far as he could see life was actually pretty hard over there. "It's not that hard," I said. I didn't like his story.

One rather cool thing I had was a tourist booklet from the White House with a photo of Ronald and Nancy on the cover.

I say, "I had"—I've still got it now, actually.

My Ronald Reagan.

You'll laugh. I never gave that booklet away because I thought that if Reagan was all right we would be all right too and that, in the end, those Communists would be defeated.

I kept the booklet between the glass doors on my bookshelves. It's still there now and always will be.

Anyway, one day the election women came over.

Election women were people who brought polling cards and reminded us to come to the Sunday election. I'm talking about Soviet elections. Again, I don't remember what year it was. I was the only one home and they left the polling cards with me. Anyway, they paused for a moment by the Reagan family photo and were quite delighted. They were just ordinary, cheery-faced ladies of a certain age. "Look, Reagan's photo," one said, "and in color, too." I made up some rubbish: "My father brought it back from America." When she heard that she was even more excited. "What was your father doing in America? Oh, such a fine woman, and I think the man dyes his hair." "They look after themselves," the other one said. "They don't even go gray."

But this story's about Sergio Leone, and you probably want me to get the point.

Next, Billy Joel came too. But firstly, Billy Joel didn't have the kind of name and fame as De Niro and Bob Dylan, and secondly, by then the state had already screened his performances on TV—Billy Joel walking down Rustaveli Avenue, Billy Joel signing young men's shirts, Billy Joel rehearsing at the Opera . . . Nothing was secret anymore. There were photos of his wife in Georgian dress hanging in the windows of an art studio on Rustaveli Avenue itself. I think it was the first picture advertisement—albeit black and white—we'd ever seen. She was Miss America, if I'm not mistaken.

Then came Ian Gillan with his shaven-headed wife and their wedding, Suzi Quatro with her bass guitar—but again, the state had already aired their concerts on TV.

But the older ones, the ones from before, weren't on TV, and they weren't doing concerts either.

The story about De Niro and the killing of the calf, though, is probably an echo of an earlier story from the time Jawaharlal Nehru was in Tbilisi and they presented him with a whole roast deer. Apparently he declined and went out to stand on the balcony until they took the meat away from the table. I don't know which story *that* is an echo of.

With foreigners you just never know, as people used to say here.

Could you imagine perestroika steaming ahead and Margaret Thatcher not coming? They took her to the main square. The whole of Chavchavadze Avenue was lined with fluttering British flags. I really wanted to get one down but you had to find someone from the regional police to give you one after they'd been taken down. Apparently some people tried to climb up and get one themselves and got dragged away by the police. I really couldn't climb that high. Turashvili wrote a great story about those flags.

Anyway, it seemed especially significant that Reagan was an actor. Back then there was a particular TV program that used to come on whenever they were screening soccer games. During halftime they would bring out respectable international journalists to make fun of the fact that he was an actor. I often wondered what kind of country it was where an actor could become president. A free country, my father would say, but I didn't really understand what he meant. A country like that simply wouldn't exist, he said, without laws to first ensure he was a decent and proper man.

Eventually we got two of Reagan's movies—both very simple Westerns—but I think by the time we got them Reagan was no longer president. Some people even said he was in *The Magnificent Seven*. I never believed them, though, because to this day I know off by heart who played who in that movie. I think the people who said it were talking about Charles Bronson, who played Bernardo O'Reilly: they probably thought Reagan had his eyes.

One day a guy from my neighborhood came up to me and said, "Oh, you won't believe what I've seen." When I asked him what, he said he'd seen the real *Magnificent Seven*, the one with Reagan in it. He was making it up, of course—in the absence of real information we all relied on fantasy instead. I told him there was no such movie, and he said he'd seen it, so there must be. It must be a different *Magnificent Seven*, he said. There was a sequel, actually, with only Yul Brynner in. In fact there were ten *Magnificent Seven* films in all. Well, that's what people said, anyway.

Call it perestroika, call it what you like—not once did I ever see anything in the movie theaters that was critical of the regime, like *Repentance*. No, they didn't release that until I was at university, but by then I'd already seen it at home. My friend's father's friend brought it over on video. He was a well-known man and ended up losing his post. Anyway, when he saw the gang of youths waiting to watch it he almost changed his mind. He wanted to see it himself though, and back then there weren't all that many VCRs around, and fewer still among people you were sure you could trust. My friend's dad said to him, "Let them watch it; they really should see it. We know it all anyway." So, down came the window blinds . . . It was the first time I'd ever seen older people behave like that. And we didn't even know what they were talking about and what it was we had to see.

We sat down and watched it.

I think perestroika started very soon after.

One summer they fired everyone at the Merani publishing house because it printed the original document of an anti-Soviet poem written by Kolau Nadiradze in the book *The Thousand Lines of a Poet*: "Snow fell, Tbilisi wore a shroud of black, Sioni stood silent, its people struck dumb." The poem was called *25 February 1921*. I don't know the details, but it was all done very deliberately and openly. It was a green book; I still remember it now.

Anyway, back then, the discussion about what De Niro did and didn't like was on a completely different level. Completely different. But these two discussions didn't interfere with each other; in fact, they actually helped each other. One was fantasy, the other one reality.

But as we come to the end of this introduction let me mention Sergio Leone one more time, because Sergio Leone died without ever knowing what effect he was to have on Georgia. Because behind the Soviet gossip and the liberal movement there existed a much more powerful and invisible system in place, which had already been around for an unimaginably long time.

Yes, let's tell the story of Sergio Leone and one or two others, real or imaginary.

II. Noodles, I Slipped

Once, on a school trip (I think) to Qvareli (I think) in Kakheti (I think), I saw a statue I have never forgotten and will never forget.

Unfortunately I don't know where the statue is now. It's just like that table which used to stand in Tabakhmela post office that they said had once belonged to the writer Nikoloz Baratashvili.

But the statue itself turned out to be completely unforgettable.

To tell you the truth, I only remember two statues from the old days, apart from the ones of Lenin: the first was a large yellow bust of the writer Alexander Kazbegi in the foyer of the Kazbegi cinema, and the second was this one.

This statue wasn't even displayed properly; it stood on a rear balcony, or somewhere half hidden like that, because times had changed and nobody really wanted to have things like that on display anymore.

It wouldn't surprise me at all if in the old days that statue had stood where the monument to the writers Ilia Chavchavadze and Akaki Tsereteli stands today, in front of School No. 1. But clever and thoughtful people decided where to position statues, and they took great care in doing so. Back then, putting that statue of Ilia and Akaki—who so openly supported Georgian self-determination—in front of School No. 1 was probably considered a great act of patriotism. Our kind of patriotism, of course, the kind of hidden patriotism that was so widespread in the Communist era.

Or maybe it's just that nobody had thought of putting a monument in front of School No. 1 until then.

But anyway, I seem to remember I was in the Ilia Chavchavadze Museum in Qvareli, and was probably about twelve years old.

The statue was white, or rather off-white, with a glossy sheen, and was as unexpected as it could possibly have been. I had never—well, rarely—seen anything that unexpected.

Ilia was seated in an armchair. Leaning slightly to one side and smiling, he was looking with hope-filled eyes toward a young man who, if I remember correctly, was standing to his left and slightly forward, and who was holding in the palm of his hand an open book and staring into space. The boy had neatly combed hair, a simple, belted smock and big eyes. If I'm not mistaken, Ilia was touching the boy lightly with his hand as if to push him toward the future. Believe it or not, the boy was a young Stalin—

Soselo, as they called him—whose poem was printed in Chavchavadze's own newspaper *Iveria*.

They taught us that poem at school. *Iveria* very rarely printed poems, on the whole.

But that's irrelevant. I remembered the statue because it was the best expression I'd seen of something which often happens here: suddenly somebody decides to try and connect together things that cannot be connected, and with this as their goal they press doggedly onward without ever looking back.

Is there, I wonder, a place where Stalin is connected not to Ilia but to Sergio Leone?

As yet I can't say with any certainty whether such a connection is even possible. Maybe in the end everything comes to resemble that statue, but anyway I suspect that such a connection probably did exist somewhere. Let's see if we can't find out where.

Somewhere hidden, to be sure, but let's try to find it anyway. I think it might even be fun.

But now it's time for another question:

When did Gorbachev and Reagan meet in Reykjavik?

It was spring, I think. It must have been the spring of 1986, in fact. Reagan stood on the veranda and smiled as he waited for Gorbachev, who turned up wearing a hat.

I remember that day because they showed it on the news, and as soon as the news had finished we put on a movie. Somebody had brought the video over to my friend's house, and we'd actually skipped lectures to watch it because it was long, very long indeed.

The movie was *Once Upon a Time in America*, and if you ask me, the only reason we hadn't watched it sooner was that we'd heard so much about it from everyone who'd already seen it and wouldn't stop talking about it— it's six hours long, it's got De Niro in it, blah blah blah.

Anyway, before we eagerly sat down with our cigarettes to watch it that morning, we saw Reagan and Gorbachev on TV. In other words, the day we watched that movie was a historic day—although I have to admit that

I didn't watch all the way to the end; I left early for some reason. Maybe I had to go somewhere, or something like that. I can't really remember.

In any event, we seemed to be watching it for hours. I thought it would never end and to this day I still don't know how long it is—although actually there's not a soul on this earth who *does* know how long it is. In fact, every time I've tried to watch that film I can't get more than twenty minutes in before confusion sets in.

I had seen gangster movies before, like *The Godfather* and a few others. There was a TV serial too, called *The Gangster Chronicles*, about Bugsy Siegel, Meyer Lansky, and various others, and then of course *Scarface*, which didn't really do much for me. I liked *The Godfather* the most, especially the parts about old New York. Before then I had read a clandestine copy of *The Godfather* and knew what it was about. I can still remember that opening line now.

Anyway, surely the roaring twenties depicted in *Once Upon a Time in America* were the same ones I fell in love with when watching *The Cotton Club*. And yet somehow I just couldn't get excited about it. I watched it, yes, but it felt almost as if I hadn't. I had no opinion about it. The jokes were very boorish and the movie had no real sense of zest.

That's probably how it was supposed to be—what else should one expect from a gang of young men like that? But I didn't realize that back then, because everyone was talking about them—including me. At least I could talk about that movie too; in other words, at least I could prove that I'd seen it.

And the music. Yes, the music—the soundtrack as they call it nowadays—was where most of the romance in that movie came from. There was that famous main theme, of course, but in fact there were many other kinds of music too. Even today, I sometimes hear that soundtrack playing as the ringtone on some loyal aficionado's phone.

But the best thing was that the movie explored the young men's emotional side. Young men don't usually express their sentimentality, after all, or at least only a select few do. That's how it was back then, anyway; I don't know about now. But that *Once Upon a Time in America* made it somehow acceptable for everybody to be sentimental, because the sentimentality of the street was somehow coarse.

There's that famous scene where the neighborhood crime boss falls out with Noodles and his gang—still a small-time outfit at that point—when he feels that they are working too independently and might start to challenge his authority. But Noodles's gang has already made some money, partnered the bootleggers, bought expensive outfits, stashed the money in the locker at the station, and so on. Anyway, this crime boss—Bugsy—attacks these well-dressed young gangsters, chases them, and opens fire.

They all flee and, needless to say, it's the smallest, funniest, most lovable member of the gang who gets hit by Bugsy's bullet: Dominic, who is also the one who really had the brightest future ahead of him.

Dominic runs for shelter, is hit by the bullet, but somehow manages to stagger to where Noodles is hiding (I hope you're following this). He dies in Noodles's arms, with the words: "Noodles, I slipped."

That scene was the movie's sentimental apex, although people talked about other less important, less dramatic moments of sentimentality too. For example, when the little hooker Peggy asks for a cake in exchange for sex and Patsy Goldberg ends up eating it himself, despite having worked so hard to buy it. Yes, they'd say, because really he's still just a child, a child who prefers desserts to women—and then they'd smile wryly to themselves.

But we were talking about Dominic's murder. That scene is particularly relevant if we think about how fashionable it was from very early on to quote lines from the movie.

There was a lot of debate about the words "Noodles, I slipped."

Some said Dominic was so young and innocent that he didn't realize he'd been shot and instead thought that he really had slipped.

And even though back then hardly anyone really knew what it feels like when a bullet hits you, some said that's what it really was like—you didn't even feel it.

But others disagreed and said that although he was young he was so tough, brave, and unyielding that while he felt the bullet hit him, he just didn't acknowledge it.

In other words, it was rather like the bit in *Gulliver's Travels* when they can't decide whether to break the egg at the larger or smaller end.

I think our young wiseguys and wannabe gangsters have always discussed the behavior of their movie heroes. It was always in relation to criminal activity, though—nobody ever discussed the bit in Fellini's *Amarcord* where Teo shouts from a tree.

This phenomenon peaked in the sixties when people saw *The Magnificent Seven*.

I read somewhere that *The Magnificent Seven* was the highest-grossing movie in the history of Soviet movie theaters. It ran in the theaters for four years straight, and would have gone on for longer if it had not suddenly been pulled on the orders of an unidentified party.

Anyway, a man who was around at the time told me that people went absolutely crazy over it. People were talking about it in the street, arguing over who showed more integrity and who was more in the right, Calvera or Chris? Those in the know said Calvera was. I don't know whether it was because he fought those who needed fighting, or maybe because while he freed the Seven after taking them prisoner, they then went straight back to their treacherous ways. Apparently the thieving fraternity said Calvera was in the right. But anyway, let's face it, who's going to stand in his way?

All this talk threatened to swallow up *Once Upon a Time in America*.

Actually there was no "threatened to" about it; it was already happening. The movie had already spawned a community of expert aficionados: young men who knew every twist and turn in the movie and who judged every action according to the laws of the Georgian street.

To be honest, you didn't really need to listen to them more than once. Once you'd heard one of these experts you already knew what the others would say. Remember that the law of the street, just like any other law, allows for no deviation in any direction, nor was there any room for liberalism either.

The greatest liberalism was to declare that when all was said and done they were still armed robbers who showed no mercy to anyone and so they couldn't be good people—but back then hardly anyone said that anyway. Those finding fault with the movie tended to do so with a single, standard phrase: "I dunno, I prefer *The Godfather*."

But *The Godfather* could never become the seminal street movie in Georgia. No way.

Yes, every now and then someone would quote the Corleones, but it never had the same force as "Noodles, I slipped."

The reasons for this are, I think, completely understandable.

Ultimately, *The Godfather* tells the story of a family, albeit one called the Mafia. It is a Mafia family—and in fact the movie never actually shows how it is the Corleones get their money. There is an almost Shakespearean feel to the way it deals with family issues. I think Coppola meant to film it that way.

In contrast, *Once Upon a Time in America* is a guys' movie through and through. Forget about family—we were all friends together and it was one long party. We were a gang. There's a big difference between a gang and family. Family means rules and a straitjacket, the gang means freedom and the street.

Some say that this movie became a manual, a sort of unwitting instruction manual.

When I was a boy one gangster, no longer alive, told me with absolute sincerity that he wanted to be exactly like Tony Montana—Scarface. Or was it Montano? "He's so cool," he said, with such enthusiasm. "He does it all. He's fucking awesome."

"Not just cool though," he said, "but a great guy too—after all, even though he acts like he's tough and crazy he refused to blow up that car with the kids in it, didn't he?"

There is actually an ulterior motive hidden behind the inclusion of children in gangster movies. They're used to they hook the viewers, to make them think they'll learn what kind of man the gangster is by seeing how he relates to the child.

That's rubbish, of course. It's just a plot device. Anyone who's ever written anything knows all about hooks and snares. Recently, García Márquez was on television talking about the tactics he uses and it was a real eye-opener.

For example, he talked about how he wrote *Chronicle of a Death Foretold*.

"I wrote the first sentence in such a way that the reader wouldn't be able to take his eyes off the page: 'On the day they were going to kill him, Santiago Nasar got up at five-thirty in the morning . . .' With those words alone I had grabbed the reader's attention. But if you write a sentence like that you can be sure that the reader will start leafing through to the last page of the book to find out how they kill him. And needless to say, by the time the reader has got to the end of the first chapter, he's decided whether or not to bother with the rest of the book, and so it was at that very point that I presented him with a phrase to make him change his mind. My main task," said García Márquez, "is to ensure that when someone reads my book only one universe exists for them—the universe in my book."

And to think some people consider artistic types to be naïve . . .

Sergio Leone was the master of that. Apparently, though, they wouldn't show the director's cut in America. It was the kind of film it was pointless to cut anyway. He had wanted to make that film for almost twenty years and in the end he didn't really manage it. I read somewhere that after a screening in the non-competitive section of the Cannes Festival it received a fifteen-minute ovation, and that both the European and American versions played to a full house.

But this doesn't concern us now and never did.

We saw the movie on video, and when much later on they showed it on state television it was apparently yet another version, which differed from the ones that had been available up till then. Mind you, I don't think anybody watched it on television—by then, anyone who wanted to had already seen it dozens of times.

I don't suppose the students who hang around in front of the Sorbonne talk much about this movie, and nor do the guys who aren't students but have nothing better to do than hang around there anyway (do guys like that even exist?). The same is probably true of students at the universities of Prague and Georgetown too. So when it played to packed theaters there, that was the end of the matter; many other movies had played to packed theaters before and many more would in the future. But here in Georgia it was different. Here in Georgia something happened.

This movie touched something in us that had been dormant or semi-dormant for a long time. It corresponded to something, and the correspondence turned out to be a painful one.

Some people's lives were amazingly reminiscent of this movie. Some people's were not, but not for want of trying.

Perestroika was just beginning. Freedom is never a matter of chance; it is entirely dependent on people, especially when it tries to sneak in by stealth. It cannot do so—people grab hold of it and drag it in. That is true whether we're talking about lions or mosquitoes, and it's not just students fighting for the independence of their country who find that it never really exists for them—it's the young men of the street too.

Anyway, wherever informal unions started to appear, gangs sprang up too: a different type of gang, not like the robbers of Soviet times who came mainly from the provinces but real, urban gangs, just like the ones in our charming criminal saga. Nobody can blame Sergio Leone's movie for contributing to their formation—they were springing up everywhere, across the whole of the Soviet Union. It's just that in Georgia the birth of gangs adopted certain elements of the movie's artistry. It founded itself on the mythos, shall we say, as well as much more besides.

The magazine *Ogonek* was one of the best things I remember from the era of perestroika and it published one article in particular that I'll never forget. It was called *The Tiger Pounces* and told the story of the famous twenties Russian gangsters Lenka Panteleev and Vaska Kultiapy. This was back before career thieves even existed.

Anyway, toward the end of the article it said, "Now Russia's great gangster tiger has pounced and is attacking us."

Tiger schmiger, I thought. I really didn't feel the article had much relevance for us in Georgia; I just assumed something was going on in Russia. So, you're in business then, are you?

But it was happening here too, in the empire's most picturesque province. To a lesser degree and more gradually, maybe, but here too.

Everything was just beginning back then, and this was beginning too.

We Georgians are an artistic people and those muscular, shaven-headed, tracksuit-clad racketeers never appeared in our country. Russia, on the other hand, was soon full of them.

In Georgia every racketeer had to be a hero, a real character, somehow unique—the kind of hero you'd find in the movies, in other words. We just can't do it any other way; we don't know how. And what would be interesting about that, anyway? Where's the fun if you don't stand out?

It was Aristotle who first said that all these creative works are the stories of what might have happened, whereas history is what actually happened.

Anyway, let's see what might have happened and not what actually did.

Wouldn't you like to take a peek inside a box like that?

There are guns in there, and weapons, and a million other things besides.

Inside it smells of old cigarettes, but unfamiliar ones. Not those low-grade Marlboros from Sokhumi. Real ones. This is the smell of the kind of Marlboro that had "For sale only in the USA" stamped on the box.

And somebody had smuggled them in.

It was back in the days when people would say, "I've smoked the American ones, you know—imported ones . . . They taste completely different."

Different?

Because in America everything really is different, isn't it?

III. Atria, aka Noodles

Atria. I had to look that up, you know. I opened the dictionary and looked it up, because it's not often you come across a word you know in a foreign language but not in your own.

I think the words Georgians use for car parts would be examples of this: *proshinebi, kalotkebi, raspredvali*—Russian words. Georgian equivalents do exist, but only a few people know them. Anyway, I'm pretty sure that even if we got full membership of the European Union we would still never adopt the Georgian terms; they are so deeply rooted in the living language and likely to live on forever in garages and car lots.

And then there are a few words which you just never hear. You could quite easily be born, grow up, become an adult, grow old and then pass away and never once come across these words. Or you might hear them once or twice when someone else utters them but not have a clue what they mean.

The word *atria* has a strange history. There are probably only a few people in Georgia who even know the word, and even fewer who have ever used it. Until yesterday I didn't know it myself, but I looked in a couple of dictionaries and there it was.

It was no problem at all to find out the meaning of this word, but the food it refers to wasn't all that common in Georgia until recently. Now, though, it's in all the Chinese restaurants and supermarkets.

I've never heard the word spoken out loud. As words go it's not that bad, and what is more it represents something else, too. Something bigger and more important.

I've heard that in Georgia a lot of new words were invented in the twenties, and I thought maybe this word was invented then too. But it turns out that's not the case.

Atria.

It's a beautiful word. In Sulkhan Saba Orbeliani's eighteenth-century dictionary its meaning is given as "dried bread," whereas according to the Russian-Georgian dictionary it denotes the legendary Chinese Five Cereals associated with ancient China, the Eastern Han dynasty, the Yellow River, and many other things. Nowadays we use it to refer to what might be termed "Chinese macaroni"—the Russians, of course, just use their own word, *lapsha*, and English speakers use the term "noodles." Noodles. Noodles. Noodles.

The Russians have a saying that goes, "Don't hang noodles on my ears"—meaning "don't talk rubbish." I don't know any sayings about noodles in English.

A man with well-boiled *atria* hanging off his ears really would be funny.

If you ask me, *Once Upon a Time in America* has a lot to answer for.

Anyway, as I was saying, I think that in Georgia the word became popular a long time before noodle soup itself, because the hero David Aronson's nickname in Sergio Leone's movie was Noodles.

Noodles.

There were a couple of unofficial dubbed versions of *Once Upon a Time in America* featuring well-known voice-over artists of the eighties who specialized in translating movies to be released on video. One was a rather shrill voice, the other a deep bass. In the end I seem to recall they both turned out to belong to the same man.

Anyway, in one version they called the film's hero Lapsha, and in the other they called him Noodles. We picked up both words.

I had never even seen actual noodle-atria soup, even in Moscow, yet I knew the word in two foreign languages. Back then you'd find young men who knew hardly any English and pronounced, "Fuck you" as "Fork you," but they all knew the word *noodles*.

The Noodles we see released from prison was played by De Niro.

David Aronson, aka Noodles, aka Atria.

The main character and hero of *Once Upon a Time in America*. His story is the film's story.

To tell you the truth, I didn't like either Noodles or his story.

It was one big useless pile of nothing. The Noodles who comes out of prison after the passion-fueled and juvenile murder of his young friend's killer and the policeman who jumped in to intervene was just an ordinary man. Just a regular gangster who probably needed to make his name among his friends with this murder. And that's what happened.

But actually this was no man. He seemed much more intelligent as a child. Once he grew up he started behaving almost as if the world owed him something. Even in old age, when trying to work out the truth after discovering he had been tricked by a friend, it seemed almost as if he were Nelson Mandela, some kind of moral yardstick. His moral yardstick was probably his devotion to his friends, which stood in such stark contrast to the total lack of loyalty displayed by his other friend, that fellow survivor and good-for-nothing Max, who married Noodles' longtime sweetheart.

And that is that.

Anyway, in Georgia the morality of friendship was just as powerful.

I don't think they wanted anything more from Noodles. The rest—what he thought and what he did—was at best insignificant, and at worst in very poor taste.

To cut a long story short, Noodles wasn't capable of development.

In his childhood he showed judgment. Once, sitting on the lavatory, he opened *Martin Eden*—but it is clear that he always preferred something else to reading books. In a neighborhood like that it wasn't likely anybody would have given much thought to *Martin Eden*. Why, then, did he have *Martin Eden* thrust into his hands? Taste. Taste.

During the entire remainder of that epic movie the book is never re-visited. He flicks through it, and that's the end of the matter. Then, in old age Fat Moe asks Noodles, or Atria, what he's been doing all these years. I think it was Fat Moe who asked him, although I wouldn't swear to it, and Atria answers that he's been going to bed early. Did that mean he'd been going to bed early to leaf through a book that might help him sleep better? The elderly Noodles/Atria really didn't look as if he'd been leafing through anything, or had even acquired such experience during his years away from New York as would make us give that idea serious consideration.

It must be the glasses, which give him the look of an academic, in con-trast to his friend Max who, while Noodles was going to bed early, trans-formed himself into Secretary Bailey, but that's all it is. Glasses and graying hair. Like at the end of Robinson Crusoe, where death turns the living dregs into dead dregs. Nothing more.

For a man in Noodles' line of work to be loveable he needs to be like Jean Valjean. True, Atria/Noodles knifed two men whereas Jean Valjean only stole bread and candlesticks, but both experienced prison.

Someone I would consider to be an authority on prison, the writer and Gulag survivor Varlam Shalamov, says that Jean Valjean does not exist and that guys like him are only an invention, ennobled by their creators. I don't really think that Sergio Leone even needed a Jean Valjean. It seems to me that the story he filmed was complete and, honestly, nobody in Georgia ever really liked his characters anyway, as compared to the ones in *The Magnificent Seven*.

Nobody ever called Noodles a great guy, or Patsy a great guy, or Bruzziani a great guy. I'm saying no more about Max. On the whole I'm surprised that a guy like him was a Mafioso, and that the Mafia still managed to get one of its own so high up in the American administration so late into the twentieth century. But please, don't take me seriously, I beg you. I think I've lost my train of thought.

In the romantic sixties, heroes like Chris, Vin, Harry, Lee, Bernardo, Britt, and Chico inspired a generation of boys and young men, who copied Yul Brynner's gait and idolized Britt and his knife-throwing skills. Similarly, the influence of Tarzan in the fifties saw young men leaping from lime trees across the city. But in contrast, the heroes of *Once Upon a Time in America* just weren't that important.

Just as in the villages of central Georgia I believe—with my limited understanding—they advocate schema and etiquette as a means of inspiring their young people to modesty, so the structures that exist in this movie inspired the youth on our streets by providing them with a kind of implicit framework within which to develop.

Maybe some people preferred Tony Montana with his total fearlessness, but *Scarface* had neither a structure nor any mythical feel.

But here the guys on the street started out together and stayed together. They conducted their business with such solidarity and honor, pooled their takings and kept no secrets from each other. I don't think anyone gave a second thought to Max, that mendacious character who completely betrayed his brothers.

Nor indeed to the great Noodles, who spends his old age tottering about feebly in the streets and going to bed early.

The movie created the impression that America was a land of gangsters. In the seventies and eighties you would never have drawn that conclusion from the American movies being shown in Soviet movie theaters, even if you had seen *The Cotton Club* a thousand times. But back then seeing things on video was much more powerful than seeing them on the big screen, and our young wiseguys put as much faith in what they saw on video as they possibly could have done.

They weren't really interested in *Bonnie and Clyde*; the films they liked were the ones where a bunch of guys banded together and did what gangsters do.

I don't think anybody really saw that movie as a fictional creation. It was a true story and the main conclusion people drew seemed to be that life, and America, were like that.

For example, one guy told me that in America gangsters are buried in large mausoleums as a sign of respect, and backed this up with the incident in which an elderly Noodles/Atria goes to his friends' mausoleum, which he had apparently had built for them.

Once, during a period when everyone was shooting everyone else, some guys I knew quite well—may they rest in peace—visited me in my holiday home outside the city. Their parents were at home, they said, and they needed to use my kitchen for a bit to dry out some weed in the gas oven. They had all those guns and nobody at home said a thing about it, but they were too ashamed to dry out a bit of weed on the stovetop. These boys spent half their time shooting at each other and everybody knew it, and that was fine, that was just the way things were in Georgia, but weed? Well no, that just wasn't okay.

We went downstairs into the kitchen and anyway, it seems that weed dries out pretty quickly, and we moved on to talking, and it was good-natured enough—pretty amicable on their part, cautious yet willful on mine.

They were praising the way things were developing at the time: "The right people are in charge of business now. You watch how we'll develop. It's not like this in America, you know. But you look at who built America in the first place: mobsters, wiseguys." No, I said, it wasn't wiseguys who built America, it was wise men, and we debated the point a bit.

I must have said something funny because they almost died laughing—although it was kind, sincere laughter. "You seem to know all about it," they said, "but it isn't really like that." If I mentioned George Washington they'd bring up Lucky Luciano, if I said Benjamin Franklin they'd mention Meyer Lansky. Anyway, in the end one of them said to me, "You've seen *Once Upon a Time in America*, haven't you? That's America, and if we do the same shit here it'll all work out fine."

What use was my picture of Reagan to me now?

I had a fixed image of America in my head, and refused to entertain the notion that America was or is like that. As if America could possibly be a world full of guys like Noodles and, what is more, run by guys like Noodles. Poor Noodles—I mean, really, what on earth would he have been capable of running?

There was a time, sure, when there was some truth to it, as when Frankie Carbo and Blinky Palermo ran the boxing. And there was Chicago, of course. But it wasn't just because it was Chicago, was it? Go and look at Chicago now.

My friend went there and said he went into one office which he was told had once belonged to Al Capone. There were some girls tapping away at computers, and even they said that the great gangsters are buried in mausoleums.

It's something to do with elevating something an artist creates and then believing it, and if you look at it like that maybe somebody somewhere does have a mausoleum.

A female friend of mine was being pursued by a rather wealthy admirer. It was during Georgia's period of economic hardship, but one day he said to her, "Come on, let's go out for dinner." This admirer of hers wasn't a city bigwig, but rather from aspiring emergent section of society. Anyway, he took her for dinner and they went into the restaurant and the restaurant was completely empty and they just sat there in front of this huge window and there was this strange silence between them and then the guy said, "I've set it up like in *Once Upon a Time in America* for you."

I imagine he meant that scene where Noodles and his longtime sweetheart are in the restaurant.

Oh, and yes, that brings me to another story.

Let's leave all that talk of structure to one side and talk about another issue—taste.

Even when something humorous happens in the adventures of Atria and his friends it is always connected to questions of masculine pride. What it boils down to is this: all the humor in this movie revolves around genitalia. And that's how it is from their teenage years onward. This isn't some kind of lecture on morals—it's just that jokes like that are worthless, because they are so easy to think up.

Noodles is a strange man. When they burst in to steal the diamonds he immediately attacks the woman. She then tries to identify Noodles from a lineup of his friends. The most lighthearted element in the whole movie is Peggy, the hooker, whom they hang around with from childhood on . . . All that is easy enough to understand. I can more or less imagine why Leone chose such light relief in this form and why he sets up this contrast between our dear Atria's violent sex and Peggy's sincere and complex love, but the whole of this episode is of very dubious taste.

In the movie Burt Young, who is one of my favorite actors and who here plays an Italian Mafioso alongside Joe Pesci, eats like a pig while the considerably more refined Noodles and Max watch and listen, forcing themselves to laugh at his boorish jokes and comments.

If you ask me, this dinner scene is the greatest scene in the whole movie, because it is the one time the viewer is able to truly appreciate the level, scope, taste, and aspirations of the people he is dealing with.

But back then it wasn't such a big deal.

The sense of style reflected in this movie permeated the sense of style present in our street society. Either permeated it or coincided with it, I'm not sure which. Later I think the obsolete gangster style was revived or modified by John Travolta with *Pulp Fiction*, but in between these two points in time our country fell apart.

The most unfortunate thing was that all this crude joking around is presented as if it were genuine, straightforward humor. It was a kind of implicit validation of the sense of taste demonstrated in these episodes, a stamp of approval.

I think that in broad terms Leone viewed these episodes quite neutrally. He just took them as part of the story and not as an indication of their heroism. And they weren't heroes. It's strange. Noodles was not a hero, he was an imitation of a hero, whose inner desires are indefinable.

Why was it like that, why?

There are reasons.

After all, nothing happens for no reason, does it?

But I cannot possibly talk about them now.

I should repeat a well-known phrase that I am particularly fond of: to understand this story you need to know the story of what's happened up till now, and you'll never understand the story of what's happened up till now unless you know the story of what happened before that.

It's basically what Professor Woland says: the girl has already spilled the sunflower oil—you're in big trouble now, Berlioz.

Anyway, that's how I see it.

Atria is already dead right at the very start. He doesn't exist.

I think the hardest thing was that some people thought this was their real life. In other words, that this is what life really is.

IV. The second wire

A friend of mine got caught up in a funny story which illustrates something about young men in Georgia at that time. My friend was born and raised in

Kutaisi and in Soviet times he was an exceptional photographer. Actually, it was more around the time *Once Upon a Time in America* came out, and why exactly he considered it a funny story I don't know, but there you go.

He was a young man back then and, like all young men, occasionally lacking in good sense, and one night he went out with some friends and got drunk, and then decided he'd pay one of his girlfriends a visit. He was so drunk when he got to her apartment building that he got the floors mixed up and started banging on the wrong door entirely.

Anyway, there was nobody in, so obviously nobody answered the door, and being drunk, he took offense. Well put yourself in his shoes—you've come all the way here with all those emotions churning around inside and your girl won't even open the door . . .

His girl was actually was sleeping soundly in her apartment on the next floor down, but by now my friend had had enough; he stopped knocking and calmly broke the door in with his shoulder.

This was the Soviet Union, don't forget—doors back then weren't as solid as they are today, with their reinforced concrete and concealed locks. My grandmother, for example, always used to say, "What's life come to if you have to lock your doors?"

So yes, anyway, he got his shoulder, broke the door down with it and burst into what he thought was his girlfriend's apartment but which in actual fact belonged to a total stranger, and as nobody was home he didn't realize he was in the wrong place, and passed out on the sofa.

Had this been an episode from the golden age of Georgian cinema, what happened next would have been amazing: we would follow the hero on his adventures, there would be romance, irony, destiny, fortune—everything. But unfortunately this was Georgian reality and not a Georgian movie where roadworkers chase butterflies through the meadows.

He was still drunk when they shook him, shouted at him, woke him and sat him up, and before he could even rub his eyes, they slapped a pair of handcuffs on him.

There were a lot of people milling around the apartment; some were in uniform, some were not. There were men sitting at a table and writing, and spread out on the table there were sheets of paper and a sack stuffed full of clothes. All the cupboards were open and all the drawers had been pulled out.

Anyway, they pulled my friend to his feet, shoved him into a car and whisked him off to the Kutaisi administration building, just a stone's throw away from the notoriously harsh Kutaisi prison. The prison has been demolished now, but back then the whole building simply shook with the horror of the unbearable ordeals people suffered within its walls. Inside the prison they had cudgels with the names of painkillers written on them. For fun, so that while they were beating prisoners they could say, "Here, take your painkillers." It was an interesting place, Kutaisi prison—one cell even had a decorative plaque saying "This was Stalin's cell."

But that's a story for another time.

So, the poor guy sobered up and found out he'd been charged with encroachment on a citizen's private property and theft, and because he was just a regular guy who'd just happened to get drunk that really worried him—how, he wondered, had he managed to get so drunk that he decided to steal these people's stuff, and what on earth had he wanted their clothes for, a nice guy like him who was studying photography in Moscow and trying to move forward in life?

But apparently that's what had happened.

When the owner of the flat came home he first saw his door broken in and then the stranger asleep on his sofa, and must have thought it was a nice opportunity to make his fellow citizen pay for his drunkenness and for breaking down the door, and to make some profit for himself at the same time.

He rearranged things in his apartment to look as if there'd been a break-in, called the police, and told them there was a burglar asleep in his flat— and of course all the neighbors came over to have a look too.

With his limited intelligence he thought he'd get the ball rolling, get some money out of a drunk young man, let the police take their share too and come out a winner, while the drunk "robber" would buy his way out of jail and be happy with that.

So what it boils down to is this: *they* all turned out to be thieves, while the young man was guilty of nothing more than breaking down a door and falling asleep on a sofa.

But there were two things the owner of the apartment could not foresee: firstly, that the young drunk and his family wouldn't have enough money to bribe everyone who needed bribing, and secondly that there was a nationwide campaign underway against thievery in all its forms, the lifestyle associated with it and the crime of theft in particular.

It was a high-profile campaign: special programs on Soviet Georgian TV, famous presenters, guest appearances by well-known thieves, interviews, the lot—and alongside this the Georgian authorities ruled that anyone found guilty of stealing would no longer serve their sentence in Georgia, but would instead be sent to one of Russia's notorious labor camps. At least I think that's what the setup was, especially for repeat offenders, and I think the objective was probably to get all of the thieves out of the Georgian labor camps.

What the result of all this was I don't know, but I think it's probably clear that for my friend, at least, everything had gone horribly wrong.

That man who'd wanted to line his pockets got nothing, and toward the end I think he was probably rather ashamed that he'd created the whole spectacle. My friend, meanwhile, got five years on charges of theft and was sent from Kutaisi prison to the Tsulukidze labor camp—where there was no longer a single thief left—and from there straight on to the Komi Autonomous Soviet Socialist Republic corrective labor colonies.

The strangest part of the whole sorry tale of this latter-day Jean Valjean was that the investigating magistrate somehow still managed to extract a bribe from the prisoner's parents, despite doing nothing in return: he just saw they were simple, decent people and thought he'd give it a go.

By the time my friend got back to Georgia it was already an independent country; he went to find the magistrate and asked him to explain just what it was he'd taken the money for. The magistrate gave the money back.

Because, as you know, this is Georgia.

I remembered this story because my friend is an expert on the "irregulars"—the criminals—of the eighties. I have other friends who know a lot more about the criminal underworld, but they weren't inside in the eighties.

Anyway, listening to him speak you would think that the traditional world of the Soviet Georgian criminal was nothing like *Once Upon a Time in America* at all. It wasn't influenced by it, didn't really understand it, didn't even pay it much attention.

The movie became the life story of those young men who were emerging onto the street scene at precisely that time, and in those exclusive parts of Tbilisi that are nowadays known by that term "elite."

For the Soviet Union this was a very strange world. Suddenly the children of the Tbilisi elite were becoming interested in the street. The world over, fearless, unabashed criminality tends to be associated with specific neighborhoods on the outskirts of a city. In Soviet Georgia, even though thieves traditionally operated out of neighborhoods on the far side of the River Mtkvari and cities in western Georgia rather than the elite neighborhoods, the latter spawned a particular breed of criminal who had close connections to those who were decidedly un-elite. Thinking about why this might be will take me off on too much of a tangent, and in any case I don't think it's something that needs to be raked up again.

A man who's served time for theft isn't going to be interested in some cinema-derived template. That was probably true in this case too, although from the seventies onward thieves knew how to make money in all sorts of ways that didn't involve theft. Racketeering was a familiar concept back then, as I think I mentioned before. So perestroika's racketeering pioneers didn't really invent anything new; they probably just needed cinema to turn what was already there into something they could perceive as artistry, so that they could then adopt elements of it.

For example, young men started used to work themselves up into a hysterical frenzy over the slightest things. These frenzied outbursts were, needless to say, meant as a show of force. Taking offense from some insignificant nothing, going completely over the top about it, getting their knives out and so on. This, I think, is still the case today.

I remember a story about one of this new breed of racketeers who, along with a friend, was stealing gas from somebody's car, in the street and in broad daylight. It was around the time of independence and it was very difficult to get hold of gas. As I recall, this racketeer was the son of a professor. Anyway, his friend told me they decided to steal some gasoline and while they were doing so the owner turned up, a man in his sixties, and just stood there looking down at them, and he wasn't even angry because they looked like decent guys, and he just said, "What are you doing, son? Aren't you ashamed of yourself?" His friend swore that's all the man said. But anyway, without a second thought the racketeer started swearing at him like crazy and shooting and shooting, and the owner was lucky to get away.

Shooting—that was a word you didn't hear very often back then, although it was not to be unusual for much longer. The friend told me this story to demonstrate how fearless the poor car owner was, because he didn't back down, but I probably remember this story out of the thousands I've heard because in my mind it was linked to Dutch Schultz—the Dutch Schultz who at that time appeared in *The Cotton Club* and later in *Billy Bathgate* and other movies.

I don't really think that such an aggressive relationship with the world around them is all that typical of southern gangsters, and it certainly wasn't a characteristic of our traditional criminals. In fact, the criminal underworld's more reticent forerunners—brigands, bandits, and outlaws—are even considered as folk heroes.

Aggression was more of an issue in the big cities. Things were just getting started there, and some kind of big noisy debut was probably inevitable, although I don't think anybody gave it any conscious thought. That's just how it happened. After all, underneath all this hysteria there's a considerable amount of pride and arrogance.

People were there at the start of an epic new chapter and probably preferred to conduct themselves in that way.

After a while this deafening aggression died down, though, and was only really noticeable in a few places. People didn't need it anymore, because now people were walking around with automatic weapons, stealing not the gas but the car itself, and so brazenly that half the time they'd do so while the driver was in it.

Of course that was not the kind of environment *Once Upon a Time in America* took place in, and our gangsters and wannabes were considerably less well-mannered than Max and Noodles, too.

This movie has an odd quirk: manners are important to the gangsters precisely because of who they are, and yet their sense of taste is quite loathsome.

That's what happened in the free world.

As a young man Larry Flint once remarked that all he was guilty of was poor taste.

It was just around that time that those Dutch Schultz movies came onto the scene.

Billy Bathgate, based on the Doctorow novel—which was even published in the literary journal *Inostranka*—and *Hit the Dutchman.*

Hit the Dutchman, directed by Menahem Golan himself if I recall correctly, made a clear and lasting impression on me—rather unexpectedly—most probably because I felt there were parallels with our own new-breed racketeers that seemed inconceivable, implausible even.

Dutch Schultz was one of those people who like to make a lot of noise. But in Golan's movie, the minute he gets out of prison he bites the nose off the first person who crosses him and hides his bloodstained shirt—a present from his mother—under his raincoat.

And that's what happens. A perfectly ordinary movie or book suddenly throws up something so incomprehensible, at first glance so inconceivable, that you're left reeling. At the time it came out *Once Upon a Time in America* somehow appeared to be in line with the tastes of our young wiseguys and wannabe gangsters, to somehow be the answer to their dreams. There simply wouldn't have been that connection, though, were there not something extraordinary about the circumstances at the time.

I think you could compare this connection to two telegraph wires. One wire carried the smell of freedom, the other carried the past, in which was hidden whatever it was that made these American crime dramas fit our template so well.

I think we can find that second wire.

For some reason I think that in Soviet Georgia traditional criminal society failed to satisfy the young men living in Tbilisi's elite neighborhoods, as well as their less-than-elite associates. I'm not sure that anyone really expressed that dissatisfaction openly after the sixties, but deep down I think it was there. In the sixties thieves inhabited a completely different social sphere than they did at the end of the seventies and in the eighties. The street gangs still used to have all manner of fights and showdowns with them, and even beat them.

I'm no expert, but I somehow get the impression that at the start of the seventies a criminal revolution took place in Soviet Georgia.

It happened first in the criminal underworld itself and then in wider society.

It brought about many changes.

The essence of this unseen revolution was that concept of "the society of thieves" (prior to that they had been known as career thieves and later, among other things, "official" thieves) spread into the provinces and took on a provincial flavor. In all my reading about the "official" thieves of Stalin's time I've rarely found any reference to any of them coming from outside Tbilisi. In other words, in the beginning the big city acted as a shelter, a hiding place—and there was only one big city. But then as time went on thievery became more widespread. This proliferation happened most commonly and most rapidly in western Georgia. There was an increase in the number of thieves everywhere, but in certain places it was more like an explosion. The proliferation was especially marked among young men in those towns that were connected with the labor camps; indeed, such towns became one of the main channels into—and hotbeds of—criminality.

In the old days thieves came primarily from the lower social classes, and it was probably only an exceptional few who chose to enter this profession because of what life had dealt them: war, hardship, and before that, repression. Anyway, thieves were people with no home and no documents, like in the old Dumbadze story—"Their address is the Soviet Union, Madam." But as it became more widespread in Georgia a story started doing the rounds about a notorious provincial thief who had died and whose funeral had been attended by old-order thieves in military jackets who'd traveled all the way from Russia.

When they saw his beautiful house and grounds they were astonished. What kind of thief lived like that?

Apparently this thief had been killed by a normally law-abiding man whom the thieving fraternity had decided needed to be punished, in other words killed. But the Russians, it seems, apparently said that the thief had deserved to be killed, because real thieves have no need for property like that—and thanks to them the thief's killer escaped death.

The killer wasn't even mentioned in the other version, in which those Russian thieves in their padded jackets just left the rich dead man right there in his coffin and told him that in their eyes he was no longer a thief at all.

In short, a huge, infinite world had been created—or, more precisely, was born, came to be. Anyway, whether they wanted to or not, these young men I've been talking about had a sense of connection to that world. It doesn't matter what you call it, whether it was on a personal level or a business one, or whether you try to explain it or not; it was there. But deep down this world as a whole did not satisfy their requirements.

Behind closed doors they probably called it parochial, unsophisticated, but I never heard anyone voice that out loud. They belonged to an entirely different layer of society and had received an entirely different education, and ultimately those thieves from the lower layers no longer existed. Almost. Two or three exceptions, of course, couldn't change the prevailing wind.

Anyway, it was about that time that the American dramas came along and, I think, showed us the way. Because as we've already established, "America" was the magical word.

V. Aerobics

One story from the Tbilisi of that time seems to have been forgotten, or maybe it's just gone unnoticed. It was this: a team of touring wrestlers came over from Poland to put on a show at the Palace of Sport.

It might not have attracted the kind of crowds the Suzi Quatro concert did, but it was a foreign show nonetheless and its Tbilisi run finished with rather a bang.

Just like the pro wrestling they show on TV, this was the kind of wrestling that normally attracted a very particular audience.

Pro wrestling comes from the older sport of circus wrestling, and in actual fact it's more of an acrobatics show, in which terrifying and unfeasibly muscled men and women set out to entertain the audience. It's all false blows and acrobatic wrestling moves. What is more, the whole thing is choreographed and scripted, with "champions" and "villains" and so on and so forth. In other words, it's circus, pure and simple.

In the Soviet Union we had a kind of wrestling called "catch"—as in "catch them any way you can"—which we knew to be a form of American no-holds-barred wrestling in which anything goes. Imagine a Tbilisi version of cage fighting and you're somewhere in the right area.

In the Soviet sports press these two things were lumped together in the same category and according to the propaganda pro wrestling shows were a bloody fight to the death—like gladiators, they said.

This happened around the time that the low-budget American movie *The California Dolls* came out on video. It told the story of two girls who take part in real, unstaged fights. Their trainer was played by Peter Falk, the actor who later became known on Georgian television as Columbo.

Anyway, the wrestling show came to town and started its run at the Palace of Sports.

It was a disaster.

Crowds of young people came to the show expecting to see a bloodbath, but found themselves instead watching acrobatic mock fighting with no real grasp of the essence of what it was supposed to be. They didn't understand it for one simple reason: they didn't know that this genre even existed. How could they? Where would they know it from?

One young guy who saw the show told me it was as if they were just pretending to hit each other, jump on each other's heads, slam into each other and throw themselves on top of their opponents, and that nobody even got knocked over properly.

Anyway, the audience felt they were being taken for idiots and started whistling and shouting that they'd bought tickets to see this and now nobody was even drawing blood, and they booed and shouted at the wrestlers to start hitting each other properly.

But the wrestlers just carried on with what they'd been doing up till then—I mean, they weren't really going to start drawing blood, were they? To make matters worse, I doubt they even did that particularly well—a group of Polish wrestlers back was never going to be of the caliber of Hulk Hogan and his ilk.

Anyway, the crowd started swearing, booing and raining down heavy brass five-kopek coins onto the wooden stage, as a way of saying "They're ripping us off, they're ripping us off."

"That was to show them just what we thought of them," the guy told me, "but some people even got their pocket knives out—thankfully still folded up—and started rushing down toward the stage."

To cut a long story short, the Poles made a muscled run for it toward the changing rooms and never emerged again. And that was the end of Tbilisi's only pro wrestling show.

They were just doing their thing, but the crowd was expecting something else.

That's the story as I heard it from the guys back then, anyway. To be honest you could probably count the number of minutes I've spent watching pro wrestling on your fingers and toes, and still have some digits left over.

Oh, there was so much we didn't know, even stupid things like pro wrestling. And that made us angry. When you don't know something you get angry. And you get angry with other people; at least, that's how it is with Georgians.

Back then, during that period they called perestroika, people heard more news in the course of a single day than they'd heard in their entire lives up till then. By now the Russian press was already printing whatever it wanted, and even the Georgian newspapers told tales of émigrés, the loss of our independence, and countless other things.

In that respect it really was a wonderful time, a time for discovering truths, although people still found a million things to be irritated by, like the pro wrestling; the novelty of perestroika was not so great that people greeted everything with joy. There was a lot of anger too.

At the same time life was getting harder and harder by the day.

By now Schwarzenegger and Stallone were on our television screens. Before that the government hadn't had a good word to say about either of them, but especially Stallone, thanks to his ridiculous action movies set first in Vietnam and then Afghanistan. The word "action" started appearing in video stores; movies were either action, comedy, or drama. Where have all the video stores gone now? The last one I remember seeing was next to Delisi metro station, inside a mini supermarket. It wasn't all that long ago. They had about two hundred black cassettes stacked up. I don't remember the year, but it was around the time Kubrick's last movie, *Eyes Wide Shut*, came out, and I asked the guy whether they had it. They did, he said, but the quality was poor and they didn't have the uncut version.

Those video stores hung on for an awfully long time.

As well as rental stores there was the odd video club or video bar. Erotic movies were passed around behind closed doors, in the back rooms of former Houses of Culture and the front rooms of houses of much less culture.

These video bars were characterized by heavy drinking, frequent brawls, culminating in stabbings or worse.

Commercial enterprises and Snickers. I think the first of those new things that started coming in was Snickers, wasn't it? But there was this expectation that the stuff coming in would be somehow unique . . . and it wasn't unique at all, not the Snickers and not anything else. It was all good stuff, but so expensive, and meanwhile life was falling apart all around us.

For me, the best thing that first appeared during those years was the Kirov Park book stalls. If there was any book published in Russia, you could buy it there. It was rather expensive, but even if you weren't going to buy you could always have a flick through, at least.

Broadly speaking, it seems to me that back then, during those years, it was a time of books. Books were responsible for an awful lot of things that happened back then. I mean in the Soviet Union as a whole—exactly what they were responsible for in Georgia I can't really say, and that's because I don't really understand it myself.

Even things that were banned or not published in the Soviet Union would be set out right there on the pink gravel of Kirov Park. I don't know how they managed to do it so quickly.

It was fabulous.

On the one hand there was this torrent of stuff flooding in, on the other hand there was this resurgence, this revival, of street society. Something in these established, longstanding relationships was changing. And at the same time, of course, the country was on the verge of collapse. The independence movement was gaining strength.

Chattanooga days. Do you remember what they were, Chattanooga days? It was early in the fall of 1988. There were Americans all over Tbilisi. The weather was marvelous. There were academic conferences, concerts and, for the first time I think, camera crews from American TV stations. There was an organization called Friendship Force which had helped arrange for Americans to come and stay with families in Tbilisi. Later on, Georgians went to stay with American families. It was basically an exchange visit.

I don't know what the Chattanooga bit referred to. I think it's a city. But for some reason I remembered they said Chattanooga. Chattanooga, Chattanooga: it was written all over the place.

That was the first time I saw how American cameramen worked.

There was one guy with the camera, and an assistant who followed him around with a little folding ladder which he'd unfold quick as a flash when needed so that the cameraman could climb up and film.

And what did they film?

Crowd dispersal, what else?

On one particular day, from the morning onward, people were holding rallies in various different locations between the university and the presidential palace. The Americans filmed them.

The only time I'd ever seen that many police was in a sports stadium. The university gardens were completely encircled. I think this was the first time a large-scale protest was broadcast to the world. There were police all over Rustaveli Avenue. In places they were pushing into the crowd and beating people. They didn't really know what they were doing themselves. Well, what could they know about rioting crowds? And because they didn't know what they were doing the crowds got even angrier and then they rioted even more. At least they had the stadium experience, I suppose.

There were only two occasions when the spectators stormed the field. The first was during the soccer game against Zarya Voroshilovgrad when the referee sided with the opposition, and the second was when we lost to Baku in Tbilisi. But both those events had taken place years before. Add to that the fact that at assemblies the police were normally able to just stand there quietly and you'll understand why they really knew nothing at all about rioting; they were learning as they went. By the following February they were coming out wearing white helmets, with shields and batons at the ready, but at that point it was still only regular uniformed police.

In places they also deployed the infamous *vasmoi polki*—the Eighth Regiment—which was made up entirely of young people, all of whom were, I think, Russian.

Our wiseguys and bad boys always took special pride in recounting how they'd fought with the Eighth Regiment. I don't know its history, but it was based in Tbilisi, at the Eighth Regiment barracks.

In short, the Americans were watching and recording what was going on. What good it would do them from here I don't know. It would probably all just end up in some documentary somewhere.

There were only a handful of people back then who understood what "media" meant.

At one point they showed a Polish movie on the private TV channel Mermisi. I think Rybczynski was the director. The movie showed people moving around, stretching out, slowly and sluggishly turning around and over.

I can remember the shots. I'm not sure it's what the director had in mind, but I had a strange sense that we are all stretching, all slowly swimming around outside something. This feeling stayed with me for a long time, although the time really had already passed for sluggishness like that. I mean, who in their right mind was still thinking about Rybczynski's broad movements at a time like that?

As I was saying, it was a strange time. People watched satire and bought books; my father even brought home a huge box to keep newspapers in. It was like a trunk.

It didn't actually hold that many newspapers and magazines. I don't know about other people, but we used to get mail by the ton and we never managed to read it all. The minute a publication became popular, you had to subscribe.

The majority of publications, though, were still in Russian.

Before then my reading matter had consisted of a couple of sports papers and a soccer magazine which was hard to get on subscription and cost several rubles at kiosks—under the counter and only to people they knew. On the other hand the kiosks sold *The Morning Star*, the English communist newspaper and *Neues Deutschland*, the German communist newspaper, quite openly. But times were changing, and who on earth cared about *The Morning Star* with its blurred monochrome photos of English soccer players printed on the back page? Now you could get real newspapers like *Echo Planeti, Novy Mir, Novoe Vremy,* and, of course, the magazine *Ogonek.*

Until then I did not think it possible for there to be anything less interesting than *Ogonek* on the face of the planet. My grandfather had a great pile of old copies of *Ogonek* and *Vokrug Sveta*—a sort of Soviet *National Geographic*—in his attic. *Vokrug Sveta* was great, and *Ogonek* absolutely useless.

But now *Ogonek* came into its own.

At the time, the whole country was glued to the TV series *La Piovra,* with police inspector Corrado Cattani. It was an Italian series about the Mafia. *La Piovra* season one, season two, season three, season four. The first—the best—was filmed by Damiano Damiani. But people watched the others seasons too, day and night.

But me, I read *Ogonek.*

What is surprising is that I knew most of the things written in it about Stalin and Soviet history from my friend's father, who'd spent a long time in the labor camps and in exile for a long time. I always believed whatever he told us. It was true, so he told us. Other people argued that things weren't like that at all, and questioned how could he know such things. I never asked where he knew things from, of course, but he told us himself; he said that in the camps everybody knew everything. And everything really was just like he told us.

The best story Uncle Nukri told us was the one about Stalin's death.

Or rather the story about how the news of Stalin's death broke in Siberia.

Many Russian writers have described how they found out. Many of their books were first published during perestroika: Dimitri Panin, whose version of events is more interesting than Solzhenitsyn's, in my opinion, even though he was not a writer and is not nearly as well-known; Lev Razgon, generally such a restrained writer; Varlam Shalamov, who—but I digress.

This, anyway, is how my friend's father told the story:

"I was on duty down the mine and when my shift ended at dawn one of the Starostin brothers came over to have a word. There were four Starostin brothers who all played soccer for Spartak Moscow; they were the real stars of the team and were being held on pretty dubious grounds. I think the real reason they were being held was so that Spartak wouldn't beat CSKA Moscow, which was the army team, or Dynamo Moscow, which was KGB.

"Well, I can't even remember which Starostin brother it was, but he told me he needed to get to the station but couldn't because he had a work shift, so he asked me to go instead. He said the train would be coming through and on it would be Kapler, who was being sent to the labor camp in Khabarovsk. The train was only going to stop for two minutes, but he'd heard from the other guys down the mine that Kapler had a message for him, that he had news.

"I was so exhausted after my shift I could barely stand, but I had to hear the news, so I went down to the station and waited for the train which, unsurprisingly, was late. But at last I saw it coming and ran out onto the platform. The train was really long, with both freight wagons and cattle cars containing prisoners, all with locked doors. I set off to find out which one Kapler was in.

"So I'm running back and forth shouting 'Alexei! Alexei!'

"You remember Kapler? He was the first love of Stalin's daughter Svetlana. She was sixteen, he was forty. Uncle Joe soon brought an end to that romance . . .

"There's that legendary phrase of his: 'Your Jew was an English spy.'

"Kapler was exiled, but he had friends in the secret police, and he actually used to travel back and forth across that vast distance between Siberia and Moscow, and relatively freely. He'd done the journey a few times since the war.

"Anyway, I get to the end of the platform, jump down, and run over. I'm crying 'Alexei, Alexei!' into every wagon and suddenly the train starts to move, I still can't find Kapler, and none of the doors will open. But then just as it starts moving off properly I catch sight of a door opening at the front and suddenly Kapler sticks his head out and starts calling back.

"So I'm still running like crazy, I scramble up onto the platform and the train's picking up speed, Kapler's getting further and further away from me and I shout to him '*Shto*? *Shto*?'—What? What?

"And he shouts '*Stalin umir, Stalin umir*'—Stalin is dead, Stalin is dead—'We'll all be going home now that bastard's gone . . .'

"'What? How? He's dead?'

"'He's dead, he's dead!' I heard him shout from the distance over the sound of the rattling train and I ran around madly in the freezing dawn light on that platform that was empty apart from a couple of station workers, and when I stopped they started running, running after me to find out what had happened.

"And afterward the Starostin brothers told me that Kapler himself had found out from a well-known KGB agent."

Yes, that's what he said. I don't know if I've told it exactly right and I lay no claim to historical accuracy.

Yes, every morning there was aerobics on TV. Women leaping around in headbands.

And aerobics helped us how, exactly?

VI. Utopia . . .

Back when *Once Upon a Time in America* came out, I think the most popular female star would have been the Italian singer Sabrina. There were posters of her plastered all over the place, and I think they even brought her to Moscow to sing.

The women from *Once Upon a Time in America* were not really considered sex symbols. There was no way Elizabeth McGovern, who played Noodles' long-term love, could match Sabrina with her ripped denim hot pants and, of course, the shirt, dutifully unbuttoned, that she made her own. And Deborah and Noodles' love was somehow so chaste, so complex, and ultimately things ended as they always do in this kind of movie: he lost his woman to his best friend.

It was another woman in *Once Upon a Time in America* who grabbed people's interest more.

This second woman appeared in some of the movie's crudest scenes, scenes which for some reason were considered comical; or at least the way people recalled the scenes always prompted them to laugh.

There was a sense with this movie that the funniest bits were the bits people forced themselves to find amusing. It was as if certain people *wanted* the movie to be funny. But the scenes which should have been funny employed such clumsy and ineffective devices that they could not possibly ever be so.

If you ask me, there's only one scene with any comic value: the scene where Patsy eats the cake on the steps. The rest of the movie isn't funny at all, and yet people still laughed.

When people talked about this movie they always mentioned the bit about our dear Noodles raping this other woman during the diamond heist.

In the Russian voice over Max calls out to Noodles during the rape, saying, "Noodles, are you here or there?" And Noodles replies, "I'm here *and* there."

I think this bit of dialogue came about as a result of that famous voice over guy doing a bit of ad-libbing during the recording. In the English-language version they don't say that at all. But there you go.

Anyway, it then turns out that this other woman—I've just watched it again; she's called Carol—was working for the gang all along, and to this day I can't understand why Noodles did what he did.

Actually not why Noodles did what he did. Why Leone did what he did.

I didn't understand the storyline back then and I don't understand it now either.

Why was it necessary?

During the heist the gangsters have handkerchiefs over their faces so that they won't be recognized and so, as you'd expect, Carol doesn't know which one of them raped her. So, when she goes to the speakeasy they start messing around, goading her to say which man raped her, and she asks how she's supposed to recognize him.

And as I've said before, these are men of taste, and there's no way they would think up something like this.

They line up in front of her and tell her to give each of them a try, as it were, so as to jog her memory, and Carol herself seems happy with this.

So anyway, a few people convinced themselves to laugh at this bit, especially the kind of people who'd never actually said anything really funny in their life.

What a terrible thing it is, forced laughter.

But there it was.

It's as if people had to like each and every aspect of this movie.

But what's the point of trying to take these crude scenes and presenting them as humorous? What's the point of inserting humor into this film at all?

I think that earlier on I talked about Burt Young and the scene where he's eating. That shows better than anything what kind of creatures these gangsters are, and yet this scene too was turned into something comical.

To cut a long story short this is a serious movie.

I am not saying that people should only see it in terms of art or great cinematography.

That would be ridiculous.

The majority of people don't know how to think about art and that's no great surprise. They have no interest in it.

It's just that you can't take something that isn't funny and make it funny—you can't take barroom humor out of the bar. You can't take it out, and that's why you go to the bar. And when you get there you force yourself to laugh.

Yes, really this is a serious movie.

As I recall, one of the first items produced by a private enterprise in our country was Samantha Fox keychains.

At the time, Samantha Fox was a well-known and rather well-endowed English glamour model. Anyway, these keychains were basically just her photograph inside a round black frame. I remember them because you'd see them hanging in newspaper kiosks almost everywhere you went.

Until then we'd never even heard of Samantha Fox. We had only heard of poor Samantha Smith.

Samantha Smith was an American girl who campaigned for peace and wrote letters to the Soviet and American leaders pleading with them not to start a war.

So obviously they brought her to Moscow. It was a huge propaganda coup. But then she died in that plane crash. Of course, in propaganda terms poor Samantha wasn't quite on a par with the astrophysicist and hunger-striker Charles Hyder, who protested over many years in front of the White House, nor the American Indian leader Leonard Peltier, who killed two federal agents on the border of his reservation over some conflict or other, but they used her anyway.

Then perestroika started and nobody gave any more thought to the American Indian leader. Prior to that the Soviet Union had sent renowned eye specialists to see Peltier because he was going blind. Then, suddenly, the interest in his blindness evaporated.

Where's Leonard Peltier now, I wonder? Is he even still alive?

During perestroika things really were very strange.

When I say "things" I mean in particular the first things produced in private factories.

For example in the very exclusive Tbilisi neighborhood of Vake, in the twenty-four-hour convenience store, you could buy molded plaster models of Sylvester Stallone, quite big, painted, and wearing stars-and-stripes underpants.

It was Rocky, of course, and they'd taken the mold from an American toy. I think that Stallone would be pleased to know that his plaster figurines triggered a new period of production in Georgia.

These Rocky and Rambo figurines came on the tail of the movies, which by that point there was no point trying to ban.

The first of these previously banned movies to appear on state television was Stallone's *Cobra*.

They showed *Cobra* and Schwarzenegger's *Commando* on the same night.

If I'm not mistaken it was a Sunday night. By then they were already showing Western films on state television, so running all over town with tons of videos was a thing of the past.

All in all they were strange times: while there were a lot of things happening there was also a strange sense of monotony in the air. Why that was I don't really know. The monotony probably came from the fact that all the old stuff had lost its significance. Well, not the old stuff, the Soviet stuff, and as yet very little had come along to replace it.

In other words, the country suddenly became empty and it took a long time to fill up again, even though there was so much stuff flooding in.

Back then they had difficulty getting the water to run up to the villages in the hills above Tbilisi. It was so bad that at night there were queues at the springs. Then there were bread shortages too, but that was a bit later on.

A friend of mine was walking down Rustaveli Avenue on his way back from a party when he was stopped briefly on the street corner by a representative of one of the political parties.

This particular party had its own way of fighting against Soviet imperialism: they said that if we all surrendered our Soviet passports we wouldn't be citizens anymore, and that would effectively take us out of the Soviet Union.

Well, as he was on his way back from a party my friend didn't actually have his passport on him but he went up to their stall anyway and gave them his full name and address and said he would most definitely bring them his passport. Needless to say, by the time he sobered up he'd forgotten about the whole incident, but then one day they came over to his apartment and told him he'd renounced his Soviet citizenship, and that if he surrendered his passport to them he'd get a genuine Georgian one in return.

By then, of course, he'd changed his mind. We still laugh about it even now.

At the time of independence the Georgian passport was a photocopy of the passports that had been issued by the independent Georgian republic of 1918. I've seen one: it's printed in French and Georgian.

As I recall, only one Georgian managed to actually travel on that passport. He got as far as the Baltic States, where his story was even reported in the papers, but because he didn't have any official documents he had some trouble with the local law-enforcement agencies and ended up going on a hunger strike. I think I'm right in saying that his story appeared in Latvia's first opposition newspaper *Atmoda*.

Atmoda was the newspaper of the Popular Front of Latvia; they sold it on Rustaveli Avenue. The Russian edition, obviously.

Back then, those informal newsagents were a breed apart. There were some very colorful individuals among them, too.

On one occasion, we went from the public library over to the consumer societies union building. They had a canteen there, and if we were working in the library we used to pop over for a bite to eat.

When we got to the union building we were met by a large crowd. Apparently there was a union meeting underway.

We looked into the hall.

There was a man standing at the podium and talking about how we should break away from Russia. He said the very same thing about our passports, that we should surrender them and break free of Russia, and even touched on the legal implications, the restoration of the constitution, and other such matters.

As he started to explain the precise procedure in more detail, a man's voice came from somewhere inside the hall:

"Utopia . . ." He said it in Russian.

The man at the podium answered him in Russian, too: "*Pochemu utopia?*"—Why is it utopia?

And the same again: "Utopia . . ."

The heckler was tall and balding, with glasses, a pipe between his fingers which he fiddled with, and white trousers. Overall, he was very smartly dressed. Back then people in Georgia hadn't really started wearing clothes of either that style or quality.

I asked my friend who the man was. He said it was Mamardashvili, and called me an idiot.

Mamardashvili was a Georgian philosopher. Shortly after that he started lecturing at the university.

We didn't have passports yet, true, but we did have passport covers. Protective sleeves, you might call them. They must have been cooperative produce like the tricolor flag badges which were sold in the foot tunnels under Rustaveli. They were plastic flags with a pin stuck on the back.

Around that time there were two flags that taxi drivers liked to stick on their grills: one was the tricolor flag of the Georgian independent republic of 1918–1921, and the second was the old white flag with five red crosses, only slightly different from the Georgian flag we have today. They were both produced by private enterprises, obviously.

The passport covers had the flag of the 1918–21 republic on the front. It was probably considered the best of all the products that appeared at that time. On the front it had "Passport of the Georgian Republic" in a nice modern font, and a picture of Saint George.

Around that time my friend's father went to Germany and put one of these covers on his Soviet passport.

"I crossed the borders, no trouble," he said. A German customs official had a good look at the cover but never asked him anything.

Yes, that's how it was back then.

Anyway, when I think about it now, I can't come up with anything from that period that has survived and remained visible and tangible. A lot of things from back then just never came to anything. The Berikoni nightclub, for instance—I think that closed so soon after it opened because one night the Communist party bigwig Yegor Ligachev showed up there and ruined its image as a cool hangout for young people.

But that was Ligachev for you. Back then he was second in command. He came to the university and asked them to increase the size of the Russian-speaking division. He had real Communist credentials, yes, but real Communists shouldn't start poking around in matters concerning languages and nations.

Anyway, when I think about it now, there is one thing that's survived from that period, and that's Georgia.

It was right at that time that Georgia came into being.

It doesn't matter anymore how it came about, what battles we had to fight, what hoops we had to jump through, and what we sent downstream.

Some things are really regrettable, that's all.

So why watch *Once Upon a Time in America* at all, when the real world is so wonderful?

In fact, I'm not even sure we ever finished watching it.

ZAAL SAMADASHVILI
Selling Books

We took García Márquez, Sartre, Camus, Cortázar, and two volumes of Kafka. Each book nearly new and in good condition. We'd never even opened Thomas Wolfe, Borges, or Hemingway, nor Salinger, nor Bradbury either.

The first things we'd need to buy were kerosene, granulated sugar, margarine, oil, and vermicelli, and if there was any money left over, beans. At first Dad didn't want to take me along. "I don't know long I'll have to stand there," he said. "You'll be tired and cold." It was the end of November, sometimes it rained, sometimes it snowed, people hunched over as they walked through the streets, stray dogs slept on piles of rubbish. My mother really didn't want us to go to the market. What if we saw someone we knew? What on earth would they think?

We set off at first light. There was a power cut so the metro wasn't working. The wind almost blew us away on the long descent down to the River Mtkvari. If we'd thought we were going to be first at the market we were wrong; we were almost the last to arrive. All the spaces were taken. We walked and walked through the hacked-back greenery of the garden and right at the far end ran into one of my father's former students. A thickset lad in glasses, with a red scarf knotted around the collar of his khaki pea-jacket, he didn't seem surprised to see us and greeted us busily. On the ground in front of him was a patterned oilcloth on which he had very precisely laid out a selection of microchips; he moved the oilcloth to one side to make room for us. Dad spread a plastic sheet out on the wet grass. While I was getting the books out of the bag the young man told us which professor was standing in which corner of the garden and what he was selling. It seemed that almost all of them had brought old dinner services and stainless-steel cutlery.

"Aren't they selling books?" my father asked with interest.

The lad seemed not to hear my father's question and held out his hand to me.

"Dima."

"Niko," I said to him, and got the distinct impression that Dima was avoiding giving us an answer we wouldn't like.

People had always sold books in that garden, books and model airplanes . . . And before that, when my father was a child, the garden had housed an enormous statue of Stalin. A political rally which lasted for many days was once held by that statue; later, those who had taken part were shot by the Red Army up on Rustaveli Avenue.

Every now and then the biting wind blew through the poplars that had survived the garden clearance and made their branches creak. The sun, hazy behind dark gray clouds, flickered weak and yellow like the lights in our flat; the cold cut through our flesh and bones. Dad pulled the hat Mom had knitted me down over my ears and brow. He wasn't wearing a hat, and his hands were freezing too.

Dima pulled a flat, flask-like bottle filled with vodka from the bag at his feet. He unscrewed the lid, poured some vodka into it, and passed it to Dad. "We need something to keep us going till it fills up around here and gets a bit warmer, don't we?"

"Here's to our meeting!" my dad said, and drank.

"Here's to a lucky day!" Dima said, and put the bottle to his lips.

When they had taken a few more swigs and emptied the bottle, Dima started speaking.

"Philology's not really a man's subject, but if you've really got your heart set on it you need to either be from a rich family, or be the kind of person who puts their own business before everything else . . . I'm neither of those. It's a good thing I've liked tinkering with stuff since I was a child. An iron, a fridge, a television: whatever you want, I can take it apart, fix it and put it back together again. I don't need an office or a fax machine, I just need a small table and a soldering iron. I've made all of these and I'll support my family with them . . ." He pointed at his microchips: metal sheets, onto which a variety of tiny cylinders and cubes had been soldered with thread-thin wires, and which looked more as if they had been made in a factory than at home.

"You're clearly very skilled," Dad complimented him.

A woman walked by carrying a sheet of plywood with a cloth draped over it.

"She's like me, too," Dima said.

The woman was young, very thin, and pale. Wrapped in a large men's jacket, she took short, rapid steps.

"Her husband's seriously ill. She looks after him and their two children. She trained as a chemist—used to work in the scientific research institute. But now she bakes *khachapuri* instead and sells it, sometimes down here, sometimes at the big market by the station."

"Doesn't *khachapuri* cost a lot to make? Flour for the dough, cheese for the filling . . . How many does she have to sell to get the money to buy more cheese, and how much for?" Dad asked.

"Cheese? What does she need cheese for? You just soak a bit of macaroni in salt water, and no one can tell the difference!" laughed Dima.

My father left the university when the students left the lecture theaters to go out onto the streets and fight for the nation's independence. For a while he taught in a private school. When the school closed he started working at the newspaper. Even though it was a political newspaper, my father never wrote a single word about politics. Instead he just wrote a few letters that stood as appeals to his readers. Like this: "If you want to bear your hardship with dignity and not let hunger, power cuts, and cold drive you to insanity, then read! Music, theater, and cinema have abandoned you; only books and literature have not!"

Eighteen months ago the newspaper ceased publication and since then my father had been out of work. At first he was fine, glad even. "At last," he said, "fate has given me the chance to live the life of a professional writer." He hoped that in the time that had been freed up he would manage to write a lot of short stories and provide for us with his fee.

It didn't happen that way. Nobody needed stories and poems—not his, and not anyone else's either. First my mom sold her earrings, then her ring, then my grandmother's old fur coat with the pockets we stuffed full of mothballs every summer . . .

"I'm looking for worming medicine for Sancho. They told me to come here," a short man in a leather cap said to my father. Like Dima, he didn't seem the slightest bit surprised to find us standing in the market. He was wearing a short overcoat with patches on the elbows and smoking a foul-smelling unfiltered cigarette through a wooden holder.

I remembered Sancho, the cheerful, golden-eared spaniel, straight away. But I barely recognized the man, my father's oldest friend, whose home we visited quite frequently at one point. He was a lot thinner and had aged a great deal.

"They had some over there yesterday." Dima pointed to the far reaches of the garden.

The man thanked him and reached down to pick up Cortázar's short stories.

"It's a good collection . . ."

"The translation's pretty good too," Dad agreed.

"I saw a film a couple of years back, it was based on *The Pursuer*. Charlie Parker came out looking less like a saxophonist and more like a basketball player—an NBA star," Dima said.

"When it comes to ruining books, film directors are the experts," the man smiled.

"Apart from Forman," my father corrected him.

The man nodded his head in agreement.

"I read his autobiography recently; he writes beautifully," he added a few moments later.

"That's probably because he pays such attention to how others write," Dad said.

"It really is a lovely collection," said the man in the leather cap, and bent down to put the book back. Dad grabbed his wrist. "Think of it as a gift," he said.

The man tried to protest—had my father gone quite mad?—but in the end it was no good. Blushing a little, and with an embarrassed smile, he said good-bye.

"You're not going to do very well if you carry on like that. Have you come here to sell stuff or hand out presents?" Dima reproached us.

"Have you any idea how extraordinary a writer he is?" Dad said.

Dima shrugged his shoulders—what did he know?—and then suddenly tapped his index finger against his forehead.

"All the time he was talking I kept asking myself where I knew him from. He was at my neighbor's house recently; he was wearing that coat with patches then too. He fixes pianos . . ."

Dima needn't have bothered with his warning; we did better than all of the experienced market-sellers, and by three o'clock we'd sold every single book.

First, some young men came over and stood around drinking beer rather noisily from cans. They complimented us on our "goods" and asked whether we had any new issues of literary journals. When we told them we hadn't they started moaning, said we were keeping them in an intellectual vacuum, drained their cans, and left.

The minute they left a guy of indeterminate age with a large bag and only half his teeth came along. He bought every single book—and he didn't even haggle. That made Dima suspicious: clearly the man was an experienced dealer who knew he was getting valuable books dirt cheap.

Dad reassured him and invited him to come for *khinkali*[2] with us. But he had work to do and declined our invitation. We didn't dare offer him any money; we knew he'd be offended even though that day nobody had gone anywhere near his microchips . . .

We went down to the restaurant that had opened by St. Nicholas' church on the banks of the Mtkvari to get some *khinkali*. Above the entrance to the cellar restaurant hung a decorative sign in the style of one of Pirosmani's paintings. It was warm in the cellar. Because very little daylight penetrated the grill on the tiny window, the oil lamps on the walls were already lit. Only one of the four or five tables was occupied, by some men who were eating *khinkali* washed down with vodka and beer; they looked like the kind of men who sprang up all over the city at times of war and revolution—heavy beards and mustaches, narrow brows, eyes darting furtively . . .

We ordered *khinkali* too—twenty of those meat dumplings—a jug of beer and a bottle of Coca-Cola.

We were just about to dig in when out of the corner of my eye I saw several small, reddened hands poking in through the window grill. Several voices came pleading at once: "Sir, give us a few *khinkali*, would you, just one or two?"

"Those damn kids are such a pain in the ass! Can't we even eat our dinner in peace?" the men drinking vodka moaned.

The waiter came dashing out from behind the bar like a large shaggy dog let off the leash, and while he tried to placate his angry customers Dad grabbed a dish full of *khinkali* and went up to the street. He came back empty-handed, of course, and in a voice that was purposefully loud said, "Let's get out of here . . ."

---

1   Boiled pockets of dough filled with meat and spiced and sealed with drawstring-type folds at the top.

On the stairs the waiter arrogantly blocked our way.

"Who's going to pay for the dish?" he shouted.

I don't know what I thought my father would do next: pay him the money, argue, maybe even apologize, but instead, and unexpectedly, he pushed his fist right up against the waiter's nose and quietly said, "This is . . ."

My heart didn't leave my mouth until we were a block away from the restaurant; when things had got tense I'd noticed one of the men drinking vodka had a handgun tucked into his waistband . . .

We went to the market and bought everything we needed. We put some money aside for the kerosene. When we got home Mom had made fried potatoes with onion for us. Dad finished his quickly and went out of the kitchen. "I'm going to do some writing," he said to my mother, "your son and I have survived an interesting day."

What my father wrote in his thick notebook that night I do not know. But I told my mother everything in detail. I complimented Dima—what a nice lad, I said, to let us share his space. Then I remembered the question Dad had asked when they were talking about the other professors selling at the market. Why had he not answered, I asked my mother. Tears came to her eyes and after a brief silence she told me, "People like us sell the books from their shelves when they've nothing else left to sell . . . That boy knew that and he didn't want to upset you." And I finally understood . . .

Surely Dad knew better than Dima that we had nothing left to sell but our books? Of course he knew, but he hadn't fully appreciated that selling his books meant he was close to crossing a very dangerous line, and that something terrible was waiting on the other side. It was only when he asked the question out loud—"Aren't they selling books?"—and got no answer back because the other person pitied him that he suddenly felt it, felt that he was teetering on the edge of a yawning chasm. He felt it and got his second wind, like a mountain-climber who loses his grip, slips, then manages to grab on, pull himself back up . . . That was what it meant to raise his fists to that waiter in front of a room full of dangerous men. His behavior since that moment had convinced me of this: leaving the kitchen to write "some stuff" where in the past he would have pleaded tiredness and gone to lie on the sofa with his face to the wall, and the phrase he used with my mother: "your son and I have survived an interesting day . . ." The emphasis was on "survived." With me by his side, my father had survived a very difficult experience. In a nutshell, he had survived selling his books . . .

NUGZAR SHATAIDZE

November Rain

"Pardon me? Pardon?" Aleksandre cupped his hand to his ear, tilted his head slightly to one side, and stared with blinking, reddened eyes at Parunashvili, who was sitting in the third row.

Outside it was raining and dark. The classroom could be seen reflected in the wet window panes; Aleksandre was reflected there too, an old man with his hand cupped against his ear, head tilted slightly to one side, and staring fixedly at Parunashvili, while the other students in the young workers' evening class sat behind their desks in silence and with their heads bowed.

"Parunashvili, stand up and repeat what you just said!"

"Don't shout at me." Parunashvili's face clouded over.

"I said stand up!"

"You're praising class enemies and spouting bourgeois propaganda and on top of that you're shouting at me!"

"Who, boy? Who is this class enemy?" A bewildered smile played on the old man's lips.

"The writer of this poem, who else?"

Aleksandre turned deadly pale, took his handkerchief out of his pocket, cleaned his chalk-covered fingers, then went over to Parunashvili, grabbed him by the ear, and shook his head violently.

A flurry of whispers swept through the classroom.

Parunashvili pulled his head back and freed his ear from the teacher's hand. Aleksandre rapped his crooked finger sharply down onto the crown of his slightly balding head.

"Ha!—" An uneven smile appeared on Parunashvili's lips.

Aleksandre turned back around, went to his desk, pulled out his chair, sat down, and gazed sternly at the motionless class.

* * *

Aleksandre struggled for a long time to get through the door with his umbrella, which was already open.

He walked home, going slowly like the old man he was. There were large puddles on the pavements; Aleksandre, wearing galoshes, walked straight through them.

In the cold, fine November drizzle the street was deserted apart from him.

As he got farther away from the school building he heard the sound of hurried steps behind him. It was Kolya Purtskhvanidze, the school principal, no doubt—he always caught up with Aleksandre at exactly the same point on the way home, after which they would carry on their journey together.

He stopped and turned to look behind him. Yes, it was Kolya: a tall, spidery man. In the darkness Aleksandre could not make out the director's expression, but he sensed that something was troubling him.

Kolya looked around as he got nearer, carefully surveying the empty street, and instead of putting his hand on Aleksandre's arm and making a lighthearted comment as he usually did, he just asked him sternly, "What have you done, Aleksandre, eh?"

"What have I done?"

"Don't you know who Parunashvili is?"

Aleksandre got angry. "Do you know what he said to me?"

"I know, I know the whole story. The whole school's talking about it."

"So?"

The director looked up and down the empty street again, ducked his head under the old umbrella and whispered, "He's with the secret police, Aleksandre!"

"I don't care who he is!"

Kolya looked startled, straightened up again, and stood looking down at the short, old man. They stared at each other in silence for a while.

It was raining. The water ran in streams off the umbrella.

"Let's just let it go, can we? After all, we're not children. I mean, how could you do that?"

"And what should I do now, then? Apologize? Maybe go over to his house and kneel down before him?"

"No, no." Purtskhvanidze didn't appreciate the humor.

"Well then?"

The director thought for a moment. "Are you staying somewhere else tonight?"

"What, I'm supposed to hide?"

"And don't come to school for the time being either."

"Are you suspending me from work, young man?"

"For a while, for a while, I said!"

The director turned around and walked off quickly down the wet pavement.

* * *

"Are you in any pain, Sasha?"

Aleksandre didn't answer; he didn't even hear his wife's question. He was sitting on a high-backed armchair with his hands on his bony knees and staring fixedly ahead, lost in thought and with his head swaying slightly.

He loved sitting in this armchair. Even as a younger man he had enjoyed quiet and calm, but when he retired he took this to extremes—he slacked off so much that he stopped even going out to buy the newspaper anymore. He shackled himself like an invalid to his threadbare armchair, and sat there either sleeping or thinking, and his wife could ask him a question ten times without getting an answer.

Elene was not concerned at first. She put it down to his age—what could she do?—but when he stopped even shaving she started to worry more seriously. She realized that Aleksandre had thrown in the towel; he had become a prisoner of old age and was now waiting calmly, uncomplainingly for death.

At first she was angry to see a strong man like him becoming so timid that he simply folded his hands across his chest and lay down in his grave, destroying his life of his own free will. Soon, though, she started to feel sorry for him—he was still her husband, they had faced life's challenges and struggles together for almost half a century, and her memories of that time were as sweet as they were bitter.

In fact she blamed herself a bit—had they had a child, she thought, he surely would have not given up like this, become so resigned, he would have focused on his grandchildren, their love would have helped him withstand and endure old age. All she could think of was what she should do, how she should help this man. She tried different ways to rouse him from his chair: she pointed out what a beautiful day it was, asked what on earth he wanted to spend it inside for, suggested he go for a walk, give his eyes something nice to look at.

On one occasion she brought him some theater tickets and made him shave and put on a suit and tie. They went to the play, mingled among the crowds, saw a couple of people they knew. Aleksandre rallied a bit, and seemed somewhat buoyed, but the next day he was back in that armchair that was so old it was fit for the fire, sitting there silent, torpid, lost in thought.

Finally, Elene realized that neither strolling in the street nor going to the theater was enough to help Aleksandre now—idleness was slowly killing him. Previously, when he worked at the school, he felt needed, felt he had a purpose. Now, though, he had become a useless burden, and that was why he was so low. When a man has no purpose, what value does his life have?

Elene bustled around and fussed over him and finally sought out his former pupil Kolya Purtskhvanidze. She explained the situation to him and told him what she wanted him to do. The very next day she invited him over to their house, where he spent so long telling Aleksandre that he had nobody to teach him Georgian and that Aleksandre was his last hope that Aleksandre actually believed him.

And that is how Aleksandre came to be working at the evening school. He only worked for a few hours, three times a week, but the change in him was so dramatic that he became almost unrecognizable—he was more positive, it was almost as if he was having a second youth—and that was why when now she saw him so torpid and pensive again she asked him if he was in pain.

* * *

"Are you in pain?"

Aleksandre didn't answer her; he sat there with a fixed gaze, deep in thought.

Elene left the table, went over to him, stood in front of him and gazed at him with a sad smile on her face.

Only now did he see his wife.

"Hm-hm!" He cleared his throat.

"Come on, get up. Let's have dinner."

"Yes, all right, all right!" But Aleksandre sat there for a while longer, staring at the pictures of famous writers that hung on the wall above the writing table: Akaki Tsereteli, Vazha Psahvela, Ilia Chavchavadze. Underneath them in an oval frame there was a photograph of his father-in-law, Colonel Giorgi Janelidze.

"Get up, don't be so lazy!"

He leaned on the armrests, suppressed a groaning that stirred somewhere within him and just about managed to stand up.

Elene had laid out a paltry feast: tea, bread, cheese, cherry jam.

He pulled up a chair and sat down.

"You don't seem quite yourself," his wife said casually.

Aleksandre stirred his tea and stared at it as if he was going to say something.

"Well?" his wife prompted him.

"I think I'm getting old, Eliko." Aleksandre smiled.

"Oh, well that's nothing new, is it?" His wife stared at him doubtfully.

"Do you know who I just thought of? Your father. I could almost see him standing there in front of me, bless his soul."

Elene smiled. She turned her own mind to the quiet, well-loved man, spirited and indomitable, even after the death of his wife.

"Do you remember when he built the house on the slopes in Aghbulakhi?"

Elene mimicked her father: "Garden? What do I need a garden for, I'll just go and stand on a boulder and look around!"

Aleksandre mimicked somebody else: "'Has Colonel Janelidze gone completely mad? Where on earth is he building that house?'"

"I can remember the smell of those apples even now. And peaches. Do you remember those peaches he used to send us?"

"Do you remember the first time we visited him what a splendid evening he put on for us? He'd invited absolutely everyone. 'My daughter from Paris!'" Now Aleksandre mimicked his father-in-law, and clearly very well, because Elene laughed out loud.

"What about when he wanted to get married again? At eighty years old, can you imagine?"

"Yes, laugh, laugh! But he managed to find himself a beautiful fiancée, didn't he! And who? Abashidze's daughter!"

"The fool! She thought he'd die and leave her his millions—little did she know he was up to his ears in debt!"

"And she was so young, so beautiful! I can't lie to you, Eliko, I wouldn't say no to a woman like that either!"

"Yes, yes, you're a veritable Don Juan too, don't worry!"

They sat there and laughed. They laughed low and hearty, just as the old should.

"Oh, Giorgi, Giorgi!" Aleksandre sighed.

Elene sipped her tea and gazed at her husband with a bewildered smile and said, "Will you look at that! Our tea's gone cold!"

* * *

After dinner Elene cleared the table, washed the dishes and made up the beds, then turned down the oil lamp and went to bed.

Aleksandre pottered about for a while longer, got his glasses, opened the day's newspaper, and started to look at it, but when his wife called him— "Come to bed, man, you need to sleep!"—he went into the bedroom, got undressed and got into bed.

He knew he wouldn't get to sleep and he was right; no matter how hard he tried, no matter how much he tossed and turned, he was unable to get a wink of sleep. Elene fell asleep quickly, but Aleksandre just lay there and thought about it all over again: he could see Parunashvili's face, deadly pale, and his evil expression; he recalled Kolya Purtskhvanidze's words, too—He's with the secret police!—and a cold, sticky liquid filled his soul. He knew that a creeping, insidious fear was the cause; he tried to fight it off, telling himself it made no difference who Purtskhvanidze was or where he worked, but at the same time he heard a second voice telling him he was wrong, that it really was a stupid thing he had done. What should he do then, go to him, fall on his knees, and beg his pardon? Aleksandre got angry with himself but there, too, the internal voice lay in wait, telling him that wouldn't help him either, that nothing would help if Parunashvili really was devious, if he really did work for the secret police, that he would not forgive Aleksandre for grabbing his ear and rapping him on the head, that it was really all over for him now. The voice sounded just like Kolya Purtskhvanidze. But Aleksandre reasoned to himself that he was a good person, that his students were not little children, that Parunashvili had verbally abused him, lambasted him if you will. Something had provoked Aleksandre to grab his ear and rap him on the head. The internal voice had fallen silent, it gave not even the slightest whisper, but Aleksandre felt that it was right there tucked away in some corner of his brain, with bated breath, watching him in silence.

In the end, finally, he fell asleep and dreamed that he was sitting at a row of desks in the classroom, and that the teacher, Evdokim Romanovich Katurov, with his ginger beard and mustache and wearing a black frock coat, was walking calmly up and down between the rows with his hands behind his back and intoning, "Our father . . ." in a sing-song voice.

"Our father!" the pupils shouted back, in a discordant din.

"All together!" Katurov ordered.

"Our father all together!" repeated the confused pupils.

"Our father, who—is—in—heaven, say it all together!"

The class followed his instruction with a low mumbled roar and Aleksandre covered his face with his hand to hide the fact that, while pretending to make an effort, he was not actually speaking at all and did not want his teacher to notice his passiveness. But Katurov recognized the deceit, walked over angrily, and hit him with the cane.

He woke up in terror. His hands were shaking.

The lamp had gone out and the room smelled of kerosene.

Aleksandre lay on his back and tried to regain his composure after his nightmare. Listening to his wife's gentle breathing, he gradually calmed down. At last he felt back to his normal self.

His dream reminded him of his childhood and school days: every day before the start of lessons the teachers would assemble the pupils in a large classroom to recite the Lord's Prayer and other prayers together. The teachers spent the first three weeks teaching the pupils these prayers off by heart, and only after that did they start teaching them the Russian alphabet. Their method of teaching was simple, and it was completely useless: the teacher held a book in his hand and broke the sentences up into individual words and recited these slowly, before the pupils repeated them back to him in short phrases, following along with their right index finger in the books that lay open on the bench as they did so. Sometimes the teacher would stop reading and check that all the children had their finger on the right word, and woe to any child that didn't! Katurov kept his flexible cane hidden behind his back, ready for them. The children found it very difficult to learn the alphabet in this way and it took two or three years for them to be able to read more or less fluently. In contrast, they finished school not knowing how to read or write in Georgian at all. Georgian was only taught in schools after 1905, by which time Aleksandre was already a teacher himself.

One day his father, a proud but illiterate peasant, brought some documents home that were written in Georgian, and after dinner he gave them to his son, saying, "Be a good child and read these to me, will you?" As he did so he looked around with thinly veiled pride at the numerous family members gathered around the table, as if to say, "Look, this is what the child's education is for; I haven't paid those school fees for nothing, you know!" Aleksandre stared down at the documents and then, since he could not understand any of it, he looked at his father rather guiltily and mumbled, "I can't read Georgian."

"What do you mean? You've been going to school all this time and you don't know how to read?" His father said in astonishment. "What kind of learning is that? Well, to hell with them. To hell with that school and those teachers! You won't be going there anymore; you can just bring a hoe and come up to the fields with me!"

His mother stepped in. "He doesn't need school to teach him Georgian! I'll teach him the Georgian alphabet within a month, you see if I don't!"

And sure enough the very next day the mother laid an open book in front of Aleksandre and said to him, "Look, this one is 'a.' See if you can find me another one like it!"

Aleksandre did so immediately.

"Yes, and that one makes the sound 'a.' Go on, find me another 'a.'"

Aleksandre found another one.

"What sound does it make, son?"

"It's 'a.'"

"Well done!" his mother praised him, kissed him, and stroked his head.

She taught him the whole alphabet that way. Then they moved onto writing; they found a large bone—the shoulder blade of an ox—cleaned it well, polished it up, and collected a pile of small sticks with charred ends. His mother wrote letters on the polished bone and told him the letter names: "This is called 'a' and this is 'b', and here we have 'c' and 'd.' Can you say the names?"

Aleksandre repeated the names of the letters back to his mother.

"Now, write me an 'a'!"

Aleksandre did so with ease; his hand was already used to writing because of the time he had spent in school.

"Now write me a 'b'!" his mother told him.

He wrote that too and then followed it with a 'c', 'd', and 'e.'"

And in that way he learned to read and write Georgian in exactly a month. His mother had brought books with her as part of her dowry—*The Knight in the Tiger's Skin*—and other great works, and soon he managed to read them even better than his mother could.

Aleksandre sighed and rolled over in bed. For some reason he always remembered his mother as a young woman whereas in fact, unlike his father, she lived long and died well into old age. He often tried to remember his mother as an old woman, dressed in an old Georgian dress, a traditional headband and pad covering her head, sitting on the floor on a rug—but he always struggled, and even now, when he really racked his brains to imagine an old woman in her eighties, her face lined with age, he could not associate that with his mother, in his mind ever young, beautiful, and with a soft, sweet voice.

His memories of his father were rather vague in comparison. Sometimes he would picture his severe face, his suspicious expression, his large, thick hands that were always, always busy doing something: holding a stick and herding cattle, or driving the hoe into the earth in the fields, or sharpening his scythe before kneeling to cut the grass, chopping wood, digging, washing out wine jars, carving a wheel rim for his cart, weaving a basket, or crumbling cold corn bread into his pot of boiled beans after a long, tiring day's work in the vineyard.

Aleksandre came back from the gold deposits in Bodaia to find his father already dead. The man had been replaced by a small, already grassy mound in the yard of the church of the Trinity. He sat by that mound all night long, smoking tobacco and thinking about his ill-fated life, the years that were wasted in prison and in Siberia, about his father lying there in the ground with his arms folded across his chest, peacefully decomposing and calmly rejoining the very earth over which he had spent his life bent double, moaning like a hard-working ox.

Aleksandre suddenly saw that such calm peacefulness was the point of existence. This was not all that surprising from a man who had spent so long in prison and exile, but from that night onward he always sought out peace and calm. Having tripped and stumbled once, he subsequently tried to walk with great care, because he remembered the horror and pain of that day with such bitterness.

He often thought about Siberia too, and the awful humiliation and suffering he underwent in prison, but he always kept those thoughts inside himself, in his head. He never spoke to anyone about it, not even Elene.

In the final days of 1906 when Aleksandre was working as a teacher at Zugdidi elementary school, his colleague Vasiko Alshibaia, who was a teacher at the same school and a member of the Zugdidi District Federalists' Committee, took him to a committee session. Aleksandre did not really want to go at all—he had decided not to get involved in politics—but felt he could not refuse Vasiko's request and so went with him to the session, where what was apparently a very important matter was being discussed: the Social Federalists were deciding whether to approve the killing of the District Leader Vasily Keghashov and his two police superintendents, Kvaratskhelia and Shengelaia. They had already passed sentence on Keghashov in a previous session and approved his killing, but the debate about the two policemen had been going on for a long time without a ruling being made. At the committee session that Aleksandre attended, Vasiko Alshibaia stated that killing the superintendents was completely unnecessary because they were clearly no more than pawns in Keghashov's hands. Aleksandre was allowed to vote, he obviously sided with Vasiko, and it was he who saved the superintendents' lives.

As already mentioned, Vasily Keghashov had already been sentenced to death at the previous session and Aleksandre was of course not consulted about this at all. On the other hand he was included in discussions about bringing a bomb from Kutaisi, told that the task had been entrusted to someone called Chkheidze, and that this Chkheidze would store the bomb in Vano Chanturia's pharmacy. But fate was smiling on Keghashov—Superintendent Shengelaia found the bomb and arrested all the members of the committee in a single night—Aleksandre among them.

In criminal law at that time, political prisoners were classified according to three categories of crime: a) verbal rebellion against the state and the government, punishable by up to three years' imprisonment without loss of civil rights; b) membership (even passive) of a secret organization opposed to the existing state regime, punishable by up to four years' hard labor and complete loss of civil rights; and c) membership of a secret organization and activity involving weapons, punishable by hard labor or death.

Aleksandre was found guilty under the second category and sentenced to four years' hard labor and exile in Siberia.

The Social Democrats' and Federalists' provincial committees hatched a plan to dig a tunnel into Kutaisi Prison and smuggle out the political prisoners before they were sent off on the long journey to Russia. The plan was to start the tunnel in the house belonging to the Social Federalist Varlam Pantskhava, which was across the street from the prison, only a short distance away.

With the help of Giorgi Zdanevich, chairman of the Chiatura Manganese Industrialists' Council and director of the Social Federalist provincial committee, they brought in professional pit tunnelers and a mining engineer. Work started on digging the tunnel from Pantskhava's basement, and on the sixteenth day it emerged in one of the prison cells, under a bed.

One by one the prisoners went down to the cell, squeezed into the tunnel, crawled a hundred and fifty meters or so and came up in the basement of Pantskhava's house, where representatives of the provincial committee were waiting for them with passports, money, and clothes. The prisoners, dressed in dinner jackets, tailcoats, and top hats, followed each other one by one out of Pantskhava's house right under the prison guards' eyes, got into a carriage that had been specially ordered for them, and then left the area as quickly as they could.

The one man who was on the list but did not manage to get out of the prison was Aleksandre.

* * *

Outside it was still raining.

Aleksandre woke up properly, then lay there for a while listening to the sound of his wife's breathing and the rain outside. Then he got up, put his feet into the slippers he'd flung down onto the floor, put on the striped shirt that was hanging on the back of the chair, and went out into the living room.

The large, wide room had two windows looking out onto the street. Outside, in front of the house, a portable gas lamp attached to a tall wooden pole flickered, casting a beam through the window and spreading its faint light from outside. Aleksandre opened the thin, sheer curtains and looked out onto the street. In the light of the street lamp he could see how lopsidedly it hung. He stood there in silence and watched the rain, the wet pavement, and the leafless acacias that lined the street, standing like strangers in the darkness.

He always thought that the weather on this cold, rainy November night was just the kind of weather in which he should die. In summer, or especially in spring, death seemed to him to be so senseless, like fate's bitter mockery. He had spent so long thinking about it that he had come to hate the rain—and indeed the month of November as a whole—wholly and entirely. Thinking about this fateful period always filled his heart with a heavy despondency; he lost his enthusiasm for life and wanted only to sit by himself next to his mother's grave by the Church of the Trinity on the hill, deep in thought, and to die his own bittersweet death right there too.

For some reason he was sure that there, in the village of his birth, on that hill next to the blue church wall, his death would be more natural, more logical, and so considerably simpler than here in this shelterless city. But anyway, what was death—the end or the beginning? Aleksandre had believed for as long as he could remember that death was a terrible force that mercilessly destroyed and devastated every earthly being in this world, that turned man into a lifeless corpse, and that terrifying thought perplexed him and made him lose his zest for life, but recently in the night skies of his despair hope had twinkled like a distant star, and true, it was as yet a small, insignificant hope that struggled against niggling doubt, but it was a hope nonetheless: the hope that death was, in fact, the beginning of a great and unknown reality.

As yet this hope was so feeble that it brought no real relief. Nonetheless it resembled a beacon lighting the course for a lost ship circling aimlessly through turbulent seas, showing it the way to the distant shore. Little by little he started to believe that he too should follow that course, he too should swim toward that shore, because right there on that promised shore was the thing he had been waiting for, the thing which would dispel his bitterness and torment.

Back then, in his distant childhood, when he repeated the words of the prayers his mother had taught him, life seemed to him to be laid out specifically to remind him that everything—every stone, every blade of grass, every living being, including him, his parents, his village, and the entire world—had one lord and master: the boundlessly kind, justly severe God the Father. He was behind everything that happened, he was mankind's shepherd and guardian, and Aleksandre only had to believe in him and follow him and everything would be all right. But as time went on Aleksandre grew up, and day by day grew more distant from his mother's apron strings and his father's caring, calloused hands, and gradually he started to believe that life was considerably harsher and more merciless than he had previously thought. God did not involve himself in man's affairs and even if he did exist, he existed for himself alone, in a corner very far removed from the world, and was not in the least bit interested in the destiny of mankind, his own creation.

He first began to doubt God's existence when he was ten or eleven and watched his elderly neighbor beat his old dog to death with a cudgel while it was tethered to a post on the cattle stall. Even as an adult he could still remember how the man had battered the poor animal, the dog's bloodied body, the horrendous moaning which sounded almost human and its eyes, in which he could read both terrible suffering and astonishing loyalty. He remembered too how the old man finished the job, washed his hands right there in a water trough and then sat down under the roof overhang with the satisfied expression of one who has done his duty to have his dinner. Later, after he had experienced firsthand the inhumanity and humiliation suffered by prisoners in Novorossiysk and Oryol prisons, and the unbearable, suffocating regime of the hard labor camps in Znamensk and Bodaia, his doubts intensified that God was nothing more than a fairy-tale character invented by man, like Snow White, Puss in Boots, or the Gingerbread Man.

But now that the distant shore was becoming ever clearer through the hazy fog of uncertainty, Aleksandre in turn became ever more convinced that he had missed the true path in life and gone off in another direction entirely, and now that he had arrived somewhere else he found himself looking at that strange, wholly unfamiliar place with great confusion.

After he had spent four years in Oryol prison he was exiled to Znamensk and there, in a local prostitute's cabin, Aleksandre had caught sight of himself in the mirror and was horrified—his own father was staring out at him from the mirror. Surprised and appalled, he realized only later that this craggy, gray-haired man, old before his time, was him. The strange sensation he felt was a lot like the feeling he was experiencing now, in his old age—it seemed to him almost as if now, too, he was standing confused and dismayed in front of the mirror, unable to recognize the reflection of his own being, because it was an entirely different man that stared back out at him. Yes, a different man, because a person always imagines himself to be slightly better-looking than he actually is, and now, looking wide-eyed at that distant shore he clearly saw a strange, completely unfamiliar person, who in reality was him.

* * *

The change within him had not actually started with him.

The year before, one bright, cold Sunday, when Aleksandre had brought the wood up from the basement and was preparing to light the stove, somebody knocked on the door and after a few moments Eliko came in with their new neighbor, Niko.

Niko was forty years old, of medium build, a slightly balding, swarthy man. He had deep black eyes that glinted constantly and very white teeth. These eyes and teeth somehow made him seem trustworthy to people whether they liked it or not. That was the case for Aleksandre, and for Elene too, who in general did not like people who grinned happily for no reason.

Niko was holding a chess set, but it soon became clear that playing chess was just a pretext for getting to know his new neighbors; after two games Niko threw the pieces back into the box, crossed his legs and started talking about himself. He spent almost the entire evening telling the elderly couple about his rather ordinary, unremarkable life very openly and with an almost childlike naïveté. He spoke with innocence about his own feelings, aims, and aspirations and it seemed to Aleksandre that this man— so much younger than his years—was showing the two of them a special degree of trust and asking for a similar degree of frankness and trust from them in return. He had only ever seen anything like this in prison—only there were people so direct, sincere, and quick to make friendships with each other. These friendships, as a rule, turned out to be short-lived; once in the outside world they were not pursued, but left inside the prison walls like old clothes no longer fit for wear. A friendship formed during imprisonment was rather like a stinking old coat, covered in scorch marks, as superfluous a burden outside prison as it had been necessary protection from the cold when inside prison.

From that evening onward they were very close, and would often sit playing chess with each other or chatting around the samovar. Sometimes, if a reason presented itself, they would drink wine, and then Aleksandre would became more frank and eloquent—he would tell his tales of the labor camps and exile, often talking about things he had never mentioned aloud before and it was almost as if by doing so he was repaying his neighbor for his own frankness. Niko, on the other hand, talked about his day-to-day life—he was unhappy with the Bolshevik regime, he worried about Georgia's servitude, he reviled those who had sold out their homeland for their political ambitions or careers.

From these conversations Aleksandre realized that his new neighbor felt like a prisoner in his own homeland, that his surroundings had become his prison walls, and that his unusual frankness and directness, which set him so apart from other people, was less an innate quality and more a means of acquiring friends. Niko needed a friend just as badly as any prisoner locked in a cell and embittered by loneliness.

Niko's wife Nunu, an attractive woman almost fifteen years younger than her husband, was pregnant and due to go into labor any day, and because of this she needed special care. Her parents lived in western Georgia, whereas Niko had lost his mother when just a child and his father a year later; his older sister had married a butcher from the city and had her own children and grandchildren to look after and so clearly was not able to help these newlyweds.

It was Eliko who helped Niko's wife—sometimes she would take her hot meals, sometimes help her with the laundry and other strenuous household chores, and in doing so made the pregnant woman's life easier. Aleksandre could see the two women growing closer day by day, and as their bond grew it began to resemble that of a mother and daughter, rekindling within Elene the motherly instinct that had died out so long before, and moreover because of it her whole attitude toward her husband, her family, and the world in general began to change.

At first Aleksandre was startled by the change in his wife; it irritated him, because it seemed that she was escaping from a fortress built over many years and whose ruler was Aleksandre himself, and as if the tenants who had settled in his tower were seizing with stubborn determination every floor, every room, and dividing up his possessions—the armchairs, slippers, crockery, and cutlery—with an almost impudent desire, but when one blustery February day Nunu's stomach began to ache, when Aleksandre spent the whole night with Niko at the maternity home in a cold, dark waiting room, when in the morning the birthing assistant congratulated Niko on the birth of his son and Aleksandre, mistakenly, on the birth of his grandson, he felt something melt in his heart and its awe-inspiring warmth course through his veins.

That day his life changed fundamentally: he tried to be with the child as much as he could, stayed close at hand, loved to watch how the women took care of him, how they bathed him, how they laid him in his cradle. Sometimes he would pick the child up and when he felt the warmth and smell of his flesh he was always filled with a strange sense of joy.

Who can say why or how, but one thing was clear: it was the birth of new life that showed Aleksandre that distant shore and that hope-giving beacon that illuminated a life which until then had been rather confused and chaotic. Now everything, every corner of his life seemed to be in order and Aleksandre felt a strange sense of faith and calm settle slowly in his heart.

* * *

Outside it was still raining. Aleksandre lit the night-light. The clock was showing half past three. Ilia, Vazha, and Akaki looked down at him from the wall. Underneath them hung the oval frame containing the photograph of Giorgi Janelidze. The old man put his palm against the warm outer wall of the stove, then knelt down, opened the round iron door, spread the dying embers with the tongs and put in some chopped firewood. Suddenly Parunashvili's ashen face and blanched lips appeared before him once again and he sat in his armchair and pulled his checked blanket over him.

He was filled with a strange feeling, almost as if this had happened before, as if he had been through something like this—exactly like this—in the past, and the feeling alarmed and perturbed him, and he must have turned cold suddenly because in the pit of his stomach there was a terrible pain which reminded him with remarkable clarity of that story from long ago, the story that filled him with feelings of shame and embarrassment and which he had spent his whole life trying to forget.

He remembered his cell in Kutaisi Prison and saw himself lying there on the bed, doubled up with terrible stomach pain, and he saw Vasiko Alshibaia and Vano Goguadze standing over him holding the list of prisoners to be smuggled out. Rendered immobile by pain and clutching at his stomach with his hands, Aleksandre was unable to move from where he lay and kept repeating one thing over and over in an exhausted voice: "You go, my brother, you go, leave me here!" But then, when it was all over and the twenty-second prisoner had safely escaped, Aleksandre's stomach pain suddenly eased off, almost as if it had been waiting for that moment, and he was overcome with the unexpected relief of someone who has escaped an ordeal that would have brought them their liberty. Now though, when he sat in his favorite armchair and thought about the events of the previous evening, it seemed to him as if the house of cards he had built up over so many years was falling down and being gradually replaced by an astonishingly real and tangible feeling of terrifying, overwhelming fear.

The stove heated up and filled the room with warmth.

He was becoming more and more convinced that they would be coming for him tonight. Maybe it would be better to wake his wife and tell her everything. If nothing else she would at least get him a clean pair of socks and some underwear. But he did not move from where he was sitting, some kind of unidentified hope stopped him, and he thought that maybe it was not raining as much as thundering, and that if he knew Elene at all she would accuse him of cowardice.

His stomach pain worsened.

He recalled the days he had spent in other Russian prisons; in his head he could hear the awful clanking of handcuffs and the shouts of men being transported in the convoy. He recalled the transit prisons in Chelyabinsk and Irkutsk, the poverty and near-starvation of Znamensk, and finally his transfer to Bodaia.

After seven years of tortuous, hellish labor at the gold deposits, Aleksandre had collected around ten pounds of gold which he converted into money in Irkutsk before sending it back to Georgia—a pound of gold fetched five hundred rubles, but when he got back to Tbilisi and paid ten rubles rather than one for two dishes in the station restaurant he realized that he had done something very foolish. At that point in time, Georgia was the closest point to the border between the Russian and Ottoman empires and so the exchange rate there was much lower than in Irkutsk, whereas on the other hand gold was valued considerable more highly; if he had brought back the ten pounds of gold instead of money he would have been set up for life. However, because he was fortunate to be returning to his homeland at all, Aleksandre did not let this realization trouble him for long.

Interminable war, economic hardship, and finally the February Revolution destroyed the Russian empire. In Georgia this led to an resurgence in political activity but Aleksandre, frightened by prison and exile, did not get involved in politics; he devoted all his energies to finding peace and quiet, and to a sedate family life, and so he brought the wife he had not seen for eleven years from the village to Tbilisi, bought a two-room apartment in Sololaki and the devoted couple, forced to spend so much time apart, finally set up a loving, peaceful home together.

Aleksandre was fifty-one years old by then and in poor health, weakened after years of hard labor and exile, but once he was back in his own environment with Elene providing such tender care he became stronger again. They did not have children, but this did not get in the way of them having a happy family—theirs was a sweet, amicable, consensual union and seemed to understand each other even without the need for words. They even worked together, in the same school; Elene taught mathematics and Aleksandre taught Georgian language and literature.

There was an unusually warm winter that year. It snowed in the first days of the new year and plastered the mountains surrounding the city in white, but on the twentieth day of January the wind blew in and scattered the clouds, and the sky was completely clear. It got warmer. The sun melted the snow, and the soft smell of spring blew into the city. The River Mtkvari swelled as it always did in spring—its muddied waters came rushing and churning, bringing with it trees torn up from the roots, carrying discarded, unwanted items, sometimes even a drowned and bloated dog or cat. But the river did not remain swollen for long and after two or three days the waters subsided again, calmed, and returned to their normal levels. The wind died down too, and one warm, dry day followed another. Everything seemed more cheerful and positive, although this joy proved premature—one morning at the end of the second week of February the citizens awoke to the roar of field guns and gunfire coming from the outlying districts of Tbilisi.

The enemy brought with it from the north a terrible wind which drove black clouds and darkness over the area. It turned cold. The unexpected winter chill penetrated people's bones. A storm swept through the deserted streets of the city. Sparrows took refuge in attics and warm smoke holes. In the evening the wind abated, but it remained cold. Then night fell, and through the impenetrable darkness snow suddenly started to fall.

It snowed heavily and with a sinister, dogged insistence. Enormous flakes of snow fell stubbornly down from on high, landing like strange, evil birds on roofs, paving stones, balcony railings, and bare branches. The city fell silent. People sheltering in their houses listened pensively to the distant thundering of field guns. In the middle of the night a small group of young people carrying torches came down the street shouting, "Geor-gia, Georgia!" And then they were gone again, disappearing back into the darkness and the snow. Nobody knew who they were, where they had come from, or where they suddenly vanished to.

The old river, which had seen so much, flowed calmly on. It, too, felt the falling snow; large, heavy flakes settled quietly onto its smooth, black surface and then equally quietly died away. But the river kept on flowing, carrying waters turned sluggish by the cold.

They did not sleep all night and when dawn came they found the city covered in a thick blanket of snow. It was snowing only lightly now; a few flakes fluttered sluggishly down from on high. It was as if the ash-colored sky had dropped down onto the snowy rooftops, and the black crows had been rammed down onto the branches of the trees.

Elene and Aleksandre went to Sololaki. There was still sporadic gunfire but nonetheless there was an unusual calm outside. The enchanting winter smells of biting cold and snow hung in the air. It was almost as if nothing had happened. The citizens were calmly going about their business in the streets, seemingly unperturbed. Yard-sweepers threw ash onto the pavements, traders used dust pans to scrape up the snow in front of their booths. Only by the palace was there an unusually large number of people, milling like agitated bees around an upturned beehive. Aleksandre recognized one member of government, dressed in a plain military coat, a rifle hanging on his shoulder, pacing up and down in front of the palace.

School was closed because everybody had gone to the university and so they too made their way there through the snow-covered streets. They went down via Kvashveti Church and the Society of Arts theater, meeting people they knew along the way. People headed toward the university in groups, and these groups were gradually getting larger. The people strode onward, faces frozen turned to stone, and underfoot the snow crunched, became compacted, and changed color.

"Geor-gia! Geor-gia!" shouted the front few rows.

"Down with the vultures of the north!" replied the rows at the back.

"Geor-gia!" the entire group roared as one.

They carried on like this until they reached the university courtyard. Standing by the main entrance to the university, at the top of the snow-covered stone steps stood professors, students, and government representatives. Among them were battle-ready military personnel. The university rector addressed the crowd. He spoke calmly, deliberately, clearly seeking to hide his inner turmoil. At the bottom of the steps people were putting together a list of volunteers. Those wanting to put their names down had formed themselves into long lines; among them there were students, old workers, and local craftsmen. The rector carried on talking, his voice gradually becoming stronger, sounding ever more forceful, and like a large, powerful bird of prey he circled in the freezing air, cawed down at the pale, silent people below him like an eagle and filled them with a strange, awe-filled power.

"I should sign up!" Aleksandre thought suddenly, stamped his feet in the snow, and glanced at his wife.

Elene was standing there with her head held high, listening attentively to the speaker and her expression—lips slightly apart, eyes lit up, and face illuminated—was one of astonished excitement.

The line of those wanting to sign up moved slowly forward, and grew longer; it now also included young girls, well-dressed intellectuals, fathers well into middle age.

"No, I really should sign up," thought Aleksandre, stamping his feet in the cold.

But now a new speaker took the stand, an elderly general. He faltered and searched for the right words, but nonetheless his steely voice carried in it the ringing and clashing of sword on sword, and the fizzing sound of hot sparks falling into snow.

"I should sign up too," though Aleksandre again and put his hand on his wife's arm. Elene looked at him, staring at him with questioning eyes, but Aleksandre suddenly bowed his head and mumbled, "Shall we go, Eliko?"

"Yes, dear, let's go."

The sound of a car engine brought him back to the present. He jumped in fright and raised his head; a car suddenly arriving in the middle of the night could not augur well, he thought. He got up from the armchair, went over to the window and looked out. It was still raining a thin drizzle; a black car came along the wet cobbled street and stopped in the pool of light cast by the single lamp mounted on the post. Aleksandre stepped back, but could not stop himself pulling back the sheer curtain with trembling fingers; he craned his neck and looked cautiously down at the car, its engine now silent, its steamed-up windows reflecting the yellow lamplight and shielding the people sitting within. Suddenly, both car doors opened and three men got out. Aleksandre let go of the curtain immediately, but as he did so he recognized Parunashvili in his leather jacket and thought he saw him nod his head toward the window as if greeting him, and give a courteous smile.

* * *

Groping around in the dark, Elene followed the damp wall and when her hand touched its slimy surface she was filled with loathing. There was a revolting foul smell in this strange tunnel and everything was covered with a kind of sticky slime. She walked barefoot through the viscous, ice-cold water. Sometimes she felt rough, teeming creatures brush against her feet and, so fearful she could hardly breathe, tried to move more quickly so that she might get out of this place as quickly as possible, but she could no longer move her body, numb with cold, and it seemed to her that she might fall right where she stood, sink into the filthy water and drown in the terrible darkness and stench.

Suddenly she heard a distant voice, a call. She stopped, listened, but the call did not come again. Instead she heard the sound of heavy footsteps coming up wooden stairs toward her, she clearly heard people breathing rapidly, panting even, and spurred on by that hope she decided to call out; she opened her mouth, but nothing emerged from her throat but a strange and unfamiliar croaking. Exhausted, she carried on her way, walking more quickly now, the water lapping around her ankles and by now longer shying from those foul-smelling slime-covered walls—she bumped against them, leaned against them with her palms and in that way went staggering onward in the dark.

Suddenly something touched her foot—she tripped, lost her balance and fell onto a dead body lying face up in the water. She recognized—or rather somehow sensed—that this was Aleksandre's corpse; she screamed in terror and woke up.

For a while she lay there with her eyes closed, trying to come to her senses, then groped about on her husband's bed, and when she found it empty she was terrified. She heard muffled voices coming from the street. She listened, heard a car engine chugging idly, somebody clearing their throat drily, and then she heard a car door slam. Elene got up from her bed, groped her way toward the window in the darkness and pulled the thick curtain to one side, and when she looked outside she saw a black car pull away, drive down the hill, blend into the darkness, and disappear.

She stood there for a while and waited for her husband to come back in. She assumed he had gone out to the toilet—he often needed the toilet at night and gradually Elene calmed back down again after her nightmare.

Outside the vexing, cold November rain fell on the street, the roofs, and the old, swollen acacias. For some reason Elene felt sorry for those acacias, old and weak and lopped so ruthlessly every autumn, and which in the spring barely managed to put out a few green branches. Twenty years ago they were still young, could still turn the whole area white in rose season and bewitch the whole street with their heart-stopping scent. But now they stood there pitifully in the rain like weak, wretched old men, they stood and waited for a peasant to come down from the village with his ax and cut them back, saw their branches short and take their wood away on a horse-drawn cart. Elene always found this wait very painful, and as soon as the man from the village appeared her heart would start to tremble with terror so much one might think it was not an ordinary peasant in the street but the archangels Michael and Gabriel themselves.

Twenty years ago Elene was young too, not so young that she could blossom, but still beautiful enough that the neighborhood men coming to the street were not only stupefied by the acacias but also bewitched by her, and that when he came back from exile after so long away from the wife he yearned for, it was with great passion that Aleksandre gazed at this good-looking woman.

Elene thought her husband should be proud that during the eleven years he was in prison and distant exile she remained faithful to him until the end despite the advances of many men, and managed to protect him from her minor indiscretions. At that time, people still valued bright, forward-looking, tortured heroes very highly and so Elene, as the wife of one such hero, was treated with special consideration and respect, and although she herself knew absolutely nothing about the underground work her husband did, she could easily believe that Aleksandre really was an important political figure. Representatives of the Social Federalists' Kutaisi provincial committee often paid her visits, helped her with money, and sometimes asked for her help too.

Once, Elene was visited by a good family friend and distant relative Elizbar Lolua, who asked her—as both a trustworthy individual and the wife of a revolutionary—to temporarily store for them a weapon smuggled in from abroad, probably for a couple of weeks. At first Elene was afraid, because at that time in Georgia the laws were extremely strict and reactionary and she knew that holding a weapon was enough to get her sent to Siberia, but because of her love for her husband and her sense of loyalty to his cause she felt unable to say no to Elizbar. Sure enough, they pulled up at her door one night in a cart hitched to a buffalo and loaded with rifles and boxes of gunpowder and shot; they hid the weapon under the kitchen, in a deep pit they had dug in advance. The housewife invited the tired, cold party workers to an impromptu dinner in front of the fire, and when Elizbar's friends threw their wet felt cloaks on the earth floor and untied their hoods and masks she was taken aback by one man's handsome and rugged good looks. He was the famous outlaw Jarisha Jgushia, known throughout the whole of western Georgia, who helped the Social Federalists bring in weapons from foreign ships and store them safely.

Importing weapons always involved great danger and so the party committee used special units of bandits for this task, but because they did not trust them completely they always appointed as leader the kind of man whom nobody would accuse of betrayal. Jarisha Jgushia was one such man. He enjoyed particular authority among the bandits and could be trusted in so much as he knew that in the event of betrayal the party committee would condemn him to death and find his executioner from among his enemies.

That night Elene looked at Jarisha twice and both times he caught her eye. After that she did not go out for several days, and then one evening when she came back from school she found the outlaw waiting inside for her. She did not know to this day how Jarisha had got into the locked apartment. He was sitting calmly on the ottoman and waiting for her to come home. Elene was enraged by his insolence and threw the outlaw out by the scruff of the neck. The next day she went to Zugdidi, found Elizbar Lolua and told him the whole story with great indignation. After that she never laid eyes on Jarisha Jgushia again but many years later when she heard the news of his death she sat down and cried bitter tears for a very long time.

On the agreed day Elizbar's men came and took the weapon away, and from that moment onward Elene found herself caught up in political activity. She carried out various jobs for the party quite happily—she went to sessions, distributed leaflets, talked to her pupils and their parents about the necessity and inevitability of overthrowing the evil autocratic regime, and eventually she became a party member; she believed she should continue the work carried out by her husband.

When Aleksandre came back from exile he poured cold water on his wife's political ambitions and enthusiasm for the party. At first he laughed when he heard that Elene had become a party member, but then he said that if she had any respect for him she should break off contact with them the very next day.

Elene did not argue; she had involved herself in party activities out of respect for Aleksandre and so leaving them behind was not particularly painful, but her view of her husband changed significantly. Over eleven years Aleksandre had slowly been transformed in her mind into some kind of knight, cloaked in a haze of secrecy, who had fought day and night for the well-being of the workers, for a bright future for them, who had devoted his life unsparingly for the achievement of this lofty goal, even if it meant facing prison, shackles, the freezing Siberian weather, or the back-breaking work of the labor camps. But when Aleksandre came back from exile he was, to Elene's surprise, a totally different man. This sick, stunted man with constant stomach pain had nothing in common with the hero she had created in her imagination; this was instead an ordinary, cautious man who sought a quiet life, had no interest in the fate of world politics and in fact did not even have a very clear idea of them at all.

For a long time Elene could not accept this change; it seemed to her almost as if gold had been transformed into a ten-ruble note, as if somebody had palmed her off with some fake money and left her disillusioned and frustrated, but when she realized that this pitiful individual, who calmed his incessant stomach pain with soda water, needed special care and attention rather than reproaches or opprobrium, she started giving him special medicines and put him on a strict diet, nourished him with porridge, kept a close eye to make sure he was not putting anything in his mouth that would upset him, and after a year she had nursed a man who had been almost on his deathbed back to health. In the course of that year Elene got to know her husband very well; she discovered so many fine qualities in him that she laughed when she remembered her own exaggerated image of him. She felt him gain color from one day to the next, and somehow the face of the martyred knight she had imagined faded from her mind and came to be replaced by a real, deeply beloved man whom she held very close indeed.

However, revolutionary work had left a deep mark on Elene's character. Those close to her knew her as a daring, direct, and forthright person who ignored no one and never let herself be ignored by anybody else. Her pupils were afraid of her, her fellow teachers viewed her with respect and fear. Because of her principled nature and indomitable character she caused a fair amount of trouble for the school directors and heads of the education department.

That was her life, and now that she was silver-haired and worn by time she was often troubled by the heavy lot fate had dealt her and which she felt more keenly in old age than she had in her younger days, when she had thought the love she felt for every child she had ever taught was like the love a mother feels for her own child. Now, though, when she thought about all those children good and bad as one nameless entity she realized she had been deceiving herself, satisfying her maternal instinct with that love, whereas in actual fact the real, divine feeling mothers felt toward their own flesh and blood was completely different. She had resisted this feeling and this eternal instinct her whole life. She resisted it when she thought she loved her pupils like her own children, when she nursed a weakened Aleksandre back to health after his return from exile, and now too when she fussed over Niko and Nunu's son Merab to stop him from getting cold—as if he really was her own child.

It was still raining outside; grim black puddles lay here and there in the street, illuminated by that single streetlamp, and the puddles reminded Elene of her recent dream. She saw that dark tunnel again, its walls covered in sticky slime. She put on her gown, opened the door and looked into the living room.

Aleksandre stood with his back toward Elene and was taking down the pictures that hung on the wall—he had already taken down Ilia, Akaki, and Vazha's photographs and was now lifting down the picture of Colonel Giorgi Janelidze, dressed in the uniform of the army of the Tsar.

Confused, Elene watched her husband in silence. She could not understand what Aleksandre needed these photographs for now, in the middle of the night, and when he took down the photograph of his father-in-law too, took them over to the stove and set fire to them, Elene cried out and rushed forward with her arms outstretched.

Crouched by the stove, Aleksandre looked around when he heard Elene's scream. Elene saw his calico-white face, dark and sunken eyes, and broken, formless face. Terrified, she stared at her husband who in the space of one night had become an enfeebled stranger. She could not imagine what had happened, what misfortune could possibly have befallen him, and when Aleksandre went to stand up but stumbled on his weak knees and had to support himself on the floor, Elene rushed over to him, helped him stand, led him to his armchair and lowered him carefully into it.

The old man's mouth gaped like a fish pulled from the water.

"What is it, Sasha? Are you unwell?" Elene asked him, but Aleksandre was unable to speak, stared blankly at his wife as if he didn't know who this woman was, where she had come from or what she wanted, and when she took out a small bottle of mint drops from the chest of drawers, tipped it into a glass of water with shaking hands and put the glass to his lips, he said to her in a hoarse voice, "They've just taken Niko and his wife!"

"Drink this, come on," his wife said hastily and only when Aleksandre had drained the glass did she ask him, "Taken them where, Sasha? What do you mean?"

"I don't know. They put them both in a car and drove them away."

Only now did Elene remember the black car. She was filled with terror, the glass fell from her hand and spilled onto the floor, but did not break.

"And the child?"

Aleksandre stared at her for a few moments without saying anything, his face tensed as if he was trying to remember something.

"I don't know. I didn't see the child."

Elene rushed to the door, turned the key, opened it, and ran quickly outside.

* * *

Aleksandre did not move, he sat and stared at the empty wall. The outlines of the photographs—three largish ovals and one smaller one—showed up against the discolored wallpaper. The wallpaper where they had hung had stayed its original color and style and he thought back to the day Assyrian craftsmen had renovated the rooms. He could smell the lime, starch, and wood glue even now. It was the smell of the past, of their happy life. What he wouldn't give to return to that distant past, to that time twenty years before when he had bought this apartment with the money brought back from Siberia and felt boundless happiness, because this was the first and only property he had bought, one which he had longed for so much when he was in exile. He had loved the smell of this house from the very first moment, its walls, its windows with their wooden shutters from which he could see the cobbled alleys so typical of Tbilisi. He remembered those spring evenings when the neighbors would sit on chairs set out in front of the windows and play chess and backgammon, or just sit and chat as neighbors do.

In nice weather wonderful cooking smells would emanate from the open windows of each house, and each house had its own specific smell, but each one mingled in with the others and combined with the slightly bitter scent of the white acacias to create one unique smell that characterized their alley. Back then people recognized their own streets by their smell, because every street, big or small, had its own particular aromas that set it apart, and in fact it was that blend of so many different kinds of aromas combined into one that somehow came to represent the ancient city itself, know from the very beginning as Tbilisi, but which for some reason people referred to simply as "the city."

Aleksandre remembered the Tbilisi of the past like some distant dream, as something different, illuminated by a different hope and, although probably still troubled by a thousand troubles, nonetheless considerably more cheerful, happy, and free. He remembered the day when the enemy entered the defeated city in their torn, tattered clothes, lousy and hungry, when a city wrapped up in the splints and bandages of entirely different laws died its death and turned to ashes.

The country was ruled by terror. The foreign power that had entered by fire and by sword turned the peasantry into slaves of the collective farm, shackled the workers with the chains of salary, destroyed the aristocracy, defrocked the priesthood, turned the intelligentsia into circus dogs trained with sugar cubes hidden inside clenched fists, and gradually turned the Georgian nation into a bullock forced to choose between two evils: either to be killed and have its meat carved into pieces and sold, or to be castrated and turned into a working animal. The nation chose the second evil over physical destruction, put its head meekly into the yoke and allowed a rope to be tied around its neck, and set off on the bumpy road to socialism, keen to avoid the stick.

This choice seemed sensible to Aleksandre. As he always said to Niko, if a bear starts circling you, you call it "Sir." He was sure that little Georgia would never survive alongside mighty Russia; he felt it would be destroyed and wiped off the face of the earth. The most important thing, he said, was to somehow save themselves; indeed it was remarkable that they had survived this time. This made Niko angry: "What, so we should just sit around and watch?" Aleksandre tried to reason with him: "Why no, not at all! We should work hard. Let's build a country, keep our traditions, not just degenerate into nothingness. Nothing lasts forever, we've seen much worse than this, and at the end of the day they'll go too, they'll leave us and our time will come again." But Niko did not agree: death was preferable to a life of slavery, he said, because slaves do not build or create; instead they one day lose everything they have, and will come out empty-handed.

In other words, they did not agree, stood on opposite sides of the fence, and debated fiercely, but it did not affect their friendship.

"All right, you two, that's enough, don't fight to the bitter end!" Elene laughed. "This empty talk is of no use to anyone." But in spite of this she often joined in their debates and always took Niko's side because she shared his opinions. Aleksandre, unable to defeat their combined forces, would wave his finger lightheartedly and say, "What will this Eliko do to me, eh? She's a little revolutionary, after all, and an old hand at political struggle."

And that would be the end of the debate, or at least they would save the rest for another day, and then they would sit down to eat the dinner Elene had laid out for them, or drink tea or wine from narrow-waisted glasses and chat quietly, and forget all about the foundations and achievements of socialism. Soon Nunu would come in too, always carrying a dish filled to the brim with hot *khachapuri* and with her smiling, chubby-cheeked baby in her arms, and would sit by Elene's side and put the baby on her lap. At times like these Aleksandre felt that there was a special warmth and love in the room.

In recent times Niko and Nunu had grown especially close to them but when Parunashvili and his associates put them into the car and took them away, Aleksandre suddenly felt a strange, shameful sense of relief and joy which stubbornly gripped his entire being, despite his efforts to resist it.

When he saw caught sight of Parunashvili getting out of the car, Aleksandre was surprised to find the feeling of fearful expectation vanish completely; instead he was seized by an unexpected resolve and peace. He saw everything more clearly, as if he had surfaced from muddied waters; he noticed with this purified mind that everything around him seemed ordered, and that somehow objects and events had regained their form and significance. Reality took the place of bittersweet memories, those pictures he held in his mind of life already past were swallowed up by the fog and the present became more tangible, and Aleksandre did not fear it anymore—he was troubled by what was in his opinion a more important matter: he regretted the fact that he had not woken his wife up before now and told her everything in advance in order to prepare her for this moment. With his mind's eye he searched through the bookshelves and drawers of his writing table, intrigued as to what might be found during a search and that in future might be used as evidence against him. He felt sorry for Elene, who would now have to face old age alone, and obviously he himself dreaded this ascent to Calvary that he had avoided once already, and he heard in his mind again the clinking of handcuffs and the crude shouts of the prisoners in convoy. But now that the long-awaited danger had become so real and inevitable, it no longer scared Aleksandre, because the expectation of danger is considerably more difficult to bear than the danger itself.

He stood in the middle of the room and in the silence of the night could clearly hear every slight noise and rustling: the soft, quiet pitter-patter of the rain, the clock ticking, a distant weak ringing and the sound of heavy footsteps on the creaking wooden steps as Parunashvili and his associates came up. He could already picture their stern faces and pursed lips, and their hands shoved into their pockets. They reached the top of the stairs and came out onto the landing. Now they would turn left, Aleksandre thought, stand in front of the closed door to his apartment and bang on the door with their fists. He listened closely, confused, craning his neck to look at his doorway, but nobody knocked and the sense of anticipation became gradually more and more unbearable and oppressive.

Suddenly, he heard a heavy pounding, but it was not his door they were banging on. The sound was coming from further away, from the end of the landing, and Aleksandre thought they must have made a mistake.

After a short time he heard Niko's drowsy voice asking who was there, and they answered him in such a cheerful and friendly way—"Open up, it's only us!"—that Aleksandre found himself wondering whether Niko and Parunashvili actually knew each other from somewhere. Then he heard the door creak, then something he could not make out, a muffled sound as if somebody was clearing their throat and then it went so quiet that once again he could hear the hands of the clock and the falling snow.

Aleksandre did not move. He stood there thinking. They had probably gone to Niko's first because they needed him as a witness, he thought, so that they could announce their intention to arrest Aleksandre in his presence and make everything legal and proper. But time passed and he could not hear any sound coming from Niko's apartment at all.

Aleksandre waited for a long time and finally decided to wake his wife. His only concern now was what to do, what things to keep from his wife so as not to break the poor woman's heart, and while he was thinking about that he suddenly heard the door creaking again, then some noise and footsteps. He listened carefully and heard men talking and a woman crying, and the sound of some sort of scuffle, but they did not come to his door this time either and instead went downstairs and then outside.

Aleksandre hurried to the window, pulled the curtain to one side and looked out into the street. The car doors were open and Niko and Nunu were being forcibly put inside. Niko stood there, frozen, staring blankly, unable to speak, whilst Nunu was crying, putting up a fight, cursing the men angrily and trying to get back to her house, but they paid no attention to her struggling and shoved her toward the open car door, and when they had finally got both of them inside, they themselves got in and the car moved off, and as Parunashvili was wiping the steam from the inside of the window he looked up at Parunashvili and smiled.

Then the car drove off down the hill, blended into the darkness, and vanished, and Aleksandre just stood there by the window holding the curtain back with one hand, and before his eyes he could see Parunashvili's clean-shaven face and his smile, menacing and mocking, but at the same time somehow amicable and amenable. He was seized by doubt. That smile could not be trusted. He remembered how they called out to Niko so innocently—"Open up, it's only us!"—and suddenly their slyness and treachery was all too clear to Aleksandre. He remembered the black car which, instead of stopping in the darkness of the street, had pulled up in the only light spot right in front of his window, and Aleksandre realized that Parunashvili had done all of this to frighten him, and that even Niko and Nunu's arrest was all part of the same elaborate performance. But there was one thing he did not yet know, and that was whether this ugly farce was over or whether the second act was still to come, still to end in its tragic finale, and once again Aleksandre was seized by that feeling of vague expectation. He turned, looked blankly around the room and when suddenly he noticed the photographs of Ilia, Vazha, Akaki, and Colonel Giorgi Janelidze he was so startled that for a moment he could not breathe and he rushed, terrified, toward the writing table.

* * *

The door creaked and Aleksandre jumped with fright in his armchair. Elene had come into the room holding a sleeping child in her arms. She walked quickly across the room without looking at her husband, briefly glanced at the now bare wall and went into the bedroom. Through the open door he saw her lay the child on the bed and wrap him warmly. Then she stood up and looked down at him closely.

Elene felt so sorry for this newly orphaned child who, like a blind puppy, was yet to open his eyes but to whom life had already dealt a terrible blow. Niko and Nunu's arrest terrified her. She could not imagine what those calm, harmless people could possibly have done to be seized from their homes in the middle of the night, roused from their beds and taken off with no consideration for the child. She had a vague suspicion that Aleksandre knew more about this than she did—otherwise why would he have pulled down those pictures and burned them in the stove? She went into the living room, closed the door carefully behind her and stared at her husband.

"How are you feeling, Sasha?"

"Not too bad."

She fetched a chair, put it next to the armchair and sat in front of her husband. Aleksandre swayed slightly in his chair. They sat there for a long time in silence, listening to the sound of the rain in the street, the clock on top of the chest of drawers and the rustling of mice nesting beneath the floor. Elene looked at her husband's face but Aleksandre avoided her gaze and stared down at the brown-stained, sinewy hands he rested on his knees, and seemed surprised, as if he had never seen them before, and when the woman could no longer stand the silence and asked him casually what he thought Niko and Nunu might have done, he lifted his head and looked toward the window.

Night had passed, dawn's pale light was seeping into the room and only now did Aleksandre think it safe to assume the men would not be coming back. It was indeed the case that "enemies of the people" were usually arrested at night; they very rarely came during the day. Normally they came by car in the middle of the night and took people away with no noise or commotion at all.

"It was one of my students," he said at last and coughed to clear the hoarseness in his throat.

"Which one?"

"You don't know him."

"In that case you should have said something to him!" Elene reproached her husband.

Aleksandre's forced smile twisted his lips. He looked at the empty wall and Elene automatically looked there too. The outlines of the places where the photos had hung until very recently were clearly evident against the worn, discolored wallpaper.

"We exchanged words yesterday, he and I, and I thought they'd come to arrest me."

"Wait, tell me everything from the beginning."

"I read them Ilia's poem *Spring*. How was I to know there was a secret policeman in my class?"

"Go on."

"He said the person who wrote that poem was a class enemy!"

"And?"

"I grabbed him by the ear. I might have hit him slightly too."

Elene covered her mouth with the palm of her hand and looked at her husband with smiling eyes. They sat looking at each other for a while. From the street they could hear the sparrows' dawn chorus; the mouse fell silent. The clock ticked quietly and from the absence of that monotonous pitter-patter they realized the rain must have stopped.

"They wouldn't arrest anyone because of that!" his wife said finally.

Suddenly from outside they heard a horn. Elene jumped up, went to the window and looked down at the street. The milk seller was coming up the hill carrying a milk can in one hand, and a nickel-plated horn in the other. When she got to the house she set the milk can on the ground, put the horn to her lips and blew.

"The wretched woman's going to wake the baby," Elene thought anxiously and went out to the kitchen to look for a container to put the milk in.

These new sounds—the sparrows' chirping, the horn, the tinkling of crockery—and the morning light coming in through the window changed the world, altered its appearance and brought relief to Aleksandre. The night's torment was in the past now and the new day gave Aleksandre a vague sense of hope. Elene's words—"They wouldn't arrest anyone because of that!"—had given him hope too, and even though he knew that people were arrested for much less, he still cast from his heart that heavy despondency which had troubled him all night and given him no rest.

He could still hear the horn from outside. Aleksandre raised his head and looked at the door to the bedroom. The child was asleep in there—an orphan, left alone in this world. For the first time in all of this he felt some compassion. He pitied the child's parents, too, imprisoned for God knows what crime. He remembered what he had thought earlier—that Parunashvili had arrested Niko and Nunu to frighten him—and laughed at his own stupidity. Things were surely not that simple. Niko must have been talking to other people too about the government's shortcomings and somebody must have informed on him. Or what if he was really was caught up in something, what if he had been unable to wait any longer and had joined some secret organization? The mere thought made him feel as if somebody had poured hot water over him. He knew that once a man had fallen into their hands he was beyond help, but still his mind searched for a way out.

Two months previously, Aleksandre had met a distant relation in the street, a man in his fifties named Manasi Tsikoridze. Manasi had been a priest in the Tskaltubo area. In 1923 when the Bolsheviks carried out their major campaign against religion, a letter appeared under his name in the newspaper *Worker and Peasant*. It read as follows: "To the Editor: Comrade! Earlier on in my priesthood I was sure that miracles and unnatural phenomena did not exist, but I still retained the moral aspects of my faith. Now I see that I was wrong in this regard too. Thus, I am leaving the priesthood, cutting all contact with the church and from this point onward I will try to be a firm believer in science alone. Experience has convinced me that the priesthood is a kind of looting and banditry of the foolish. Therefore from today onward I am abandoning it entirely and have decided to serve the workers and to provide for myself through honest work."

In actual fact, the village activists and members of the Young Communists League had defrocked Manasi Tsikoridze by force and the letter had been clearly been written by one of the editorial staff.

Aleksandre was so pleased to see Manasi that he invited him to a restaurant. They drank a bottle of wine each, caught up with each other's news and reminisced about the old days. In the middle of the meal the former priest suddenly started to cry; tears rolled down from his eyes and he could not stem the flow. It was a long time before he calmed down, at which point he told the bewildered Aleksandre that he had come straight from a meeting with the secret police and that they had made him sign something saying that he agreed to spy on unreliable individuals and provide information about them to the secret police. He asked Aleksandre, as an experienced former revolutionary, to advise him on what to do and how to behave.

Aleksandre was lost for words. Suddenly he hated himself and Manasi Tsikoridze. He sat there immobile and could not wait get away. But Manasi would not let him go and begged for advice. In the end Aleksandre stood up and told the former priest to behave as his own conscience dictated, paid the waiter, left the confused guest with a table full of food, and went.

Aleksandre knew that Georgia was full of agents like Manasi Tsikoridze and it was clear that one of them had informed on Niko.

Elene came in carrying a pan full of milk. Aleksandre noticed that his wife avoided looking at him and instead kept glancing at the empty wall. He felt very ashamed of his recent behavior, but he still justified it to himself—he had burned those photographs to destroy the slightest shred of evidence against him and now he was sure that if he was arrested they would not be able to find anything incriminating—but then suddenly something seemed to explode inside him, and it was as if a dazzling light had suddenly come on. This feeling was so sudden and unexpected that Aleksandre leaped up and stared at the bedroom door; there, on the other side of that door little Merab was sleeping peacefully, little Merab, the son of enemies of the people and a piece of evidence big enough to get him and Elene exiled to Irkutsk, Znamensk, or Bodaia.

* * *

He remembered that Nunu's parents lived somewhere to the west, near Kharagauli, but he could not remember the name of the village. He thought intensely, and the excessive tension made his head ache. Finally he came to the conclusion that Elene would know, but realized immediately that by the time a telegram got there, by the time they packed to come to Tbilisi, and finally by the time they actually got here it would be much too late. Then he remembered Niko's sister, who lived in another part of Tbilisi. He did not know her address either but Niko's brother-in-law was a butcher called Leo and that would be enough information to find him. He should go right now, he thought, find Leo the butcher and give them the child—but suddenly he felt his wife's suspicious eyes on him. Elene must have read his mind again because she was standing in the doorway to the bedroom, eyes blazing, looking for all the world like a lynx protecting its cub from an attacker.

Aleksandre felt weak, sank down into his chair bereft of all strength and stared over to the window, where the light was coming in. The relief he had felt a few moment before vanished and in its place he felt the strange, animal fear of the startled wild beast which huddles in a dark corner, encircled by hunters, waiting for the final blow.

This fear was completely different, it created new thoughts and unexpected wishes that did not shock Aleksandre but rather gradually subdued him and oppressed him with a strange power that seemed to be compelling him to leap up, to disappear without trace, to run until he collapsed somewhere tired and exhausted. But right now he did not even feel like standing up from his armchair, let alone fleeing, because he seemed to have been running for a long time already, running from that loathsome filth and dirt which he had been avoiding for as long as he could remember and now, tired and drained of strength from that incessant running, he could not take a single step more. He sat there, forlornly thinking that this running and this infinite torment had been entirely in vain, because there was nowhere he could go, no way he could hide without them finding him anyway and finally, inevitably, forcing him to confront that slimy, stagnant water that he had been hiding from like such a stupid fool.

Tired and bored of the eternal longing to be elsewhere, his village now came to mind, and the old church with the cracked walls on Trinity Hill, and not too far away, fenced in by a rusty iron palisade, his blessed parents lying in the sand and clay, his life's greatest lesson, and he felt as if he was there too, sitting at the long-neglected grave, looking at the November rain falling onto the ground, still covered in green grass, the grave stones blackened by the rain and the whole graveyard, veiled in mist coming up from the valley and turned a milky white. In his mind's eye he saw his father, his expression thoughtful, fatigued from the daily grind, and he heard his mother's sweet and lovely voice: "This is 'a'!" she was saying, "Find me another 'a' and tell me what it's called, son.'"

"It's called 'a.'"

She smiled at Aleksandre and affectionately stroked the top of his head with her palm.

His heart pounding, Aleksandre felt the gentleness and tenderness of her hand and its warmth that moved him so deeply, his body drained of strength and hot tears welled up in his eyes.

* * *

His thoughts were interrupted by a banging on the door. Startled, he lifted his head and stared at his wife.

Who else could it be at daybreak? He did not want to believe it but he knew that "they" must be standing behind the door. He was surprised that he had not heard the sound of the car; supporting himself on the arm-rests of his chair he struggled to his feet and shuffled over to the window. His legs were like lead. Outside by the lamp post there was a black car; the leather-coated driver had got out, was cleaning the windscreen with a piece of rag and kept looking up at the window of Aleksandre's house.

Elene was already opening the door. Standing with his back turned to her, Aleksandre could hear the jangling of the keys and squeaking of the rusty hinges, and when he turned around he saw Parunashvili had entered the room. He was a tall, handsome young man who was staring at Elene and smiling.

"Please forgive me, Madam, for troubling you so early in the morning," he said and then turned to Aleksandre. "I've come to apologize to you, Aleksandre!"

The old man raised his eyebrows in surprise, and glanced at his wife. Elene stood, confused, looking back and forth between the uninvited guest and her husband, and waiting for Aleksandre to say something in response to Parunashvili's words.

Parunashvili went over to Aleksandre, stopped in front of him with his head bowed and finally looked up at him, his face rather flushed, and said with a smile of shame, "Shall we settle our differences, Aleksandre?"

Aleksandre was dreadfully confused. He was genuinely surprised: instead of the blood-thirsty executioner and monster who had tormented and tortured his mind all night, there was now a polite, remorseful young man standing in front of him and asking for forgiveness for his unseemly behavior the evening before.

The unlikely nature of the circumstances moved the old man deeply and soothed his tense nerves just as like the spring rain soothes the drought-parched, barren earth. He relaxed so suddenly and completely that he felt his knees weaken beneath him and he burst out laughing, so suddenly that it surprised even him—his whole body began to tremble, he put his hands on his waist, bent over, and started to chuckle the rasping chuckle of an elderly man.

He laughed and even though he could feel how absurd and awkward his senseless, involuntary laughter was he could not stop, because he felt as if they were wiping the earth back off him and that he needed this laughter like someone brought up alive from the grave needs cool, fresh air.

Parunashvili, smiling but rather confused, was still staring at his unexpectedly cheerful host and gradually infectious laughter affected him too; he glanced at Elene, who was scowling and deep in thought, and suddenly gave out such a loud guffaw that the walls of the old house, the crockery in the cupboards, and the glass in the windows shook.

Now both of them were laughing, tears in their eyes, bent double in front of each other, exhausted from laughing, sometimes patting on the arm and side and laughed so much that they almost seemed to have become one.

Elene stared at the two men in dismay and bewilderment. She already knew who this guest was and she could not understand the reason for her husband's cheerfulness; she found their laughter troubling and irritating and when suddenly she heard the child crying in the bedroom she could no longer stand it and shouted, "Sasha, what on earth is wrong with you?"

Aleksandre fell silent immediately but Parunashvili carried on laughing, rummaging in his pockets as he did so, searching for a handkerchief to wipe the tears from his eyes.

Exhausted with laughter and with no strength left in him, the old man sank into the armchair and only then did the men hear the child's crying.

The smile disappeared from Parunashvili's face, he went to the bedroom door, opened it and looked inside. Elene followed behind him; she wanted desperately to get to the child but Parunashvili blocked her path. Agitated and upset, Elene tried to pass him first on one side and then the other, but try as she might she could not get into the room.

Meanwhile the child gasped for breath, then screeched with the voice of a child whose fate was sealed. Parunashvili did not move from the spot, and stood silently with his hands leaning against the door frame and his head stuck into the bedroom, paying absolutely no attention to the infuriated woman, who rushed at him like an agitated, broody mother hen.

Aleksandre surveyed the scene and he felt a great anger toward his own wife, who was hitting their guest on his back in an attempt to get past him.

Suddenly Parunashvili turned around, let the woman pass, and stared at Aleksandre with a woeful smile.

"I wasn't expecting this from you anymore, Aleksandre," he said at last and shook his head with regret.

Aleksandre fell into his armchair, devastated, lifeless. Only now did he realize that he didn't even know the man's first name and he was filled with remorse. He stared at the handsome, imposing young man and was filled with a remarkable sense of faith in him and when Parunashvili reproached him and asked him what had possessed him to bring into the family the child of an enemy of the people and a traitor, he called angrily to his wife in the bedroom, "See, woman, see what I told you!"

Parunashvili went to the window, pulled the curtain to one side, looked out and nodded to somebody.

Suddenly Elene came rushing out of the other room, her hair disheveled and her face contorted, and grabbed her husband, yelling: "Who is that man, Sasha?"

"Eliko!" Aleksandre warned her.

"Who is he, and what does he want in this house?"

"Stop, Eliko, just stop!"

"Tell him to leave right now!"

"Calm down, Madam," Parunashvili interrupted. "It would be best if you got yourself dressed and then got the child ready too."

Suddenly the door opened and two strange men came into the room. Elene turned deathly pale.

"Wrap the child up well or he'll catch cold," Parunashvili advised her.

* * *

From then onward Aleksandre saw everything as if he was in a dream, almost as if everything was happening underwater: everybody moved in slow motion, opening and closing their lips like fish, but he was unable to hear what they were saying above the continuous rumble and rustling in his ears. He saw the men in leather jackets take Elene out of the bedroom. He watched as she stood in the middle of the room, dressed in her raincoat, not even looking at him and it seemed to Aleksandre that she could not wait to leave; indeed, when the men sent her on in front of them, she left the room without a backward glance.

Then he was sitting in the armchair again, watching Parunashvili go into the empty room and look around, and finally when he came over and stretched out his arms as if to calm him, Aleksandre tried very hard to move, and yet his limbs were so stiff that he was unable to detach his right hand from the arm of his chair.

Parunashvili stood with his arms stretched out like that for a short while, then slowly turned around and went.

* * *

How long he sat there for I do not know, but when he stood up he felt a strange, miraculous sense of lightness, and it brought him an indescribable relief.

He looked out of the window.

The car was nowhere to be seen.

The clouds cleared from the sky and the large red sun rose in the east. Its rays radiated light across the rain-soaked street, the wet roofs, the whole city. A villager from the hills above Tbilisi came slowly up the street and looked calmly, purposefully up at the acacias which gave shelter from the rain.

Aleksandre turned around slowly. The whole room was bathed in golden sunlight, every corner of it shone and suddenly he almost screamed in terror: sitting motionless in his high-backed, threadbare armchair was his stiff, lifeless corpse, his eyes now extinguished but still open, and all around those eyes crawled big, green autumn flies.

NINO TEPNADZE

The Suicide Train

I find it very hard to remember everything now, but when I close my eyes really tight—till I see green circles—I can just about remember what happened.

Me and Ana are lying in bed, clutching each other. I am eleven, Ana is fifteen. Ana's not feeling too good because Mom's just told her off. She's always telling her off. Because Ana gets home late and always smells of vodka, because she talks all night long on the phone and because she doesn't look after me when Mom's on night duty and we're home on our own. I don't even need looking after, the only thing that matters is that Ana mustn't cry, because that's when she starts saying crazy things to me.

"Nin, if I killed myself would you cry much?" she asks me quietly.

"You mean if you died?" I ask her, confused.

"No, if I killed myself."

Ana's really tough, if she decides she wants to do something she'll do it, and the fact that Ana's really tough scares me.

I tell her I'll cry. No, I'll cry loads and Mom will cry too, and we'll never be able to laugh with all our heart ever again. Ana tells me that's stupid, and that I won't be sad for long. But she's only saying that to hear me say it just once: Ana, if you died I'd die too. When Ana cries, I feel like crying too. And I'm not even drunk.

Ana's a free spirit. She's only friends with boys and once she even told me that she touched a boy "there." Whatever Ana tells me I keep secret. If I ever say anything Mom hits her, then Ana starts crying and then . . . So basically, I mustn't say anything. If I say anything Ana won't be my sister anymore. When she comes home drunk Mom always yells at her. If she's really drunk she doesn't answer, if she's not really drunk she answers Mom back and then she doesn't get away without a slap. Then she runs into her room and slams the door. Then Mom feels bad, sits down stiff with shock and unable to speak. And from the other room I can hear the sound of Ana crying. I don't know what to do. In the end I decide to go and see to Ana.

Then Ana calms down. I take her clothes off. Ana waves her arms around. When she comes home the alcohol seems to affect her more. "Shh, Ana, shh," I say to her and remember how she used to comfort me when I scraped my knee.

I take off her jeans with the holes in the knees, then take off her T-shirt and stare for a while at her beautiful chest. "Leave my bra alone," Ana tells me, and I don't take anything else off. I help her into her nightgown.

I sleep by Ana's side and wonder what I'll be like at her age. I fall asleep thinking about it.

Here my thoughts fade away. I close my eyes tighter still, until I see blue dots.

It's night. I'm woken by a strange wetness and an even stranger sound. Even before I open my eyes I try to work out what could have happened. Then I open my eyes and scream, loudly. Ana is swimming in her own vomit and there's a rattling sound coming from her throat. I shake her awake and call for help: "Mom, help me!" Mom's not home. I try to get Ana upright. I put pillows under her back and fetch water. I pour it onto her face and just when I think it's all over Ana starts to cough.

"Nin, did I die?" she asks me, dumbfounded.

"Nearly," I answer and hug her close.

It doesn't bother me that she's making me dirty. It's better that she's alive and dirty than dead and clean.

Then we change the sheets together and clean everything up. Mom mustn't find out anything about this. It's our secret.

Ana keeps a diary. I'm strictly forbidden from reading it, but sometimes I can take a quick peek. But there's so much blood and death in Ana's diary that I don't even want to read it anymore.

Since I started reading Ana's diary I've been having bad dreams, and I wake up crying. In the daytime Ana cries and I comfort her; at night it's the other way around.

I dream of a huge train, and a track that skirts around the edge of the city and runs toward the main rubbish dump. The only people on the train are people who are going to kill themselves. On the far side of the track stand their family members, loved ones, and others, and everyone's comforting each other, strangers and acquaintances alike. After a while there's a huge bang and everyone kills themselves on the rubbish dump. For a while the city is lifeless.

I dream that I am standing at the edge of the city, waiting for the train to pass by so that I might catch a glimpse of Ana, because as soon as I hear the sound of shooting Ana's life will be lost to me and mine to her.

Then I wake up crying. Ana strokes me. Her hair smells of cigarettes, her skin of vodka. I think that one day the smell will remind of this time; one day, when Ana's a big girl and I'm a big girl too, only not as big as Ana.

Mom comes home from work when it's nearly morning. I run to her, throw my arms around her. But Ana won't look at her. Mom greets her stiffly.

Ana shuts herself in her room and puts her music on loud.

"Mom's got a headache, An, turn it down a bit," I ask her.

"I've got a headache too. I'm hungover," she replies.

After that I remember everything in detail, but I close my eyes anyway—until I see red spots—only this time it's out of grief.

That day Mom found Ana's diary and there was more written in it than she could ever have imagined. Ana smokes weed and she's in love with the neighborhood bad boy.

That day Mom slapped Ana so much that blood started pouring out of her nose. I couldn't stop her. Eventually Ana got away and locked herself in her room. She wouldn't let me in. Mom told me to sleep in a different room, she said that Ana would do some thinking and then come out by herself. I really wanted to be with her but in the end I changed my mind; if she didn't want to see me, why should I go and see her?

The same thing came to me in a dream. But this time it was not just me seeing Ana off. Mom was there too when Ana smiled sadly at us from the window of the train.

I heard the sound of the train's wheels so clearly it woke me up. I opened my eyes, but the sound carried on. It was following me from my dream. I was very scared, I thought my heart would burst if I didn't go and see Ana, and that rhythm kept beating in my ears: dgd-dn-dgd-dn. I went out into the street and climbed back in through Ana's window. "Ana, I'm here. Ana!" I shook her violently. Dgd-dn-dgd-dn. Ana didn't reply. My knees give way with dread. I ran to the light, switched it on and saw her: Ana, lying there, eyes open, foaming at the mouth. There were pill bottles scattered all around her.

Dgd-dn-dgd-dn.

The train passed by.

AUTHOR BIOGRAPHIES

MARIAM BEKAURI was born in 1990 in Tbilisi. She is currently in her fourth year of study in the Faculty of Social and Political Science at Tbilisi State University. Her writing has been appearing in periodicals since 2008 and has been included in several published collections of short stories. She has achieved success in several Georgian literary competitions and also works for the publishing house Diogene.

LASHA BUGADZE was born in 1977 in Tbilisi. He studied in the Department of Painting and Graphics at the Nikoladze Art College and subsequently studied playwriting at the Shota Rustaveli Theater Institute. He is a playwright, novelist, newspaper columnist, and television and radio presenter. He has authored four novels and numerous plays and his works have been published in Georgian, Russian, Armenian, French, German, Polish, and English. In 2007 he was Regional Prizewinner (Russia and Caucasus) in the BBC World Service International Radio Playwriting Competition with *When Cabbies are Attacked*, and in 2011 he won the English as a First Language category of the BBC World Service International Radio Play-writing Competition 2011 with the translation (by Maya Kiasashvili) of his play *The Navigator*. An English translation of his short story *Song for Tbilisi* was published in 2011 as part of the residential literary project *citybooks*.

ZAZA BURCHULADZE was born in Tbilisi in 1973. He graduated from the Georgian State Academy of Fine Arts in Tbilisi. He has been publishing short stories in Georgian newspapers and literary journals since 1998 (until 2001 under the pen name "Gregor Zamza") and since 2001 has also published eight novels, two screenplays, and three collections of short stories. His translations of Russian authors including Dostoyevsky and Sorokin have been published in Georgia, and his own works have been translated into Russian and Polish.

DAVID DEPHY is a Georgian poet, novelist, performer, and multimedia artist. Born in 1968, Dephy studied architecture at Tbilisi Academy. Since 1994, he has published novels, essays, and poetry; his writings have been praised by Georgian critics for displaying the phonetic and syntactical possibilities of his native language. In 2011, Dephy participated in the PEN World Voices Festival in New York, performing live with Salman Rushdie, Yusef Komunyakaa, and Laurie Anderson. His short story "Before The End" was selected by Aleksandar Hemon for inclusion in Dalkey Archive Press's anthology *Best European Fiction 2012*.

GURAM DOCHANASHVILI was born in Tbilisi in 1939. He graduated from Tbilisi State University and subsequently worked for the Institute of History, Archaeology, and Ethnography as an archaeologist. His first work was published in 1966 and he has since published numerous short stories and novellas. From 1975 he spent ten years managing the prose section of the literary magazine *Mnatobi*, and since 1985 he has been director of the Georgian Film Studios. His most popular work is the 1975 novel *The First Garment*.

TEONA DOLENJASHVILI graduated from the Department of Journalism and Filmmaking at Tbilisi State University. She presents Arts programs on Georgian television and works as a reporter and political correspondent for the Georgian press. She writes novels, short stories, and screenplays and has been publishing since 2003. She has won literary prizes in Georgia for her prose and screenplays and her novel *Memphis* won the SABA award for Best Novel in 2009. Her stories have been translated into German, Italian, Russian, Ukrainian, and Azeri.

REZO GABRIADZE was born in Kutaisi in 1936. He is a renowned theater director and screenwriter who has written more than thirty films since the late 1960s. Since 1981 he has been director of the Tbilisi Marionette Theater which has toured worldwide with Gabriadze's play *The Battle of Stalingrad*. His play *Forbidden Christmas, or The Doctor and the Patient* has been performed in the United States and he has also spent periods living and working in France and Switzerland. He has been awarded numerous awards within Georgia and was also awarded the French Legion of Honor.

KOTE JANDIERI was born in 1958 in Tbilisi. He graduated from Tbilisi State University in Geography and Geology and now works in the Department of Arts and Humanities. His short stories have been appearing in Georgian literary periodicals since 1977. Since 1983 he has also written the screenplays for twelve films.

IRAKLI JAVAKHADZE was born in 1968 in Tbilisi. He graduated from the Philology Faculty of Tbilisi State University. He started publishing short stories in literary journals in 1990. Adaptations of his works have appeared on Georgian radio and on stage. He also works as a translator and has translated the works of Charles Bukowski and Quentin Tarantino's screenplay for *Reservoir Dog*s into Georgian.

DAVIT KARTVELISHVILI was born in 1976 in Tbilisi. He trained as a lawyer but has never worked as such. He has been publishing short stories in Georgian periodicals since 1988. He is mainly known for his short stories but has also published a novel. In 2007 he won the SABA prize for Best Book of Short Stories and in 2008 the SABA for Best Prose Work. He is president of the Georgian PEN Club.

BESIK KHARANAULI was born in Tianeti in 1939. He graduated from the Department of Philology at Tbilisi State University. Best known for his poetry, he has been writing since 1954. His first collection of poems was published in 1968 and since then he has published numerous collections of poems and short stories and received a number of prestigious Georgian literary awards. He was nominated for the Nobel Prize for Literature by the Georgian government in 2010. His works have been translated into French, German, Russian, Czech, Hungarian, Bulgarian, and Azeri. His 1971 poem "The Lame Doll" is due to be published in English translation and his poem "Death of my Grandmother" appeared in the journal International Poetry Review in 2009.

MAMUKA KHERKHEULIDZE was born in 1959 in Tbilisi. He studied in the Journalism Department of Tbilisi State University and has worked as a television and radio reporter as well as a print journalist. He has also worked in the Lexicology Department of the Georgian Academy of Sciences. He writes short stories and has published a collection of these. One of his short stories formed the basis for the 2010 Georgian film *Street Days*.

ARCHIL KIKODZE was born in 1972. He studied Armenian at Tbilisi State University and screenwriting and photography at Tbilisi Institute of Theater and Cinema. He is a novelist, professional photographer, and ethnographer. He has authored four books of short stories and won the Gala award for Best Book of the Year in 2008 for his collection *Cozy*. He has also written various guide books on Georgia and has published articles on environmental, ethnographic, and social themes.

ANA KORDZAIA-SAMADASHVILI was born in Tbilisi in 1968. She published her debut in 2003, for which she was awarded the SABA Best Debut prize. As well as two collections of short stories, her works have also appeared in various anthologies. She works as a critic and literary translator of German into Georgian and in 1999 was awarded the Goethe Institute prize for Best Translation (Elfriede Jelinek, *Die Liebhaberinnen*).

ZURAB LEZHAVA was born in Tbilisi in 1960. After leaving school he worked in a state-owned printing house. He spent sixteen years in jail from 1982 and much of his work was written during this period. He has published three books—a novel and two collections of short stories—and numerous short stories in different literary magazines. He now works carving and selling wooden statues. His short story "Sex for Fridge" was selected by Aleksandar Hemon for inclusion in Dalkey Archive Press's anthology *Best European Fiction 2011*.

MAKA MIKELADZE was born in Georgia. She writes prose and verse and has published several collections of short stories and poems, including *Me and My Kusturitsa* which was awarded the SABA prize for Best Prose Collection in 2011. In addition to her writing she works as a psychiatrist.

AKA MORCHILADZE is the pen name of Giorgi Akhvlediani, who was born in 1966 in Tbilisi. He is a graduate of Tbilisi State University where he studied Georgian History. He has published twenty novels and two collections of short stories and has won the SABA award for Best Novel on four occasions. His 2005 novel *Santa Esperanza* has been translated and published in German and several films and plays have been based on his works. He has also worked as a presenter of arts programs on Georgian television.

ZAAL SAMADASHVILI was born in 1953 in Tbilisi. He graduated from Tbilisi State University with a specialization in Mathematics and since then has worked as an engineer, editor of a newspaper and literary journal, lecturer, school principal, and chair of the Tbilisi City Assembly. He has published numerous short stories, essays, and a screenplay.

NUGZAR SHATAIDZE was born in Tbilisi in 1944. He studied at Tbilisi State University and later in the Polytechnic Institute in the Physics Faculty. He wrote short stories, essays, and screenplays. His first story was published in a literary journal in 1968 and his first collection of short stories appeared in 1979. He published nine books in all. His story "November Rain" was awarded the SABA prize for Best Prose Composition. He produced five screenplays including that of the 2009 Georgian film *The Other Bank*, which won the awards for Best Script at the Festival International de Cinéma à Gonfreville (2009) and Best Screenplay at the Moqavemat International Film Festival (2010) He also wrote several radio plays. He died in January 2009.

NINO TEPNADZE was born in 1992. She is studying Georgian Philology at Tbilisi State University. She writes poems and short stories and is also an active blogger.

ELIZABETH HEIGHWAY holds a BA in Philosophy and Modern Languages from the University of Oxford and is currently studying for an MA in Translation Studies at the University of Birmingham. She translates from Georgian and French.

SELECTED DALKEY ARCHIVE TITLES

PETROS ABATZOGLOU, *What Does Mrs. Freeman Want?*
MICHAL AJVAZ, *The Golden Age.*
The Other City.
PIERRE ALBERT-BIROT, *Grabinoulor.*
YUZ ALESHKOVSKY, *Kangaroo.*
FELIPE ALFAU, *Chromos.*
Locos.
JOÃO ALMINO, *The Book of Emotions.*
IVAN ÂNGELO, *The Celebration.*
The Tower of Glass.
DAVID ANTIN, *Talking.*
ANTÓNIO LOBO ANTUNES, *Knowledge of Hell.*
The Splendor of Portugal.
ALAIN ARIAS-MISSON, *Theatre of Incest.*
IFTIKHAR ARIF AND WAQAS KHWAJA, EDS., *Modern Poetry of Pakistan.*
JOHN ASHBERY AND JAMES SCHUYLER, *A Nest of Ninnies.*
ROBERT ASHLEY, *Perfect Lives.*
GABRIELA AVIGUR-ROTEM, *Heatwave and Crazy Birds.*
HEIMRAD BÄCKER, *transcript.*
DJUNA BARNES, *Ladies Almanack.*
Ryder.
JOHN BARTH, *LETTERS.*
Sabbatical.
DONALD BARTHELME, *The King.*
Paradise.
SVETISLAV BASARA, *Chinese Letter.*
MIQUEL BAUÇÀ, *The Siege in the Room.*
RENÉ BELLETTO, *Dying.*
MAREK BIEŃCZYK, *Transparency.*
MARK BINELLI, *Sacco and Vanzetti Must Die!*
ANDREI BITOV, *Pushkin House.*
ANDREJ BLATNIK, *You Do Understand.*
LOUIS PAUL BOON, *Chapel Road.*
My Little War.
Summer in Termuren.
ROGER BOYLAN, *Killoyle.*
IGNÁCIO DE LOYOLA BRANDÃO, *Anonymous Celebrity.*
The Good-Bye Angel.
Teeth under the Sun.
Zero.
BONNIE BREMSER, *Troia: Mexican Memoirs.*
CHRISTINE BROOKE-ROSE, *Amalgamemnon.*
BRIGID BROPHY, *In Transit.*
MEREDITH BROSNAN, *Mr. Dynamite.*
GERALD L. BRUNS, *Modern Poetry and the Idea of Language.*
EVGENY BUNIMOVICH AND J. KATES, EDS., *Contemporary Russian Poetry: An Anthology.*
GABRIELLE BURTON, *Heartbreak Hotel.*
MICHEL BUTOR, *Degrees.*
Mobile.
Portrait of the Artist as a Young Ape.
G. CABRERA INFANTE, *Infante's Inferno.*
Three Trapped Tigers.
JULIETA CAMPOS, *The Fear of Losing Eurydice.*
ANNE CARSON, *Eros the Bittersweet.*
ORLY CASTEL-BLOOM, *Dolly City.*
CAMILO JOSÉ CELA, *Christ versus Arizona.*
The Family of Pascual Duarte.
The Hive.
LOUIS-FERDINAND CÉLINE, *Castle to Castle.*
Conversations with Professor Y.
London Bridge.

Normance.
North.
Rigadoon.
MARIE CHAIX, *The Laurels of Lake Constance.*
HUGO CHARTERIS, *The Tide Is Right.*
JEROME CHARYN, *The Tar Baby.*
ERIC CHEVILLARD, *Demolishing Nisard.*
LUIS CHITARRONI, *The No Variations.*
MARC CHOLODENKO, *Mordechai Schamz.*
JOSHUA COHEN, *Witz.*
EMILY HOLMES COLEMAN, *The Shutter of Snow.*
ROBERT COOVER, *A Night at the Movies.*
STANLEY CRAWFORD, *Log of the S.S. The Mrs Unguentine.*
Some Instructions to My Wife.
ROBERT CREELEY, *Collected Prose.*
RENÉ CREVEL, *Putting My Foot in It.*
RALPH CUSACK, *Cadenza.*
SUSAN DAITCH, *L.C.*
Storytown.
NICHOLAS DELBANCO, *The Count of Concord.*
Sherbrookes.
NIGEL DENNIS, *Cards of Identity.*
PETER DIMOCK, *A Short Rhetoric for Leaving the Family.*
ARIEL DORFMAN, *Konfidenz.*
COLEMAN DOWELL, *The Houses of Children.*
Island People.
Too Much Flesh and Jabez.
ARKADII DRAGOMOSHCHENKO, *Dust.*
RIKKI DUCORNET, *The Complete Butcher's Tales.*
The Fountains of Neptune.
The Jade Cabinet.
The One Marvelous Thing.
Phosphor in Dreamland.
The Stain.
The Word "Desire."
WILLIAM EASTLAKE, *The Bamboo Bed.*
Castle Keep.
Lyric of the Circle Heart.
JEAN ECHENOZ, *Chopin's Move.*
STANLEY ELKIN, *A Bad Man.*
Boswell: A Modern Comedy.
Criers and Kibitzers, Kibitzers and Criers.
The Dick Gibson Show.
The Franchiser.
George Mills.
The Living End.
The MacGuffin.
The Magic Kingdom.
Mrs. Ted Bliss.
The Rabbi of Lud.
Van Gogh's Room at Arles.
FRANÇOIS EMMANUEL, *Invitation to a Voyage.*
ANNIE ERNAUX, *Cleaned Out.*
SALVADOR ESPRIU, *Ariadne in the Grotesque Labyrinth.*
LAUREN FAIRBANKS, *Muzzle Thyself.*
Sister Carrie.
LESLIE A. FIEDLER, *Love and Death in the American Novel.*
JUAN FILLOY, *Faction.*
Op Oloop.
ANDY FITCH, *Pop Poetics.*
GUSTAVE FLAUBERT, *Bouvard and Pécuchet.*
KASS FLEISHER, *Talking out of School.*

FOR A FULL LIST OF PUBLICATIONS, VISIT:
www.dalkeyarchive.com

FORD MADOX FORD,
  The March of Literature.
JON FOSSE, *Aliss at the Fire.*
  Melancholy.
MAX FRISCH, *I'm Not Stiller.*
  Man in the Holocene.
CARLOS FUENTES, *Christopher Unborn.*
  Distant Relations.
  Terra Nostra.
  Vlad.
  Where the Air Is Clear.
TAKEHIKO FUKUNAGA, *Flowers of Grass.*
WILLIAM GADDIS, *J R.*
  The Recognitions.
JANICE GALLOWAY, *Foreign Parts.*
  The Trick Is to Keep Breathing.
WILLIAM H. GASS, *Cartesian Sonata*
    and Other Novellas.
  Finding a Form.
  A Temple of Texts.
  The Tunnel.
  Willie Masters' Lonesome Wife.
GÉRARD GAVARRY, *Hoppla! 1 2 3.*
  Making a Novel.
ETIENNE GILSON,
  The Arts of the Beautiful.
  Forms and Substances in the Arts.
C. S. GISCOMBE, *Giscome Road.*
  Here.
  Prairie Style.
DOUGLAS GLOVER, *Bad News of the Heart.*
  The Enamoured Knight.
WITOLD GOMBROWICZ,
  A Kind of Testament.
PAULO EMÍLIO SALES GOMES, *P's Three*
    Women.
KAREN ELIZABETH GORDON, *The Red Shoes.*
GEORGI GOSPODINOV, *Natural Novel.*
JUAN GOYTISOLO, *Count Julian.*
  Exiled from Almost Everywhere.
  Juan the Landless.
  Makbara.
  Marks of Identity.
PATRICK GRAINVILLE, *The Cave of Heaven.*
HENRY GREEN, *Back.*
  Blindness.
  Concluding.
  Doting.
  Nothing.
JACK GREEN, *Fire the Bastards!*
JIŘÍ GRUŠA, *The Questionnaire.*
GABRIEL GUDDING,
  Rhode Island Notebook.
MELA HARTWIG, *Am I a Redundant*
    Human Being?
JOHN HAWKES, *The Passion Artist.*
  Whistlejacket.
ELIZABETH HEIGHWAY, ED., *Contemporary*
    Georgian Fiction.
ALEKSANDAR HEMON, ED.,
  Best European Fiction.
AIDAN HIGGINS, *Balcony of Europe.*
  A Bestiary.
  Blind Man's Bluff
  Bornholm Night-Ferry.
  Darkling Plain: Texts for the Air.
  Flotsam and Jetsam.
  Langrishe, Go Down.
  Scenes from a Receding Past.
  Windy Arbours.
KEIZO HINO, *Isle of Dreams.*
KAZUSHI HOSAKA, *Plainsong.*

ALDOUS HUXLEY, *Antic Hay.*
  Crome Yellow.
  Point Counter Point.
  Those Barren Leaves.
  Time Must Have a Stop.
NAOYUKI II, *The Shadow of a Blue Cat.*
MIKHAIL IOSSEL and JEFF PARKER, EDS.,
  Amerika: Russian Writers View the
    United States.
DRAGO JANČAR, *The Galley Slave.*
GERT JONKE, *The Distant Sound.*
  Geometric Regional Novel.
  Homage to Czerny.
  The System of Vienna.
JACQUES JOUET, *Mountain R.*
  Savage.
  Upstaged.
CHARLES JULIET, *Conversations with*
    Samuel Beckett and Bram van
    Velde.
MIEKO KANAI, *The Word Book.*
YORAM KANIUK, *Life on Sandpaper.*
HUGH KENNER, *The Counterfeiters.*
  Flaubert, Joyce and Beckett:
    The Stoic Comedians.
  Joyce's Voices.
DANILO KIŠ, *The Attic.*
  Garden, Ashes.
  The Lute and the Scars
  Psalm 44.
  A Tomb for Boris Davidovich.
ANITA KONKKA, *A Fool's Paradise.*
GEORGE KONRÁD, *The City Builder.*
TADEUSZ KONWICKI, *A Minor Apocalypse.*
  The Polish Complex.
MENIS KOUMANDAREAS, *Koula.*
ELAINE KRAF, *The Princess of 72nd Street.*
JIM KRUSOE, *Iceland.*
AYŞE KULIN, *Farewell: A Mansion in*
    Occupied Istanbul.
EWA KURYLUK, *Century 21.*
EMILIO LASCANO TEGUI, *On Elegance*
    While Sleeping.
ERIC LAURRENT, *Do Not Touch.*
HERVÉ LE TELLIER, *The Sextine Chapel.*
  A Thousand Pearls (for a Thousand
    Pennies)
VIOLETTE LEDUC, *La Bâtarde.*
EDOUARD LEVÉ, *Autoportrait.*
  Suicide.
MARIO LEVI, *Istanbul Was a Fairy Tale.*
SUZANNE JILL LEVINE, *The Subversive*
    Scribe: Translating Latin
    American Fiction.
DEBORAH LEVY, *Billy and Girl.*
  Pillow Talk in Europe and Other
    Places.
JOSÉ LEZAMA LIMA, *Paradiso.*
ROSA LIKSOM, *Dark Paradise.*
OSMAN LINS, *Avalovara.*
  The Queen of the Prisons of Greece.
ALF MAC LOCHLAINN,
  The Corpus in the Library.
  Out of Focus.
RON LOEWINSOHN, *Magnetic Field(s).*
MINA LOY, *Stories and Essays of Mina Loy.*
BRIAN LYNCH, *The Winner of Sorrow.*
D. KEITH MANO, *Take Five.*
MICHELINE AHARONIAN MARCOM,
  The Mirror in the Well.
BEN MARCUS,
  The Age of Wire and String.

SELECTED DALKEY ARCHIVE TITLES

WALLACE MARKFIELD,
  Teitlebaum's Window.
  To an Early Grave.
DAVID MARKSON, *Reader's Block.*
  Springer's Progress.
  Wittgenstein's Mistress.
CAROLE MASO, *AVA.*
LADISLAV MATEJKA AND KRYSTYNA
  POMORSKA, EDS.,
  Readings in Russian Poetics:
  Formalist and Structuralist Views.
HARRY MATHEWS,
  The Case of the Persevering Maltese:
  Collected Essays.
  Cigarettes.
  The Conversions.
  The Human Country: New and
  Collected Stories.
  The Journalist.
  My Life in CIA.
  Singular Pleasures.
  The Sinking of the Odradek
  Stadium.
  Tlooth.
  20 Lines a Day.
JOSEPH MCELROY,
  Night Soul and Other Stories.
THOMAS MCGONIGLE,
  Going to Patchogue.
ROBERT L. MCLAUGHLIN, ED., *Innovations:*
  An Anthology of Modern &
  Contemporary Fiction.
ABDELWAHAB MEDDEB, *Talismano.*
GERHARD MEIER, *Isle of the Dead.*
HERMAN MELVILLE, *The Confidence-Man.*
AMANDA MICHALOPOULOU, *I'd Like.*
STEVEN MILLHAUSER, *The Barnum Museum.*
  In the Penny Arcade.
RALPH J. MILLS, JR., *Essays on Poetry.*
MOMUS, *The Book of Jokes.*
CHRISTINE MONTALBETTI, *The Origin of Man.*
  Western.
OLIVE MOORE, *Spleen.*
NICHOLAS MOSLEY, *Accident.*
  Assassins.
  Catastrophe Practice.
  Children of Darkness and Light.
  Experience and Religion.
  A Garden of Trees.
  God's Hazard.
  The Hesperides Tree.
  Hopeful Monsters.
  Imago Bird.
  Impossible Object.
  Inventing God.
  Judith.
  Look at the Dark.
  Natalie Natalia.
  Paradoxes of Peace.
  Serpent.
  Time at War.
  The Uses of Slime Mould:
  Essays of Four Decades.
WARREN MOTTE,
  Fables of the Novel: French Fiction
  since 1990.
  Fiction Now: The French Novel in
  the 21st Century.
  Oulipo: A Primer of Potential
  Literature.
GERALD MURNANE, *Barley Patch.*
  Inland.

YVES NAVARRE, *Our Share of Time.*
  Sweet Tooth.
DOROTHY NELSON, *In Night's City.*
  Tar and Feathers.
ESHKOL NEVO, *Homesick.*
WILFRIDO D. NOLLEDO, *But for the Lovers.*
FLANN O'BRIEN, *At Swim-Two-Birds.*
  At War.
  The Best of Myles.
  The Dalkey Archive.
  Further Cuttings.
  The Hard Life.
  The Poor Mouth.
  The Third Policeman.
CLAUDE OLLIER, *The Mise-en-Scène.*
  Wert and the Life Without End.
GIOVANNI ORELLI, *Walaschek's Dream.*
PATRIK OUŘEDNÍK, *Europeana.*
  The Opportune Moment, 1855.
BORIS PAHOR, *Necropolis.*
FERNANDO DEL PASO, *News from the Empire.*
  Palinuro of Mexico.
ROBERT PINGET, *The Inquisitory.*
  Mahu or The Material.
  Trio.
A. G. PORTA, *The No World Concerto.*
MANUEL PUIG, *Betrayed by Rita Hayworth.*
  The Buenos Aires Affair.
  Heartbreak Tango.
RAYMOND QUENEAU, *The Last Days.*
  Odile.
  Pierrot Mon Ami.
  Saint Glinglin.
ANN QUIN, *Berg.*
  Passages.
  Three.
  Tripticks.
ISHMAEL REED, *The Free-Lance Pallbearers.*
  The Last Days of Louisiana Red.
  Ishmael Reed: The Plays.
  Juice!
  Reckless Eyeballing.
  The Terrible Threes.
  The Terrible Twos.
  Yellow Back Radio Broke-Down.
JASIA REICHARDT, *15 Journeys from Warsaw*
  to London.
NOËLLE REVAZ, *With the Animals.*
JOÃO UBALDO RIBEIRO, *House of the*
  Fortunate Buddhas.
JEAN RICARDOU, *Place Names.*
RAINER MARIA RILKE, *The Notebooks of*
  Malte Laurids Brigge.
JULIÁN RÍOS, *The House of Ulysses.*
  Larva: A Midsummer Night's Babel.
  Poundemonium.
  Procession of Shadows.
AUGUSTO ROA BASTOS, *I the Supreme.*
DANIËL ROBBERECHTS, *Arriving in Avignon.*
JEAN ROLIN, *The Explosion of the*
  Radiator Hose.
OLIVIER ROLIN, *Hotel Crystal.*
ALIX CLEO ROUBAUD, *Alix's Journal.*
JACQUES ROUBAUD, *The Form of a*
  City Changes Faster, Alas, Than
  the Human Heart.
  The Great Fire of London.
  Hortense in Exile.
  Hortense Is Abducted.
  The Loop.
  Mathematics:
  The Plurality of Worlds of Lewis.

FOR A FULL LIST OF PUBLICATIONS, VISIT:
www.dalkeyarchive.com

The Princess Hoppy.
Some Thing Black.
LEON S. ROUDIEZ, *French Fiction Revisited.*
RAYMOND ROUSSEL, *Impressions of Africa.*
VEDRANA RUDAN, *Night.*
STIG SÆTERBAKKEN, *Siamese.*
LYDIE SALVAYRE, *The Company of Ghosts.*
Everyday Life.
The Lecture.
Portrait of the Writer as a
Domesticated Animal.
The Power of Flies.
LUIS RAFAEL SÁNCHEZ,
Macho Camacho's Beat.
SEVERO SARDUY, *Cobra & Maitreya.*
NATHALIE SARRAUTE,
Do You Hear Them?
Martereau.
The Planetarium.
ARNO SCHMIDT, *Collected Novellas.*
Collected Stories.
Nobodaddy's Children.
Two Novels.
ASAF SCHURR, *Motti.*
CHRISTINE SCHUTT, *Nightwork.*
GAIL SCOTT, *My Paris.*
DAMION SEARLS, *What We Were Doing*
and Where We Were Going.
JUNE AKERS SEESE,
Is This What Other Women Feel Too?
What Waiting Really Means.
BERNARD SHARE, *Inish.*
Transit.
AURELIE SHEEHAN, *Jack Kerouac Is Pregnant.*
VIKTOR SHKLOVSKY, *Bowstring.*
Knight's Move.
A Sentimental Journey:
Memoirs 1917–1922.
Energy of Delusion: A Book on Plot.
Literature and Cinematography.
Theory of Prose.
Third Factory.
Zoo, or Letters Not about Love.
CLAUDE SIMON, *The Invitation.*
PIERRE SINIAC, *The Collaborators.*
KJERSTI A. SKOMSVOLD, *The Faster I Walk,*
the Smaller I Am.
JOSEF ŠKVORECKÝ, *The Engineer of*
Human Souls.
GILBERT SORRENTINO,
Aberration of Starlight.
Blue Pastoral.
Crystal Vision.
Imaginative Qualities of Actual
Things.
Mulligan Stew.
Pack of Lies.
Red the Fiend.
The Sky Changes.
Something Said.
Splendide-Hôtel.
Steelwork.
Under the Shadow.
W. M. SPACKMAN, *The Complete Fiction.*
ANDRZEJ STASIUK, *Dukla.*
Fado.
GERTRUDE STEIN, *Lucy Church Amiably.*
The Making of Americans.
A Novel of Thank You.
LARS SVENDSEN, *A Philosophy of Evil.*
PIOTR SZEWC, *Annihilation.*
GONÇALO M. TAVARES, *Jerusalem.*

Joseph Walser's Machine.
Learning to Pray in the Age of
Technique.
LUCIAN DAN TEODOROVICI,
Our Circus Presents . . .
NIKANOR TERATOLOGEN, *Assisted Living.*
STEFAN THEMERSON, *Hobson's Island.*
The Mystery of the Sardine.
Tom Harris.
TAEKO TOMIOKA, *Building Waves.*
JOHN TOOMEY, *Sleepwalker.*
JEAN-PHILIPPE TOUSSAINT, *The Bathroom.*
Camera.
Monsieur.
Reticence.
Running Away.
Self-Portrait Abroad.
Television.
The Truth about Marie.
DUMITRU TSEPENEAG, *Hotel Europa.*
The Necessary Marriage.
Pigeon Post.
Vain Art of the Fugue.
ESTHER TUSQUETS, *Stranded.*
DUBRAVKA UGRESIC, *Lend Me Your Character.*
Thank You for Not Reading.
TOR ULVEN, *Replacement.*
MATI UNT, *Brecht at Night.*
Diary of a Blood Donor.
Things in the Night.
ÁLVARO URIBE AND OLIVIA SEARS, EDS.,
Best of Contemporary Mexican Fiction.
ELOY URROZ, *Friction.*
The Obstacles.
LUISA VALENZUELA, *Dark Desires and*
the Others.
He Who Searches.
MARJA-LIISA VARTIO, *The Parson's Widow.*
PAUL VERHAEGHEN, *Omega Minor.*
AGLAJA VETERANYI, *Why the Child Is*
Cooking in the Polenta.
BORIS VIAN, *Heartsnatcher.*
LLORENÇ VILLALONGA, *The Dolls' Room.*
TOOMAS VINT, *An Unending Landscape.*
ORNELA VORPSI, *The Country Where No*
One Ever Dies.
AUSTRYN WAINHOUSE, *Hedyphagetica.*
PAUL WEST, *Words for a Deaf Daughter*
& Gala.
CURTIS WHITE, *America's Magic Mountain.*
The Idea of Home.
Memories of My Father Watching TV.
Monstrous Possibility: An Invitation
to Literary Politics.
Requiem.
DIANE WILLIAMS, *Excitability:*
Selected Stories.
Romancer Erector.
DOUGLAS WOOLF, *Wall to Wall.*
Ya! & John-Juan.
JAY WRIGHT, *Polynomials and Pollen.*
The Presentable Art of Reading
Absence.
PHILIP WYLIE, *Generation of Vipers.*
MARGUERITE YOUNG, *Angel in the Forest.*
Miss MacIntosh, My Darling.
REYOUNG, *Unbabbling.*
VLADO ŽABOT, *The Succubus.*
ZORAN ŽIVKOVIĆ, *Hidden Camera.*
LOUIS ZUKOFSKY, *Collected Fiction.*
VITOMIL ZUPAN, *Minuet for Guitar.*
SCOTT ZWIREN, *God Head.*